A SINGLE GIRL'S GUIDE TO WEDDING SURVIVAL

MELISSA BORG

VERSLIUS PRESS

Paperback: 978-1-947725-03-4

eBook: 978-1-947725-02-7

First paperback edition published in November 2020.

Edited by Justine Covington and Randi Klein.

Cover art by Mariah Sinclair.

Layout by Jennifer Windrow.

Ornamental Break Image by Please Don't sell My Artwork AS IS from Pixabay.

Printed by Versluis Press in the United States of America.

For two of my favorite people, my Parental Unit. Dad, for the people skills and the constant support. Mom, for the word obsession and the endless stream of sass.

Expressions fail to convey how much I love you both.
Miss you, Mom, and I wish you could have been here to see this book you inspired published and complete.

*T*he office had closed ten minutes for their lunch break and Victoria could hear the deep rumble of the veterinarian's voice as he took a call in his office. She should quit sorting medical files, lock up, and get something to eat. But if she finished her work first, hopefully she would get out on time tonight. She twirled in her comfy office chair, her back to the phone, and kept filing paperwork.

Her desk phone rang. She kept on working, willing the person to hang up. They did. One point for Jedi mind tricks.

Handling calls for a veterinarian's office instead of being a vet was not what Victoria Shaw imagined she'd be doing. Yet after dropping out of school, the closest she got to her dream job was being the front-office help. No stethoscope, just paperwork and phone calls. Maybe she could get her vet tech license at least. At almost twenty-five, she had a loser job, she'd never been on a date, and she was a virgin. Her life was whine- and wine-worthy.

Worse, her datelessness had caused a rift between Victoria and her mother, and her mother's family. The Alburgas expected all members to marry early and upward.

In the front lobby, the temperature spiked slightly. Yet in Arizona, blasts of heat were frequent, and Victoria stashed her pity party and focused on her job.

Hands covered her eyes. Her pulse rose, but the scent of leather and lace and trouble staved off her panic attack. "Well, if it isn't Sandra, the original sass slinger." Victoria's tone was a mix of truth and sarcasm.

Sandra removed her hands from Victoria's eyes. "In the flesh, She-Who-Ignores-the-Phone, I saw you let that call go."

"I didn't ignore, we're closed for lun—" Victoria stopped mid-word and mid-swivel to stare at the stranger in front of her. The woman looked best-friend-esque, but a few sizes thinner than Victoria remembered.

Sandra beamed as bright as a kindergartener on their first day of school. "Can you believe it? My new clothes are a size 13-14."

Victoria had always been bigger than Sandra, though they were never more than a size or two apart. Now, she felt stranded in the mid-20s' sizes, alone.

During the six weeks that Sandra had endured stuck with her family in Chicago dealing with her sudden surgery and recovery, Sandra's fat had vanished. Her cheekbones were high. Never in the decade that Victoria had known Sandra had she seen those cheekbones.

"You...How? You're a mini-you."

"I am. And check out this ass." Sandra shook her booty at Victoria. "I don't recommend the Emergency Appendectomy Diet. I do recommend the results."

If Victoria had a stash of Jelly Bellies, they'd be her sugar Valium. She skipped denial, barreling into instant jealousy. Sandra wore a black off-the-shoulder shirt, knee-high riding boots, and war-torn skintight jeans. Very fashionable. Not an ounce girlie, very edgy, and a hundred percent Sandra.

Victoria's green work polo appeared drab in comparison. Dr. Yaz, the clinic owner, was old-fashioned. Whereas most vets wanted all staff to wear scrubs, he wanted Victoria to be more professionally attired. Her dress code landed in the nebulous space above scrubs, but below full business attire. The plus was that she could wear her smaller hats to work, like the green Peter Pan hat she donned today because she hadn't felt like being an adult or arguing with her wavy hair this morning.

But the polo material looked like it had been shrunk and stretched to accommodate her five-year weight gain. Victoria pulled her focus off her clothes and onto Sandra's. "Going for millionaire refugee chic?"

"I'm smokin' hot." Sandra struck a pinup pose and leered. "Makes you question staying straight, doesn't it?"

"Nope. I'm not swimming in your gay party pool." Mustering an ounce of happiness, Victoria spoke through her moat of envy. "Seriously, you look amazing and I missed."

"Missed you, too. Glad to be away from the fam in Chicago and back home." Sandra plopped a brown bag onto the counter. "I brought a kick-off weight-loss meal to you."

"Good. Otherwise, I'd never get to eat. Today's been one for the litter box." Victoria peeked inside. "What is this? Dried leprechaun poop?"

"Kale chips."

"Did you try them?"

"They're for you," Sandra said, the *duh* implied.

"Am I your taste tester?"

"Toxic level barometer."

Victoria sniffed them. Nothing horribly offensive. Low calorie count. Why not? "Saluté." She popped one in her mouth and crunched.

Sandra leaned over, scrutinizing her expression. "Thoughts?"

"It's bitter. Bitter. Bitter. And my taste buds may never forgive me." Victoria's mouth felt coated in a sour powder. She snagged the nearest drink to wash away the rank flavor.

Pounding the counter, Sandra whipped her head back, laughing.

"Don't laugh at me when you feed me healthy poison. Out, wench." Victoria lobbed the shriveled green missiles at her best friend.

"Check the bottom of the bag." She batted away the flying kale chips.

Victoria pointed to the doors. "Stop laughing and leave. Or I'll make you eat these."

Sandra slunk out, yelling through the glass lobby door, "Check the bag, you'll love me again. See ya."

Crossing through the lobby and flipping the lock, Victoria vowed she'd have a quiet lunch.

Surprise time. She slipped behind her reception desk, dug into the bag and found something cold and plastic. The surprise turned out to be a Greek salad. Greens? Greens wouldn't buy her love.

Salads were healthy. Extremely healthy. Too healthy. The new mental image of Sandra with a fresh pixie cut, thinner waist, and high cheekbones depressed her.

If Sandra could lose weight. If Sandra could gain a better figure. If Sandra cared enough to bring her along on the shedding-weight train, how could Victoria not eat the stupid rabbit food?

A salad would help her get slimmer. And once slimmer, she might manage to get a date.

Thoughts Victoria swore would never possess her, would never take her over, plagued her now. She channeled her advice-doling, pain-in-the-brain mother, Millie, who had taken over her synapses, her serenity, her sanity.

Her mother, her grandmother, and her cousins equated losing weight with getting a date. Dieting was the most popular family pastime. Every conversation between Victoria and her mother, in the last five years, had revolved around her mother offering unsolicited advice about how to spruce up Victoria's nonexistent love and social life.

Victoria had a plain-yogurt life. No hidden hunks of fruit, just plain white yogurt, bland and sour.

The phone rang. She'd prefer to work off the clock since work meant safety. Work was much better than listening to her mother's advice in her head. She plastered on a smile, lifted the receiver, and answered with forced pleasantry. "Noah's Haven, this is Victoria. How may I help you?"

"Tori, are you sitting down?" Her little sister, Dessie, asked, her voice nearly dog-whistle sonic.

As if Victoria's day wasn't bad enough. Eighty-five out of ninety times, her sister called to ask for a favor or to brag. She didn't know if she could fake her way through caring about either. "I'm at work. Not cha-cha-ing at the Ritz."

A sharp boat horn blared over the phone and nearly took out Victoria's eardrum. She went from annoyed to irate. "Are you on the wharf during class time?"

"Not important. Focus. I've got break-into-your-favorite-daytime-soap-type news."

Per usual, Dessie sounded curt and impatient, which was the same as every other time she called, but Victoria's snotty, privileged sister thought she could skip her education to go boating without care?

Victoria felt her lecture tone activate. "Not important? In your last semester of college? You better have your cute little trunk-with-no-junk in every class, from today until May."

She could hear Dessie rolling her eyes, yet Victoria's duty was to ground her sweet and flighty sister.

"You're not Mom. I'm almost done. And you're one to preach. You never finished college."

The truth punctured Victoria's heart. A hot shot of shame erupted in her belly and burned.

She tugged down today's hat choice and turned from the empty and locked lobby. "Yes, I know how stressful a communication major can be. Nothing like my easy-breezy pre-med major. Ah, the troubles and woes of the College of M-R-S Hunters."

"Quit badgering me. Listen. I have very important news." Dessie's puffed-up voice sounded bouncy and typical.

Victoria slumped back into her office chair. Dessie loved to surprise people with these news flashes. "You think everything you do is important."

"This is."

Uneasiness crept into Victoria's stomach, upsetting the shame lava and made her sit up straight.

"I'm getting married!" Dessie sang her news to the childhood taunt tone of *na-nana-naa-nah*.

Shrieks poured out of the receiver and Victoria's brain echoed her baby sister's marriage announcement. Dessie, only four years younger than Victoria, had always led a bejeweled-tiara life. The skinny genes, the looks, and the men drooling after her.

Cats hacking up hairballs would be better than these happy, harpy squeals.

Dessie rambled on.

"Isn't that great? Me in a white dress. A-ma-zing." Dessie squawked in ferret-on-crack speed.

Dread set in. This sounded real. Engagement. Engaaagement. Engaaaaagement.

"Can you hear me? Aren't you happy for me?" she asked, her tone catclaw sharp.

With Dessie's supersonic squeals, Victoria was surprised the dogs in the back hadn't started howling.

Before her sister started spewing out how *"Victoria never cares about me,"* or *"she only wants to ruin my happiness,"* or some other lame line Dessie had been repeating and screaming since childhood, she'd better find her rah-rah-rah switch and cheer.

So lie.

Victoria swallowed her second helping of jealousy for lunch. "Lucky you. You've been with Greg since Thanksgiving, a whole four months, right?"

"God no. Greg was over weeks ago. Damien asked me."

Even the best mind reader at a psychic hotline would have had trouble keeping straight the men in her sister's love life.

Dessie scoffed. "Don't you ever check any social media? I'm on them all. Seriously, you need to be more active in life."

That's Dessie code for all ears, minds, and TV sets must be tuned into The Dessie Show.

"B-T-W, Damien calls me Esmeralda." Dessie's words were chipper and boastful. If her sister had a spirit animal, it would have to be a rooster, since she was full of egotistical cries.

"You're using your real name? The name you've hated your whole life?"

"Damien says Esmeralda is a beautiful, grand name, which fits me perfectly."

Somehow, Victoria's head was still upright and not slamming against the metal desk. "When are you planning to get married?"

"I had our star charts done and the best day to get married is March eighth."

Her sister had easily fulfilled the family's "marry early" edict and here she sat having never waded into the dating pool. Sick. Victoria felt sick.

Big paws scratched the locked glass lobby doors. Relief

flooded her. Never had Victoria heard such a delightful racket. She turned to see who had saved her. The chunky bulldog waiting outside dented her relief.

Princess slobbered at the door and, unfortunately, where the dog went, the owner, Fran Zann, a matchmaker monster, would be only a leash length behind. Yet at this moment, Victoria would happily trade devils. Into the receiver, she said, "Well, Dessie, you have a little over a year to plan your wedding. Currently, I need to work."

"Wait, I—"

"Later." Victoria slammed the receiver into the phone cradle. She was as likely to continue that conversation as she was to agree to a drug-free root canal.

Leaving her salad untouched, Victoria scurried around the desk to unlock the door and let in her unlikely saviors.

Fran, the thin-built and thin-faced bulldog owner barreled through the door. "Victoria, love today's hat choice. Got a hot date tonight?" Fran's upturned lips and tilted face said sweet and sincere, but her syrupy voice belied that.

"Not unless you count my cat, Ralph. Let me see how long you and little Princess will have to wait." Victoria had forgotten that the only reason this small, mousy woman spoke to her was to play Aphrodite or Cupid or Venus.

"No date? How sad." Fran's fake caring tone continued.

Chin thrust out in denial, Victoria clutched Princess's patient folder to her chest. "Not really. Plenty of twenty-five-year-olds are single and love the freedom."

A disbelieving snort and head jerk from Fran told Victoria she didn't buy the lie either. Princess panted and flopped to the tile floor, cooling off from the early spring Arizona heat.

Fran tapped away on her phone, not paying attention to Victoria. "I could call Donnie or Danny to take you out."

Victoria pasted on her best business smile. "Thoughtful. But no thanks."

The double D's, Fran's nephews, or as Victoria thought of them, Dimwit and Dippy. Not a judgment, only truth. The one time they had come in, they had refused to look, speak, or breathe in her direction. Fran had to pin them to the counter to even squeak out a hello, their wan faces covered in a sheen of sweat. Later, Fran told Victoria that the spineless boys had wanted her to ask them out.

Fran peered over the phone. Her stance widened and her shoulders squared ready to fight. "You're single?"

"Yes."

"They're single."

"Sure." Victoria's single word response dripped dread.

Fran rocked on the balls of her feet, her tiny frame looming within inches of Victoria. "Then how aren't you compatible with either one of my sweet nephews?"

Victoria leaned away from the protective aunt love. "Because rule number one of my dating rule book is: Girls don't ask guys out."

"How very Victorian of you." Fran laughed at her pun.

Victoria winced. "Let me re-phrase that. This girl doesn't ask guys out."

A night from hell in high school had taught her well enough.

*F*inally, a perfect exit line, which Victoria took full advantage of by abandoning Fran in the lobby and sprinting into the kennel. The swinging doors snapped shut behind her. Hiding in the back of the vet office, Victoria left Fran alone to scheme. That was mañana's problem and she had enough Monday drama to fuel a soap opera. The kennel area was her refuge.

She scanned for the doctor and checked the exam rooms because the good doctor needed catnaps.

Winner. Exam Room Two. She found him dozing. She tiptoed closer and shook him softly. "Princess is here with Fran."

Dr. Yaz bolted upright. His filmy eyes blinked, recognition dawning, his gray hair disheveled due to his naturally rumpled state. "Right. Send them to me." He ran his fingers through his thinning hair in a futile attempt to tame it.

Victoria dragged her feet toward the lobby and witnessed Princess run at full-tilt for the exam room until she reached the end of her leash lead and jerked to a stop and then repeated the process. Odd. Victoria bent down to pet the pup. "Guess you're looking to meet someone new."

"So could you, if you'd let me set you up with one of my nephews." Fran was as subtle as a rocket launcher.

For once, something went right in her life. Dr. Yaz eyed the obese dog and delivered a few condescending *tsks*. "Fran, are you feeding Princess the prescribed amount of food?" He marched Fran away. For that, Victoria thanked the gods.

With her desk organized and neat, no one in the lobby, and the phone silent, Victoria did what any employee with an impending crisis would do—she opened her phone to check her email account and social media notifications.

Seventy-two new notifications responding to the news of Dessie's engagement and heaps of emoji-laden comments remarking how wonderful the two lovebirds looked together. Between the social media alerts and the texts, her phone morphed into a swarm of angry bees humming and buzzing.

Victoria thought to herself, *please let this wedding announcement be just another ploy by my pesky sister to be the center of the galaxy.* For Dessie, the world's attention would be too small a goal.

The only message Victoria cared about was a text from Sandra.

Salad's great, right? Work is crazy. After I escape the warden, ur place or mine?

Victoria's thumbs hovered over the phone. Normal Crappy Day Protocol would mean junk food and plenty of alcohol. With Sandra's weight loss, Victoria didn't want to be That Friend. The friend who tried to fatten you up so you'd revert to being heavy. Misery loved empty calories dipped in self-loathing.

Victoria texted back.

Mine. Bring sorbet after u bail from the loony bin

Sorbet could be billed as healthy. Healthy Crappy Day Protocol was achieved and supported Sandra's new body.

Evening plans solidified, she did not need to connect with

the rest of the world. Victoria set her phone to silent. Even Fran's matchmaking would have been better than all her sister's social media friends posting happy little heart emoticons.

Filing and greeting incoming patients kept her busy until closing time arrived. With the office locked behind her, Victoria turned up and blared her car radio. Time to hole up with her best friend and catch up after Sandra's medically-induced family togetherness. Six weeks felt like forever for Victoria, but Sandra had been out of town visiting her family when her appendix burst, and texts weren't enough.

At her overcrowded faux stucco apartment complex, she spotted Sandra's bright blue Mini. A spare key cost Victoria five dollars, yet as a best-friend investment, it was priceless knowing that Sandra could come and go as she pleased. A lone open spot sat next to the dented, tagged dumpsters. Victoria whipped in and trudged up the three flights of stairs to home.

Before she could put her key in the door, a text came in. She dug her phone out, a message from Dessie.

When I come home, I challenge u to swing races

The memory of them eating lunch at the park by her dad's work made Victoria laugh. No question that dealing with her sister led to headaches, yet there were times when her kid sister showed her sweet side like now.

Ur on

Inside her apartment, Victoria heard Sandra singing an Ol' Blue Eyes song. Victoria pushed open the door to see Sandra's brown-haired pixie-cut head swaying to the beat in the living room. She had ditched her new designer threads and sported a comfy tee and basketball shorts.

Victoria dropped her stuff on the entry table and glanced at the mess. The sight of her and Sandra's matching ten-year-old battered half-heart best friends' keychains lying next to each other in the key bowl lowered Victoria's blood pressure.

"Honey, I'm home." Victoria shouted over the music in her best Ricky Ricardo *I Love Lucy* impression.

Sandra turned, her butt still shaking to the tune. "Go. Jettison work." Greeting over, she picked up on the chorus with Frank Sinatra.

Walking past the living room, Victoria detoured to the right and into the tiny kitchen. She dumped dry kibble in her cat's bowl and coffee beans into the grinder. The beans whorled and crunched.

Sandra continued to channel a Vegas impersonator as she belted out Sinatra. She had snagged one of Victoria's many fedoras and attempted to roll the hat down her arms.

Victoria shook her head and went down the hallway to her bedroom. Unpinning her hat from her head, she opened her closet and carefully placed it on its stand. She loved her hat collection. She had started it in high school with a single silver fedora, and now she had over two dozen hats of all types and styles and for every occasion.

She could hear Sandra opening and closing the cabinets in the kitchen. Time to stop admiring her collection and warn her best friend about Dessie. After a quick change, she came out barefoot in a tank top and black running shorts.

The music transitioned from Sinatra to Michael Bublé, his silky voice warming up her apartment with "Fever."

Sandra shimmied her shoulders and crooned, *"You give me fever when you kiss me."*

Victoria had never been in love as swooned about in songs, but watching Sandra shake her booty made her frown vanish.

Her best friend's ability to play the starring role in her own life constantly impressed Victoria. No matter where they were or who they were with, Sandra never hid herself.

In high school, they were a matched set. Sandra was the star, regardless of her heaviness. Victoria was the no-name walk-on. Not much had changed since then.

Sandra finished big, her chest heaving.

Victoria whistled and clapped.

"Thank you, you're too kind." Sandra bowed, curtsied, and tossed the fedora at Victoria. "I'll be here all night, tip me since you enjoyed the show. I'll sign autographs after my scheduled coffee break."

Victoria swooped the hat out of the air and with a flourish donned it on her head. "You're not a ham, you're the bacon of entertainment."

"At least I'm yummy and the candy of the meat world." Sandra waved her hand to the breakfast bar behind Victoria.

Two blue bowls, each with a scoop of orange and raspberry sorbet, sat next to two thick ceramic mugs of coffee.

Sandra snagged the smaller helping of cold goodness and plopped down at the dining table. "Did you enjoy lunch?"

Lunch reminded Victoria of the phone call from Dessie, which caused her face to constrict and her Cortisol levels to spike. If Sandra had been less averse to social media, trending algorithms would have warned her of the impending Tropical Depression Dessie instead of Victoria having to be the broadcaster covering the brewing Dessie disaster.

"I thought you loved Greek salads?" Sandra asked.

Her words, uncorked, rushed out. "Forget the salad. Dessie is getting married."

Sandra almost choked on her spoon. After hacking and coughing, an I-don't-believe-it smile spread across her face. "The dweeby guy from Thanksgiving?"

"Greg."

Staring into her sorbet, Sandra shook her head. "I'm trying to imagine Dessie marrying him. Instead of a boutonniere, he'd wear a pocket protector."

The thought squeezed a chuckle out of Victoria. "According to the social media comments I read, she ditched geeky Greg right before finals. Booted for not making enough time for her. She's marrying a guy named Damien."

"Who knew college would be such a treasure trove for hot dates? You went there for four years and came away with nothing: No dates, no prospects, no degree." Sandra was so matter of fact with zero heat, giving a simple statement of gospel.

Victoria's body and spirit wilted. Her best friend's words shredded her heart. Breathless. Defenseless. Ten years and Sandra still said whatever the Hades popped into her mind. "A coffee pot has a better filter than you do."

Sandra grabbed Victoria's clenched fist. "There is nothing wrong with not finishing your degree."

"Yeah. I'm only upset about not getting a degree." Victoria dripped sarcasm. She had been within one semester of graduating with her bachelor's when she got sick from all the constant stress and dropped out. Now, she'd have to repeat a few of her courses, plus she'd need to complete the last two dropped classes.

"Look at me. I went. Got bored, and got a life working in a tech start-up." Sweet, clueless Sandra kept on spewing rainbows trying to make everything better.

Victoria withdrew from Sandra's touch and pushed her hair back from her face. "Dessie says that she and Damien's stars line up for a March eighth wedding." Her voice wobbled. "This means I have a little over a year to get off life support and rustle up a date for the wedding."

"A year sounds doable. Knowing Dessie though, before the invites are printed, the whole thing has a high probability of being called off."

"A year is a short time to prove my family wrong about me, to not attend the wedding alone, and to avoid major family judgment."

In the kitchen, her landline rang. She fidgeted. The only people who called her landline were solicitors or her mother.

The machine clicked on.

Her mother's voice oozed through the speaker, pelting her with questions. "Victoria, isn't the news great about Esmeralda? Where are you? Why aren't you picking up?"

"Survival instincts," Victoria replied to the answering machine.

"Call me as soon as you get this." Her mother sent her an air kiss and disconnected.

Victoria stabbed her spoon into her sorbet. "Not. Going. To. Happen."

Sandra draped her arm over the back of the kitchen chair. "You always complain about your mother, but you fold faster than a camp chair when it comes to her."

"I do what she wants because once she tells you to do something, she'll harp you to death if you don't do her will."

"Admit it, you want your mother's approval and that's why you do her bidding. Also, you will talk with your mother tonight."

"Not this time. If I pick up my phone, the entire conversation will be her gloating about the impending marriage and how happy she is that one of her daughters is living up to the Alburga family expectations. Then next would come the threats of shoving me through the thirteen levels of blind-date hell."

"You know Dante only depicted nine levels of hell, right?"

Victoria sulked in her chair. "Nine levels would never be enough for my mother."

"Truth."

The "Wicked Witch of the West" theme pealed from her cell phone, hopping next to Victoria's bowl. They both stared.

Victoria covered the phone with her hand and, although muffled, it tolled on. "You could earn best friend points by answering for me and claiming that I'm dead."

"Wimp. I'd say the call won't be bad. But I won't lie."

"Thanks." Victoria tried to Jedi-mind-trick the phone, willing her mother to give up. But her meager control of the Force couldn't match the Dark Side.

"Answer it." Sandra took another bite of her sorbet.

"You're right. I must answer or be tortured by the inquisition later." She caved and stabbed the green answer button. "Hello."

"Oh, Baby." Her mother gushed in a register that almost made Victoria believe her mother cared about her eldest daughter. Almost.

She used the word "baby," which in Mother Code translated to asking for a favor or to deliver a terminal diagnosis. But Victoria knew about Dessie's nuptials, so she lowered her internal warning from battle stations to stand-by panic.

"There you are. Why didn't you answer your landline?" Her mother's pouty huff transmitted perfectly through the phone.

"Because you never listen to me." Victoria pointed to the phone.

"Now that I have you on the line, aren't you excited about Esmeralda getting married in three weeks?"

Victoria's lungs seized. Her heart froze. Her vision clouded.

"Three weeks?" she numbly repeated.

Sandra's eyes widened. She leaned forward like a lifeguard who spotted potential trouble and stood ready to sound the alarm.

Twenty-one days before the eternal photograph evidence that would display Victoria as being alone. Massive hanging-over-the-mantle Alburga family wedding pictures. All of which would be taken under the judgmental gaze of her perfectly married and successful cousins and now sister.

"Exciting times." Her mother's words boomed against her ear.

The air thinned. Each inhale brought less oxygen than the one before. If only Victoria could move beyond freeze and into fight-or-flight. She couldn't show up without a degree, without a life plan, and most critical to her family without a man.

Her mother prattled on with apocalyptic happiness, not knowing, or caring what havoc she was gifting her eldest. "Dessie will be flying in next week to make the arrangements."

Knockout. Victoria's world spun.

Her pathetic life strobed behind her eyelids. All her shabby life achievements colored and filled her black vision.

Technicolor downer.

The conversations and her family were too much for her today. Victoria was amazed the phone was still in her hand and not flying across the room, not smashed against the wall, nor dashed to small bits, though the plastic case groaned. "Isn't three weeks a bit too soon?"

"It works with her spring break."

She must think. If Victoria could convince her mother how bad the wedding could be for her impulsive sister, there was a chance to stave off this ceremony of disaster. Then Victoria could escape the whispers she'd hear at the wedding about her spinsterhood. She must find some way to get her mother to stop the newest Dessie catastrophe.

"Dessie won't be able to find a decent venue to hold the wedding."

"Don't worry. Damien lent her his black card. That will be enough incentive to make cancellations happen. Everything will get arranged." Her mother's voice was so unnaturally bright, Victoria thought she should be wearing a welding mask.

"Power of the buck is what you're relying on, Mother?"

"Yes." She spoke plainly and honestly.

Her mother most likely salivated over the groom's limitless credit card, because with plastic, she and Dessie could do what they do best: shop, plan parties, and spend other people's money. With that thought, any possibility of this wedding not happening vanished. Her mother would sleep well knowing her cherished youngest was getting hitched to a guy willing to pay for everything Dessie wanted. For life.

If Dessie wanted to elope, Victoria could shrug it off as a questionable life choice and move on. But if Dessie wanted to get married, for real, that would mean all the family would come and suddenly want to pry why the eldest daughter hadn't walked down the aisle first. The Alburgas acted as though they lived in the freaking Victorian age where children got married in birth order.

Her mother broke through Victoria's anxiety haze, saying, "Plus, you'll be your sister's wingman to make sure she remembers everything. You're always so good with the details, dear."

Victoria panicked. "Wait, I have to help her plan the wedding? I thought with a big-shot credit card, Dessie would get an event planner to help her, not me. I have a job."

"We Alburgas couldn't possibly outsource the wedding details to an outsider. It is too important a day to trust others to do the work. You keep telling me you have unused days off; now you have a reason to use them. It's so great…" Her mother kept rambling. The words stabbed Victoria, yet the barbs couldn't pierce her misery.

Dessie had found her charming prince. Victoria couldn't find a fat frog. Every family holiday conversation about her being the single, older sister was true.

Victoria had to release her pent-up need to break something. She wouldn't miss her shattered mind or dreams, so she allowed her head to drop and bounce on the table. She banged her head in time to the internal jingle of loser. Loser. Loser.

Her squawking mother clattered to the floor.

Sandra snatched up the phone, made crackle and popping out-of-range sounds, and hung up. Then Sandra grabbed both sides of Victoria's neck, stopping her self-flagellation.

Her mind had cracked. Sandra's fingers anchored her to reality.

Reality sucked. Victoria wanted to bang away this moment and this day.

"Come with me." Sandra pulled her out of the chair. "Come away from the table, away from the phone, away from sharp implements."

She steered Victoria toward the living room and around the coffee table. Sandra left her marooned on the sofa.

A blender whirled faintly in the distance.

Victoria studied the white ceiling and reviewed the current lowlights of her life.

Her younger sister married before her? Check.

Never been on a real date, let alone having one lined up for the wedding? Check.

Must deal with her narcissistic sister for the next three hellish weeks? Check-a-dee-check-check.

A cold hand tilted her chin down. Sandra and Victoria were eye-to-glazed-eye. Sandra shoved something at her. She blinked at the chilly glass that had materialized.

"The drink will help." Sandra was only inches from her face but sounded continents away.

It was cold and convenient, and the liquid singed her throat. She forced the frosty sludge down, gagging. "What did you put in here, rubbing alcohol?"

"No, you had almost no hard liquor. I had to improvise with

your vodka-based lemon balm tincture and orange juice."
Sandra took a tentative swig and sputtered.

Her best friend's face contorted, contracted, compressed into a sour grimace. Victoria giggled, rolling off the couch. Sandra joined in the manic laughter.

Sandra wiped her eyes. "Alright, nervous breakdown is over. What's next?"

Sprawled out on the floor, Victoria lifted her head, squinted at the last of the slushy in the blender, and waved her empty glass in the air. "I'll have another."

TIP # 3
NEVER GIVE UP ON YOUR DREAMS: KEEP SLEEPING

*T*he smell of coffee primed Victoria's brain for Awake Mode. *Please let yesterday be a nightmare.* She opened her eyes and her white living room ceiling stared at her.

Wait. Coffee is brewing? Damn.

Someone else made the coffee. Double damn.

Verified: all those phone calls happened. Dessie was getting married. Triple-plus-infinity damn.

Rolling off the couch, she almost broke her nose. Right. After the second pitcher of Sandra Surprise, Victoria never made it off the couch. Hungover on a Tuesday, the rest of her week promised to be brutal.

She stumbled into the kitchen, dodging her cat, Ralph, and inhaled deep. Her nostrils lead her to her savior and found a star sticky note taped to Mr. Coffee.

WENT HOME. THOUGHT YOU COULD USE THIS. IF YOU NEED ME, CALL. LOVE, S

Coffee dripped one drop at a time. She fed Ralph and decided to shower first. Twenty minutes later, she faced off with her closet, her head pounded, and her forehead was tender.

When feeling like roadkill collided with being an adult, it was time to fake feeling fine.

Victoria pulled out her power outfit: her favorite bohemian style skirt, a white work polo, and a sunny cap. One of the positives of living in the hot desert was that, even in February, she looked ready for a picnic by the lake.

Sunshine spilled over her windowsill. Anything seemed possible in this sunlight. Victoria could breathe a little easier this morning. A smile bubbled up, softening the memories of yesterday's wedding announcement and her mother's manipulating ways.

Her phone started singing "White and Nerdy" by Weird Al. Victoria's already good mood brightened. Her dad never called. She snatched the phone before the call went to voicemail.

"Hi ya, Daddy."

"You OK? I heard about your sister." Her dad's voice sounded calm, but underneath Victoria detected a distress quiver. Then again, her dad always tensed up when he talked about Dessie.

She didn't force a smile. She did force a lie. "I'm OK."

The phone stayed silent. Victoria knew the signal was good, so her dad must have shut down. Typical. After the divorce, her dad, left with two preteen girls, had used silence as a shield against the estrogen.

She heard him shuffling papers. "Are you at work before noon? Do you have a circuit board design due to a client or something?"

Her dad was fantastic with electrical circuits, but awful with people and rising early.

More paper rustling came through the phone. "No, I have a new hire."

Time to dig into the reason why he phoned. "How are you with the news of Dessie's marriage?"

A low rumble, a cross between a wounded lion and a lost

kitten, warned Victoria that this conversation needed to be in person. "Daddy, do you want to grab lunch today?"

More silence.

When fifteen-year-old Dessie had started to date, their dad had had no idea how to respond. He would open the door to meet the boy, shake the date's hand, and set a curfew. No threats. No crushing handshakes. Just wide-eyed parental terror.

A ritual he never had to do for Victoria.

"I'll even stop by and pick you up. My treat." Though her dad could be cranky and moody, she loved him. And love waited.

After a long pause, her dad huffed, "Fine." Then he hung up on her.

She'd better head out the door before anyone else could dim her morning. As soon as her key hit the ignition, the cursed Barbie ringtone played, chipping away at her morning cheer.

Couldn't Dessie leave her alone?

She dropped the car into reverse. How sad she couldn't answer since driving and talking would be illegal and dangerous. Saved by the accelerator.

The Barbie song died. Victoria's smugness at avoiding her sister became crushed when the "Wicked Witch of the West" theme song came from her phone. Playing no favorites, Victoria ignored her mother. She continued on to work as her life and self-esteem weren't imploding.

If Victoria answered her mother, she knew what she'd hear: "Get off your duff and snag yourself a man," or "How can you stand being alone at your age?"

No need to visit the house of mirrors to reflect on her faults.

In the past, Victoria had been stuck in the "friend" box by guys. Especially by her big crush in high school, Garett. He most likely saw Dessie, her bubbly, outgoing, beautiful sister, and never saw her. In high school and college, guys called her if they needed tutoring, not a date.

She could fix the future. A plus-one at the reception in three weeks would be a great start to the new her.

Three weeks. Yeah, she could do this. But not alone. Victoria couldn't fight off her personal cataclysm on her own. She shelved her pride and self-vows.

She'd bend her dating rule number one and ask friends for help securing a safe date.

Sitting in her work parking lot, she dialed. Call one to a college buddy she had saved from failing math courses a few years was a bust. Call two to an old coworker was also a bust.

Work beckoned and so she got out of her starting-to-roast car, slipped into the deserted lobby, and stashed her purse in the bottom of the gray desk drawer. Within minutes, owners began to flow in and out of the office bringing in sick cats, dogs, and birds. In between filing, ringing up patients, and answering the phone, Victoria kept up the mayday calls to find a date.

All her SOS's resulted in no rescue. Someone had to have a single guy to lend her for a date.

One of the last calls yielded a match.

An old roommate texted. She knew a single guy, Mateo. A date was set up for that night. Bonus: since Mateo and Victoria had once shared the same English 101 class, the date couldn't be labeled a blind date.

Yet her stomach still churned out acid, her body felt tense, and her brain freaked out. Victoria had never spoken to Mateo in college. She only remembered that he was a little geeky and always wore black-rimmed glasses.

A thousand insecurities and questions hammered at her for the rest of the morning.

THE MENTAL HAMSTER wheel of dating troubles bounced around her head all morning and through her lunchtime run to her dad's office. She even missed the freeway exit and had to turn around.

The lobby of the engineering research company was a brightly lit Fort Knox. The front receptionist, Karen, buzzed Victoria through security, and her freckles framed her welcoming grin.

Standing behind the key-swipe glass door, Karen pointed to the R&D section. "Your dad's most likely holed up in his office."

But Victoria couldn't move. She could only stare at the guy by Karen's sleek metal desk. He had to be lost. Victoria knew no one that good-looking worked in her dad's building because she came by at least twice a week to pry him out of his office cave.

Mr. Hot was tall and wore a snug black T-shirt, perfectly showcasing his lean, muscular body. Victoria inched closer and heard him ask for directions to the HR office.

When he leaned over pointing at something on Karen's screen, Victoria's vision locked tractor-beam style on his snug jeans. She could handle doing Karen's job if he was the type of specimen she could see daily.

She was afraid of stepping into the shallow end of the dating pool and he was clearly a shark who hunted in the deep end. To him, she must be chum to be gnawed upon.

Karen caught Victoria's gaze and mouthed, "I know."

Internally, Victoria screamed at Scotty to disengage her eye lock. She managed to break away and went toward the R&D offices and her dad. She stopped to pull herself together, unseen by the dedicated employees who sat behind the hallway's heavy metal doors. Inside each room, engineers hunched over tiny circuit boards, oblivious to the rest of humanity and her.

In the quiet, she shook off the dangerous attraction she'd had to the stranger. The last time she had been that attracted to a guy had been in high school, to Garett, the friend of her sister's boyfriend. Older than Dessie, he was Victoria's age.

Once Sandra had uncovered her interest in him, she had forced Victoria to invite him to the Girls-Ask-Guys dance. Sandra, betting that he'd accept, drug Victoria dress shopping. Garett had declined, devastating Victoria. Dessie had poked fun at her for the failed attempt.

In truth, Garett had already agreed to go with another girl. Sandra had insisted she and Victoria should go to the dance together to have fun. Since she had the dress, Victoria let Sandra convince her to go with her best friend as her date.

After Sandra had left behind her forced beauty-pageant days in elementary school, she'd sworn off dresses, makeup, or fancy hairdos, so it was no surprise to Victoria when Sandra rented a tux. The dismay at Sandra's choice of outfits came from her beauty queen mother.

On the day of the dance, Garett's date had gotten sick. He had called, asking if Victoria was willing to still be his date for the night. They agreed to meet at the dance.

Sounded like a beautiful beginning, but reality was cruel.

When Victoria had gotten her first glimpse of Garett, she'd pulled up so short, her heels stuck to the flower-strewn entrance. Sandra plowed into her back.

Garett was dreamy—tall, handsome, and dashing—in his pressed suit. They had less than one dance before the magic vanished.

Once he had opened his mouth, the illusion shattered. During their first dance, he puffed up and admitted to "taking one for the team" being with her to gain favor with Dessie.

Victoria had waltzed him over to Dessie, spun him out of her arms, snagged Sandra, and left the dance.

By Monday, Dessie started dating him and rubbed it in Victoria's face, too. As a couple, they lasted for a nanosecond.

Per the norm, her sister flitted to a new boyfriend. Victoria had been grateful she never had to talk to Garett again.

She shook off her past and pushed away from the hallway wall and her crappy high-school drama. Tonight, she had a date and could move forward. Her stomach felt knotted. She tamped down her rising panic. Squaring her shoulders, she continued down the hall to her dad's office.

The last door had the window covered with blank pieces of paper taped together. Victoria pressed the intercom to her dad's office and in her best Frankenstein voice said, "I'm here for your brains."

After a few moments of cursing and slamming drawers, her dad opened the door. Right next to the door was his overflowing desk, papers laid over with wires, making the piles haphazard and in danger of falling.

"Lunchtime already?" His hair was spiky and wild like Benjamin Franklin after the lightning experiment, his rumpled polo shirt faded with a small tear on the sleeve.

"When was the last time you trimmed your whiskers?" Victoria brushed crumbs off his coarse, slightly overgrown beard. "Did you sleep here?"

"Time drift. Absorbing project. Plus, a new technician is starting today." Her dad's stomach interrupted his excuses with loud rumbles. He eyed his stack of tattered take-out menus that poked through the mess by his office phone. His gaze slipped to his computer and then to her. "Well, we could..."

Victoria tapped her fingers on her hip and she could feel her face solidify into a nag mask. A look she'd learned from her mother. "Go ahead. Finish what you were saying, Daddy."

He raised his hands. "Right, out it is. You pick, I'll pay."

"I said I'd pay."

"What? Can't hear you." He offered her his arm to loop hers through.

She nudged his shoulder. "Liar, I know you have sharp hearing. I'll let it slide since we're going onward to food."

PITA STOP WAS two doors down and Victoria's choice. They walked over, ordered, sat in silence, and it was perfect. Customers filtered in for the lunch rush. For most people, the quiet at their table would have been pressure enough to fill the space with nonsense noise. But between Victoria and her dad, the lack of conversation was peaceful. Relaxing. Normal.

Being in her dad's presence soothed her. After the divorce, if Victoria had a rough day, her dad would come in and watch over her until she fell asleep. Of course, he had plenty of excuses for why he was in her room. A light bulb to change. A lost shoe in her closet. Missing nail clippers.

Her dad knew to just be there for her. No words needed, and today was the same. She knew they needed to talk about Dessie. Not yet though. She wanted to tell him about her first date, but her stomach cramped thinking about saying the words, *I have a date*. She refused to pop this bubble of tranquility.

A small, absentminded smirk lined his lips, yet this face looked more haggard today. He seemed stressed enough without her laying down her drama on him.

The "Wicked Witch of the West" theme song blared from her phone. Her relaxation bubble burst as the imagery of the witch riding in a tornado slammed Victoria into crisis mode. One button and her mother was banished to voicemail. Time to discuss the Notre Dame-sized wedding bells in the middle of the room.

Tact was never the way to go with her dad. A tackle-and-pin move was necessary to discuss messy things in life. Messy things such as emotions or daughters.

Victoria opted for the sneaky body slam attack. "Are you OK with Dessie getting married?"

His fork froze halfway to his mouth. His jaw hung open. Eyes dilated.

"Dad. Don't even try to deer-in-the-headlight me." Before he could retreat, she dove in with rapid words to press her advantage. "Are you alright with giving your youngest away? In a few weeks?"

He dropped his fork. He scooted his chair back as though distancing himself from the subject. "No, I don't know this boy. I don't know how they met. I don't even know what her last name will be. But the marriage is what Dessie wants. Knowing that, can the wedding be stopped?"

Victoria blinked. Long speech for her dad. She mirrored him, leaning back from the table. "It's Dessie. And Dessie listens to no one."

"Except maybe your mother."

"Don't bring up Mother."

"What she'd do now?" His soft, caring tone made her revert into a lost and lonely teenager again.

"She's not going to talk Dessie out of this wedding." Victoria stabbed her Greek side salad, her voice as brutal as her lettuce-spearing. "You said Mother could stop this. This mistake. And does she? No."

He put down his food and gave her his patent parental stare. "Why must you always think the worst of your mother?"

"Because I know her. Remember, she left us, walked out, for no reason. Did she move across the country to start over or pursue her dreams? No, she moved a few streets away. Mother is the runway model, the poster child, the epitome of selfishness, and thanks to her, Dessie is, too."

"You've never gotten along with her. I'll be the first to admit it. Millie's not good at showing her emotions well. But she loves you more than you know."

Victoria snorted. "Right, because her constant harping is her being a caring mother."

He raised his hands, palms out. Two stop signs directed straight at her. "You won't believe me, so I won't listen to you belittling your mother anymore. I hope one day you'll understand her better and go easy on her." His words were tinged with sadness.

"Go easy on her? She never was easy on you or me."

His narrowing eyes, flaring nostrils, and threatening eyebrows made her shut up.

She knew he wouldn't hear another syllable against Mother. "She's Glenda the Good Witch. Happy?"

Her dad nodded and let his stern face drop. "How's Sandra?"

"Thin. Fine. Thin."

"And the vet?"

"Busy. I love being around all the animals." Her shoulders relaxed. She was the luckiest lady, getting to work in the field she loved. All she needed to do was find a more meaningful job in the field she loved.

"Good."

The rest of the lunch, they sank into their old routine of silence peppered with surface conversations about work and, well, more work. By the time her dad walked her to her car, they were sharing inside jokes, not worrying or arguing about either her mother or sister.

"Have a good day, Daddy."

"I will, and don't let Dessie or your mother twist you up. I love you." He deposited a quick kiss on her cheek and slammed her car door shut.

Head down and hands shoved in his pockets, her dad beelined toward the safety of his family-free and drama-free lab.

Victoria laughed. His momentary emotional confession of love must have triggered a PTSD-like reaction in him.

Though distant and wrapped up in his work, her dad was a softy and made her feel as though the world was hers to conquer.

Victoria needed the Mighty Conqueror vibe. Because tonight was her first official date. She checked the clock and booked it back to the vet's office.

WORK WAS a furry battlefield all the way until they locked the doors. Her body went through the motions with minimal absentminded mess-ups. Her conquer groove vanished completely once she drove home. Her mind fretted about her upcoming date. She forgot her keys in the ignition and had to traipse down the three flights of stairs to get into her apartment.

Inside, she and the mirror stared at each other. She felt uneasy and queasy. Maybe she should cancel. But the time was too close, she couldn't cancel. Her mother, Miss Manner's mini-devil, would never let her call off an appointment with less than a thirty-minute notice.

Her phone rang, derailing her mental inventory of what not to wear and viable excuses she could use to not go. She answered. "Hey, Sandra."

"You all prim and prowl-ready?"

"No, and I have thirty to dress, drive, and dash into Jake's BBQ." She held up a pink shirt and discarded it with the rest of her crappy clothes. "I have nothing date-worthy. I should have canceled."

"*Brawaaaakkkk.* Chicken. Are you sprouting feathers?" Sandra's taunting tone would do any schoolyard bully proud.

Her friend's slam jolted Victoria. Sandra's secret weapon

against her. Once she started heckling, Victoria could never renege. *Curse the woman for knowing how to make me do things I would rather not do.*

Victoria took a deep breath and returned fire at Sandra. "If I am growing feathers, I hope you're allergic to 'em."

Sandra's words softened. "Seriously, you'll be fine. You'll wow him with your witty charm. If you wear your ass jeans, you'll also wow him with your curvalicious body."

"You mean the dark jeans with red patches on the pockets? Could work for a barbecue place." Victoria paused, trying to remember if the pants were clean.

"This is what a lesbian best friend is good for: impeccable fashion tips and truth-slinging."

"Your ego is bloated. Got to go."

"Flirt like a champ." Sandra always threw in the last word.

Victoria tossed her phone on top of the reject-clothes mound, unearthing said jeans from the pile. Jeans, a white button-down shirt tied in the front, and her red cowboy hat. She was ready for the night.

Final mirror check. Success. She looked good and the jeans were the best decision. Her phone alarm sang, "*Time is on my side.*"

Her ten-minute warning blared. Her pulse accelerated. Sweat ran down her neck. Her vision blurred, and the room whirled.

"Move it, woman." Fear, hope, and keys in hand, it was time for her first real date.

TIP # 4

DATING ENDURANCE: EQUAL PARTS AWKWARD AND ALCOHOL

*T*he day after her sister's phone call, Victoria drove to Jake's BBQ to meet Mateo. Her stomach was tighter than a fresh suture and just as comfortable. The restaurant's neon lights washed her car in red and white. She had three weeks to get a date for the wedding.

"Squat, Squat, find me a parking spot." Victoria prayed to the benevolent parking god. "I will sacrifice fries, beer, and my right shoe."

A spot miraculously opened. *Thank you, Sandra, for showing me The Way of Squat.*

She slipped into the prime curb spot. "You're the best, Squat. Right next to the door. I'll totally drink a beer to your awesomeness, you sweet parking god you."

A chalkboard sandwich sign on the sidewalk by the front door advertised the daily specials. Big, bold letters at the bottom announced the Dixie Vixens started playing at 7:30.

One minute until Victoria was late. All she had to do was get out and go in. The ten feet between her and the entrance could have been ten thousand feet, because she couldn't move.

Her body started quaking. Closing her eyes, she blocked out the neon lights and tried to tame her anxiety. "Be cool. Be flirty. Be engaging. You finally have a date. You can do this."

Pep talk over, Victoria gathered her jittery, spastic energy and entered Jake's BBQ.

Inside, the scene muted all thoughts. The place was the definition of down-home. A blaring jukebox and a wooden dance floor sat in the heart of the place. Cowboy hats were everywhere. She swallowed. Roughnecks, sawdust, antler chandeliers.

A quick scan of the room didn't reveal anyone who could have been Mateo. The last time she had seen him, he was tall and thin and wore black-rimmed glasses. Geek chic.

She created a confident façade, wove around families and couples waiting for tables, and stepped up to the hostess stand.

The hostess, from her boots to her Texas-sized hair, was pretty and perky.

She read the lady's nametag. "Hi, Mary. I'm meeting someone here named Mateo. Party for two. Has he been seated yet?"

Mary checked the table list. "Nope, no one here by that name."

Victoria hooked her thumbs into her pockets and tapped her index fingers on her jeans. "Do you have a table where I can see the front door?"

"Sure thing." Mary grabbed menus, strutted toward the dance floor, and stopped at a table.

The table happened to be next to the stage. Victoria picked the seat that gave her a clear view of the front door and dance floor.

Her skin itched. She shied away from the dance floor. She loved to dance, but not in public. The heaviness of people watching her, judging her, made her leery.

Mary handed over the menu to Victoria. "Susie is your waitress. She'll be along shortly."

On Mary's way to the front of the restaurant, all the men ogled, their drunken and brazen stares glued to her sexy wiggle.

The patrons were a mix of multi-generational families and clusters of young friends out to have a fun night. They all flowed into the restaurant in waves. Being seated to her left was a party of fifteen who laughed and shouted. Victoria could hear every other word even over all the restaurant noise.

The table in front of her had a sweet older couple holding hands. All around her, raised voices sounded joyful and yet she sat alone.

Mateo would arrive soon. Her stomach rumbled and quivered.

Perfect, she was starving and nervous. For the one high school dance date, they hadn't done dinner. What was the proper dating protocol?

If Victoria ordered now, would she be perceived as a fatty who couldn't contain her ravenous, gluttonous appetite? Living in a heavy body left her in constant awareness of how people thought her too lazy to lose weight. It wasn't for lack of trying. If only she could get her sluggish metabolism to work, she'd drop the pounds.

Susie the waitress appeared, as though her hunger pangs had summoned her in all her teeny denim shorts, yellow cowboy boots, and blonde hair glory. Great, another woman who outshone Victoria's plainness.

Where do all these perfect specimens of women come from? The distant planet of Hotness?

Susie opened her thick, stripper-on-a-pole red lips and asked, "You waiting for one more, honey?"

She slumped in her seat. "Yes."

This must have been what happens when she broke her own dating rule of not asking a guy out: humiliation.

"Can I get you a drink while you wait?"

"Tempted to order a margarita bigger than a bathtub. I'll substitute a sarsaparilla instead."

"Coming right up." Susie gave Victoria a fake Texas smile and wandered off to her next table.

Two sarsaparillas and thirty minutes later, Victoria checked her phone. Again. Finally, she broke down and texted Mateo.

R u OK? I'm here

Susie swung by to double-check her drink level, an empty tray balanced on one hand and her other on her hip. "This a first date?"

Victoria couldn't hide her shock or her grimace. "Is 'never been on a date' tattooed on my forehead?"

"Shug, this isn't just a first date, but your First Date? Don't fret if he doesn't show." Susie's voice was sunny. "I saw a few guys at the bar eyeballing you."

Victoria managed a half-smile, distrustful of the men who'd be "eyeballing" her. With her twisted luck, they would have no hair, teeth, or hygiene. "Thanks."

"Sure you don't want anything to eat while you wait?"

Victoria caved to emotional munchies and ordered. "The potatoes skins loaded with everything."

"Sounds good." Susie glided away.

"And a margarita as big as a ten-gallon hat," Victoria called after her.

Calories and carbs be damned, she needed a pity party. Tears threatened. Deserted on her first real date. Victoria fidgeted with the brim of her red cowboy hat.

She couldn't wait to get her infusion of adult courage. Adult courage could muffle the crappy little voice that listed all her flaws.

Out of the thick dance crowd emerged a thin, tall man who waved at her. Only the stage was behind her, so he had to be Mateo revised.

Gone–the geek chic. Gone–the tattered Nintendo game shirts. Gone–his Converse high tops.

He'd gone country. Black cowboy hat tilted like he was a George Strait throwback, jeans plastered to him, highlighting his non-existent butt, and his codpiece-style crotch, thrust forward. Not an attractive view.

"Glad I made it." His greeting was as fake as NutraSweet. He plopped onto the seat across from her and seemed to have forgotten that he was forty-five minutes late. "Did you order already?"

Victoria dug out her brightest smile. She wouldn't let his lateness ruin her first date. No matter him not texting her or his lack of manners. "No problem, I just ordered some potato skins."

"My favorite." He went from interest to ignore, his tight, flinty posture anything but welcoming. There was nothing. No talking. No eye contact. Did he even remember her from their English 101 class?

Since she initiated this date, she'd get this disaster started.

"Did you finish college?" Victoria mentally whacked herself for such a lame conversation starter.

He continued to scrutinize the thickening crowd, flaring his nostrils like a skunk marched up his nose. Mateo scoffed and swung his eyes to Victoria. "College sucked. I didn't finish," he said, his tone ticked off. His lips locked into a smiling position, yet the expression wasn't friendly.

Then silence descended but, unlike with her father at lunch, this quiet frayed Victoria's nerves.

She longed for the nearest exit, yet she plowed on trying to make this date work. "I know how you feel. I didn't finish either."

He took her hand and with icy fingers drew circles on the back of her hand. "You do understand me."

After ignoring her for minutes, why was he scrutinizing her now?

Susie swung by, dropped the potato skins and margarita, took Mateo's order for beer, and left. Victoria shifted in her seat, withdrew her hand, and took a sip of her drink.

"Where are you working?" Mateo's voice dropped to 1-800-Lov-U-Lot husky.

The tone should've warmed her up. It didn't. Victoria dug into the appetizer. "I run the front office for a veterinarian."

His eyes tracked something behind her. "Really?"

Victoria resisted turning around again to see what he was watching, or yelling at him to stop being squirrely, and instead, she answered his question. "I like the work. Today was a mess. A little wiener dog spooked Mr. Emerson's parrot."

"Interesting." Mateo scooted back into his chair, phoning in his attention.

This date had a similar feel to the date in high school she had with Garett. Both Garett and Mateo acted distracted. Thankfully, Mateo wasn't obsessing over getting into her sister's pants.

Unsure what to do, she played with the condensation on her massive margarita and continued talking about her work. "The poor parrot flew around the lobby saying all the words in its vocabulary. The owner is an old sailor. The parrot recited haikus. Kama Sutra haikus. Recited them at the top of its little feathered lungs. Parents covered their children's ears. Heck, there were X-rated things I wished I could unhear."

"You don't say." Histone broadcasted disinterest as did his stupid nod. The type of nod you'd give a rambling child.

She tried again to entice him to pay attention with her funny story. "When the frazzled bird finally landed on the front desk, it pooped all over the counter. And a unicorn flew around my head." Victoria's story should have ended in a jovial flourish. Instead, her tone was flatter than roadkill.

"Weird."

One word. After the whole story, a single word. Maybe she should bail on this date.

Behind her, the band warmed up, drowning out any possibility of conversation, even if she had wanted one. She would have taken the cursing parrot over this guy. At least the parrot would have talked back.

People around them hooted, hollered, and catcalled.

Mateo straightened, snagged her wrist, and pulled her up and out of her chair. Not once did he look at her. His attention was on the front mic.

"Hey," she shouted over the roaring crowd.

He barreled onward, dragging her behind him. She ended up hemmed in by her crappy date and the overcrowded dance floor.

The glamorous lead singer strutted to the mic in her stiletto heels like she was hotter than the Arizona sun. Her poured-into jeans accented every steamy curve. She opened her red lips and the throng exploded into cheers.

Victoria raised her head closer to Mateo's ear to suggest maybe they should go somewhere else. But he forced them closer, closer, closer until they were plastered against the raised stage. His head and body seemed fixated on the lead singer.

Her one and only date with Garett was loads better than this disaster. She slid under Mateo's arm to leave. Not that he cared.

"Damn, the singer is smokin'," the beefy guy next to Victoria screamed to his buddy.

Red, spiky heels planted themselves in front of Victoria and Mateo. The singing vixen gripped the beefy guy by the shirt and puckered her lips. The guy followed the lips, vaulting onto the stage. The singer laid a big kiss on him.

Kissing a stranger so easily sent a shudder down Victoria's spine.

Dazed, sporting a slobbery puppy-love grin, the guy stretched his burly arm toward the hottie with the mic. "I love you."

Without missing a note, she easily dodged, passing him to security, then beamed out to the crowd, still singing.

The singer zeroed in on Victoria and she blew a kiss right at Victoria, fluttering her long lashes.

Thoroughly creeped out, Victoria leaned away and felt Mateo's chest pressed into her back, his temperature scorching.

She turned toward him. His throat veins bulged worse than a rabid dog.

Mateo watched the lucky guy who was wearing the singer's fire engine red lipstick weave his way down the steps, and then his eyes latched onto Victoria.

She felt like a trapped mouse. She wiggled to escape.

Mateo reeled her in closer. "You'll do."

She'd do for what?

His breath was beer-saturated like he'd sucked on a hops Tic Tac.

"This isn't happening." No one could hear her. She wasn't going to let those thin lips touch hers. Panic mobilized her. Victoria reared back and slammed her head into his.

Cursing, he let go.

Pushing, shoving, and hollering, "Excuse me," she slipped through the undulating crowd. Though a rough and rowdy bunch, they had manners enough to scooch over and let a crazy-eyed lady through.

She hit the door so hard, it slammed against the brick wall.

Never in her whole life had she been more grateful to be sans a purse. She had her keys out of her pocket and was gone, her escape complete with squealing tires.

In her rearview, no one came after her.

Once the glow of Jake's dissipated, Victoria focused on the road. If only she could have shed her date symptoms—the gasping and the shaking and the tremor snaking up her spine. Home now. Breakdown later.

*N*o good breakdown was complete without a sugary soother. Victoria swung by the nearest ice cream drive-thru and ordered two quarts of soft serve, one vanilla and one chocolate. "Lean on Me" played on her phone.

Sandra. Her internal panic eased a little.

With her ice cream safe on the passenger seat and an emergency cone melting in her hand, Victoria put Sandra on speaker.

"How's your date going?"

"Bad." Victoria's voice trembled.

"How bad?" Sandra's tone dropped to mama bear dangerous.

The thought of Sandra mauling Mateo made her brighten. "I just bought two quarts of crappy-date eraser. Want some?"

"I'll pop over to your place and have spoons waiting for you. Screw the bowls."

Twenty minutes later in Victoria's apartment, Sandra and Victoria ate a quarter of each flavor at the kitchen table. She recounted her horrible night. Sandra fumed until Victoria got to the horrible part: her hitting Mateo hard enough to produce whiplash. Then Sandra gave her a high-five.

"I swallowed humiliation and asked friends to help me find a date. And this is what happens." Victoria's voice was a high-pitched, low-gusto whine.

"You improved your reaction time from Garett. You just left Garett to hook up with your sister. With Mateo, you delivered your answer clearly, straight with a little head-to-head communication."

An annoying song about partying with Barbie started singing on her phone.

"Dessie, voicemail land for you." Victoria slid the phone icon on her screen to the left.

The kitchen phone rang.

"Your sister is as persistent as your mother."

"Both as stubborn as a foot fungus."

"You going to answer?"

"I refuse to answer."

The machine picked up. Her mother's voice stopped their conversation. "Victoria, are you home? I'll try your cell."

Victoria jumped to the defensive with Sandra before she could start heckling her about avoiding her family. "I'm currently ignoring both family headaches, not out of unlove, but out of self-preservation."

A deep *uhm* was the only response from Sandra.

The "Wicked Witch of the West" played on her cell, each note a pickax stab to her brain. Sandra must have registered Victoria's facial twitch because she intervened.

Sandra scooped up the singing cell and slid the phone icon to the right. "Hi, Millie. What? Your friend has a son you want Victoria to meet?"

Victoria crammed more chocolate ice cream down her throat to keep from screaming. The screams built, squeezing her lungs. This couldn't be happening. Her mother setting her up would be a certified disaster.

"A blind date for this Saturday?" Sandra asked into the phone but stared straight at Victoria, aiming for her ego.

Victoria knew Sandra wanted her to accept the date. She swayed from side to side, her whole body objecting to the match.

Her mother might mean well. Yet nothing her mother did for her *went* well.

Case #2563 of her mother's Mothering Gone Wrong was Victoria's sweet-sixteen gift. The present had sounded great. A day spa package and an hour-long shopping spree with a style expert. By herself. By the end of the day, she had been plucked, kneaded, embarrassed, and shoved into uncomfortable clothes she would never wear, truly an adventure for the therapist's couch.

A date planned by her mother would be horrific. So horrific only multimillion-dollar special effects could come close to capturing the terror.

Sandra pantomimed Millie's flapping mouth and contorted her features at the phone. Finally, she broke into the phone monologue. "Yeah, well, we're a little busy."

Her mother screeched. An explosion of words flew at Sandra. Victoria rocked a little faster.

Millie versus Sandra. Not going to be pretty. Hell, Victoria wasn't even sure who would win. Millie had years of guilt-slinging on Sandra. Sandra had youth and a slicing wit that scarred.

"What? Can't hear you." She stabbed the screen to disconnect and missiled Victoria's phone onto the couch. "Ugh. Your mother."

"Selling sin to the devil. I know all the horrors of my mother."

Sandra got up from her chair, squeezed Victoria's shoulder,

and walked toward the living room. "Well, don't expect the devil to die just yet. She has a date all planned for you on Saturday."

Victoria shuddered. "From the moment I was birthed, my mother has had a plan for me."

Flopping belly-down on the couch, Sandra watched her best friend. "Nineteen days till the wedding. What's next?"

With the calendar mocking her, Victoria mustered all her dignity and answered, "I'll troll for men tomorrow night at the bar." She laced her voice with enough straw-house confidence to fool any wolf.

Sandra gaped at her. A gape that could've doubled as a shocked fish. "A bar?"

"Yes."

"A bar bar?"

"You always come home with dozens of numbers when you go out." Victoria shrugged, all nonchalant, but her hands, hidden under the table, were clenched together. "Fairly straight forward, low lighting, and low expectations."

"Vi, trolling for a date at a bar is a Hallmark movie plot and so not you." Sandra downgraded her lecture tone and shifted into worrywart mode. "Your fear of going to your sister's wedding without a date is making you desperate."

"I'm afraid. Afraid of not having a date, and then all the whispers about me always being alone will be true." Victoria shivered at the thought of how her family would judge and pity her if she showed up at the wedding alone. She could imagine the polite and condescending smiles they'd heap on her. Her resolve solidified. "I have less than three weeks to find a date for this wedding."

Sandra raised her hands palms outward showing Victoria she was on her side. "I don't want to see you taken advantage of. You're new to cruising the dating scene, which can be dangerous."

Victoria gathered her righteousness. "You go out all the time. I know it can be dangerous. I'm not looking for true love, but a decent warm body to be my date. So tomorrow I'll go bar hopping." Her words were quick. Clipped. Final.

"How about I go with you?" Sandra's olive branch was clear in her warm tone.

The offer for help made her sag. She didn't have to brave the troll den without backup and said, "I'd appreciate a capable wingman. Thanks, Goose. How about seven?"

They set a time for their visit to the On Q Bar. How much further could her shredded dignity slip?

AT PRECISELY 6:59 P.M. Wednesday, Victoria sat in her car hyperventilating and ordering herself to get inside On Q Bar.

Sandra Freddy Krueger-ed her window. Victoria's pulse spiked over a hundred beats per minute. She glared at her soon-to-be-departed best friend.

That didn't faze the Krueger.

In her standard jeans, Keds, black T-shirt, and jacket, Sandra should be too casual for the bar scene, yet she projected an image of a slumming, slightly heavy model. Regardless of what Sandra wore, or her weight, every eye followed her.

"Come out, come out, it's heart-breakin' time." Sandra tapped on the window again.

With an adjustment to her '50s pillbox hat, Victoria got out and they headed into On Q.

The bar managed to be both mellow and lively. People lounged on overstuffed couches around glass coffee tables. Dim lighting in blues and greens mixed with the brightly colored clothes of the patrons lining the bar.

A few twiggy girls hung all over each other and grinded

away on the dance floor. They must have been newly minted twenty-one. No one over the age of twenty-four would've been that blatantly grotesque, in public at least. Most people averted their gaze from the spectacle—well, except for the men.

Victoria soaked in the vibe of the bar and decided age-wise she fit in here. Most patrons dressed as though they had come directly from work. No one was outrageously garish. No attention whores. Well, minus the grinding newbies.

Decked out in a cute knee-length black skirt and a lacy cream tank top, she felt the part of an adult cruising for a date. If only her heels would stop pinching. Made of black lace, they were too adorable not to wear. Cute or not, they were strictly sitting shoes. Time to find a seat...soon.

Guys tracked Sandra. Nobody seemed to notice Victoria. She felt like a nondescript drop in the bucket of beauty. She forced herself to smile, refusing to show her dread at being in this dark level of Dante's Inferno.

She wouldn't go alone to the wedding. A catwalk attitude flooded her body. Victoria mentally demanded that every eye track her as she faked confidence and paraded to the bar. The tiny torture devices strapped to her feet struck against the hardwood floor, trumpeting her approach.

The bartender was yummy in a salmon-colored shirt and with thin sideburns, beard, and a pencil mustache.

Victoria caught the bartender's eye and ordered. "I'll have a Seven-N-Seven."

"Coming right up, doll," he called from down the bar, flashing a killer smile and starting an elaborate show concocting her drink.

Sandra popped up behind Victoria. "Don't be fooled by the bartender. He's sweet and as gay as his shirt advertises."

Her facial muscles froze, which worked out well, otherwise her jaw would have hit the bar top. Her eyes remeasured the approaching glittery bartender. In his hand rested a squatty glass of bravery.

"Here you are, Beautiful. I love your Jackie O hat." His husky, sexy voice didn't match the fashion statement his silk shirt advertised. "Are you planning on opening a tab or pay cash?"

Sandra laid a twenty on the bar. "Cash and make it a ditto on the order."

"Well, Starry Lips, I haven't seen you in ages." The bartender took the cash, handed Sandra her change, and turned to whip up her drink.

Oh, no way Victoria could let the nickname disappear without comment. "Starry Lips?" Victoria managed to hold in the giggle fit.

Sandra ran her palms across the smooth wood and studied her reflection in the bar mirror. "We met at Swing By, a lovely little bar in the gay community when I dropped in for drinks with coworkers. All the straight men in the building were hanging off my every word, hence the nickname."

All Sandra had to do was exist and the men came a-flocking. All Victoria had to do was smile and the men went a-fleeing. Sandra and Dessie were twins in this respect. Most likely why the two never got along well.

Victoria stared at her drink, wishing she were home. "You are the definition of humble and modest."

"Can't argue with truth." Sandra shrugged.

Though Victoria could drink the truth into oblivion.

*T*he bartender pushed Sandra's drink across the bar to her.

With liquor in hand, both Victoria and Sandra snagged two barstools at the bar.

Checking out the men in On Q, Sandra sipped her Seven-N-Seven. "I'll be your guy filter. He hits on me, I'll check him out, and I'll only bounce along the good ones to you."

Within minutes, Soothsayer Sandra was proved right. Men materialized at her elbow. Asking her to dance, asking to buy her drinks, asking her to conceive their firstborn.

Sandra declined as only a dating pro could—there were smiles, waves, and no cursing when the men left, alone.

In between guys number five and six, Victoria grabbed Sandra's arm, pulling her in close for a quick heart-to-knife talk. "This isn't working. Half the single men in here swung by and not one is fit to know my name?"

Sandra didn't flinch at Victoria's harsh tone or words. "I don't want to lob you a dating STD."

The hot bartender floated down to their side of the bar. Without them ordering, he came bearing two more Seven-N-

Sevens. He grinned, oozing sexy vibes. "What brings you ladies in tonight?"

Sandra hooked her thumb at Victoria. "Her baby sister's wedding is in three weeks."

Victoria's cheeks must have radiated dayglow embarrassment even in the low light, because the drunk lady next to her laughed loudly, filling the space with the sound of judgment. "I'm in a bind."

"So, you're trolling?" He nearly shouted to be heard over the drunk giggling next to them, as he slid the drinks forward.

"She'll take the troll." Sandra raised her glass.

"I asked you to come why?" Victoria's question had no heat but loads of regret.

Sandra and her newest buddy ignored Victoria's comment and continued to conspire.

The bartender nodded to the couch section by the door. "See those two men seated by the dance floor?"

Sandra and Victoria tracked his gaze to an L-shaped couch on a little platform.

He tapped the two new drinks on the bar. "These are from them. They're regulars and aren't too bad."

"Pick one, doesn't matter to me." Sandra drained her old cocktail and reached for the new one.

Squinting in the low light, Victoria checked out the two guys. "The left one in the dark business suit looks young."

Sandra glanced at the guys, disinterested. "The right one has tattoos. See the wrist tat? I can't make out the image in this light."

"You're right. The guy on the right is a softer version of the punk living a floor down from me." Victoria liked his pale-yellow shirt, rolled up to the elbows. The look made him more approachable than the suit.

"Don't struggle too hard, Vi. Go for the one you think you'd be more comfortable with. Neither one is my gender type."

"The suit is yours to distract."

"Poor doggy, he's going to leave here alone tonight. Things you endure for friends." Sandra hugged Victoria.

Victoria rearranged her features into what was hopefully a pleasant, inviting expression and strolled over to the couches with Sandra, her wingman, in tow.

Sandra plopped down next to the suit on the left. "I'm Sandra."

The suit drank her in, starting from Sandra's Keds, up her long legs, and ending at her breasts. He turned his shoulders toward Sandra with a happy bulldog grin minus the slobber. He had the puppy-dog enthusiasm down pat. "I'm Wes." Wes hitched his thumb at his buddy behind him. "That's Nick."

Up close, Nick seemed older than Victoria first thought. He had a thick, gold watch and neatly pressed pants.

"Nice to meet you, Wes. Nick." Victoria's voice stayed steady, but she slipped down onto the couch before her knees gave way and her fake bravado drained away. "I'm Victoria."

Nick raised his glass to her. "Pleasure to meet you."

She looked over to her wingman for a little friendly comfort, yet her view and support were obscured by the hulky suit of Wes.

No problem. It's only a conversation. Easy. Open mouth and talk. "What do you do?" Victoria asked Nick.

"Real estate. And you?" Nick's icy blue eyes were clear, and they never wavered from scrutinizing her.

"I work at a vet's office." She answered automatically and winced. Here at almost twenty-five, her greatest achievement was that she could single-handedly run a front office.

Time to enhance her truth. Enhance her life. Be what she

always wanted to be. "I'm finishing my doctorate in veterinary medicine." The lie left a burning trail up her throat.

Nick's smile was welcoming and encouraging. "Very impressive."

His interest warmed her belly like straight whiskey.

Sandra peered around the suit, her eyebrow cocked, asking a silent question of aren't-you-being-a-soap-star liar?

Victoria widened her smile to keep the truth from springing out. She'd always dreamed about becoming a veterinarian. Then she could run her own clinic.

"Tough field of study." Nick lounged on the couch, his arm behind her.

He was Hollywood cool. She was a jittery crack addict. Victoria wished she could be like him, so composed and confident.

His fingertips brushed down her arm, the touch faint and delicate.

Goosebumps rose to meet his gentle caress. Boy, she did need to get out more often.

She fidgeted with her cell phone, checking the time. "Yes. Lots of years of school to become a vet." She wished she could wash down the burnt taste of that lie. Too bad she downed the drink at the bar.

"I thought you looked smart." Nick shifted closer, the space between them turning more intimate. "That's why I sent you a drink. My invitation for you to come and meet me."

"Smart. Yep, that's me." The desire to run built inside her and to keep from chickening out, she inched closer to him, too.

His eyes shifted to a darker blue. "Want to catch a movie tonight?"

Nick's warm clove scent made her want to say yes and accept his offer.

She wanted to say yes? No. She couldn't say yes. Panic

flooded her synapses. All her controlled terror she'd been suppressing busted out, tap dancing on her fight-or-flight trigger.

Movie characters could flirt like this. Sandra could do this. She couldn't do this.

Victoria didn't know this guy. She only had a bartender's word saying he's a good guy.

Accepting his offer would lead to more embarrassment. More disappointment. She didn't need anymore. Not after Mateo's serving of self-esteem deflation.

Victoria clutched her purse and held it between the two of them. "I-I-I just remembered I have a test tomorrow."

Nick set his glass down. He scooched closer, closing the tiny gap between them. His knee brushed hers. His contact startled her.

Distance, she must have distance. Her mouth moved faster than her feet. "Sorry. Thanks for the drink. Sandra and I need to leave."

The guys exchange a doomed SOS look.

Yes, the forecast was cloudy with a ninety-nine percent chance for rejection.

She sprung up, snatched Sandra, and ran away.

The door snapped shut behind Sandra and Victoria, cutting off the bass hum of On Q. The February night was nippy.

"I'm stupid." Victoria's tone crackled, thick with irritation. "The second a guy shows interest in me, I run. Pathetic."

"Yep. Normally, you're unflappable with your polite smile and your distant teacher tone. But tonight was fun watching you quake in your cute heels."

Victoria stopped walking and stared at her deranged best friend. "Tonight, fun? Terrifying. Hellish terror."

Sandra winked. "Maybe next time I could be training to be a doctor."

Neither Dessie nor Sandra ever let her off this easy. "Aren't you mad at me for turning Nick down?"

"You don't have to go out with anyone you don't want to. I'm not mad. Unless you turned him down because you feared trying something new." The force of Sandra's words slammed into Victoria.

"No. No, that wasn't the reason."

"Excellent. I hear my well-earned nightcap calling me from your apartment." Sandra skipped past her, heading for the car.

Victoria lost sight of Sandra's brunette head bobbing down the aisles of the shadowy lot.

She sharked for a date, managed to snag one, not as a set-up, not as a last-ditch date, and then turned down the invitation because she was a coward. Her spirits plummeted.

A touch on her arm stopped her.

Shock kicked her ribs. A scream climbed up her throat and she flipped around.

Nick reached out, steadying her. "I didn't mean to scare you."

Heat from his touch radiated up her arm. The electricity traveled up her spine and fried her ability to move. She let the warmth spread over her like a dry blast of summertime wind, raw and scalding.

She could smell his cologne. Clean, yet dark and dangerous. With him a breath away, her body flushed.

"You dropped this." He had her bright blue cell phone.

"Thanks." Victoria took her phone, hugging it to her chest. Just seconds ago, she was glad to be away from him, then kicking herself for throwing him aside. She had planned never to go out with Nick. She had lied to herself. The second time she'd lied tonight. What the hell is wrong with her?

A cool breeze blew, yet she shivered for so many reasons. "Sorry I had to leave in such a hurry."

"No problem. I tucked my number into your phone case."

His voice had a pinch of playfulness. "I hope you'll call me for dinner tomorrow. Your choice for when and where."

His offer weakened her resolve to not see him again.

"Yo, Vi, you coming to unlock the car or what?" Sandra's question echoed in the dark parking lot.

Swallowing the butterflies, Victoria mustered her courage, saying, "I'll call you."

He turned and threw a little salute to her. "I hope you do." And then disappeared into the bar.

Sandra popped up, snapping her fingers in front of Victoria's face. "What is going on, space cadet?"

"Nick came out." His branding touch still burned. She looked down at her hands. "I dropped my phone."

"Nice of him. But what's with the mooning expression?" Sandra asked.

"He wants to go for dinner tomorrow."

"Score one for Victoria. Let's go eat dinner tonight to celebrate." She herded her to the car.

Later, when she was alone at home, Victoria took a deep breath and texted Nick.

Tomorrow sounds good. Can't wait

FROM THE MOMENT Victoria woke the next day through her office opening duties, she worried about her first real date. With Garett, there wasn't food, or a full dance shared. He didn't count. Mateo was a setup. He didn't count. Nick asked her out. He counted.

Outside the office the sky turned dark. A storm threatened. It had been months since Phoenix had had its last recordable rainfall.

Rain tonight would be awesome. Victoria could have her

first kiss in the rain and it would be just like in the old romantic black-and-white movies.

Her thoughts cycled through what to wear, where they'd go, how to keep up her lie.

A baseball bat of reality bashed her. She wobbled, resting her forearm on the kennel chain-link fence.

The lie.

Vet school.

A warm hand landed on her shoulder.

She jumped.

Dr. Yaz's gray hair was unruly, his white doctor coat perfectly pressed, and his face concerned. "Morning, I haven't seen that look on your face since Boxy the cat tried to swallow the poor sparrow whole in the lobby."

"Too much caffeine."

"I got your text about needing to leave early the next few weeks for the wedding. No worries. Our afternoons right now are light, so go ahead. You mentioned you may need to leave early tonight. Fun plans with Sandra?"

"No, I have a date."

His eyebrows shot up into his thinning hairline, but he kept his tone neutral. "Have a good and safe time." He squeezed and let go of her shoulder.

"Thanks for the time off and acting like dad number two." Victoria gave him a grateful smile.

Dr. Yaz must have had at least forty tasks to do, but he settled against the kennel facing her and waiting for more. Even the dogs stayed quiet. "You're not nervous about your date, are you?"

The truth gushed out of her. "I told him I'm getting my doctorate in vet med. I didn't mean to lie. My life is boring."

He laughed. "That's why you look like you're about to be put down? Finish your bachelor's and apply to vet schools."

A shame tornado tore through her gut causing her to snap at

him. "There are only twenty-eight accredited vet schools in America."

"My buddy is piloting a local partnership with the University of Arizona to fast-track students to increase the number of licensed veterinarians in the valley. You already took your GRE, right? Why don't you apply?" He smiled. The condescending smile he used on owners who lie and say they didn't spoil their pampered pet.

His facial expression ratcheted up her frustration. "I have my scores, but to get into vet school can take multiple applications. Years to get accepted." Her words shot out, rapid-fire.

"Difficult, yes. Not impossible." He headed for his office, evidently done dishing lame advice.

Her phone sang, "*Come on, Barbie, let's go party.*" Victoria pinched the bridge of her nose and suppressed a why-me sigh. Dessie *would* text her now. Her sister had spidey senses and knew the moment Victoria needed to be kicked because life wasn't slamming her hard enough or with the intent to kill.

Bowing to the enviable, for one cannot ignore The Dessie, she dug her phone out of her pocket and read the text.

Booked. B there Monday morn @ 9:30. Pick me up

Naturally, she had to be her bratty sister's chauffeur from the airport. Even though she was employed, everything was always about Dessie.

Victoria could hear the doc greeting patients. She put her cell away and went to do her job and request more time off.

During the quiet moments after she checked in patients or hung up the phone, Dr. Yaz's question of why didn't she enroll echoed in her mind. His nagging morphed into an infected sliver. Time to pluck the irritant out. Victoria researched veterinarian programs every spare moment between greeting people, taking pets back, or doing paperwork.

Research done. Office hours done. Work done. Victoria

walked to her car. The sky was blue and white, not gray like it was on her drive in that morning. The rain threat had fled. No Hollywood kiss in the rain. One less dream that will never become a reality.

"Strangers in the Night" started playing on her phone. Nick. Butterflies in her stomach. He sent her a text.

7 @ Jake's BBQ I'll c u then ;)

Apparently, it wouldn't be her choice for where and when to meet for dinner like he had mentioned last night. The fluttering butterflies morphed into a line of cancan frogs.

Go back to Jake's? No problem.

No one would remember her, right?

TIP # 7
BRACE FOR THE WORST

$\mathcal{W}$ith the time and place for tonight's date confirmed, Victoria left early. She channeled inner peace and her inner Deepak Chopra on her way to the apartment to prepare. Since she knew Jake's atmosphere, that made dressing easier. She donned a black T-shirt followed by a forest green suede vest and paired that with a long, black skirt and her dad's old Stetson hat, and she sauntered out the door.

The nervousness bouncing around her body was due more to her lie than the man she was meeting for dinner. She questioned whether she was doing enough to engage in her own life.

Cruising into Jake's crowded parking lot, her phone began singing "Great Balls of Fire," startling her. Unsure of who was texting her, she pulled her phone out and laughed hard. Sandra had changed her ringtone.

Victoria invoked Squat for a parking spot. "Squat, Squat, find me a parking spot. I will sacrifice a beer and a burger."

An old, gold Cadillac's reverse lights flashed on and backed out in front of her. "Gotta love Squat."

Parked, she read the text from Sandra.

Knock 'em dead! Give Nick a big kiss 4 me! Goose

Well, Sandra's sign-off explained the "Great Balls of Fire" choice for her new ringtone. If only Victoria could feel like Maverick.

One last lipstick check and Victoria strutted toward Jake's.

The chalkboard sandwich sign announced the nightly specials and the Dixie Vixens were playing again. This time she was prepared to see the country bar in all its glory, as a horde of cowboys and girls waited for tables.

Nick waved her over to the hostess stand. "Perfect timing, our table is ready."

In On Q's dim light, he had looked to be in his late thirties. His wide, full lips softened his tattoo image, making him less punk rocker and more playful and very youthful. Seeing him at Jake's, he looked like she could present him to her family.

A ribbon of excitement ran through her as she headed for him.

"I hope you don't mind, I got a table by the dance floor," Nick said.

She caught the edge of her chunky heel and wobbled. Did he expect her to dance? Yesterday, Nick sat by the dance floor at On Q, yet Victoria hadn't seen him dance. No, he wouldn't ask her to dance.

They weaved through the packed tables. Nick sidestepped a darting kid. "I'm glad you texted me."

"Me too." She sent him a happy and nervous smile.

Nick was here on time, had a table ready for them, and he stood holding her chair out. Points to him.

Victoria slid into her seat. "Thank you."

"Always there for a pretty lady."

It was exciting to be at a dinner where she didn't have to beg for a date. But she felt jumpy.

He lowered the menu and pinned her with a flirty smile. "What are you going to have?"

His attraction ignited a Rockette response right in the lining of her stomach. Victoria shifted in her seat and studied the entrees as if she hadn't memorized them while waiting for Mateo to arrive last time she was here. "The fiesta mushroom burger looks amazing. Same with the spicy chicken wrap, too."

He closed his menu and leaned forward, propping his chin into his hand, his gaze hawkish.

She edged her menu up, but the flimsy plastic couldn't wall off his intensity. Victoria began to sweat under his scrutiny. She braved a glance at Nick. He was still watching her, measuring her, unnerving her.

His carnivorous stare was not unwelcome. Only unexpected.

Susie, the yellow-booted bombshell, was her server again. Their waitress's neutral presence convinced her stomach to simmer down again. Victoria couldn't believe how stressed she felt tonight.

She shot Susie a subtle we-don't-know-each-other head shake, pleading silently that Susie wouldn't make any reference to the disaster from two nights ago.

That farcical date had ended a few feet from where they sat.

"Hi ya, are you both ready to order?"

Nick's appraisal rode up Susie. He seemed to be taking a slow, scenic tour of Susie's long, tan legs up to her teased Texas do.

Victoria was relieved to no longer be watched like a science experiment. But she was not relieved by his scoping out their waitress. Victoria crossed her arms over her chest. Ten-point date deduction.

Susie said nothing about the leering, just tapped her notepad and kept her smile professional.

Nick leaned closer to Susie. "I'll have the fiesta burger, medium rare."

"Anything to drink?"

"Two Blue Moons." His tone was preening.

Susie scribbled the order down.

"And no mayo or onions." He swung his gaze to Victoria's breasts then slimed his way up her neck, across her lips, and finally stopped at her eyes and sent her a saucy wink. "Don't want bad breath later."

Wow, presumptuous much? Victoria kept her thoughts to herself and focused on how close it was to the wedding.

Susie shifted only her eyes to Nick. Her smile went from Zen to *Really?* with a side of a raised eyebrow. "Anything else?"

Nick grabbed Victoria's menu from her hands and passed both menus off to Susie. "My date will have the spicy chicken wraps with mixed vegetables." He'd ordered for Victoria.

The hostility radiating off their waitress was sweet and lethal.

Defuse time. Once Dessie landed in Phoenix on Monday morning, Victoria's time wouldn't be her own. Nick might be her last chance at finding a date. "No, nothing else. Thanks, Susie."

Victoria was unsure if she appreciated that he just ordered for her without her consent. Wait, no, he had asked what she wanted. She had said either choice looked good. Her irritation wilted, and she willed herself to have a good time. At least he'd been listening and paying attention to her, unlike Mateo.

The band started their set, playing a slow two-step. The singer from the other night belted out a sultry ditty. Victoria tapped her feet along to the beat. Nick stood and held his hand out to her.

Her sweat glands blasted into production. He wanted to dance? In public?

She did love to dance, except without an audience. Victoria scanned the restaurant. No one watched them. Time to be a little adventurous and stretch her comfort zone.

Having decided, a warm feeling bubbled up, both dangerous

and liberating. Victoria placed her hand in his. Nick led her to the center of the floor and everything felt different from two nights ago. Whereas Mateo was vacant and angry, Nick seemed sweet and attentive.

She could dance in public with this man.

Nick steered her around the wooden floor. He wasn't too bad of a dance partner. A whirl of sensations shot up her spine.

The band died down. Nick stepped closer. People clapped around them. The dreamy space around them shattered.

She slipped out of his embrace and applauded the band.

His voice was quiet, as he said, "Let's sit down. The food is here."

Victoria should have felt warmed by presence and attention. Instead, she felt ice layers forming. Nick slung a casual arm around her waist as they walked the ten feet to their table. Then he vanished from her side. She pivoted.

Nick was Eskimo-kissing-close to an incredibly angry redheaded woman. Her hair and attitude matched, fiery and wild. No conversation, only a right hook directed at Nick's jaw.

The force flung him into Victoria's arms.

"You slimy bastard, how dare you show up here with your newest floozy." Ripping her eyes off Nick, the woman snapped her head up and glanced at Victoria. "He's married to me, until I can divorce him, that is."

People's heads swiveled. Chairs scraped the floor. Everyone stared.

Victoria looked down at Nick. He cradled his jaw in her white arms. They stayed locked in this moment. Revulsion churned her stomach. Her green gaze steeled. "How dare you ask me on a date. And be married. And be scum." Her voice felt stuck in her throat.

Heart hardened, she dropped her arms. Dropped him.

Distanced herself from him. From his lies. From her mortification.

He tumbled to the floor with a deep, satisfying *thunk*, which reminded her of front tires hitting roadkill. The woman clenched and unclenched her big, red-tipped hands looming over Nick.

Big Red, as Victoria named her, barreled on. "That's what I thought. Did he sell you a line he worked in real estate?"

A slick dread coated her belly. Victoria could barely nod her agreement.

"Such a big shot." She snorted, tossing her thick red curls around like a wild mare stomping. "Nicky here cleans the vacant houses for them."

The venomous tone from Big Red inflamed Victoria's embarrassment. Whispers and judgment crept in from the surrounding tables.

"Let's calm down and sit down." Nick's big eyes were wide with a thousand apologies and aimed straight at Victoria.

Seeing Nick ignoring the big, red, angry lady (who was most likely his wife) snapped and cracked and shattered her calm. All the humiliation she channeled downward and outward, directly into her foot, itching to kick him.

Susie shot her arm across her path before Victoria could make him a hockey player reject. "Shug, don't waste your time on this tomcat."

Victoria swallowed her fury and pain and slumped down at the table. Her brow drew up tight, locking the tears up, and she tried to keep the typhoon of regret at bay. Loser, failure, disaster —all the words her family used to describe her were true.

Lucky her, she didn't need death to go to hell. No, for her, dating was hell. Or maybe her dating life was only a warm-up for hell, her own personal purgatory.

Dating must be a barometer of just how much torture she could survive.

Her sight blurred. Her head drooped over her plate. She'd have to pay for this disastrous dinner.

Boots scuffed on the wood and sawdust floor behind her. Victoria concentrated on her fuzzy surroundings. Cowboys in Wranglers and worn hats encircled the snake man trying to slither away. Nick was then "helped" up by a few of the roughnecks. Hauled away was a better description. They bounced him toward the exit with Susie leading and making way through the packed place.

"I'll sue you. Unhand me." Nick's voice went high and shrill. "You can't do this to me."

The waiting crowd split and the trash was chucked out the front door. A loud cheer went up around the restaurant.

Yep, her disaster and joke of a love life was something to celebrate. Humiliation wrapped her up in a warm blanket of comfy hell.

A married man. The world wobbled. She flattened her hands against the cool table, but the world continued to do its tilt-a-whirl-going-to-make-Victoria-hurl revolutions.

"You OK?" Big Red came over and placed a hand on her shoulder.

She managed to maintain her manners. "No, and I'm Victoria. You want to eat? I'm going to need to buy all of this food and it shouldn't go to waste."

The woman's face transformed. Her ruby lips spread wide in a welcoming smile that reached all the way into her eyes, making them crinkle. "Thanks, I worked up a fierce hunger kicking my lousy husband's butt."

Victoria toyed with the condensation on her thawing beer mug. "I'm surprised you aren't mad at me." Her words were mouse tiny.

"Why would I be mad at you?"

"I went on a date with him." She pushed her full beer away from her.

Susie appeared tableside, calm and cool like no marital or dating disturbance happened and she hadn't led the crazy parade outside. "He's the cheating bottom feeder. Not you, Shug."

"If you knew he was married and had accepted, that would be different from you being a sweet thing and trusting Nick." Big Red picked up Nick's drink and chugged it.

"Agreed. Now can I get you, ladies, another beer? A mixed drink? Or the most expensive scotch tonight? The nice man escorted off the premises was more than happy to pay for it all." Susie waved a worn brown wallet at them and rocked onto her toes.

Shock and guilt filtered through Victoria's mind. She couldn't run up a bill on someone.

Big Red tapped the table with one of her long nails. "Beer and a shot of whiskey to start with. Keep our glasses filled; my husband won't mind treating us ladies right. For once. You in, Victoria?"

If Big Red felt fine making her husband pay for their night out, how could Victoria argue? "I'm in."

"I was hoping you'd say that." Susie scribbled on her notepad.

The three of them high-fived. The laughter drained the tension, the ugliness, the doubt out of Victoria. By the end of the meal, the three women became fast friends. Drinks came, and Victoria swapped out Big Red's empties with her undrunk one.

Susie swung by to drop off the latest round. "By the way, Victoria, Mateo's ex was the lead singer of the Dixie Vixens, and after you left, she made sure to leave the bar with men hanging off both arms, waving to Mateo. He turned an angry red color and stormed out of the parking lot."

So, Victoria was a rebound and revenge date. The hurt stung, yet it was smaller than she thought it would be to know she was used, again, by a date. "That explains how intent he was on the band."

"You're better without him," Susie called over her shoulder as she headed to a beckoning table.

Nick's wife turned down one, two, nope, make that five dance offers from the orbiting cowboys. No one had asked Victoria.

Big Red's nightcap order was a round of twenty-year-old Scotch on the rocks. At only seventy-five dollars a pop.

With a ceremonial sip, Victoria let the smooth liquid burn a trail to her belly. Time to let the Wranglers have fun dancing with the fiery redhead. She waved goodbye to Susie and headed outside. Her drive was quiet.

Dating. How the hell do people get through this torture and become married? Or do people get married so they never have to go on another date again?

Seemed legit. Maybe that's why Dessie jumped on the matrimony train like a monkey on a banana. To stop the dating freak show.

*V*ictoria withstood the dating tornado last night without flying shrapnel impaling her. Maybe she should prepare and buy a rocker and adopt a litter of cats. Twenty cats in twenty years, that's what she was destined for if these were the types of dates she had. Actually, to be surrounded by loving felines sounded purrfecto.

While getting ready for work this Friday morning, "Wicked Witch of the West" pealed from her phone. Not what she needed. Two dates and two big, big, big strikeouts, and yet she knew that going rounds with the devil now was better than to have any hell demons hunt her down, later.

Victoria slumped against her kitchen counter, suppressed the urge to try hari-kari, and hit the green answer button. "Hello."

"Glad you could make time for me."

Oh, to be greeted by Mother Dearest's cannonball of sarcasm.

"About the date I set up for you on Saturday. Make yourself free." Each of her words were bitten off and stored in her motherly guilt arsenal.

"I never said I'd go tomorrow."

"Listen, I love you and this is to help you leave your single-hood behind. This date is with my friend Windy's nephew."

She mounted a defense because she couldn't handle her mother setting her up on a blind date. She couldn't possibly be that desperate or pathetic or hopeless. Yet. "Not everyone is like your family and needs to be married by twenty-five."

Her mother delivered rapid kidney shots over the phone. "You listen to me. Your younger sister is getting married. In three weeks. You do not have a date lined up. I want to show off how great you are both doing to all my friends. Plus, I want grandkids."

Grandkids? Air couldn't get into her lungs. The thought of kids—a right-hook, left-jab combo aimed at Victoria's internal panic button. She squeezed the phone harder with one hand and, with the other, steadied herself against the counter. Her mother constantly pressured her and Dessie to be married, yet the grandkid missile was new.

"You're going on this date." Her mother sucked in a breath to no doubt launch another verbal assault.

Still in the grandkids' tailspin, the truth of how this conversation would end became blatantly clear. Victoria rubbed her temples. "You win."

"You'll go?"

"You want me to change my mind?" Her words were testy.

"You said yes so quickly." Wonder infused every word like her mother was seeing farting leprechauns.

"I did, as long as you're sure he's single." Victoria flipped on the coffee maker.

"Victor is single. Never married." Her mother's bubbly voice boomed out of the little speaker. "I'll let his aunt know the good news."

Then, like Victoria's dignity, her mother was gone.

Ambushed and defeated by her mother, all before caffeine, was not a fantastic start for her day. Victoria looked out the window and debated about how far her phone could fly. Most of her problems stemmed from this infuriating technology. Her brain processed the time, she cursed loudly and flew down the hall to hop in the shower. Awesome, she was officially late for work.

Work that day was akin to the casting call before the Ark boarding, with a myriad of animals moving in and out of the office. Dogs, cats, a ferret, a turtle, a snake, and a horde of rats.

Victoria refused to even think about the disaster the night before, or the pending date her mother forced on her for this weekend. At closing time, the office had a funky smell.

Her feet thanked her when she sunk into her driver's seat. A text came in from Dessie.

U have a date on Saturday???? Good 4 u

Thanks, Mother, for blabbing. Weird though, a civil text from her sister? Her phone chirped again.

He won't be half as great as Damien but cheers for finally having a date

The Dessie Victoria hated appeared. This Dessie was always condescending and always needing everything to be about her. Victoria sure did miss the sweet, caring sister that died in high school. She saw rare glimpses of the old childhood Dessie. Those glimmers of her hidden sister made Victoria hang on and hope that one day, they could have a real connection.

She drove home without responding and had a tantalizing dinner of frozen ravioli. Ralph, the big black king in her life, claimed his throne—her lap—and declared naptime. Full and calmer, she scrolled through her missed texts. All were familiar names and numbers except for the first one. Selecting the unknown number, she read the text.

Victoria, I got ur number from ur mother after my aunt n her took me out 4 coffee. We r being shanghaied into a date 2morrow night. Heard u like bbq, Jake's @ 7? Victor

Was Jake's a Top 10 must-do for a first date in Phoenix? The place must be billed as "romance amongst sawdust."

She appreciated his humor. Going to Jake's for a third time, people would remember her. But if she went, she'd have Susie, the waitress, and Mary, the hostess, as backup bailers.

Victoria texted back.

Sounds good. Sorry about my mother. I wouldn't put that curse on anyone

Her finger hovered over the gray, send-arrow button. The last two failures bruised her ego. If she didn't at least respond to the text, her mother would continue to harp and scheme. One serving of silencing her mother, coming up. Victoria hit send.

Her phone chimed with his response.

I was lucky. I escaped out the window n shimmied down the fire escape 2 garner my freedom. :) Plus I got ur number out of the meeting

She laughed. Her heart beat quicker. Maybe she would have a reason to thank her mother after this date. Not wanting to stop this connection, Victoria wrote back.

U r 2 nice. No one should have 2 go through the torture. Quartering, the rack, n my mother: 3 things that should have died in the dark ages

She bit her bottom lip waiting for him to respond, and he did.

LOL, I'm glad u have a sense of humor. I can't wait 2 meet u. Good night n c u there

With that, Victoria's body heated up. Excitement pumped through her veins. She scooped up Ralph, pressed him to her chest, and sang, *"The sun will come out tomorrow."*

Her smile inflated, and her fingers flew over her phone, texting Sandra.

Help! I've got a date n nothing 2 wear

SATURDAY AFTERNOON ARRIVED. The bubbles of excitement from their text exchange had gone flat because Victoria had to get through clothes shopping in a short time. Sun streamed through the mall skylights. Foot traffic was sparse. Children scampered down the walkway with balloons jerking as they hopped and skipped. She dragged herself by another store while Sandra, in her baggy shirt and holey jeans, window-shopped.

Sandra stopped, tilting her head to study a rhinestone dress in the window display. "Any direction on what you want to wear to Jake's this time?"

"No idea. Why are all the cute clothes for size 16 and under?" Victoria's voice was filled with equal parts bitterness, anger, and vinegar.

Sandra ignored the rant, leading them further into the bowels of the mall toward Nancy's Closet. Nancy's was the only store in the eastside mall that carried a large stock of clothes in her size. There was no time to shop on the other side of town, which had better stores for those who were in the twenty-plus size range.

Victoria's anxiety and insecurity and foreboding sent her self-confidence burrowing for China.

The storefront reeked of blah. The full-figured mannequins had no panache, dressed in nondescript jeans and bland stretchy shirts. They stood in the windows warning the customers of the caliber of clothes inside. Nancy's may have been a clothing store, but the clothes forgot to be stylish. At least for anyone under the age of sixty, since the surrounding area had mainly retiree homes.

Sandra noticed Victoria's sour face and tugged on her sleeve. "Don't worry, we can find something that's perfect."

"I might be blue-lipped, purple-faced, and dead from holding my breath," Victoria grumbled.

The closer they got to the entrance, the heavier the judgment of the mall strangers weighed on Victoria. Her foot crested the threshold, she paused mid-step, swallowed a groan, and slunk inside and away from everyone's eyes.

A perky salesgirl with a waist the size of Victoria's calf materialized. "Welcome to Nancy's. Can I help you find anything?"

Maybe Victoria should go out and get the salesgirl a dozen doughnuts to fill her out a little. That way, the customers might accept this slip-of-a-girl's help without wanting to hide their bodies from her.

Victoria shook her head. This wedding was corroding her synapses. She needed to stop being nasty.

Sandra shoved Victoria in front of her. "She needs a date outfit, they're going Jake's. Do you think you can help us find something?"

The waif's feet shuffled as though she was getting ready for a race. "We just got a new line this spring, and I have an idea."

Somehow Victoria scrapped together enough inner calm not to bowl over Sandra to escape. No matter how excited those two acted about shopping, Victoria wasn't fooled. No trip to the plus section could make any woman feel thin or flirty or sexy. No spry, happy music played as her internal shopping soundtrack. No, the soundtrack for this disaster was a dirge, dry and sorrowful.

The salesgirl walked deeper into the store.

Here, reality twisted. In this plain, plus-size store, Victoria stood surrounded by things she would love to try on. She searched for the cameras because this had to be a sick prank. "When did you guys get this section?"

"Isn't the selection amazing?" The salesgirl's smile lit up her face.

Victoria tentatively touched a silky red shirt. The material was real and cool and sensual. She wanted to rub the shirt on her face like catnip. The feel was decadent. "Everything looks ripped out of a current fashion magazine."

"We got a new store manager. She came in and said we were going to experiment with this store. She is also..." The salesgirl paused and blushed.

With her hip, eyebrow, and attitude cocked, Victoria supplied the word hidden under the salesgirl's blush. "Heavy."

The girl tilted her chin up and looked right at Victoria. "I was going to say, understands our clientele. We're having a hard time keeping things in stock."

Sandra pulled a cute dress off the rack. "Let's find you something to wear."

The three of them split up and tag-team shopped. Victoria wandered down the aisles and touched all the pretty clothes.

After three trips to the dressing room, they stopped for a break. Sandra and Victoria got a drink from the coffee shop next door, returned to Nancy's, and wove through the clothes racks.

"What do you think, Vi?"

"I feel awkward in the dresses. There are a few shirts and pants that are nice."

Rolling her eyes, Sandra smiled. "Surprise of the century, you didn't pick any of the date-worthy outfits."

The salesgirl ushered Victoria into a room, snapped the door shut behind her ass, and called over the wall. "I found one last thing you must try on. The items came in last night and aren't even out on the floor yet."

Victoria stared at the checkered material hanging in the dressing room. "Um, I don't think this is my style."

Sandra piped up. "Your style is my style, an old T-shirt and jeans. Try it on quick enough and we'll have time for hat shopping."

Hats always motivated her. She stripped and slipped on the latest outfit. Turning to the mirror, she felt exposed and stupid.

"Let us see." Sandra tapped on the door.

She debated.

Sandra pounded on the door.

"Alright, alright, stash the stalker knocks for your next date."

"Quit. Stalling."

Victoria, like a good Band-Aid removal, ripped the door open.

Sandra and the salesgirl stopped mid-motion. Both talked over each other.

"That's the one." Sandra raised her hand to the salesgirl.

"I knew it would be." The salesgirl and Sandra high-fived and hustled Victoria over to the three mirrors in the center of the dressing area.

In the red and white checkered dress swishing around her knees, Victoria studied herself. "I don't know."

"It's perfect." The perky salesgirl looked over Victoria's shoulder and talked to her through her reflection. "It has a wide V-neck, which showcases your great shoulders."

"And her nice full rack."

Victoria snorted. "Simmer down, my little gay friend. Never going to turn rainbow."

"I only speak the truth."

The salesgirl coughed and said, "The skirt is an A-line, which accents your waistline and lengthens your legs. The dress really takes the country girl and spices her up for the city."

"What do you think, Sandra?" The reflection showed just her. In a dress.

"I agree. This is the one, Vi."

The two fawned over the dress.

She peered harder into the mirror to see an eighth of what

they said about the dress. "I feel funny, but if you both think I look good, how can I argue with that?"

Sandra checked the time. "Crap, we have an hour and a half to get you new shoes and dolled up for the big night."

By the time Victoria dressed and wove her way to the register, Sandra had a bag in hand. She flashed a smile that was full of wicked plans. "We'll be back soon. Then we can exorcize your closet of high school."

"You paid."

Sandra moved the bag away. "Say thank you."

This could go two ways: fight with Sandra or acquiesce to the friendly and thoughtful tyrant.

Victoria playfully slugged her arm. "Thanks, Goose. Now, I also need a new hat."

Seventy-five dollars later they had found the perfect hat and shoes, both white. Strappy sandals with a little wide heel and a straw cowboy hat with three small sunflowers on the side. With forty-five minutes till her date, she and Sandra rushed to the apartment.

Sandra finished her makeup magic on Victoria. "Check out how good I am. I gave you a very natural application to bring out the green in your eyes."

Victoria checked out her reflection.

Staring back at her was a facsimile of someone softer and more glamorous than she was on a normal day. Her dark-blonde crazy hair had been tamed into sleek curls, framing her pale face and doing something it never did. Behave.

"Wow. I couldn't replicate this makeup masterpiece."

"You don't have time to bask in my awesomeness, cause you have fifteen minutes to get down there and deliver a wow punch to your date."

They went through the lock-up routine and flew down the

stairs. The white sandals were comfortable and didn't make her wobble.

Sandra stood with one hand on Victoria's open car door. "This dinner date will be better than your last two atrocities."

"Because the odds are ever in my favor?"

"Smartass, you're dolled up better than Katniss, and she got her man. In book three. Believe in the power of threes. Any man who walks away from you is an idiot." Sandra leaned down and kissed Victoria's cheek.

A wave of anticipation rose. Victoria felt empowered. With a quick squeeze of Sandra's hand, she slipped into her car. "You're right. I look hot. Power of threes and makeup."

Sandra backed away from the car, laughing. "Correction. You ARE hot."

"Thanks."

"Any time, Maverick." The name felt right. Sandra sent her off with a small salute and a saucy wink.

Minutes later, she cruised Jake's parking lot, again praying to Squat. He must have accepted her offering because a spot appeared.

Car in park, she checked herself in the driver's side mirror. "Go get 'em, you vixen," she told her painted-up reflection.

Couples and families crowded the entryway of Jake's waiting for tables to open up. Her phone buzzed.

@ the bar, table is ready. Just need u

Instantly, her gaze gravitated to a tall hunk at the bar. Well, hell-o, Hottie.

His black shirt hugged his curves, not ripped, but he had a lean muscle look about him like Hugh Jackman. His shoulder-length hair was in a thick ponytail. All the ladies were watching him, either through the edge of their vision or straight up with stalker eyes. Even the bartender was hitting on him. She bent to mix a drink and flashed her cleavage at him, most likely asking him if he wanted her number or a lifetime commitment, no doubt.

A kid bolted through the crowd causing a cowboy to bump into Victoria when he dodged the little guy. "Sorry, Miss."

"No worries." Victoria waved off the cowboy. Focus. Find your date. Who's not Mr. Sin-in-Black. That man wouldn't need to be set up by his aunt.

Victoria hit reply.

Just walked in

The hottie dropped his eyes from the bartender's boobs to his phone. He shifted to scan the entryway and homed in on Victoria. He waved at her.

He couldn't be Victor. No, he wasn't waving at her. He's waving at someone behind her. She checked. No one was behind her.

She waved back on autopilot and her mind raced. There was no way this was going to go well tonight. Her knees softened. Her courage wavered. Too bad her feet weren't flying out the door.

Victor should be a sloucher, wearing thick glasses. A retainer. Balding. He shouldn't have wavy black hair pulled tight in a sexy, Highland-style ponytail or have wide kissable lips.

She was in jeopardy of swooning or at least drooling uncontrollably, and they hadn't even spoken.

His long, jean-clad legs kept striding over to her.

Her legs became one with the sawdust-covered floor. Courage evaporated. Gone. Her mouth transformed into the Sahara.

This could be someone besides Victor. This still could be a mistake. A huge mistake.

"Victoria?" The man's voice shattered her inner tirade. "It's very nice to meet you."

She lied. "You too."

He held up a little blinking coaster at her and stepped over to the hostess. "We're ready to be seated."

Mary undressed him with a hungry once-over. "This way."

"After you." Victor placed his hand on the small of her back and they followed the hostess.

Oh, sweet baby Jesus, he was touching her. Her low heels allowed her to stay upright. The crowd faded. The laughter. The kids. The happy couples all faded. All she could hear was her luck changing.

Thank you, power of threes.

*M*ary led them into the heart of the restaurant on a busy Saturday night. Victoria's mind bounced along on repeat, chanting *he's touching you, steering you, touching you.*

Though she might have to thank her mother for this miracle, his touch meant nothing. He was here as a favor, not because he knew her or liked her. Nothing would happen. This date was only a layover stop for him. Not the destination.

By the time they made their way to the table, she turned down the panic flames in her brain and slid into the booth.

To whatever deity didn't put her by the dance floor, she sent up a silent thanks. Nestled in a nice corner, the table had a quiet fountain bubbling nearby. A jukebox played softly in the background. No loud band tonight.

The hostess, Mary, leaned over a little too far and handed Victor his menu. Mary shamelessly flirted, so she handed Victoria her menu by reflex, not by sight. "Susie will be right with you," Mary announced and then left.

Victoria twitched in her seat. Trying not to fidget, she imagined she was sitting across from Sandra and relaxed a bit. Yet the silence built to an uncomfortable pitch. She busted the quiet zone. "How does my mother know your aunt?"

"My Aunt Windy needed fun and creativity in her life and took a painting class your mother taught. They got to talking and here we are." He peered over the top of his menu at her. "I love your hat. There aren't enough people who dare to wear hats these days."

She felt lost. Since when did her mother teach painting, and did he compliment her or give her a backhanded compliment?

"Thanks." She borrowed her head further into the menu, afraid that if she looked up, his expression would be mocking like her sister or her mother would have done. They judged her for wearing hats.

"Where do you work?"

Victoria lowered her menu, folded her hands in her lap, and studied the spot over his right shoulder. Time for the truth. All the words surged out of her in a stampede. "I'm the receptionist for a vet. I planned on becoming a veterinarian. But with one semester before I could apply to vet school, I wigged and dropped out. I'm thinking about going back, one day."

The judgment. Victoria could feel the judgment for her giving up and playing dead building. Not many people could understand why, with only one semester from getting her degree, she quit. She waited for his disgust.

"College is hard. Glad you're thinking about finishing up your degree. Working with animals is interesting. I read somewhere animals are great balancers for people's emotions. Dogs exude happy, joyful energy, and cats suck out the negative."

She braved looking at her date. His face was open and understanding. Shock threaded throughout her body. She'd never expected him to be understanding. She'd never received understanding.

"I researched colleges this week. I've never heard about animals and people's energy."

"I read it in *Cutting Science*." He hung his head a little. If Victor were five and on a playground, he would have been staring at his feet and kicking dirt. "I know the publication is geeky, but they have some of the coolest articles about new research."

"You're freely admitting you're a geek? That is the first step to recovery." Victoria teased.

His shoulders sagged back against the booth seat. "The geek rabbit hole is so deep, the first rays of our sun's birth haven't illuminated the black pit of where I am." He let loose an unguarded conspiratorial smile at her that froze her lungs and added, "I'll spill a secret: geeky is in. All the girls swoon over complex math theories."

"I would have to say my favorite is Stokes' Theorem. The boundary curves make me all aflutter." She fanned herself like a starstruck teenager.

"You know calculus?" His tone implied he disbelieved his ears.

Victoria shrugged. "My university allowed us to take three semesters of advanced math in place of the four semesters of a foreign language. I took Calc 1 to 3."

"I would have never pegged you for a math geek."

"I'm not. I enjoyed the challenge of the material."

Being smart and heavy never made for a good combo growing up. Thankfully, she was lousy with music or she could have had the trifecta of geekdom. Pulling herself out of the past, she focused on the surprising man across from her.

He put down his menu. "I got the prize mad bag accepting this blind date."

She flinched, feeling reprimanded and reminded about her

pathetic situation because he was *only* here on this blind date as a favor. Being a "mad bag" didn't sound good.

He continued, apparently not registering her lopsided, unsure smile. "You're interesting. You're training to be a veterinarian, you enjoy advanced mathematics, and you look beautiful in your country dress."

His sweet compliment and his candid expression warmed her. She grinned.

Susie appeared. "Hi ya, Vi. You both ready to order, Hon?"

Victoria straightened. That saved her from floundering for a response and she was grateful for the reprieve. "I'm ready if you are."

"Go right ahead, Vi." His left dimple appeared with a sly half-grin.

Mindful of the white on her dress, Victoria ordered a chef salad. Then, kicking herself for ordering rabbit food, she added a side steak.

His smile deepened, uncovering the fact Victor had not one but two dimples. Victoria didn't fan herself, but her pulse rate rocketed. With him flashing those white teeth and those dangerous dimples, he was much too charming.

Too charming to be with her. Victoria rubbed her wrist under the table.

He ordered a porterhouse steak. Susie left with promises of drinks.

"For a moment, I thought you were going to order only weeds. By the way, call me Iggy, all my friends do."

Had she just been dumped into "friend" purgatory? She kept her face pleasant while her brain and emotions sagged at the reminder that this man only sat across from her due to his aunt's request, not because of her. "Iggy? What's the story behind the name?"

"Only my barber knows for sure." He did a Groucho Marx impression, complete with flicking ash off an imaginary cigar.

Victoria giggled. "Who says that anymore?"

"Me. Apparently." He wiggled his eyebrows up and down, continuing the Groucho love.

"Where did you go to college?"

Iggy dropped his gaze away from hers, placed his right hand on his left arm, and pushed away from the table. "I started here at ASU for my undergrad, but three years into the electrical engineering program, I transferred to the University of Texas at Austin. Once I finished my EE there, I decided to do my grad work there, too."

She leaned forward. "What made you want to go to U-T?"

"Life got complicated and I wanted a fresh start." Iggy blinked and waved away the discussion. "Do you want to dance?"

Hell no, yet she heard herself saying, "Sure."

Please let this not be a huge mistake, she silently wished.

She placed her hand in his. Moving together toward the dance floor, Victoria felt something bubbling in her belly. She could be happy or giddy or gassy. She wasn't sure which.

Iggy led the way, weaving their way around the packed tables. "I'm a horrible dancer. I have the incurable geek syndrome."

"Don't worry, just go along with the beat."

"I've heard those illuminating instructions before, and somehow, those words don't translate into body movement." On the dance floor, Iggy pulled her to him.

Through the first song, Iggy hammed up his moves and danced around with all the classic no-rhythm guy moves, complete with uncoordinated arms and flailing legs. He made her laugh and forget about everyone else and her insecurities.

"When You Say Nothing at All" started, Victoria grabbed him.

"Follow my lead." She looked up at him from under her eyelashes like she had seen her sister do a billion times with the men she dated. Victoria led him around the dance floor. They fell into an easy rhythm of sway, step, and turn.

The song finished with Iggy's hands on her waist. Heat radiated between them.

Her skin soaked in his warm embrace. She felt dizzy, excited, cherished.

"Only one toe stomp, that's a record for me." Iggy's voice was smooth and intimate with him being inches from her.

"I can still wiggle my toes, so you're good."

"Thank you for the dance. I've worked up an appetite and I think Susie is heading for our table." He dropped his hands from her and stepped backward.

Victoria cooled down without him near, and they headed to the table in silence. Susie slid their plates onto the table.

Iggy slipped into his side of the booth.

Susie stopped Victoria a short way from the table, leaning in close to her. "Mary, the hostess, said he's a keeper. She hit on him. He flashed her a sweet smile and moved along." Lowering her voice, she added, "And he seems immune to my Southern charm. We're just looking out for you."

"Thanks?" She had never had anyone besides Sandra looking out for her with guys. Dessie was only looking for a way to get all the male attention for herself.

"Anytime." Susie winked at her and wiggled her way through the tables.

Victoria checked out Iggy. He drooled over the slab of meat, as happy as a dog with a tennis ball.

She sat down, realizing that a few days ago, she had barely noticed anything about Jake's, and now her waitress and hostess were hitting on her date to protect her. Life had more surprise plot twists than a soap opera.

Iggy pulled her out of her musing. "I don't envy Susie's job. She works hard for those tips."

"Did you ever wait tables?" Victoria tried to imagine Iggy whirling around a packed restaurant, tray raised high.

He shuddered. "No, I don't have that type of patience for humanity. In college, I worked for a florist."

Victoria snorted, stifling a giggle behind her hand.

"Yuck it up, Chuckles." He flexed his fingers, grunted, and strained, showing off his imaginary bulging hand muscles. "Yes, I know how to make a killer floral arrangement for any occasion."

An idea struck.

"Is your former employer here in the valley? Do they do weddings?" Victoria flipped through a mental list of things they needed to do for the wedding. Crossing off "Find florist" from the checklist would be great.

His animated face fell into a rocky and gloomy expression. "I'm sure they still do."

He stabbed his steak with extra vigor. His entire focus became eating. Never mind that another human being was a foot away, eating with him. Supposedly on a date. Victoria tried to regain the nice vibe they had lost.

"I'm asking because my sister is getting married in a few weeks, and we have to plan her wedding quickly." He had clearly checked out. His withdrawal hurt worse than when Mateo ignored her, because Iggy and she had been connecting, or at least Victoria felt there was a connection.

Mentally kicking her own ass, Victoria shoved her salad around, not eating anything. Within her, disappointment waged war with despair.

Around them, couples, rowdy friends, and families all talked and had a good time. The cheeriness was almost deafening.

Susie sauntered over and shot Victoria an inquisitive brow, a what-the-hell-is-going-on-here brow. "Can I tempt either of you with one of our desserts?"

Victoria hadn't made it through dinner with a date yet. To dessert or not to dessert? Now she had a way to break Iggy's frigid silence and asked, "What are the options?"

Susie snagged the sample dessert tray off the cart going by. "We have a chilled chocolate mousse cake, carrot cake, lemon meringue pie, pecan pie, and hot apple crisp with two scoops of vanilla ice cream."

Iggy was as involved as a TV viewer. He was either unable or unwilling to break the fourth wall and engage with her or the world. Let him sulk. Let her indulge.

"The chilled chocolate mousse cake looks divine." Somehow, she unlocked from the gravitational pull of the sugary tray, finding some willpower. "Except for my sister's wedding is in two weeks. I'll pass."

He piped up and ordered. "Mousse cake with two forks. Also, two cups of coffee, to cut the calories."

Susie nodded and whisked the tempting display tray and herself away.

Iggy leaned across the table and to Victoria whispered, "I'll split the cake with you."

"Really? Generous of you. No, thanks." Her tone was as brittle as her heart. Victoria sat up and raised her hand to wave Susie over.

He snagged her hand, brought it to the table, where he covered her hand with his. "I'm sorry I porcupined on you."

"I'm listening." Optimism bloomed in her speech and in her heart.

"A memory surfaced of a rotten old relationship and triggered me."

She wanted to believe and wanted to protect herself.

"Please forgive my brief bad mood and share dessert with me?" He sounded sincere.

"I shouldn't splurge with the wedding."

"Victoria, I don't want to hear about fitting into a dress, because you're lovely the way you are. Plus, a few bites of sin cake won't make you explode." His voice was steel rebar.

Stunned silent, she processed. He called her lovely. She could build a house of hope on the honest way he complimented her.

And the way he said her name made her stomach do a flip-flop. She could stand to have her knees sag until she grew accustomed to his voice. Liar. With the way her name rolled off his tongue, she'd never stop swooning.

"I yield." Victoria's hands and words rose in a childlike surrender as if he had just captured her castle. "I could never deny a hottie who calls me lovely and says that cake and I shouldn't be parted."

Iggy cocked his head in a confused, puppy-dog tilt. "Hottie? Moi?"

"Don't play coy." She nodded at the bar. "Most of the women in this place hope you leave me here, alone in this booth, before the end of the night. That way they can snatch you up."

He rubbed his chin and dropped his eyes, a bit bashful. "I doubt that. But I guess that makes you very fortunate, in their minds, to be here with me."

He unleashed his impish one-dimple grin again, scooted to the edge of his seat, and traced Victoria's fingers with his.

The table wasn't on fire. No, but a deep burn flared up in her, snaking up her arm and diving into her belly.

"Ahem." Susie subtly announced her presence. "I hate to break you up, but here's dessert."

She placed the cake in between them, then unloaded the

cups of coffee, along with sugar and creamer containers. She threw Victoria a parting thumbs-up.

Victoria's cheeks were hotter than the steaming coffee. Unsure of where to look, she added a teaspoon of sugar and a dollop of cream to her drink. Her spoon clanged around the thick, porcelain mug.

"You're cute when you get flustered." Iggy scooped up a bit of the cake with an easy flick of his wrist.

She sipped her coffee and desperately tried to regain her composure. "So, you're an electrical engineer."

He chuckled. "Uncomfortable getting a compliment, are you, Vi? I'll play along. Yes, we covered I'm an electrical engineer."

She ignored the tug in her heart at the dreamy way he called her Vi. She distracted her emotions with cake.

The moment the cool, silky cake hit her tongue, nothing could stop her body from relaxing or her eyes from fluttering closed. Victoria could feel Iggy's scrutiny. Curiosity bubbled up inside her and made her peek at Iggy. His eyes had darkened to a deep, honey brown.

Victoria licked the last bit of chocolate off her lips and silently pleaded with herself, *Get your mind together. Say something, you twit.* But she shouldn't talk about the flower shop. That subject shut him down faster than a cat smelling menthol. "Are you currently working as an electrical engineer?"

Shifting in his seat, he cleared his throat. "I just started at a new job, this week in fact. I don't want to bore you."

She shook her head. "You wouldn't bore me. My dad is an EE and runs an R&D research company that deals exclusively with hardware circuit design. Engineering is a typical dinner table talk."

A shadow crossed Iggy's face and his tone sharpened. "Your sister's name isn't Esmeralda, is it?"

"Yes."

"Your father's name is Robert and he runs Quinn Research in Tempe." His hands balled up and his shoulders were around his ears.

"Didn't my mother tell you all this?"

"No." Iggy's jaw snapped tight.

The three large cowboys in the booth next to them pounded on the table, laughing. The explosion of noise shuttered off all conversation between them.

Victoria's head spun from the turbo change in his personality. "Is everything OK?"

"I'm perfect." Iggy flagged Susie over. "Check, please."

A child bawled a few tables away, his tiny fists clenched at his sides. With every breath, he screeched louder. Victoria flinched at all the crushing noise.

Susie swung by with the black bill holder. He shoved his card at her without glancing at the amount, continuing to sip his coffee, his fork abandoned.

Victoria struggled to keep the flood behind the levies. "Iggy? Did I do something wrong?"

His arctic, rigid body softened. He cast her a sad ghost of a smile. "No. I had a great time with you. I had a horrible experience in the past dating a boss's daughter. I'm not ready to try that again."

"There would be no problem, my dad isn't—" Victoria caught his closed expression and switched tracks. "Are you sure we couldn't talk about this?"

"I am."

Susie dropped off the check for Iggy to sign. She shot Victoria a puzzled frown. Iggy scribbled his name.

Half the cake untouched on the plate.

Iggy stood. "I'll walk you to your car."

"No need." Feeling like his words sucker-punched her, Victoria slunk out of the booth and followed Iggy through the dense crowd. By the time they were outside, the music was a vague clamor, barely background noise. Stars sparkled above them. Faint moonlight lit up the night.

They parted at the doorway.

She found her car, managing to get the key in the ignition and to drive home. Her mind rewound to earlier this week at her dad's office and the hot guy who had been talking with Karen, the receptionist. That must have been Iggy.

Victoria arrived at her apartment parking lot, her heart heavy, the world outside her car dark and windy.

She got out and limped up the three flights of stairs to her apartment. Inside, she wadded up the new dress and the new shoes and chucked them into an unlit corner of her room. Her feet had three new blisters. The earlier euphoria had acted like novocaine, but the effect had worn off.

And she never should have believed the salesgirl or Sandra. That dress didn't suit her at all.

Ralph protested over his empty dish. Victoria went into the kitchen, picked up her cat, and released the dam of tears into his black fur, her hope for a plus-one at the wedding dead.

TIP # 10

DON'T GROW UP, IT'S A TRAP

*S*till in a sleepy haze the next morning, Victoria snagged the bag of coffee and set it brewing. To quiet the rumbly in her tummy, she shoved a handful of dry cereal into her mouth. She stood at the counter, cabinet open, eating and waiting for the coffee to beep.

Her Sunday started perfectly—no one bothered her. The rest of the day she could do anything she wanted. The couch called to her to flop down and drone her day away.

"Great Balls of Fire" played in the other room. Ignoring Sandra's ringtone, she shook some food into Ralph's bowl.

Being alone was freedom. She could buck her mother's side of the family, the cursed Alburgas and their expectations of believing the only way one could be an official adult was by getting married and starting a family.

Who needed a boyfriend? Or at least an arm to hang onto for the wedding? Not her. Nope. She'd show up liberated and alone.

A tear weaseled its way down her cheek. Three dates down and all the "Prince Charmings" had been scratched off her to-date-again list.

According to Susie, Mateo's entire reason for the date boiled down to revenge. His ex happened to be the hot lead singer of the Dixie Vixens. Victoria should have followed up the head butt she gave him with a swift boot to the knee.

Mateo was dead to her.

And the lying cheater Nick was another corpse.

Her coffee maker gurgled the last few drops, spewed steam, and beeped. Fresh coffee in hand, she went over to snuggle into the couch, the cereal box tucked under her arm.

Victoria pondered her third frog prince, Iggy. It started well, yet he clammed up after he talked about his old florist job. On the dance floor and over dessert, they recovered and flirted. Then the mood went up in a Hindenburg fireball once he realized who her dad was.

Her dad would never have interfered with her dating life. Hell, since she had never had one before, he had never had anything to disturb.

She banished all thoughts of dating and turned to school. Somewhere in the house, she had her GRE scores.

"Great Balls of Fire" pierced the quiet again.

Sandra could be more tenacious than her mother. Victoria better pick up before her phone exploded. She dug the singing contraption out of her purse and answered. "What's up, Sandra?"

"You're up. Hopefully, basking in the dating amazingness of last night."

Slouching against the couch, Victoria petted her cat. "Nope. I'm currently drinking coffee with the most stable male in my life, Ralph." There was a light rap at her apartment door. She moved toward the door to check the peephole.

On the phone, Sandra said, "Sucky. Open up. Salvation is on your stoop."

"No need for missionaries of the Jehovah or Mormon or gay variety."

"Shut up and let me in."

Victoria did so. Sandra came in dressed in black yoga pants and a white shirt that said, *You go, girl! And don't come back.*

Her anxiety plummeted thanks to Sandra's presence. "Your collection of sassy shirts. Where do you find them all?"

Sandra looked down, reading the phrase. "The Internet is a beautiful thing."

Victoria poured out another mug of coffee and they curled up on the couch.

"Greetings over. So, the guy...was he a classic loser?"

Victoria sighed at the could-have-beens. "No, he had movie star looks. All the women at the bar tried to pick him up while he waited for me. He's definitely stepping down going out with me."

Sandra slugged Victoria's arm. Hard. "Shut it."

"Ow, violence isn't the answer." She rubbed her abused arm.

"To your stupidity, violence is the answer. Now, dish. When's the next rendezvous with Mr. Movie Star?"

"Never. We found out he works for my dad and that's a dating no-no for him."

"Wow, talk about a coincidence."

"Isn't it? I can't believe my mother didn't mention that little fact."

"But your dad would never have a problem with one of his engineers seeing you."

"Tried to explain. He shut down the conversation."

"Rough. Fourteen days and counting until the big day. Who's up next?"

Victoria swatted at Sandra's arm. "Thanks for the doom countdown. Dessie's in tomorrow."

"Is she staying with you again?"

At the suggestion of Dessie living with her, dread shot down Victoria's spine and she said, "Aren't you set to Happy Newscaster mode today?"

"For you, always."

"Two stressful weeks till I can pawn her off on her husband. Don't you wish you could be me?"

Sandra drained the rest of her coffee. "Only if you had a pot of gold to bestow on me would I wear that hat. Good luck tomorrow."

"What happened to being my wingman, Goose?"

"Men, yes. Your sister under normal circumstances, maybe. Her prepping for her pretty and perfect wedding day? Let's not push the insanity defense case." Sandra shrugged. "Just throw water on her if she gets a crazed gleam and her head spins."

"Helpful."

"Honest."

Victoria sent a text to Dessie asking about her pre-wedding living arrangements, though the acid pit in her belly already assumed the worst. Her sister responded swiftly.

Roomie! C u @ 9

She sunk into her couch and shot Sandra an *eee-villl* glare. "I hate it when you're right."

"Which is daily. Dessie staying with you is the only option. Your dad is a recluse math genius. Towers of take-out boxes decorate his studio apartment."

"That only happens when he's engrossed in a work project." Victoria's voice was little-girl-defending-her-daddy stubborn.

"The other option would result in the famous Mom vs. Dessie battles."

The thought of her mother and sister living together lifted Victoria's spirits. "I can picture the crash-n'-smash derby between those two perfectly. Mother would be the monster truck and Dessie the clown car. Mother packs enough guilt-fuel to keep her spewing gravel in the air for a century, and if needed, she could pack a pound or two of nagging in reserve to nitro herself up if she runs low on guilt."

Sandra snorted up coffee. After relearning how to breathe, she asked, "What are you doing today?"

Victoria looked around. The bottom shelf of her bookcase was dusty. Not only could she draw in the dust, but she could also scrape off layers and made a 3-D painting out of the surface. "I better clean. Dessie will be here with a suitcase full of judgment. Just like Mother."

"I'll help for a bit then." Sandra got up, went into the kitchen, and came back with the cleaning supplies.

Victoria started dusting and, as she pulled out photo albums and yearbooks, she flipped through the pages and watched herself grow up. The first album showed her family intact, a whole unit—mother, dad, two sisters, and various animals. After the divorce, there were pictures with mom or dad, but never the whole family again, unless the day was a mandatory family holiday such as Christmas or Easter. Even then, her parents never stood together. They'd frame the picture with themselves on the outside.

Sandra grabbed another album and leafed through the pages. "Even after your parents split, they still smiled at each other in all the pictures."

"They're divorced and yet they love each other. Whenever Dessie or I spoke badly of Mom, Dad would quietly listen to our complaints and then tell us one day we'd understand better and to have patience with her. He still does that."

A blank white envelope fell out of the album Sandra was looking through. The paper cracked and crinkled. She flipped open the unsealed flap and pulled out a piece of notebook paper. "What's this lost treasure?"

"What's on the page?" Victoria continued to clean.

"Hm, it's your handwriting." Sandra began reading.

DEAR VICTORIA,

TODAY IS MY FIRST DAY OF MY SOPHOMORE YEAR IN HIGH SCHOOL. AND I FOUND OUT THAT TOMMY IS DEAD.

Tommy. Her heart vised. His name teleported Victoria to the day she wrote the letter. The teacher had walked in from the teacher's pod, her face scrubbed clean, eyes puffy, to deliver the news to the class.

Sandra stopped reading. "I don't remember him."

Tears filled Victoria's eyes. "With over a thousand kids in our graduating class, no surprise. We went to junior high together. He was a sweet, shy guy who was always talking about all the things he knew he would never get to do."

"Why not?" Sandra reached over and squeezed her hand.

She sniffled and squeezed back. "He had stage four cancer. I'm curious what I wrote, go on."

Sandra unfolded the letter all the way and kept going.

TOO MANY PEOPLE HAVE DREAMS AND EITHER BURY THEM DUE TO LIFE CHOICES OR THEY DIE BEFORE THEY CAN SEE THEIR WORK AFFECT OTHERS. IN HONOR OF THE MOST TALENTED ARTIST I'VE EVER KNOWN, I HEREBY PLEDGE TO:

1. GO TO SCHOOL TO BE A VETERINARIAN. BECAUSE NOTHING MAKES ME HAPPIER THAN BEING AROUND AND HELPING ANIMALS GET WELL.

"I kind of completed that pledge. I took my GRE test in preparation for applying to vet school." The best class she'd had was in her last year of premed when she interned at Noah's Haven and eventually became Dr. Yaz's receptionist.

Sandra smiled. "For the attempt, half a point to Gryffindor. But there's more advice you left for yourself."

2. DO SOMETHING BIG EVERY YEAR THAT SCARES ME: PUBLIC SPEAKING, ROCK CLIMBING, BASE JUMPING, SKYDIVING. BECAUSE LIFE IS TOO SHORT TO LIVE IN THE SHADOW OF MY PETTY FEARS.

EVERYONE NEEDS TO QUAKE IN THE KNEES TO REMEMBER WE ARE ALIVE TO LIVE, NOT BE COMFORTABLE.

Victoria broke in. "Base jumping?"

"Outrageous, for sure. If you had a superhero name, you'd be the Couch Cruiser." Sandra's light tone was meant to rib her; instead, the direct dis irritated her.

"I did something scary last week. Dating," Victoria spat out.

Sandra nodded in agreement, but her facial expression sang *liiiiar*. "And in the last ten years, you've made chickens seem brave."

Victoria crossed her arms. Her life stalled in the last few years. After she dropped out of college, she couldn't find the drive to achieve anything anymore. Stupid inertia. "Fine, zero points for Gryffindor."

Sandra cleared her throat. "No, negative five points. Onto things-you've-never-done number three."

3. FIND SOMEONE WHO YOU CAN LAUGH WITH AND WHO WILL SUPPORT YOU IN YOUR DREAMS. BECAUSE I'M SICK OF GIRLS WHO, ONCE THEY START DATING, LOSE SIGHT OF THEMSELVES AND THEIR OWN LIKES. IT'S CALLED A PARTNERSHIP, NOT A DICTATORSHIP.

"My current self agrees with my past self." She leaned closer to Sandra.

Twisted to block her view, Sandra peered over the yellowed paper. "Maybe you should listen to your high school self and use this list to get your next date."

Victoria sank onto her heels. "If I found such a fantastic guy, I'd run out and find the nearest single gal to hook him up with because I wouldn't deserve him."

"Self-sabotage for a negative twelve-thousand points." Sandra's teasing tone vanished. Her words were serving up disappointment by the wheelbarrow.

"Shut up. Is this tortuous flashback over?"

"You want me to go on?"

"You'd go on anyways. Just swing the ball-peen hammer to my toes now."

"As you command." Sandra continued.

4. DON'T LET YOUR DREAMS GO STALE. BECAUSE NOTHING IS WORSE THAN A PILE OF COULD-HAVES OR SHOULD-HAVES OR WHAT-IFS. LIFE IS MEANT TO BE AN ADVENTURE.

"I'd like to punch my pontificating, naïve self. Please tell me I'm done being wise."

"A little bit left."

LOVE, VICTORIA

"Good." Victoria reached for the letter.

Sandra swatted at her hand and flipped the page over. "Oh, look, a postscript."

P.S. YOU DESERVE EVERYTHING YOU WANT AND MORE. NEVER BELIEVE ANYONE WHO SAYS OTHERWISE.

Victoria dropped her head to her chest. Disappointment curled her shoulders inward, hiding her heart from her own failures. Four simple to-dos and not one had she actually completed. A hot sludge of rage climbed up her esophagus making it hard to think, speak, or breathe.

Sandra wrapped her arm around Victoria's shoulders and brought her in for a side hug. "You do deserve everything on your list. I know you've been scared, but I'm here for you. I'll help you be courageous."

"Got any brave-it-all potion?"

Sandra chuckled. "I could make you a screwdriver with lemon balm tincture again."

They both cringed and shared a smile.

Sandra's phone alarm went off and she silenced it quickly. "I'm sorry, I've got to go. Are you OK?"

Ralph climbed up into Victoria's lap and purred. She scratched under his chin. "I've got my backup best friend."

"I would be jealous, but he's a handy lap warmer. I love you.

Call me, if you need me." Sandra got up, grabbed her stuff, and left.

The door clicked shut. The letter sat on the coffee table. Her younger, innocent, and idiotic self hadn't understood how hard life could be outside of school. How impossible it was to stay true to herself and believe everything will work out. Plus, challenging herself to be better than she was yesterday was like kayaking into a tsunami.

Victoria picked up the crinkly, stiff page, and, instead of ripping the insipid drivel into twelve thousand-and-one tiny confetti pieces, which she'd have to clean up, Victoria stuffed the letter into the album and slipped it onto the shelf. She didn't have time to wallow.

The smell of cleaners, a steady sponge, and a soiled heart filled the rest of her day.

BEFORE THE SUN woke her on Monday, Victoria's phone did. The ringtone sang about Barbie partying. That and the residual irritation reminded her of the weekends past where she had to pick up her drunken sister's SOSes.

Victoria focused her glassy vision on the blinding screen and read Dessie's text.

I'm off 2 the airport. Don't b late. XOXO

As if she cared. She had time to sleep still. Her phone screeched the "Wicked Witch of the West."

She hit the green button and slurred into the receiver, "What?"

"Don't be testy with me. Esmeralda will be here soon. Don't forget your darling sister at the airport."

Victoria's comfy pillow muffled her voice. "She just texted. Dessie won't be here for another few hours, which I could use for sleeping, so what do you really want, Mother?"

"How'd your date go?" Her mother sounded like she downed an entire carafe of espresso.

Victoria hated chipper people before she'd had her morning coffee fortification. "Date sucked."

"Did I set you up with a loser? He seemed nice."

"No, not a loser. He had issues, so no second date for me."

"Oh, Baby." Her mother cooed her fake sympathy.

Victoria twitched. Her mother called her "Baby" again, paired with the coo. Victoria hated being on the receiving end of that too-bad-you're-not-your-sister pity, like when she went stag to prom. "Did you know Iggy worked for Dad?"

"No. I knew he just started a new job, but his aunt couldn't remember the company's name. Small world."

"Tell me about it. And now, we're going to stop talking about my dating disasters."

"Don't fear. I'll be on hot date patrol for you."

Victoria shivered at the idea. "No, Mother, I'm—"

Cut off by kissing noises and a click, she finished her sentence into her empty apartment. "—fine."

Couldn't her mother stop trying to guilt, fix, or mold Victoria into a mini-Millie? Victoria had never been good enough to be her mother's clone. Hell, that's what her mother had Dessie for. Not her.

*T*he early Monday morning irritation left Victoria too awake to go back to sleep. After a shower, a vat of coffee with a nutritious Pop-Tart, and an argument with her closet, she drove herself to the airport.

She loved her sister, even if Dessie was hard to love. Victoria didn't feel that Dessie had to attend a crazy expensive college in California. Victoria had stayed in-state, so her dad hadn't needed to raid his savings to pay for her tuition.

But life at USC had called to Dessie. For her, college meant having the dorm room experience the first year, then the sorority house the next year, and, of course, she couldn't come home for spring breaks. No, she had to go to all the hot spots with her new sorority sisters.

Cha-ching! More money dished out to fulfill her dream adventures. Their dad's money. Dessie owned all of easy street. Now she'll hear wedding bells before she finished college.

After parking her used Civic in the airport garage, Victoria filtered through the crowd at the baggage claim. A shrill shriek made her turn slowly toward the deafening glee.

She caught a blur of Dessie wearing skinny jeans and a curve-hugging tank top before her sister launched herself at Victoria long-jump style, shouting, "Tori, Tori, Aaaaaaah." Her sister's arms and legs were thrown wide and then she wrapped herself around Victoria's torso.

Not an unusual greeting, so Victoria had braced herself and kept them both upright. The bone-crushing hug her little sister gave her would make any WWF wrestler proud.

Dessie was the antithesis of Victoria—petite and radiant with blonde hair, a thin waist, and bright blue eyes. Her hair curled in big goddess spirals that framed her high cheekbones. Perfection. The word described her sister's outside.

Victoria was frumpy next to such perfection. No makeup, lips rice-paper thin, her dishwater-blonde curls corralled in long pigtails topped with a sailor's hat. Her navy blue pea coat hung open to catch the spring breeze. It happened to be the third outfit she'd tried on that morning. Still, in a side-by-side comparison, Dessie was a demigoddess and she was beige paint.

"Hey ya, Dessie. Let's get your baggage."

The mighty midget disengaged and squealed like an excited toddler. "We have a wedding to plan." Dessie sent her a little salute, bounding over to a mound of bright yellow suitcases. "A nice man who sat next to me on the plane got these off for me. See the man in the green shirt?"

Victoria followed Dessie's French-manicured hand to see a small man limping off. "Why does he look like you stole his favorite fetch toy?"

"We chatted on the flight. He insisted on hefting my luggage off the belt for me."

"I'd be slumped over from a pulled back, too. You always exceed the weight limits." Victoria verbally poked her with two-thirds sibling love and one-third pointy truth.

"Har har. He handed me his business card with his home

number scribbled on the back." Dessie raised her right shoulder in a meh gesture. "I told him to keep it, that I was here to plan my wedding."

"You're going to disappoint a lot of men in two weeks." Victoria readjusted her sailor hat, her tone teasing and full of older sister wisdom. "Must be hard for you to find a place to step with all those men lying at your feet."

Dessie didn't brag, but delivered the simple truth, saying, "Naw, I just walk on 'em."

"Same old Dessie. Going to be a tight fit with both your luggage and your ego in my car."

Dessie ignored Victoria's comment and flipped her platinum curls over her shoulder with one fluid move. The move had silver screen written all over it, a mix of Shirley Temple innocence with a dash of Vivian Leigh vixen.

If Victoria had tried the move, someone would have stopped and asked if she was having a seizure.

Her sister started toward the elevators, texting. "Load up the bags for me."

"Yes, Master." Victoria dragged her right leg and hunched over while she piled the retina-burning yellow luggage onto a rolling cart. To argue or ask her sister to help would've been useless.

Squished and loaded into her Civic, Victoria cranked the radio as she eased out into the petering morning traffic. After the last few days, she wasn't ready to deal with her sister. A conversation could spark a Dessie time bomb. Better say nothing to save the world from an IED. Irate Explosive Dessie.

Back in her apartment's parking lot, Victoria snagged a primo spot.

"You still chant to that stupid parking god?" Dessie stopped texting and put her phone away.

"Pays off, too. Squat gifted us with an open spot right next to the stairs." She got out, popped open the back hatch, and all the luggage launched right at her in a Kamikaze death dive.

Dessie got out, propped herself against the car, and checked her nails. She didn't even raise a pinky to help Victoria hold back the tidal wave of suitcases. "Don't worry, carrying my luggage up won't be too bad." Her sister delivered the words with no hint of irony.

Dessie stooped to pick up her carry-on bag, plus her gigantic makeup box. This left three massive pieces of luggage for Victoria to wrangle. Neck craned to the heavens, she hoped to hear a benevolent voice of the One whisper wise words or at least a reason for why she was stuck with this demon.

All she heard was Dessie singing to herself.

Only two weeks to the wedding, Victoria chanted over and over and over again to herself as she rounded up the suitcases.

"Let's go, I'm tired," Dessie said, her tone resembling the whine of a terrier.

"Carry more and we'll be done faster."

"I could hurt myself."

"I could do that for you."

"What?" Dessie asked.

"Nothing. Catch." She threw her keys to Dessie. "At least open the door for me since you have a free hand."

"I can do that." Dessie started up the three-story staircase without glancing behind her.

Victoria trudged up to her apartment with a heavy case in each hand and the last one shoved precariously under her armpit. The breeze was cool and refreshing. But whereas Dessie's hair fluttered angelically around her, Victoria's hair viciously attacked her. Dirty-blonde curls whipped around her face and she had no extra hand to fix the problem.

Halfway up, two high-school boys popped out of a nearby

door and gaped at Dessie. Camped on their doorstep, Twiddle Dee and Twiddle Dumb twitched as though a tick infestation existed in their shoes.

Here we go. Dessie smiled, switching on her patented men-bamboozling tricks.

Step 1: look tiny, cute, and in need of being rescued.

"Do you need any help?" Twiddle Dee asked.

Did he ask the person closest to him loaded down heavier than a pack mule if she needed help? No. He asked the pretty blonde who carried a pittance. Victoria could've written a heart-felt country song about the unfairness of the situation.

Not to be outdone, Twiddle Dumb puffed up his chest. "I could carry your case."

Dessie stepped down to them, lightly brushing her fingers down Twiddle Dee's arm. "That's sweet. I would love some help."

There was Step 2: touch the arm acting coy and sweet.

She shot them a blazing smile, one that hardened war veterans wouldn't have been able to stand against, and shooed them down the steps. Behind their backs to Victoria, Dessie threw a giddy thumbs up. "And help my favorite sister with hers? Thank you so much for helping me."

Sliding into Step 3: thank them and make them feel special.

"Favorite?" Victoria gripped the handles tighter and continued to mutter to herself. "How about the only."

"You men don't need to take everything. I can help." Dessie's voice seemed sincere only to those who didn't know her. Yet she had moved into Step 4: ask to help, but never follow through and actually do it.

"We're good." Twiddle Dee and Dumb plastered two dopey grins on their faces and relieved Victoria of her yellow suitcases.

They huffed and half dragged all the suitcases up the three

flights of stairs. The boys departed with red lipstick on their cheeks, courtesy of Dessie. Marks of the final step, Step 5: give them a token of gratitude, which could range from her number to a dazzling smile, then dump them onto the heap of men groveling for her affection.

Dessie's ways were effective, simple, elegant, and a powerful example of world domination technique.

Besides looking petite, Dessie's steps were something Victoria could try exploiting later.

Dessie closed the door behind her love lackeys. "Tori, I told you it wouldn't be bad to get these up here."

Victoria locked the door and turned to Dessie. "Only because you snookered defenseless boys into doing your work. Speaking of getting others to do your work, have you thought of hiring a wedding planner?"

"This is my wedding and I'll plan it," Dessie sneered.

Taking a calming breath, Victoria tried another way to get her sister to see reason. "There are lots of details to get done in such a short amount of time. You should have a professional to handle and help you have the day you've dreamed of."

"I've been waiting and planning for this day for years, so I don't need a planner, end of discussion."

Ralph came out, investigating all the luggage.

"Your cat better not pee on my bags."

Victoria picked him up. "He won't, and remember, Ralph can't go outside—his previous owners declawed him."

"Jeez, I remember the lecture last time about not letting him outside, even though he's a cat." Dessie collapsed on the couch. "I'm hungry. Got anything good to eat?"

"Nothing that meets your low-fat, low-sugar standards. I have an idea."

A text later and keys in hand, she herded Dessie to the car. Within minutes, they pulled up in front of their dad's offices.

"Lunch with Dad? He adores you and loathes me." Dessie's voice was stuck on pout.

Victoria snorted. "Nice temper tantrum. You're mad because there's one person who isn't circling, waiting for your commands, and that's Dad."

"Am not." Dessie locked her jaw, staring straight ahead, and gripping her biceps.

"Stop with the baby act. Dad doesn't know what to do with you. You're his kryptonite, all emotional, girlie, and dramatic."

Rife with indignation, Dessie puffed up, ranting. "I am not theatrical or fake." She jumped out of the car and stormed off down the street, heading away from their dad's office.

Victoria locked up the car, dashing after her demented sister. They walked a few paces in silence, pierced by the noise of Dessie's heels snapping on the sidewalk.

Dessie stopped and deflated. She flipped her hair out of her face. "Kind of melodramatic, huh?"

"Could've been your middle name." Looping her arm around Dessie, she steered her toward the entrance.

Karen, the front receptionist, spotted them coming through the glass doors. She let out the girl's war cry, a squeal, then propelled herself over to them at the speed of light. Dessie caught Karen full in the chest, and somehow, in spiked heels, she still stood upright.

They bounced on their toes and squeaked, talking over each other, catching up. How did they become such good friends?

Victoria cocked her head and studied the pair. With their lewd jokes, pithy cut-downs, and bad pickup lines, she and Sandra were apparently abnormal.

Dessie always acted like everyone's best friend. Victoria stopped by her dad's office at least once a month and the most she got from Karen was a wave and a polite, compulsory greeting. No personal questions about how her weekend or how her work went or if she'd done anything fun in the last five years. Victoria felt transparent, sad, and alone in a sea of smiling humanity.

Clearing her throat of her clawing pity party, Victoria interrupted them. "I'm going to collect Dad."

Dessie stopped mid-sentence and to Karen said, "I'll be back after lunch. You want me to pick you up something while we're out?"

"I brought a salad, I'm good."

Salads. Karen's food choice reminded her of the healthy surprise lunch Sandra brought her minutes before Dessie called about the engagement and wedding, which started the insanity ball rolling.

The two sisters walked to their dad's office-slash-electrical engineer's boneyard. Victoria raised her finger over her mouth in the universal sign for "be quiet" and hit the intercom. Lowering her voice, she said, "Clean up the bloody body parts. You have a guest."

Cursing and slamming drawers greeted them.

"Good to know he was expecting us." Dessie leaned against the white wall.

Dessie gestured for Victoria to come closer. They pressed their faces into the door jamb, snickering and whispering like they used to when waiting for their dad to come home. In a fit of giggles, they kept hip bumping each other.

Victoria couldn't remember the last time they had fun together. The heaviness in her chest lightened. Some days having her sister around was great. Maybe the next few weeks wouldn't be so torturous.

Dessie whacked her a little too hard, sending Victoria through the now-open door. She sailed inside and slammed chest-first into a solid wall of a man. Straightening, she found herself eye-to-eye with her last date.

Victoria swallowed hard. "Fancy running into you here, Iggy."

*V*ictoria and Iggy stared at each other in the doorway of her dad's office. He looked shocked. She enjoyed being so close to him.

"You know my Victoria?" Her dad's bearded face popped up between them.

Iggy jumped back. A small sheen of sweat sprung up on his forehead.

Her dad had caught that she knew his nickname. Her dad might be a scatterbrained engineer, but he was like Rain Man in his observations. Yet he didn't seem to know they'd gone out on Saturday.

Iggy's mouth floundered open and closed.

Initiate WWDD, What Would Dessie Do, to see if she could earn her own brass lipstick case. Iggy was clearly the one in duress, so Victoria jumped straight to Step 2: touch men to distract 'em and make 'em bendy.

Victoria linked her arm through Iggy's, channeling her best Dessie impression by looking up at him through her eyelashes, and flirted. "I met him last week."

With Victoria practically shoving her breasts on Iggy's arm, he went into rigor mortis.

Her dad's face brightened. "Iggy is a fine young engineer."

All Iggy's color drained. "Robert. Sir—"

Her dad patted Iggy on the shoulder in one of his you're-doing-well-and-be-proud reassurances Victoria remembered from growing up. "I'm sure he'll be in *Cutting Science* one day. Soon he'll be besting my designs with his own."

"You're too kind, sir. Have a good time with your daughters." He extracted his arm from Victoria's trap. With the quickness of an Olympic sprinter, he disappeared around overstuffed bins of circuit components.

Deploying Dessie charm had sort of worked. Iggy himself was wooden and not the least bit bendy to Victoria's will. But what was she expecting Iggy to do, declare his intent to woo her? Her life leaned more toward being a dry, nod-inspiring documentary than a romance.

Dessie wrinkled her nose at her dad. "His name is Iggy?"

Their dad shepherded them out of the building. "Where to, ladies?" He popped both elbows out for his daughters.

Victoria threaded her arm on his left side. Dessie looped her arm through his right. Three abreast, they claimed the sidewalk as theirs.

"If I know Tori here, she'll vote for the Pita Stop." Dessie scrunched her features in a sour pucker.

"And if I know Dessie, she'll want the new, posh restaurant The Fox." Victoria stuck her tongue out *blahing* at her little sister.

He steered them both towards the green expanse at the end of the block. "Well, since I'm paying, we're going to the park to have hot dogs."

Dessie swiveled her head over toward Victoria. Their gazes locked.

They both yelled, "Race ya."

"I'm gonna beat you," Dessie shouted, propelling herself forward on her stilettos.

Victoria sprung forward. "Baby sister, you're in heels, keep dreaming."

A couple stepped out of a shop. Victoria swerved to avoid them, causing her to drop behind Dessie.

"What was that? La-hoo-za-her." Dessie sang.

Victoria closed the distance and the park loomed close. A family with a toddler was dead ahead. She zigged left around the pokey bunch. Dessie chose unwisely and was sidelined by the little one jumping in front of her.

"What was that again? You be the sore la-hoo-za-her. Flats for the win." Victoria pulled ahead, pumping her arms and legs, hands outstretched, slamming into the park wall.

By the time their dad caught up, they were both sitting on a chest-high wall, drumming their feet along the stucco.

"What took you so long, Daddy? Feeling old today?" Dessie's face was flush from the sprint.

"With the way the two of you just acted, I feel mighty vigorous having two ruffians as my spawns." He offered them both a hand to hop down.

From there, they meandered over to the old hot dog stand. Big Gabe owned the stand and had been serving them their hot dogs, no matter the weather, for the last twenty-plus years.

"Afternoon, Gabe." Her dad leaned on the metal lip of the cart.

"Where did you find such beauts?" Big Gabe wiggled his eyebrows at the sisters.

With his simple waggle, Victoria felt transported to a time when she could barely see over Gabe's metal ordering window.

Their dad stood a bit straighter. "You remember Esmeralda, my youngest daughter. And you know Victoria."

"Let me see." Big Gabe rocked onto his heels, pointing to Dessie with his tongs. "Dog with chili, cheese, onion, and mustard."

Dessie nodded.

Swiveling to peer at Victoria over his thick, black plastic glasses, he started fixing the food. "For your dog, ketchup, and relish."

"You know me well." Victoria did her best villain voice, rubbing her hands together.

Big Gabe erupted in a big belly laugh, his chapped lips spreading wide, revealing his chipped teeth. "Couldn't forget you, your pigtails, or your hats."

Victoria tipped her sailor hat at him. "Glad to be remembered by such a charmer."

He waved away her comment with a dismissive flick of his wrist. "The usual for you, Robert?"

Her father, Robert, reached for his wallet. "Yep, today's a special occasion. My Esmeralda is getting married in a few weeks."

Victoria could swear the grizzly bear swallowed a tear. Big Gabe placed the dogs on the metal lip of his serving window and pushed them forward. "Take 'em."

"How much?" Her dad dug into his billfold.

"They're on the house. Congrats, Ms. Esmeralda. Soon you'll be a Mrs." He shook his head. "Man, when did I get old?"

Dessie smiled up at the sweet, balding guy. "You're still my favorite part of the park."

"Go on with you." Big Gabe wiped down his hot dog cart with a white rag. "Get outta here."

With Big Gabe's back to them, her dad slipped a big tip in his jar.

They made their way over to the abandoned swing set. Their old haunt.

When they were little, their mother would bring them down here to share lunch with their dad. As soon as Victoria and Dessie saw the park, they would beg to go on the swings, but food came first. With the promise of playtime itching under their skin, they would inhale their hot dogs, then race to the swings to see who could reach the sky first. For Victoria and Dessie, the sky always seemed one more swing pump away.

Whoever got the highest first would turn to the other and say, "To the moon and back." Then they would hurl toward the earth and try to beat the other's swing height.

And now here they sat, eating as they had in the past, everything similar and yet alien. Life in the past had been straightforward. Even in high school, when Victoria wrote the life-advice letter to herself, life was linear. Being an adult made everything harder and complicated.

Time to plow forward in the now.

Polishing off her dog, Victoria shot her dad a nail-gun glare. A glare that was fast, pointy, and painful. She tilted her head toward Dessie and to her dad, whispered, "Talk to her."

Her dad blinked.

Victoria's eyebrows pitched upward in a warning as she tapped her wrist where her nonexistent watch ticked.

His body slumped. His posture radiated reluctance. He turned to his youngest. "Tell me about your fiancé."

"He's Italian, twenty-nine, and has his own stock trading company, D's Bet."

Victoria sat up straight and stared at her sister. From all the social media posts, she thought the two were the same age because they had met at a college party. Victoria kept her mouth closed and let her dad do the talking.

Her dad coughed and asked, "Does he have a name?"

"Damien Volpé."

Dessie spun herself one way and then the other in the sun-faded plastic swing seat. Only the scraping and twisting of the swing's metal chain could be heard.

The two of them couldn't seem to carry on a conversation without her. Victoria sighed a deep, martyred sigh. "Soon you'll be Mrs. Damien Volpé?"

Her new name must have snapped Dessie out of dreamland because her eyes went wide. "I love being Esmeralda Isabella Shaw. I don't want to take his last name."

"You don't have to take his name if you don't want to." Her dad's voice was calm and placid. He'd had years to perfect the tone, having been married to their temperamental mother. "You could even hyphenate your name to be Shaw-Volpé."

Dessie gagged.

Her dad's phone rang. He answered so quickly you would have thought his own personal savior was on the other end. Victoria knew the call had to be work by the distant set of his shoulders. Once he hung up, they dusted the crumbs off their laps and the dirt off their pants and escorted him to work. The walk felt nostalgic and their dad waved them off at the lobby.

Back at the apartment, Victoria drafted a game plan and split the tasks. She took ten wedding venues and handed Dessie another ten to check their availability. If any of them were possible then set up a site visit for the next day.

Two hours later, Dessie had booked four tour appointments for the next afternoon. Victoria had struck out on all ten. She texted Dr. Yaz to let him know she'd need more time off.

"Great Balls of Fire" blared from her phone. Victoria read the text from Sandra.

How's Dr. Jekyll or is it Hyde? Need backup? Goose

Dessie poked her head around her laptop. "Isn't that song from *Top Gun*?"

"Yes." Then Victoria replied to Sandra.

Thankfully, hanging w/ Dr. Jekyll. How about u stop by Pita Stop n bring reinforcements?

Sandra responded.

K, b there in 45 w/ dinner

"Sandra offered to bring Pita Stop for dinner."

"Great, I know how much you love her and Pita Stop." Dessie's voice dripped snake venom.

"I ordered you the Greek Salad. Healthy enough for you?" She matched her sister's nasty tone.

Dessie's gaze moved to her computer screen. "Fine."

Sandra and Dessie had a tenuous truce. In high school, Dessie dated Sandra's little brother. The two broke each other's hearts, ending with a brawl between Dessie and Sandra, which took a can of mace, a dart gun, and a water hose to stop.

Eventually, Dessie and Sandra's brother discovered a friend had tricked them into believing the other had cheated. Once the truth came out that neither had been unfaithful, Sandra apologized to Dessie, as well as to their dad, for giving him a black eye when he broke up their fistfight.

DINNER TURNED INTO A MOVIE BINGE, which ran late, and Sandra stayed over. Victoria got up first. Before the arguing started, she was thankfully caffeinated and showered.

Raised voices bounced down the hallway toward the now-vacant bathroom. Sandra and Dessie were still sandbox bullies. Victoria peeked into the hall to see them steamrolling toward the bathroom.

Sandra hip-bumped Dessie. Hard. Dessie ate the wall. Sandra darted into the bathroom.

Dessie hammered on the door. "Hey, I'm the one who is getting married. I should get the shower first."

Sandra popped open the door and thrust her face through the crack. "Bride Card won't work here. You told me yourself last night you don't have to be anywhere until two o'clock. I have a job to go to. We poor folk have to sully our hands to get by." She slammed the door shut. Right in Dessie's face.

That left Dessie millimeters from the painted door, her teeth grinding.

Victoria ducked back into her room for her safety. "Morning, Hyde." Picking a battle she might win, Victoria faced off against her wardrobe. Most days, she'd be in slacks and a semi-nice office shirt. Today, she chose jeans, a work polo, and a fedora.

She tiptoed down the hallway to check the Dessie Barometer. Dessie sat on the kitchen counter, her hands wrapped around a mug.

Victoria thought she should tread lightly to keep Hyde at bay. She headed for the door and to Dessie said, "I'm off. Text if you need anything."

Her sister didn't say anything. Just studied her coffee. Good, no feeding frenzy.

Slow traffic all the way into work and opening the office was a breeze. The morning slipped by.

As the gods loved messing with her, Princess, the bulldog, heralded Fran's coming a mere thirty minutes before Victoria's first scheduled appointment with Dessie.

"How's the wedding planning going?" Fran's thin, reedy voice carried over the threshold. "Manage to snag a date yet for the wedding?"

"I'll go see if Dr. Yaz is ready for you." Victoria's polite mask cracked. Her face slid into a testy pucker and she bolted for the kennel.

The quick escape left Fran no room to throw another jab at her fragile ego. After three crappy dates, she couldn't handle

Fran's needling and meddling. Safe in the backroom, she beat her forehead into the wall. The exam room door opened.

Cool plaster under her brow, Victoria rolled her head to the side.

Dr. Yaz wore a knowing and concerned half-smile. "I take Princess and your favorite dog owner are in the lobby?"

"You're psychic." She unglued from the wall and pulled her fedora down over the red welt she could feel forming.

"Yes, be careful what you think around me. I'll take care of Fran. Why don't you lock up and leave a little early?" Patting her shoulder, he made his way to the front.

He greeted Fran, and Victoria could hear their steps echoing down the hall. Once the exam room swung shut behind Fran, Victoria sprinted for her desk and shut down her computer. The front door opened, which snapped her attention to the lobby area.

The unknown man had shaggy brown hair hanging over his brow. He wore a button-down shirt and black slacks and was leading a small mop of dog. A dog Victoria had never seen before. She might forget human faces, but fuzzy faces? She knew them all.

He didn't seem the type to turn heads, yet there was a soft allure to him. Victoria stared into the nicest pair of blue eyes. "May I help you?"

His gaze focused on her. "Daisy here alternates between being a ferret on crack or an angry little snail. I thought the change was because of the stressful cross-country move, but her pattern hasn't returned to normal," he said, concern in his every word. "I know I don't have an appointment. I'm new to town and my neighbor recommended Dr. Yaz as the best."

Victoria appreciated his style. "Flattery can get you far."

"Does it?" His worry lines fell away, and he hit her with a smile set to stun.

With him beaming at her, she amended her first impression of him. Happiness morphed his unremarkable features. If he flashed that smile again, she was afraid any woman within fifty feet of the blast radius would wobble on her heels.

Handing him a clipboard, she wrote a note on the office calendar. "Fill out these papers. I'll see if he can squeeze you in."

"I appreciate you checking."

Leaving him to his paperwork, she headed down the hall.

Dr. Yaz spotted her peering into the room through the square window and stuck his head out. "I thought you left."

Victoria stepped out of view of Fran, explaining, "You have a new walk-in, seems routine. Can you squeeze him in after Fran?"

"Yes, and then leave for your appointment." He shooed her away and went back to work.

In the lobby, the completed clipboard lay on her desk. She reviewed the form.

Before she could exit, Fran steamrolled down the hall, this time almost choking Princess to get to the front. Victoria could feel her blood pressure rise.

Dr. Yaz steered Fran to the side counter to check her out. To Victoria, he asked, "Could you show our new patient to exam room two for me? I'll take care of Princess here."

"Sure thing." She offered a thankful you're-my-personal-Jesus grin to Dr. Yaz.

When they were safely in the exam room, Victoria petted Daisy, the little mop dog. She brushed off her hands, glancing out the exam room window checking the lobby.

"I'm Ethan, in case you missed it on the paperwork." He stuck his hand out to her.

She shook his hand. "I'm Victoria. Nice to meet you and Daisy."

Ethan propped his shoulder up against the wall. "If you don't mind me asking, why are you avoiding that lady out there?"

She spread her hands out wide in front of her, unable, unwilling, and unsure of what she could or should say about her stalking matchmaker. Victoria settled on a copout. "It's kind of complicated."

"What is?"

"Maybe 'complicated' isn't the word. Embarrassing is. She wants to set me up with one of her nephews."

"That can't be all bad." Ethan's voice may have been low and pleasant to her ears, but his words were not.

"She's tenacious and unrelenting like a rat after cheese." Victoria watched as Fran finally let Princess tug her outside.

On cue, her cell sang as the doctor stepped into the exam room.

"I've made you late. Have fun today." Disbelief must have been stamped and underlined and triple-starred on Victoria's face because Dr. Yaz chuckled. "Maybe not fun. How about don't have the cops called on you?"

"Alright, nice to meet you, Ethan. Night, Doc." Victoria left the room, gathered her stuff at her desk, and read her text message from Dessie.

The Sanctuary of the Lily called, we need 2 b there @ 12. The owner will personally take us around. Don't b late 2 get me

She checked the time and calculated whether she had time to grab something to eat beforehand. Nope. Oh well, the first place shouldn't take too long to check out.

*W*ith her long, red nails and tight suit, the owner of the Sanctuary of the Lily was as subtle as a freak show. It must have been a slow Tuesday because once Victoria and Dessie set foot on the property for the tour, the owner threw them a hard sales pitch. Dessie just oohed and aahed about the place, encouraging the woman to prattle on.

As she did, dread settled in Victoria's stomach. Dessie could barely drink legally and yet was getting married. Heck, Dessie wasn't adult enough to rent a car for a long weekend, and here they were, planning the start of her forever.

It took two mind-numbing hours to get free of the horrible woman's clutches. Dessie left undecided.

All aboard the loco wedding train. Next stop: Wind Song Gardens. The property sat on the edge of red rock boulders in the middle of the Tempe desert preserve.

"Dessie..." Victoria bit her lip. How could she ask Dessie if she was really, really ready for marriage without causing her sister to explode?

"What?" The single word dripped with bitchiness.

Dessie sounded primed to reward Victoria's questions with

lethal jabs like the super classic response, "*Right. Your life is so perfect, you need to fix mine?*" Victoria gave up and hit her blinker to turn into the empty side road.

The grounds showcased native desert plants. Gray-green stalks with bright yellow flowers bobbed in the wind. Roadrunners and jackrabbits darted around the gardens.

"It's like a carpet of desert flowers and we're right by the zoo," Dessie said, kitten excited and, magically, her sour mood evaporated.

"Yes." Victoria's voice was loaded with a dog's sigh worth of disappointment. She couldn't even talk with her sister.

A middle-aged man in cargo pants greeted them at the wrought-iron door of the garden. "Hi, I'm Zack the manager and I'll be showing you around." He was one of those nouveau hippies, too young to be the original, but he still had that I-worship-the-Mother-Earth vibe.

They made their way toward the outdoor amphitheater.

"The back garden is where we have all the big weddings." The manager led them down the packed dirt pathway.

Yellow dots fluttered around the suspended canvas sail, providing much needed shade. Butterflies danced in the light breeze, blotting out the bright green tree branches with their colorful wings.

"Beautiful place." Dessie's head kept swiveling, drinking it all in.

With forests, people can get overwhelmed with all the green and browns. In the desert, there is less color and more space between the plant life, so any small splash of color is accented by the muted background. That's what made the desert alluring to the eye—the surprise pops of color.

Taking in all the raw beauty, Victoria shoved her elbow into Dessie's ribs. "Reason number 145 of why I still live here."

"I don't remember the desert like this. A hidden treasure of textures."

Victoria chuckled inwardly. "You never liked to be outside."

The manager gestured to the west with the low red rock hills. "Sunset is spectacular, then at night, we turn on the clear lights, which are strung throughout the trees, for soft lighting. We're projected to have perfect weather in March."

Dessie turned in a slow circle, taking in the red rock and cactus. "It is picturesque."

Victoria stepped closer to her sister. "Could you give us a moment, please, while we talked?"

"Sure, here are our brochures and price lists. Take your time and then come find me. I'll be at the entrance." The manager walked back the way he came.

Victoria flipped open the price list. Her world tilted. "How many are on your guest list?"

"A small party of two hundred." Dessie read over Victoria's shoulder and gave a low whistle. "That's a huge chunk of change."

"More than I paid for all my cars, combined. I need to sit down."

They staggered over to the amphitheater steps and sat. The concrete radiated warmth from baking in the sun all day.

"Glad Daddy isn't with us." Dessie giggled.

A laugh. No better time. Praying for no outburst, Victoria barrel-rolled into a real conversation with her sister. "Where is Dad going to get the money for all of this?"

Dessie tossed a rock. The pebble bounced across the concrete, skidding into the tan sand. "Don't worry. Damien's family is paying for the wedding."

Judging by her sister's loose throwing arm and the relaxed line of her body, Victoria was safe to forge ahead. "Does Dad know he's not doing the traditional father-of-the-bride thing and paying?"

Dessie tossed the next rock into the air, watching it go up and down. "I haven't informed him yet."

Well, that talk with their dad was one hundred percent all Dessie's.

Doves cooed in the distance. A mommy quail darted across at the edge of the stage with five fat babies chugging after her. They zigzagged their way, disappearing into the brush.

Initiating conversations with her sister had similarities to being dropped behind enemy lines with land mines littering the area. Victoria had to keep her objective clear: no fighting, only ask a single honest question.

"Are you sure you want to get married?" The question came out in one full exhale.

Dessie stayed quiet, unnaturally still. When she spoke, her voice quivered. "Yes, we love each other. He buys me gifts and opens doors for me."

Crap, her baby sister was basing a lifetime commitment on gifts and manners? "Listen, I have no place to ask, but this is a big deal. This is real. This is the whole death-till-you-part. This is forever."

Dessie hugged her knees, turning her sapphire gaze on Victoria. "I love him."

The happiness that lay deep in her sister's soul ripped the questions right out of Victoria. Dessie beamed and brimmed with joy and something Victoria couldn't even name.

What qualifications did she have to question the depth of her sister's love for her fiancé?

Victoria would rather have gone through a Hyde-tide tantrum. Guilt flooded in, reminding her how heartless she was being. She felt happy for Dessie. Yet, at the same time, Victoria thought her sister too reckless. Plus, deep down, she wanted to be in love, too. Real love.

No need for a pity party. They were planning Dessie's wedding adventure. Victoria stood and dusted off her pants. "Good enough for me. It's your life. Now, where do you want to get married?"

She chewed her lip. "I don't know. They both have their pluses."

"How about this? Close your eyes and imagine your wedding at sunset in the first place. Got it?"

"Yes."

"Now, release that and imagine this place lit up at night. Which looks better to you?"

Dessie's shoulders relaxed. "This place. I want to get married here. I want to show Damien how wonderful the desert can be."

Victoria offered her sister a hand up. "Then let's go rent this baby. How are we going to pay?"

Dessie grinned, reaching for her sister's hand. "With plastic, my dear Watson."

Victoria hoisted Dessie to her feet.

"I couldn't have decided on a place without you." She launched at Victoria and squeezed her tight.

The sweet sister Victoria recalled surfaced and she was relieved to see the softer side of Dessie again. She hugged her back, saying, "You're welcome. Get moving though, I'm starved."

AFTER DROPPING A RIDICULOUS DEPOSIT, they headed to home base. Dessie texted Damien to let him know the date, time, price, and place of his wedding. Victoria mentally rebuilt the list of wedding tasks. Contact hotels to reserve rooms for guests, prepare invitations to be emailed or Tweeted or instant messaged, and rent limos. And hunt for The Dress.

Once Dessie crossed into the apartment, she squealed down the hall to her room. The first thing Victoria did was crack open a beer.

Dessie flew into the kitchen, clutching a scrapbook to her chest. The devil's book.

Beer was not going to be strong enough.

Inside, its bright pages detailed Dessie's wedding inspiration. For fourteen years, she had been saving clippings from newspapers, brochures, and magazines—all ideas for her big day. Random ideas. Besides the cut-outs, there were enough stickers and glitter to entertain an entire kindergarten classroom for a year.

Hip resting on the counter, Victoria drank her beer, taking in the swirl of madness building before her. Once this glittery hell book opened, Tropical Storm Dessie would be upgraded to Hurricane Bridal Beast.

Without making any sudden moves, she one-hand texted Sandra.

It begins. The book is in my house. Tell my dad I loved him. Maverick

Her sister looked feverish. Eyes dilated and glazed. Hands trembled.

Hello, Hyde.

Dessie opened the book, pointing to a 1920s-style sheath dress. "Won't this be amazing on me?"

The deafening first gale of the bridal hurricane had hit land.

Bottle upended, Victoria checked the bottom of her beer. Her drink had magically evaporated. "Drape a potato sack over you and you'll be catwalk ready. Want a beer?"

Engrossed in the crumbled clippings in front of her, Dessie waved her sister, the giant gnat, away. "You can keep the pointless calories and carbs to yourself. I need to lose a few pounds."

Insulting much? Victoria swallowed a retort. No use stirring up her sister.

Not glancing up from her scrapbook, Dessie said, "I'm hungry. Get me healthy food. The wedding is soon." Her mouth stopped. She dropped the book and slowly, scarily slow, swiveled her whole body toward Victoria.

Ice cascaded down Victoria's spine. Maybe she should ship Dessie off to stay with their mother. The two were crazy and deserved each other.

"Tori, I'm getting married in two weeks." Each word came out faster and an octave higher than the one preceding it. Dessie thrust the book at her.

Victoria caught the book square in her chest and rubbed her sore breastbone. "That hurt."

"I'm going to be wearing one of those down the aisle in two weeks." Then she detonated into a tear bomb.

"Everything will be alright." Victoria shoved a kitchen towel at her leaking sister. With Dessie's waterworks gushing, she couldn't leave or Dessie would pop a lung yelling at her, so she waited out the sob storm. "What do you want to do tomorrow?"

Nose buried in the towel, Dessie cleared her sinuses. "We go dress hunting." Her voice was thick and nasally.

"Where?"

Dessie's puffy eyes sparkled and glazed over. "Ms. Z's Gallery. I'll email them to set up an appointment." Her tone hardened like a hawk's talons. "If they dare say they can't fit me in, I'll tell them I'm taking my limitless credit card somewhere else for my dress."

This was not a calming subject. Detour time. Victoria tried again. "Who are your bridesmaids?"

"Avon, Connie, and Joy."

Victoria's sisterly concern evaporated. Dessie's friends were the worst and brought out the worst in her.

The four of them stood at the center of everything in high school. They were pretty, popular, and scheming. Dessie, the undisputed leader, ran the group with her sweetness and looks. If Dessie went somewhere or wanted something, magic happened.

Avon hated being the sidekick to the marginally nicer and more attractive Dessie. The few times Victoria was unfortunate enough to be left alone with the three sans Dessie, they were brutal to her.

Nothing personal, they simply judged everything as either posh and worthy of them or trash. Avon, Connie, and Joy judged Victoria as trash since her hair was too curly and she weighed too much.

Time to escape. She wanted to drown this whole headache with some mindless TV. Nonchalantly, she crept away. "I bet the four of you will have a great time tomorrow. Why don't you call them and talk about your plans?"

"And, obviously, my maid of honor is you."

Victoria felt like Thor's hammer just took out her knees. "Me? You want me to be in your wedding?"

"Well, you're my only sister." Her words sickly sweet. "Aren't you excited to be in my wedding?"

This excitement was akin to walking over a high wire strung between two skyscrapers with no safety nets.

Dessie's phone chirped and saved Victoria from responding.

Fantastic. Not only was her little sister getting married before her, but now she had the duty to be the maid of honor of this fiasco. The rest of the bridal party's favorite pastimes were partying and backstabbing each other with their stiletto heels. Well, as their queen, Dessie would at least keep the frosted flakes inline and focused on the wedding. Not focused on Victoria.

This still smelled of impending disaster. She texted Sandra.

Goose, SOS. STAT. Maverick

Dessie hung up her cell and started texting and walking to her room. "Thanks to the limitless card, we have an eight to eleven slot tomorrow to try on dresses."

The world spun on Victoria. She stood, staring at her kitchen tiles trying to noodle this all out. Tomorrow. Three hours. With Dessie in hyped-up Hyde mode. Plus, Dessie's best buddies, the three piranhas, circling, waiting to draw first blood, and she had to get yet more time off work. This had to be the downside of the power of threes.

Victoria's phone rang. She hit answer.

"I can't help tonight. I've got a date. Your sister can't be that bad." Sandra's tone was short and dismissive.

The glib response snapped Victoria out of her stupor. "Not that bad? Quick recap. One, my little sister's getting married. Two, she lives under my roof with her terrifying puff-painted wedding book."

Sandra's shudder flowed through the phone. "The battered scrapbook that your sister slaved and obsessed overgrowing up designing the best wedding ever? That's a high bar of hell."

"I can pole vault over the book nightmare because there's ever so much more. Three, I have no date lined up for the wedding. Four, my sister's transforming into everlasting Hyde mode. Five, tomorrow we go dress shopping with the fantastically bitchy Dessie posse. At Ms. Z's."

"Ms. Z's? Dessie's fake high-school friends would kill to go shopping there." Sandra's voice got further away. "How did your sister get an appointment there? The shop is movie-star-catering expensive."

"Limitless credit card." Victoria's voice escalated into the strangled cat register. "But I'm not done with my list. The coup de grace, six, I'm her maid of honor."

No noise emanated from the phone.

She checked her phone screen to make sure she hadn't dropped the call. "San, are you there?"

"I retract what I said. This is a chugga-chugga-choo-choo train wreck. When is the dress catastrophe slated to begin?"

"Eight a.m. begins the freaking torture session."

"I'll be there at seven. I'll bring the food. You make the coffee." Sandra sounded way too happy.

"You want to come?" There was naked disbelief in her question.

"I should do humanity a favor and record the trip for posterity. There will be enough blood and gore that Roman gladiators would have fainted at the brutality. I'm in." With her declaration of joining the blood bath, Sandra hung up.

Of course, this disaster would be entertainment for her since Sandra would be able to watch from the relative safety of a corner and not in the middle of the dress wars. Phone in one hand and a beer in the other, Victoria debated her options for tonight. She could be in Mexico in less than five hours.

Her cat meowed.

Scratch Mexico. She couldn't leave Ralph by his sweet and fuzzy self to deal with the demon who lived below the surface of Dessie's skin. Her sister may eat him.

Ralph howled at his bowl. She fed him.

She spent the rest of the night avoiding Dessie by feigning a headache and whisking Ralph to the safety of her locked bedroom.

*U*nusually punctual, Sandra came over the next morning at seven in standard Sandra attire: jeans, sneakers, and a black T-shirt. She delivered a breakfast of fruit, bagels, and cream cheese as promised. "Swap ya for coffee."

"Yours is right there." Victoria grabbed them small plates for the food.

"I swear we could do well as a couple." She sprayed bits of bread with her words.

"Except for two things: unlike you, I don't do girls, and manners are foreign to you."

"I'm cultured."

"I don't mean your diverse dating tastes."

"I'm well-mannered." With an exaggerated eye roll that would have made any teenager proud, Sandra Vanna White-ed her breakfast. "See, I even have a napkin under my bagel. Not resting in my palm. Manners on clear display."

Victoria wiped her mouth with her napkin. "Want to back up the claim with a friendly wager?"

Sandra flounced into a kitchen chair. "Easy. I'll bet you I can handle anything Dessie and her evil triplets throw at me for a few hours."

Victoria smiled wide and hit Sandra in her forbidden-tiara pride. "If you can't keep your cool today, you'll have to wear a girlie, hot-pink dress with all the froufrou accents to the wedding. The price of failure must include heels that hurt, makeup that shows, and hair that's runway ready."

She knew she set the bar too high for Sandra to bite. The thought of butch Sandra all dolled up at the wedding was hilarious.

"Done."

Punching the arrogance button for sure, Victoria wanted to make sure Sandra understood what she was agreeing to. "You'll have to pass off as a real, live girlie-girl for the wedding. You would need to revert to your forced child-beauty-queen ways."

Sandra drew herself up and shook her bagel at Victoria. "I hate you for bringing up my pageant torture, so as a bonus F-you, challenge accepted."

A dress. Sandra said yes to the dress? There had to be a hallucinogenic drug in Victoria's cream cheese. "Stilettos? Toe crushers? You know, the things you constantly monologue about how they weren't even created for women. They were created by men in the Middle Ages to show off their big, dancing calf muscles to impress the ladies."

"All true. And yes, heels will be worn, if I lose. Which I won't. I won't back out. How about what I'll get when I win? You brave enough to handle my counter?" Sandra dropped her bagel to the table.

Victoria felt ready to step into the ring over the mere implication of cowardliness, and her tone came out as stubborn as a pit bull. "Are you implying I'd back out? I won't."

Sandra lit up. "Good, because naturally, you'll lose this bet. And when you do, you'll have to kiss a guy. By Sunday."

"I'm sorry, what?"

"Time's a-ticking. I figure I can scare you into finding a man."

Victoria's shoulders sagged. "I'm already outside of my comfort zone."

"Kudos for guy trolling and dating. Yet I want you to be time zones away from the shell you've been hiding in for the past seven years. Since high school. As a safety precaution, if you force me to be unladylike, we both lose. My final offer." Sandra popped a chunk of bagel into her mouth.

For three solid hours, Sandra had to keep her temper with Dessie and her three minions while trapped in one room. For Sandra, that was mission nigh impossible.

"Deal." Victoria's voice was giddy. "Hot pink isn't in this spring's fashion catalogs. You might have to hire a seamstress."

Sandra snorted. "Don't count your pink monstrosities before they give birth. But you should work on your come-hither look and do some lip exercises because I am majestic as a cat."

They both swung their eyes over to Ralph, who sat spread-eagled on the chair, cleaning himself. He glanced up, dismissed them, and continued his royal bath time.

"I can see the resemblance." Victoria laughed.

Dessie whipped out of the bathroom, cutting off whatever Sandra's pithy comeback could have been. The bride-to-be looked regal and seamless whereas Victoria felt scruffy and glued together.

Victoria hadn't even donned a hat that morning, figuring she was going to put on a lot of dresses. To keep her wild curls corralled, her hair was in a low ponytail. At least she put on a cute sundress with flowery sandals she had bought a few months ago.

Dessie floated past them, heading out the door. "Come on, I don't want to make Ms. Z wait."

Her sister's demeanor seemed downright pleasant. Victoria

and Sandra sat in stunned silence. No demands, no shouting. This could go well.

Sandra recovered first. "We better go before the kind Dr. Jekyll hotwires your car."

Pulling up to Ms. Z's Gallery to find Dessie her dress, a valet hopped forward and whisked the car away. The building looked slick and modern, painted black and white with gold trim and oozing money.

Stopped to let Dessie take her selfie before going in, Victoria asked, "Is Mom going to meet us here?"

"She is out of town until tomorrow, but I couldn't get another appointment for another month." Dessie straightened her spine and slipped her phone into her purse. "It's fine. I have you and the girls to help me find the ideal dress."

A small woman waited by the door. She looked about forty and was dressed stylishly with a thick leather book in her hand. "I'm Olivia. Which one of you is Esmeralda?"

Dessie put her hand out to Olivia. "I am. Nice to meet you. This is my maid of honor and sister, Victoria. And her best friend Sandra. She's not in my wedding party, of course. My three bridesmaids should be here shortly."

"I will be your personal gown assistant." Olivia held the door open for the three of them, then walked them through a plush front area. Massive portraits of brides lined the walls. Gigantic teeth shone out at them. No racks. Not even other brides flitting around cooing and crying. Only a reception area with a slip of a girl manning the phones and the creepy pictures.

Past the lobby area, they entered the dressing rooms. Each door had a different style and paint color. Olivia stopped in front of a black door with gold and silver paint swirls and an elegant number seven displayed on it and pushed it open. "I have us in my favorite room."

A glass-beaded chandelier lit up the fitting room. Who knew a dressing room could be elegant and swanky?

Victoria could have thrown an intimate soirée with one or two tuxedoed waiters in this dressing room. She and Sandra stood straighter.

Dessie beamed. The light illuminated her features, making her profile romantic and tinted with a rosy glow.

"Do sit down to discuss where and when the wedding will take place." Olivia arranged herself at the small table. Her pencil skirt lay flat against her thighs, even when she crossed her feet at her ankles.

"I bet she only has one butt cheek on the edge of that minuscule chair," Sandra whispered directly into Victoria's ear. They both suppressed giggles.

Dessie was a mirror image of Olivia. She sat on the edge of her chair, her back ramrod straight, head up, and, yes, her ankles locked around each other. In her lap, the unholy book of wedding planning insanity.

"Come on, Tori. Sit down next to me." Dessie patted the chair to her right.

Crap, Victoria was stuck in the bride's claws. She slunk further away from the only exit. Sandra came, too. They flanked Dessie in the open chairs on either side of the bride.

Dessie squared to Olivia. "I am getting married at Wind Song Gardens in a sunset wedding."

Olivia cracked open her large notebook and took notes.

"On March the eighth." Dessie's chin and voice raised, her challenge clear.

"On March eighth, which is in two weeks?" Olivia's voice remained calm and steady, but they all could feel the heat underneath the cold exterior. She removed her glasses from her nose. They fell to her chest, attached around her neck by a diamond-encrusted chain.

This did not bode well. Were they going to need to find another place to go dress shopping? Victoria prayed not, because they didn't have time to bounce around place to place.

Dessie laid a protective hand over her wedding planning book. "Is that a problem?"

Olivia tapped her leather notebook with her pen. "Well, the timeline is very tight. We might not be able to help you."

Reaching into her purse, Dessie pulled out a plain black card and slid it across the middle of the table like she was the star of a bad mob movie. "I guess I will have to go to someone who is willing to work with me." She started to retrieve the credit card, her ticket into this exclusive shop.

Olivia placed her hand over Dessie's. "Don't be hasty. We can work something out. Be aware, there'll be rush charges to get everything here in time."

Dessie retracted her hand and perched on her seat again. She bared all her teeth. "I had heard such wonderful things about Ms. Z's. I'm glad to know all those glowing referrals weren't wrong. For a moment there, I had my doubts."

The limitless card still rested in between them. "My dear Esmeralda, let's see what ideas you have. Then we'll know where to start. What are your bridesmaid's names? I can leave their names at the front and have them brought to us."

Ten minutes later, they strolled out to the dress area. Olivia threw open the double doors. Chandeliers sent diffused light around the massive area, sprinkling rainbows on the racks of white dresses.

Victoria peered to see the end of the sea of white and felt snow blind.

Turning to Dessie, Olivia asked, "Where do you want to start? Sheath dresses, ball gowns, A-line?"

Dessie glanced down at her body and threw Victoria the lost puppy-dog expression.

Dessie normally ordered everything and everyone to bend to her whims, but as a bride, she couldn't decide. Very bizarre.

"She wants to try the sheaths first," Victoria answered for her sister. That's the style Dessie had pointed to in her devil book earlier.

"Good choice." Olivia grabbed a sleek control pad by the rack. There were only two buttons—one red, one green.

Olivia pressed the green button. The rack churned. White dresses whirled by.

Watching the dresses fly by made Victoria slightly nauseous. Numbers flicked by and dresses continued to spin.

Dessie paced in front of the bridal-dress blizzard. "I'm not going to wait. The girls should be here in a few minutes."

Olivia punched the red button. Silently and smoothly, the racks shimmied to a halt. "Here is the sheath section. See the numbers above the rack? That is the dress size. Any of them you want to try on, let me know. I'll get them placed in the dressing room."

Dessie shoved Victoria and Sandra to the side. Eyes dilated, glazed, and crazed, she stared at all the dresses, her breath coming in short bursts.

Madness pulsed. The crazy leaked out of Dessie's pores. The bride dove headfirst into the nearest rack of dresses.

Olivia sighed, her sigh layered with a mix of resignation and reluctance. "Be careful."

Every few seconds, foraging sounds of *oh!*, *ah!*, and *beautiful!*, drifted to Victoria and Sandra. Olivia scurried by, unloading dress after dress onto a smaller portable rack.

"Tori, don't be useless, find me dresses." Dessie's shrill notes would have made a banshee cringe.

Here was the sister Victoria knew and struggled to tolerate.

She walked the plank to her sister and her white demise, dragging Sandra with her to wade into the bridal hunt. Untold time later, Olivia called them out of the white maze and showed them to the dressing room. Inside lay a horde of beaded and beautiful dresses.

Sandra and Victoria huddled around the tray of fruit and champagne on the back table.

"We're never going to leave here alive," Victoria whispered.

"I am." Sandra popped a grape without a wrinkle of concern.

"You'd leave me here. To wither and die."

"Absolutely."

Victoria slugged Sandra's arm. "Whelp."

"Again, there are limits to my wingman status." Sandra gestured with her full champagne glass to Dessie. "I've got no jurisdiction to extract you from death by sister-turned-bridezilla."

The bride in question launched herself at the closest dress pile. She moved in a desperate rush, emulating a feral predator.

Victoria downed her champagne. "Just say something nice at my wake."

"I'll be there in my brightest dress with the New Orleans style dirge all tuned up, just for you." Sandra's voice was serious, solemn, steady.

What a good friend to think ahead to her demise.

*D*essie stripped to her body slimmer in a nanosecond and stood in the middle of the raised mirrored platform. Like an actor in a speed costume change, she shimmied into the first dress.

Her head popped out and she reached around, struggling to zip it up. The first dress turned out to be a slinky velvet number, hugging every curve of her body. Victoria stepped forward, pulled the zipper, and tried to describe the dress.

Sandra raked her gaze up and down, most likely cataloging the cut and color with her finely-honed woman measurer. "Not you, Dessie. Unless you want to be a lounge singer in cream."

"Agreed. The 'no' pile has the first offering." Victoria shuffled through the dresses and extracted another. "This is the one."

Dessie tugged off the first dress. "A randomly picked dress is the one? I doubt a dress picked by you, of all people, could be The One."

Victoria's back stiffened. She let the insult roll by, taking the dress offered from Dessie and starting the reject mound. In a moment, Dessie had the new dress on.

"What do you think?" Dessie's eyes stayed glued to her

reflection.

Victoria knew this dress was The One. Her stomach churned, fueled by a lifetime of burning jealousy. The feeling tasted coppery. She swayed, overpowered by this demonic possession of resentment.

Jealously Victoria felt all the time. This felt different. She kept her hands clasped in front of her and addressed the bride-to-be. "You look stunning. Simple, yet elegant, and it will be breathtaking in the desert garden."

Regardless of the turmoil inside her, Victoria spoke the truth. Her sister shined.

Olivia surveyed Dessie from the top of her loose ponytail to her bare feet. "This has an option to add a train, which unfortunately we don't have in stock. The train comes in various lengths and all of them can be hitched up during the reception."

"I'll want the longest one you've got. I can imagine the train against the red carpet and in the pictures." Dessie swooned.

Victoria dropped her gaze from Dessie. The tears gathered. Never never never in all her life of dealing with her sister had such bottomless envy crushed her. Keeping her eyes averted, she forced herself to take the two steps toward Dessie and thrust a new dress at her. "Next."

An hour clawed by. Dessie gabbed about how awesome she looked in all the bridal dresses. Victoria and Sandra sagged in their chairs, wiping out the last cookie crumbs.

Olivia hung up the newest casualty on the no rack. "We only have an hour left. Do you want to try on the ball gown style or change over to the bridesmaids' dresses?"

Dessie twirled in one of the yes dresses. "I like these simple dresses that I started with. Let's narrow the important dress down first, mine. I'll call the bridesmaids and see why they're not here yet."

Watching the bride check her phone, Sandra leaned over to

Victoria. "They didn't call your sister at all. Heartless vipers."

"Are you mad for Dessie?" Victoria's sky-high question mark accented her surprise.

Sandra used her champagne glass to point to Dessie. Standing there, dressed in white, she looked like her cat died. "She's called them. No one answered. She's texting them. They're supposedly her friends and they're not here for her."

Dessie received an almost immediate response via text. Her body posture softened. "Silly. They had breakfast planned and forgot to put the appointment in their calendars." Her voice was hopeful and gullible. "They'll be here in thirty minutes. And they say to start without them."

"Two and half hours after we started," Victoria muttered into her glass of champagne.

"They just forgot," Dessie whispered to herself.

Victoria had never seen her little sister lie to herself so brazenly. Dessie had to know those reptiles were late on purpose because they lived to bully and torment others. Tolerating such bad behavior from her friends was new and odd. The high-school Dessie would've been in a snit, fuming over them being even five minutes late.

Maybe she'd grown up being away at college.

Between Victoria, Olivia, and Dessie, they shoveled the bridal blizzard until there were only three wedding dresses left. With Dessie still undecided, Victoria stood firm on her initial dress choice from the beginning of the dress hunt.

Dessie beamed at her sister through her mirrored double. "You're right. With my hair swept to the side in a 1920s pinup and with one single flower behind my ear, the image would be divine."

"Damien is going to have to fight off all the men at the wedding who will object to the marriage." Victoria's voice was raw and honest.

The bride teared up. "I can't believe this is happening."

After a few moments of quiet, Olivia stepped up and helped Dessie out of the dress. "I'll have my assistant verify the shipment dates and draft up the cost. Let's get to the bridesmaid dresses with the rest of the time."

All four of them moved to the dress arena. Dessie picked out all the bridesmaid dresses, an eclectic mix ranging from lacy to faux tuxes.

Dessie wanted to view the dresses quickly, so Victoria challenged Sandra to a dress duel. They flounced and strutted in front of the mirror, being the biggest dorks known to man. All of them laughed so hard, they could barely breathe.

It was the most fun Victoria had trying on clothes. She pursed her lips at Dessie and sent her sister a kiss.

The door blew open. With it blew away all the fun.

Three anorexic women surveyed the room. Their faces all had one lip curled up in disdain, which they must have thought made them appear discerning and important. The facial expression made them look like they had to pass gas.

Once the three finished their mandatory dramatic threshold-pause, they swarmed the bride. Squawking over each other, the three worked to capture Dessie's attention.

"Oh, this is exciting," Avon said.

"I can't believe you are getting married," Connie said.

"We're so incredibly happy for you," Joy said.

Sandra put her hand on her bow-covered hip and addressed the three stooges. "Sorry to pull you away from your meal."

Avon, the second-in-command, snapped her head up, narrowed her eyes, and crinkled her button nose at the sight of Sandra.

Sandra let out a sharp, cruel, mirthless laugh. "I wouldn't sneer, Avon, you'll get wrinkles, aging you a good ten years in an instant."

Avon forced her face to relax. "Your archenemy is in your wedding, Dessie? I bet she's enjoying the peep show." The words slithered off Avon's forked tongue.

Victoria charged forward. "You slimy—"

Sandra shut down Victoria's outrage by throwing her arm in front of her.

"She's not in the wedding party. She's here helping me." Dessie's words were weak and her spine retracted.

Victoria couldn't believe her ears or her eyes. Dessie should be seething, ripping snide, caustic remarks, not cowering. Her sister never cowered. And yet, she cowered now.

Avon crossed her arms and put on a smug face. "Did I strike at the truth of why you're here?"

Sandra stepped off the mirrored platform. Victoria knew the tight body posture she displayed. Sandra prowled forward ready to maim, regardless of the bright yellow, puffy dress with floppy black bows she wore. "Dessie's too young for me. As for you clowns, you're sun-bleached carcasses. None of you have half an ass cheek or a full set of real breasts between you."

The three lobster-faced blondes sucked out all the air.

Dessie hugged her stomach, her face a mask of defeat.

Before anyone else could open their sass traps, Olivia stepped in front of the offended bridesmaids, bearing the tray of champagne. "Ladies, why don't you all sit down. We only have five minutes. Victoria, please show them the dresses that are in the 'yes' pile for the bridesmaids."

Sandra gathered up her clothes and stormed out the door, her black bows bouncing in fury.

Again, the disgust Victoria felt at Dessie's meekness radiated. She couldn't believe her sister's unwillingness to voice her thoughts. Dessie stood there as useful as a garden statue. All she needed to complete the picture were decorative poop droppings.

The fun that they'd had was now long gone. After that aggravation, poor Sandra had lost the bet and hopefully found somewhere to cool off. Olivia asked Victoria to model the five dress contenders. Hands balled at her sides, but Victoria dutifully donned each dress.

The judgment from the three about her every fat fold and lumpy section as she stretched the material to its tension limits was palpable. Even though the dresses were in her size, they just didn't suit her body style. Yet under Olivia's quick talking points, the other bridesmaids sipped champagne and said little.

Standing in front of the mirror with nothing but her flaws for company, Victoria bristled. Dessie had yet to say one word of rebuke. One would have thought Avon ran the four girls, not Dessie.

The bickering began over options one and three. Joy, as usual, had no opinion. Connie loved option one, a simple sheath dress with a slit up to the thigh, which showcased every flaw on Victoria. Avon wanted option three, a minidress with a plunging V in the back and the front which left little to the imagination. Doubly unappealing. Barely better than a fancy bikini.

To the three vultures circling her, Victoria said, "If I had to go with either, I would say dress one."

Avon lifted her hand to pat Victoria's bare shoulder. The condescending little snake left her hand millimeters from skin contact. "That's sweet of you, thinking we care about your opinion."

"You better care about what I say because I'm the maid of honor." Victoria's voice bit.

Avon cocked her head at Dessie. Her twin could've been a confused yippy dog. "What did she say?"

Joy, the quietest and nicest of the three, handed Avon a champagne flute.

"She's my maid of honor." Dessie's voice shriveled like a child forced to admit they stole candy.

Victoria's fingernails bit into her palms. Gutless sister.

Avon channeled a pufferfish and expanded to about a size two. "I see. I'm glad you chose your best friend to be your maid of honor. We have somewhere to be. Sorry, but we've got to bounce." She downed the entire glass of champagne in one gulp.

Chins jutted out, they marched out of the room. Not one of them glanced at the bride.

"Slime." Victoria pointed at the retreating line of sniveling friends and said to Dessie, "You're letting them leave?"

"They're busy." Dessie's tone flat.

"Why are they in the wedding?" This time Victoria's voice went from disbelief to anger.

Olivia gave Victoria a warm, sympathetic smile. To Dessie, she steered her away from the door. "What dress do you want them to wear?"

Words clipped, Victoria said, "They deserve the salmon-colored dresses with the big flowers on the ass."

Dessie scrunched up her nose, laughing uncomfortably. "They're my friends, I can't."

"*Pff.*" Victoria wanted to know what alien cloned her cowardly sister and when did this abduction happen.

Olivia opened her notebook. "Let's start with the colors. The pale green, dusty rose, or light yellow?"

"The pale yellow would go with their skin tones. I would look dead." Victoria winced at the image.

"What do you think?" Dessie asked Olivia.

Olivia picked up the dresses. "Put the bridesmaids in the pale yellow with the plunging V and add a green band of material to lengthen it to the knee and we can add an insert, bringing the plunging neckline up."

Victoria winced, imagining the same dress on her.

Olivia checked her watch. "For Victoria, I suggest a different dress style. If you two will trust me, I'll pick something out to match the theme and look great."

Dessie exploded. Her energy magically returned. She hugged Olivia. "Thank you. We'll trust your professional eye and leave you to your next appointment."

When Dessie acted all sugary and sincere, it was no wonder everyone loved her. She floated to her wedding dress and ran her hands over the soft material.

With the cut and color, the dress made Dessie starlette-esque, flawless and glowing.

Victoria's heart shriveled. She'd never have her wedding fever. There would be no carpeted walkway with her dad on her arm. No, for her, her future would be a rocking chair. Gray hair. Twenty-five cats. Her destiny awaited.

Task accomplished, Dessie glowed with excitement and she pranced out of the elegant portal of hell.

Anger and disappointment about her sister and her three "friends" lay tucked tightly under Victoria's skin. She slumped along following behind Dessie's heel clicks.

Once outside, Sandra joined the sisters standing by the valet. "Which one did the floozies pick?"

Checking herself in the storefront window reflection, Dessie fluffed and fixed her hair. "They didn't. I picked. The V-neck minidress in a light yellow with pale green accents."

Sandra gave Victoria an are-you-really-going-to-wear-that eyebrow raise.

Victoria shrugged. "Actually, Olivia picked the dress, Dessie gave her approval."

"I did decide. I asked for her professional opinion and then agreed." Dessie took a selfie and focused on her phone.

The valet pulled up in Victoria's car. This appointment has been rough but fruitful. With the place and dress down, the rest of the wedding to-dos should be easier.

Victoria dropped everyone off at her apartment and drove to work. The dash clock informed her she had about fifteen minutes before they opened for the afternoon. She rested her head on the steering wheel and sorted through her morning without crying. Seeing her baby sister in the gorgeous dress, beaming, reminded Victoria that she would be stag and have her confrontation with the Alburga family tree in a little under two weeks.

The whole morning, Victoria felt brittle enough that a feather stroke could shatter her heart. Couldn't someone just come up and ask her out and cut through all the hoops of blind dating or trolling?

She sighed. She would have to face the whole family on Dessie's wedding day alone. It was weird knowing that being in her mid-twenties meant she would be heckled for being a spinster. Her family's norm was to marry no later than twenty-two. The only one who didn't follow the rule was Uncle Aggie, who escaped to the military.

She needed to order sanity glue.

Wallowing complete, Victoria picked up her bag and rolled into the clinic to prep for the afternoon. Dr. Yaz came in from lunch and immediately disappeared into the back.

Her stomach rumbled. She rooted around her bottom desk drawer and unearthed a tuna lunch pack. Giving a victorious whoop, she blew off the dust. She froze mid-happy dance. Fran's nephew, one of the double Ds with a buzzed head and lean body, ramrod straight, gawked at her.

"Hi, I'm Danny. My Aunt Fran left her credit card here yesterday and she sent me to pick it up for you." Face scarlet and running over his words, he continued, "I mean from you, not for you. And, I um...wanted..."

She cut off his dithering, certain he was trying to ask her out. "About her card, I'll check."

Dr. Yaz, the fool, had left the door unlocked after he waltzed in. She should have been eating in peace, not dealing with Danny.

Victoria popped through the kennel doors and snagged the doctor by his white coat. "Did you let Fran leave something here yesterday?"

"Not that I recall."

"You're aware that I love to keep my Fran-free days in the double digits because she insists I date her nephews."

He blinked at her. "Are her nephews rude or mean?"

She peeked out the round window to see Dippy, er Danny, in the lobby, straightening her pen cup. She blew out all her air in a big horse sigh. "No."

"Are you seeing someone?"

She snapped her gaze to the doctor. "You know I'm not."

"Do you have a date for the wedding yet?"

"No." The truth tasted like acid.

"Then maybe you should expand your horizons and let the boy take you out." Dr. Yaz handed Victoria the rogue credit card, patted her hand, and walked away.

"But I don't think it's a good idea." Her voice shrunk to a whiny whisper.

"How's your way going? Have an adventurous spirit." He slid into an exam room.

Her spine felt a shock. Adventurous. The stupid insipid letter she wrote to herself talked about living an adventurous life. What was she, a pirate going to sail the high seas?

With the letter triggering her mind, Victoria couldn't let her self-doubts drag her down to Davy Jones's Locker. She better go and see if her naïve self was right.

TIP # 16
BE KIND

*V*ictoria marched into the lobby and offered Danny his aunt's credit card. "It's very nice of you to pick this up for your aunt." Her voice was bright like condensed sunshine.

He grabbed the plastic card. And stood there. The ticking clock reverberated off the walls. *Tick, tick, tick.* Danny stood rooted to the tile.

His pale face shifted to green and with knuckles gripping the counter, he spewed out the question. "Want to get some food tonight?"

She hated to admit it to herself, but the doctor and her irritating letter were right: her life smelled worse than a cat lady's litter box with doing things her way. Time to live her life as dictated by her high-school self and choose to be different. She said, "Sure, we can grab a bite together."

"Really? I mean cool." He trailed off, his body trembling.

Victoria stepped in to save him from himself before he passed out. "I'm off at five. We could go somewhere to eat from here."

"I'll be here." Danny backed out of the lobby, bouncing as though he was a kangaroo. He dashed to his car and peeled out.

Victoria exhaled. She slumped over her canned lunch. Embarking on an adventure felt similar to holding a cat baptism. Cold, scary, and it went in clawing.

"That was nice of you," a deep voice in the lobby said.

She snapped her head up. Ethan, the killer-smile guy from yesterday's walk-in appointment, sat in the corner. When did he ninja into the lobby?

Fighting claustrophobia of embarrassment, Victoria straightened, locking her knees. Being upright drove the dove-gray walls back and let her body steady itself. There had been an audience for her social shipwreck.

Ethan unfolded himself from the small chair. "I didn't mean to eavesdrop on your personal life. Dr. Yaz asked me to bring in a sample of Daisy's urine to see what is wrong with my little girl." The plastic container made a dull smack as he slid the sample across the counter to her.

She kept herself rigid and professional and most likely was as red as a cardinal. "OK, I'll get this sent off today. As to overhearing my lousy social life, it's no big deal." No matter what words flowed out of her, heat and shame radiated throughout her body. Wednesday's new task: devour chocolate to curb her crying fits.

The stupid high-seas journey that her letter had sent her on sucked. Five minutes into living life by that cursive drivel and Victoria already had the urge to pitch herself overboard and swim back to the shore.

He flashed his devastating grin. "It's cute. Did you know your ears get red when you get embarrassed? Have fun on your date tonight."

"Thanks." She touched her ears. He thought of her as cute?

He headed for the door and turned around, facing Victoria.

"Your hair is very pretty today. I can see it without your hat on." He strolled out into the afternoon light.

Compliments. That was new. With him gone, the weight in her chest released.

Dr. Yaz stuck his head out into the front. "Did our first appointment come in?"

"No, it was Ethan, Daisy's owner. He brought in the sample you asked for. He told me I'm cute and that my hair looked good." Victoria felt as unconnected to reality as a lost balloon.

He collected the urine sample from her outstretched hand. "Nice fellow. You should ask him out on a date after the one tonight falls through."

"You told me to go out with Danny! And now you tell me my date won't go well?" Her lips flapped fast enough to leave speed-boat wakes.

"Simmer down. I told you to go out with Danny because doing so would be good for both of you. Someone accepted the poor boy's proposal and someone asked you out. You keep complaining about no one asking you out. I figured it was win-win."

Victoria wished she had a saber to cut down this scallywag doctor. He smartly whisked his bony butt far away from her striking radius.

Clients walked in. She tacked on her office face to deal with them while she seethed on the inside. Meddlesome doctor. Stupid letter.

About a half hour before close, the lobby was dead. Her phone chimed. She received a text and a picture of a hot pink punk dress from Sandra.

I found it @ a boutique in Tempe going 2 check it out tomorrow. N since u made me lose the bet good luck puckering up. Goose.

What? Hitting reply, she texted.

How did I make u lose the bet?

Sandra sent another message.

U challenged me 2 a runway duel. Then the plastic women came in n yelled @ me 4 wearing their dresses AKA ur fault. I admit what I said wasn't 2 most people's standards of ladylike bhavior, unless u'r in a biker bar. Again happy hunting 4 ur 1st kiss. U have 4 days. Tick Tock!

Dread crept up her spine and nestled in her heart. Four days. She had to kiss someone in four days.

Or what?

The response was quick and dire.

The consequence will only get worse 4 u. XOXO

Victoria counted the ceiling tiles in hopes of lowering her blood pressure. By the time she reached fourteen, she could think and see straight. If Sandra promised the outcome would be worse, it was a guaranteed masterpiece of pain. She had four days to kiss someone.

Someone opened the lobby door. Victoria saw a forty-something barreling in. "Good after—"

"You overcharged me." His deep, accusatory voice cut her off.

If the man breathing fumes was any indication about how the rest of her day would go, she was ready to rabbit home and skip her date. Victoria offered him her serene office smile, working to reset the situation. "How can I help you?"

"Answer me this, how could my girlfriend spend three hundred twenty-eight dollars and nineteen cents on a single rabies shot for her bratty dog?" He slapped a wrinkled invoice on the counter.

"Let me review the receipt and see what I can do." Victoria tugged the paper from his hand.

He stabbed the counter in a fast, angry rat-a tat-tat. "You'd better fix this problem."

"Do you have the second page?"

The tapping stopped. He ran his hand through his thinning hair. "Second page? There's only one."

With a click of the mouse and a quick whirl of the printer, Victoria handed him the complete invoice. "Your girlfriend wanted a full work up on your dog."

"Her dog. Not mine." He scanned the pages, the outrage gone by the time he reached the end of the invoice. "Sorry I blew up at you."

"No worries. Glad I could help you get everything straightened out."

He folded the paperwork and shoved the invoice into his pocket. "Since everything was right, I'll allow her to come back."

"We appreciate your business."

He left. If only she could defuse events in her life with such ease.

AT FIVE MINUTES TILL FIVE, Danny crawled into a parking spot right out front of the lobby and hunkered down in the driver's seat.

Sandra's threat bubbled up. Victoria tried to imagine Danny leaning over to kiss her and winced.

Dr. Yaz stuck his head out. "I can close up."

"I've still got five minutes."

"Go. Have a fun time."

With no delay tactic left in her arsenal, Victoria left the office and approached his car. Danny's fingers were white as mashed potatoes on his steering wheel.

"Hi." He coughed and tried talking again. "Where do you want to go?"

She could feel it on the damp air. One word. Jake's. Before his mouth could form the word and say Jake's, Victoria took charge. "How about this great place around the corner called River Runner? They have killer fish and chips."

Screw you, karma, she wasn't going to let fates lap her around with another surprise Jake's date.

His hands loosened, and his shoulders relaxed. "Sounds good."

Victoria explained how to get there. They caravanned. Trying not to fall into a pit of angst in her car, she had a heart-to-heart with herself. *There's no pressure. He's a nice kid. With this date, Fran would finally stop hounding her.* This could be a very productive night.

They both parked easily. By ten after five, they sat with a little pole in between them in the pleather booth.

Danny kept alternating between scratching the back of his hand and tapping the table. *Poor thing*, Victoria thought, *there were zero reasons to be nervous being out with her*.

Time to try something new, Dr. Yaz said. *Be sociable and nice*, she lectured herself and jumped into being different. "Danny, what do you do?"

His table tapping slowed down. "Nothing big. I work at a movie theater most days and on my off time I work on cars."

"I'm very efficient at filling my car with gas and can change my tires. Anyone who can decipher cars is amazing in my book."

Danny's spine straightened. His shoulders relaxed and Victoria liked his soft smile. "I love being able to take a broken engine and breathe life into it." No more fidgeting.

Dinner arrived. They ate, chatting about life like buddies with no romantic spark.

Danny piled his plastic silverware and napkin onto his empty plate. He swallowed, suddenly serious, sending his Adam's apple bobbing. "Why did you say yes to me?"

Heat crept into her cheeks. "If I'm being truthful, I was told that I should get out more."

His soda cup clunked on the table. "You're galaxies out of my league and you still don't go out often?"

Victoria nearly snorted up soda.

He whacked her on the back so hard that her spine met her front sternum.

"I'm out of your league?" She sputtered. While he was thin and tall, she was stocky and heavy. She knew loads of girls in high school who would mark him as exactly their type.

"Duh, you're smart." He shrugged like the one statement explained everything. "I figured you date all the time."

"Me? You've got the wrong Shaw girl."

Danny froze, staring behind Victoria, his color drained from his cheeks, and his eyes widened.

She twisted around to follow his gaze. The object of his frozenness was a brown-haired girl wiping down a table across the room. "I take it you know her?"

His ability to speak vanished, though he could still gape like a fish searching for water. Danny merely nodded.

"Old girlfriend?" she asked, amused.

His face exploded into a red wash. "Dream girlfriend. Went to school together. I heard she hooked up with an agent in L.A."

Victoria decided he needed her push. "Why don't you go and say hello to her?"

"But I'm here on a date with you."

"Yes, you are, with someone who is 'out of your league.' Go talk to Miss Dreamy." Her tone sounded like she was channeling her mother again, yet channeling her mother felt helpful.

He started to tap the table again. "I don't know."

Victoria unleashed a devilish grin. "How about this. You go over there and talk to her while I leave, or I will get her attention for you. I can guarantee you don't want me to get her attention. I'm known for being loud and irritating and embarrassing."

He stood and drank a final swig of carbonation for courage.

Victoria gave him a nod saying *go on* and bused the table.

At the trash bin, she watched Danny approach his dream girl. They talked. Leaving, she spotted Danny typing something into his phone. Hopefully her number. Victoria got into her car and headed home.

Driving toward her apartment, her positive vibe lasted until she realized, once again, she was alone in the dating cesspool. Panic built in her stomach. Her shoulders curled in toward her breastbone like a scared rabbit. *Relax*, she told herself, *I still had ten whole days before the wedding.*

As for her voyage out into Adventure Land Bay, it could have been worse.

Darkness greeted her when she stepped into her apartment. "Hello, Dessie? Anyone home?"

Nothing. Relief flooded her system. Break time from Dessie and her wedding mayhem. Shoes shucked off at the door, Victoria basked in the quiet. No squeaks, squeals, or meows. Hold it. Ralph always greeted her. "Ralph, here kitty, kitty. Where are you, pumpkin?"

Dessie could have fed him before leaving. She checked his food dish. Empty. Crap, him without food and not yelling at her was impossible. Sweat beaded up on her forehead. Dread settled in her bones.

No cat on her bed. No cat asleep in his tower. With panic pumping through her, Victoria scoured the entire apartment. "Come on, friend. Come here."

Call Dessie. See when she last saw Ralph.

Dessie's phone rang and rang and rang. Finally, Victoria heard Dessie's voicemail. After the tone, she left a message. "Where's Ralph? I can't find him. Call me. Immediately."

She followed up with a text to Dessie.

Call me. 911. I can't find Ralph. Did u let him outside?

Back to hollering and moving things around, she found a

lost sock, key, and cat toys. Yet she couldn't find a furry bundle of trouble. Her phone chimed. A text from Dessie.

He bolted down the stairs n refused 2 come when I called. I figured he's a cat n he'd b fine outside

Wishing she could kick her sister, Victoria texted.

He has NO front claws. Don't u remember my rants when I got him or my reminders when u come over ever. Every stinking time?

Again, her phone chimed.

Oops, my bad Sorry :)

Victoria bit the inside of her cheek to relieve the pressure to maim. This wasn't going to help her find Ralph. She blew out a huff and focused. It was time to do the search-and-rescue outside. It was time to round up the reinforcements.

Number three on her speed dial left her listening to Sandra's voicemail. She cursed loudly, hung up, and sent off a quick text to her instead.

Victoria stepped outside to see if she could coax her cat to come home.

"Ralph? Come here, kitten." Her voice echoed around the darkened grounds. She checked under the shadowy staircase, shaking treats. Nothing.

Next, she tried speed dial number one, her dad's cell number. She counted the rings. "Answer the phone, dad."

Her cat wasn't under any playground equipment, nor under any stairs, nor under any cars. Everywhere appeared to be Ralph-free.

After five rings, her dad's voicemail picked up and hung up. No texts for him. Her dad could barely answer his phone, let alone navigate texting. When she called his home phone, he didn't answer either.

She hit the last number for him, the office, and prayed. "If you pick up, I promise I will never complain again about how late you work."

The last place to search was in the dark area of the apartment complex.

Victoria heard a faint meow above her. Adrenaline pumped.

She squinted, searching in the barren trees around her and spotted Ralph. He laid flat against a branch about twenty or thirty feet up.

"Ralph, come down here," she hollered at her cat. She popped open the can of treats. The stinky seafood flavor, his favorite, should entice him to come to her.

"Hello." It was a male voice, not her dad's.

"I need Robert."

"Sorry, he's gone. It's Iggy. Is this Victoria? You sound upset."

The blubbering began. "Ralph, my cat, is stuck in a tree. I'm going to climb up after him."

"No, I'll come help. Where are you?"

Victoria could hear keys jingle over the phone. "I'm at Lindsey and Brown, The Estate complex. If you aren't here in ten, I'm going up after him." She ended the call.

For the next few minutes, she scoped out the best path up the tree to Ralph and continued bribing the cat to come down for the smelly fish bites. Refusing capture, he growled.

*A*fter eons of Victoria circling the tree, begging her cat to come down, and plotting a Ralph rescue, her phone rang. Iggy. She answered. "I'm around back. Follow the sidewalk on the left side of the buildings. I'm standing under a big, barren tree."

"I'm on my way."

Minutes later, a tall figure jogged around the corner. When Iggy popped out of the shadows, Victoria shook herself to focus on the task at hand and not how good he looked in his ripped blue jeans and maroon T-shirt.

"Do you have a plan to get Ralph down?" His long strides ate up the ground.

Relief flooded her. Having him come out to help her tugged at her heart, but instead of analyzing the feeling, she tugged him to the darkest corner by a tree. "Here's the plan: host me up onto the first branch and I can get him down."

Iggy cocked his head at her and touched her arm. "Let me do the climbing. We had a pecan grove in my backyard growing up; ergo, I have lots of practice with scratches and torn pants."

"If you're sure." Her tone was hopeful. She didn't think the old branches could hold her weight.

"Don't worry, I'll have Ralph down in a flash." He jumped, grasped the lowest branch, and swung his legs up. Easily, he scrabbled up the tree.

If Victoria had tried to climb up in her sundress, the sight would've left Iggy scared.

He climbed steady as a monkey on the banana hunt. Limbs creaked and rolled under him. From branch to branch, he moved slowly upward. Ralph lay plastered to the gray tree. Victoria covered her mouth with her hands, suppressing her anxious squeaks.

Iggy neared the black ball of fuzz. "Here kitty, kitty."

Ralph puffed up, indignant. He let off a dull rumble in his throat, clearly not impressed with his savior.

He inched closer to the cat. "Come on, cat. I'm here to help you."

She shouted up at the fur ball, "You go with him, Ralph. I want both of you down here in one piece."

Iggy's right hand slipped under the cat's ribcage, prying him off the tree. A high-pitched growl split the air.

Ralph freaked, used Iggy as a springboard, and launched himself down, bounding from branch to branch, a fuzzy Ping-Pong ball. He landed with the smallest of thuds, sauntered away, and decided now was the appropriate time to indulge in a bath.

Victoria rushed to him and cuddled him for the two seconds he allowed the smothering. Once Iggy came down, she would be relieved to have everyone's feet and paws securely on the ground. Speaking to the cat savior, she yelled up, "Iggy, are you alright?"

He struggled to keep his balance and cradled his right arm to his chest.

"Never better. I see the cat is down safely." Disgust and irritation came thick in his words.

The cat jumped out of her arms.

Iggy descended the tree with slightly less ease than going up. His feet now rested on the bottom limb with about seven feet between him and the ground. The branch snapped.

Time stretched. Iggy hung in the air. Victoria acted. She grabbed him. Time sped back up. He slammed into her. She slammed into the ground. Iggy, right on top of her.

They laid in stunned silence as they regained their ability to breathe. Iggy's body heat crashed over her. Both of their breaths were heavy and intermingling.

He was nose to nose with her. "Are you OK? Are you hurt?"

Ralph meowed. Iggy rolled off with a fluid grace he shouldn't have possessed after that fall and after his body had been intimately tangled with hers. He should be as stunned as she was.

He bent down and hoisted her up, unaffected by their collision. "You alright?"

"I'm fine. How are you? You're the one who fell."

"A bit battered, but good." After a quick inspection of his arm, he added, "Though your cat bit me, little vampire."

Victoria stepped forward to assess the damage. But once her right foot hit the ground, her mouth shaped an O and she inhaled sharply.

Iggy caught her bicep before she fell.

"My ankle. I think I twisted it." She touched the outside of her right ankle and hissed.

"Let's get you inside."

She called for Ralph. He trotted over, obedient and most likely hungry. Iggy slipped under her right arm, wrapping his strong arm around her waist.

He scanned the apartment buildings. "Where to?"

The heat from his skin seared hers. Their shared warmth sent tremors down her body.

Her brain kicked into gear. Victoria pointed to the closest stairs. "I'm on the third floor, right there."

After a few stops and about ten minutes, they managed to hobble to her apartment with Ralph dutifully trailing behind them, meowing.

Iggy helped her limp over the threshold, closed the door behind him, and steered her toward the couch.

Victoria could only imagine what he thought of her place. It wasn't company ready, with a few dirty dishes hanging about on her coffee table, but it was too late to boot him out.

He gently lowered her onto the couch. "Do you have a first aid kit?"

"Go down the hall and through the door on the left. In the bathroom, under the sink will be a tackle box of goodies." She watched his long legs vanish into her bedroom.

His disappearance left an ache in the pit of her stomach. She wasn't sure whether the feeling was attraction or fear. She drummed her head against the back of the couch and fretted. With luck, there wouldn't be any bras or underwear lying on the floor.

The only sound in her apartment was the quiet *crunch crunch* of Ralph inhaling his dry kibble in the kitchen.

With a white box in his hands, he emerged, knelt beside her, and opened the box. "Whoa, this is organized and professional looking. Were you a medic in a former life?"

"No, in high school I was a sports trainer."

"Sports trainer, eh? Was that before or after your advanced math classes? Let's secure your ankle, shall we?" Iggy smiled slightly, pulling out the ACE wrap.

"You remembered the factoid about advanced math, did

you?" Victoria's eyebrow rose as did her awareness that they sat here alone. Late at night.

Iggy laid his hand on her bare ankle. His touch sent a jolt of tension up her leg, making her shiver. He reached behind her, stripped the couch of its blanket, and pulled it across her lap.

"Thanks."

His eyes focused on the task of wrapping her injury. "No worries. Your piggies aren't going to turn blue, are they?"

To check her blood flow, she wiggled her toes and rolled her ankle. "You did a good job. I appreciate your help tonight getting Ralph down."

"No problem. Sorry I body checked you earlier." His embarrassment was evident in his pinky cheeks.

She could feel her temperature spike, remembering their bodies colliding. "Accidents happen. Can I pay you for your trouble?"

Iggy nudged her purse, skidding it across the floor and out of her reach. "No need to pay me."

"Let me at least bandage up your arm." With one hand, she hauled the med kit into her lap. With the other hand, she hooked her finger through Iggy's belt loop and tugged to stop his backpedaling. "Cleaning up your wound is the least I can do to say thanks."

"Fine. I just didn't want to trouble you." He sat next to her and held out his arm.

Victoria wiped the wound down with alcohol and dabbed on a topical ointment.

"What is this?" He bent to smell his arm.

"It's an herbal salve with a mix of plantain and comfrey oils with beeswax. The plantain helps draw out any infection and reduces scarring. The comfrey helps regenerate skin cells. I made it." She was babbling.

"You're a multifaceted woman." He pressed the edge of the tape down and grimaced.

"Want me to kiss your owie and make it feel better?" She laughed at her nervousness.

Iggy locked gazes with her. His eyes darkened. He leaned toward her, closing the gap between them.

Her flippancy shriveled, clogging her airway, and yet she leaned in, too.

The door slammed open. They both jumped apart like two teenagers caught necking when the parents came home.

"You won't believe the day I've had." Dessie dumped her mounds of shopping bags onto the table.

"I should be going." Iggy stood stiffly and shot out the door. His departure tarnished the moment they'd almost shared. Whatever that moment could've been, melted.

Victoria groaned. She could have had her first kiss with someone, if not for her sister.

"Who was that?" Dessie stared at the closed door.

"Iggy, the guy from dad's work. He came over to help me rescue Ralph." Victoria's voice shifted into righteous ire. "Since you let my cat outside."

Dessie kicked off her heels. "Why do you always blame me? What's between you and Iggy?"

"Not blame, truth. Ralph being out was your fault. And don't imagine things, there's nothing between Iggy and me." Except for mixed signals.

"I'm blonde. Not blind." Dessie waved her hand like she was trying to catch a whiff of something. "I can smell hot chemistry. Don't think I missed how close and cozy you two were when I came in."

"What? No. Ralph wounded him. I patched him up."

"Here I am getting married and no one thinks I'm pretty

enough to give me that smoldering look Iggy gave you." Dessie flounced down on the couch.

"Get your eyes checked. Iggy most certainly didn't give me a look, and no one but your fiancé should be shooting kissy eyes at you." Victoria stood and started to hobble toward her bedroom. "I am pooped. I withstood three solid hours of crinoline and lace for you. The bride and bridesmaids' dress hunting was stressful, exhausting, and pointless."

"My wedding is not pointless." Dessie puffed up.

Dessie sucked in a room full of air, ready to verbally attack her, Victoria was sure. But before she could start bitching, Victoria cut off the windbag. "You're right, your wedding is not pointless. Yet the backstabbing drama you allowed in the dressing room sure was. Don't get all pissy because your friends didn't show up for you. I did. Sandra did. Now I am going to bed. Good night."

In her wake, cupboards snapped open and slammed shut as Dessie went on a tirade.

Victoria disappeared into her room and propped her foot up on a stack of pillows. She ignored the destruction, leaving Dessie to her peevishness.

If this wedding wasn't over soon, Dessie would be in traction.

*C*offee aroma informed her that Thursday morning had come for her. After a quick shower, Victoria slathered a layer of arnica salve on her ankle and foot, and she rewrapped her injury. Her outfit was black pedal pusher pants and an emerald green tank top topped off with a cream sun hat. Victoria felt armored and ready to take on Dessie and her barrage of bridal demands.

A peace offering coffee in hand, Victoria knocked on her sister's closed door. "Which places did you pick from the list I gave you?"

No rustle of sheets, she cracked the door open. No missiles launched, she poked her head in. The bed sat empty. Clothes were scattered everywhere, making the room look as though the Huns had ransacked it. Victoria checked her cell. One missed text message from Dessie.

Got Mom 2 pick me up last night. Meet u @ Mario's in Chandler 9 am 4 cake shopping. If that isn't 2 big a problem 4 u

She texted back.

On my way

The urge to make her coffee an Irish booze-fest was undeniable. She denied her Irish heritage, muttered about passive-aggressive sisters, and left.

The stairs multiplied while she slept. With a gimpy ankle, three flights meant descending in phases. Thankfully, the Arizona morning was crisp and perfect to enjoy the slow trek on the stairs and the drive to the appointment.

Parked outside the bakery, she had arrived five minutes early and, naturally, she was the only one here. Victoria limped into the cafe part of the shop, grabbed a doughnut and a coffee refill, plopped at a table where she could see the sidewalk outside and the door, and waited.

By the time her mother's yellow convertible pulled in, she had crammed the evidence of the unapproved breakfast into her mouth.

Only fifteen minutes late, what a surprise. Victoria had expected to sit there for at least another fifteen minutes waiting.

Even before they passed through the doorway, Victoria could tell her mother was in a mood. Her mother fidgeted with her long, pearl necklace and tugged on her pale pink jacket, which barely overlapped the top of her pencil tweed skirt. Always ready for world domination or a professional photo shoot.

Victoria waved.

Her mother entered first, locked onto Victoria, and crossed to her. "I'm glad you could clear some time for your baby sister."

She suppressed an eye roll. "Good morning to you, too, Mother."

"You ate something before you came, I hope. I don't want you to fill up on sweets."

The patronizing tone made Victoria sit straighter. The sharp words threw her into a time warp to when Victoria and Dessie visited their mother after the divorce and Victoria felt alone and an outsider.

"I had something before you came." Victoria sipped her coffee.

Dessie flowed in like the sun. A bright yellow sundress hugged her body. The cut and color would've been disastrous on Victoria, but Dessie carried off the look flawlessly.

"Benvenuti. I'm the owner." An older man with a thick Italian accent greeted Dessie. "You must be the beautiful bride Esmeralda."

They kissed each other's cheeks. Reverting to her teenage self, Victoria couldn't stop her eye roll.

Dessie pointed to the table where Victoria sat, sipping her coffee. "Over there is my sister and mother."

The owner bustled the bride-to-be over to the table while balancing a tray of cake to taste. "Try this one first. It's a dark chocolate cake with raspberry cream cheese filling."

The owner rocked onto his toes waiting while they nibbled. A small woman came by, serving them coffee.

Her mother beamed up at the owner. "This is delicious."

"Grazie. Here, the next sample." The owner handed out a pink cake with pale yellow cream.

The second cake dissolved on Victoria's tongue, her taste buds were in dessert heaven. "This is mind-blowing. What is this?"

The owner perked up. "Fresh peach pound cake with almond whipped cream."

"I don't need to try anything else. I'd order this cake for my wedding. This is the cake." Victoria dug into her slice again.

The owner straightened, dipped his chin in a silent nod of thanks.

"I don't know." Dessie fidgeted with the plate.

Victoria took a second bite. "The tartness from the peaches pairs perfectly with the cream. If not for the wedding, this would be perfect for any of your pre-wedding parties. Can I have my own slice with a cup of tea?"

Her mother patted Victoria's hand. "Don't you think you tasted enough, Dear? You want to fit into your dress next week."

Years of repetition should have dulled the impact of such comments, yet they still stung. Dropping her head, Victoria chose to lick her fork and pride.

Dessie tried the third cake. "This one is different and the winner. Is this a carrot cake with coconut cream frosting?"

"You have a good palate. This is my family's specialty." He glanced briefly at their mother before asking, "Are you sure you want such a unique cake flavor for all of your cake?"

"This. Is. My. Wedding. My verdict is the only one that counts." Her words melted steel: hot, hard, and harmful.

"As you wish. How many will there be at the wedding?" The owner pulled out a notepad.

"A small affair. Three hundred guests." With no hint of sarcasm, Dessie glanced at her nails.

"I thought you said two hundred guests when we were renting out the venue." Victoria couldn't imagine inviting three hundred guests. She would've had to invite all the vet's clients, both the fuzzy and humankind, to get close to that body count.

Dessie shrugged. "We had a few additions to the list. The cake must be something grand. Elegant. Chic. The colors need to be spring colors—gentle blues, yellows, and greens." She drilled him with instructions.

"What's the date?"

"March eighth at Wind Song Gardens."

The owner tapped his notepad with his pen. "*Boh*, that's only ten days away."

"Make it happen." Dessie waved his comment off and stooped to retrieve something from her massive purse. A wave of glitter wafted over the table.

The book had arrived. Victoria leaned away, knowing no escape existed.

"Here, I have a few ideas." Dessie burrowed her nose deep into the crumpled pages.

The owner kept a smile on his face and took more notes.

Victoria sat back, realizing this must be a common occurrence for him. No wonder he could take Dessie's snappiness without forcing his happy twinkle and broad, warm smile.

After thirty agonizing minutes, one of the baker's helpers rescued the owner from Dessie's clutches.

Her mother rose. "We better get to our next appointment."

Trailing behind her mother and Dessie, Victoria felt a tap on her shoulder. The owner stood at her elbow, a white bakery bag in his worn hands. "Thank you for your enthusiastic enjoyment of my creations. I always appreciate people with a good appetite. Enjoy."

She opened the bag. The tangy smell of sweet peach rolled out. "Oh, I will. Grazie." She hugged the little man.

"Tori, come on, we have much to do." Dessie's shrill command bounced back to her.

The owner patted her forearm. "Don't tell them I gave the treat to you. It's only for you. God help you, you'll need all your strength to deal with her." He turned and greeted incoming customers.

"We need to go find flowers. Speed it along, Tori." Dessie ordered her to come like an errant dog.

"Ruff," Victoria muttered.

Dessie slipped into their mother's two-seater convertible. "We'll meet you at Peacock Diamonds in Scottsdale."

They zoomed away from the bakery. Victoria limped to her car. Her phone sang again about the stupid Barbie girl. She read text from Dessie.

1213 N. Goldwater Blvd. Suite 103 then we r off 2 lunch @ Fox's

Lunch and more family time. Reading the text made her want to do a body check in front of a moving vehicle. Her mind drifted to last night with Iggy doing his own body check. She fanned herself at the memory.

Sandra's ringtone played. She'd have to wait. Victoria chucked her phone, purse, and goody bag onto the passenger seat and eased into the car. Carefully, oh so carefully, she positioned her foot inside the car and headed to the next stop.

Victoria parked and lugged her way into the florist shop.

Once Dessie spotted her, she popped her hip up, annoyed. "I can't decide. The orchids or the calla lilies or maybe yellow daisies and peach roses?" Her words were shrill and hysterical, exactly in line with her totem animal, a yippy purse dog.

The salesperson shifted from foot to foot, waiting for Dessie to decide and order.

Hobbling her way to the center of the overpowering arrangements, Victoria ran her fingertip along a sunny tulip. "How do you want the wedding to go, traditional or funky?"

"The whole affair must be unique. Classic."

Her ankle throbbed. She wanted to move this wedding train on. "Your dress is white. I say pin your hair back with a colorful orchid and carry the calla lilies in a bouquet. They're both fragrant and beautiful. For us, maybe white roses with yellow flowers and an orchid or two to tie everyone together."

"Listen, this is my wedding. Stop trying to steal my wedding," Dessie shouted.

Victoria rubbed her forehead, tired of this constant irrational nagging.

"You wanted my advice. I'm not stealing your wedding." Heavy emphasis on stealing. Dessie always believed that someone was trying to steal from her. All Victoria wanted to steal was a chair to sit down.

The poor shop assistant slunk toward the wall.

Dessie marched over to Victoria. "Don't you give me attitude. I have been nothing but nice to you. Since you're my sister, I even made you my maid of honor."

"Made me? If you don't want me in the wedding, you can have one of your five billion friends fill the role. See if any of them would be willing to cart you everywhere, research, and arrange all the details to be completed to your uncertain specifications."

Dessie started to cry.

Their mother stepped up to Dessie's shoulder. Just like the rest of their lives, her sister and mother against her.

Dessie shifted from crying to bawling. Tears streamed down her face open-tap style, blubbering on about how her friends and family were deserting her.

Wrapping the wailing bride-to-be in a tentative hug, their mother made sure her jacket didn't get rumpled or smudged.

The shop assistant ducked into the back. Victoria wished she could hide also from her sister's fits.

The manic bride broke free of her mother and stormed outside, her head down and her fingers flying across her phone screen.

Her mother straightened her brooch, smoothed her hair, and after sending Victoria a silent raised eyebrow of disappointment, walked out after the bridal tsunami.

The quiet refreshed Victoria, but she knew the silence was momentary. Her mother would goose Dessie back on track. Less than two minutes later, with a purposeful stride, Dessie stormed back into the store. "I made up my mind."

Victoria wondered what exactly her mother said to flip Dessie from desperate and dysfunctional to determined and demanding. While the methods were mysterious, she couldn't argue about her mother's effectiveness and usefulness.

The shop assistant gulped, clutching her clipboard to her chest.

Dessie caressed the silky flower petals of an orchid and paused with a wistful expression, relaxing her pinched facial muscles. "Go with a single large orchid for my hair as my sister suggested. Must be blue or purple. My bridal bouquet must have calla lilies with pale yellow roses and pink orchids. I don't actually care much about the toss bouquet, since I'll be throwing the bunch to the masses."

The way Dessie hit the word *sister* as though it was a high cymbal struck a nerve.

"What about the rest of the bridal party?" Scribbling, the shop assistant must have had her pen set on warp speed.

Dessie continued issuing orders.

Victoria was impressed that the shop assistant kept up, writing a novella of instructions.

The girl shook out her hand. "When is the wedding? Where are they to be delivered?"

"Wing Song Gardens on March eighth." Dessie checked her nails as if a wedding just days away wasn't a big problem.

"March eighth is tight." The shop assistant's hesitation was clear in her wide eyes and her wrinkled brow.

Wrong answer. Victoria cringed. With the expression Dessie wore, a mix of rage and disgust, she knew Hyde had arrived.

"You can't make my flowers for me?" Her words cut and lashed.

"No, we can. Since you came in before we've placed our order for next week, we should be able to get this in by next Friday." The shop assistant shoved the form for the bride to sign.

Dessie initialed and tossed the shop assistant Damien's limit-less black credit card.

Receipt in hand, order signed, and copies doled out, their florist task was complete.

Victoria felt good about this morning. "How does it feel to have more wedding tasks marked off your to-do list?"

"Starved. Meet you at Fox's." Heels pounded into the tile as Dessie and her mother made a grand exit, purses over their shoulders and sunglasses on their faces.

After Typhoon Dessie dissipated, the shop looked pristine. Glad to see the bride's tantrums weren't leaving a lasting mark on these poor businesses. Whether Victoria could survive the stormy and dark clouds until the wedding was the question.

Staring at a somewhat masculine blue and green arrangement, an idea took root. She waved the shop assistant over. "You deliver, right?"

Time to send a little thank you to someone who helped her withstand the gales of the wedding typhoon. She placed the order and felt better.

She wondered what Karen would think when the bouquet zipped through security at her dad's office. Too bad Victoria couldn't be there to see Iggy's face.

As much as she had tried to evict Iggy from her mind, he starred in every fourth thought.

Her phone had a missed text from Sandra. On her way out of the florist's shop, she read the message.

How'd last night go, any luck lip-locking w/ a stranger? 3 n 1/2 days left, tick tock

Not willing to even respond to her best friend's veiled threat, she swiped the message off her screen and left it marked as unread. Then off to lunch with her archenemies.

Dropping her car off at the restaurant valet was both a treat and a simple way to take care of her ankle. She waded through the packed restaurant toward her family and squeezed into their booth. "Since your wedding announcement, I've eaten out more than I normally do in a year."

Her mother sipped her martini. "Don't worry, I ordered you a salad."

Victoria wasn't surprised and had set herself up for that one. Moving on from the normal mother hazing, Victoria asked Dessie, "Where did you find a hundred new people to invite?"

"Your sister forgot to invite your cousins from my side." Their mother's voice dripped disappointment.

Ice filled Victoria's stomach. Their cousins excelled at the Alburga family expectations to marry young, live lavishly, and spawn often.

Dessie cleared her throat. "Yes, Mother fixed the oversight and invited all of her side. They're flying a few days before to join us for all the wedding festivities. Plus, Damien added some business contacts he had to invite."

The chill spread, freezing Victoria's body. "The whole Alburga horde is coming?"

Her mother stared at her like she was new to the family. "Of course. They know how important this day is for their family."

The sisters shared a grimace. Their salads came out, closing the conversation down.

Dessie ordered another cocktail. Their mother shot her a disapproving glance. If Victoria had tried to order alcohol before noon, she would've been chided for the calorie count and given the what-would-others-think tirade. Victoria resisted pointing out the double standard. Instead, she shoveled the rabbit food as fast as she could chew. One course and she could escape.

Dipping her lettuce in the served-on-the-side salad dressing, Dessie ate tiny bites exactly as their mother had taught them to impress future partners. After exactly half the meal was gone, she stopped eating and dabbed her lips, looking at Victoria. "You will have a plus-one for the wedding, right? You've gone out enough to find a patsy for the night."

Behind Victoria's eyeballs, the red rage started. "I'm already the black sheep, being overweight and single. Why not flaunt my defects a bit more and show up stag?" She laid on the sarcasm thick.

Her mother's hand stilled on her cocktail glass and pinned Victoria with a stern look. "I've offered at every birthday and Christmas to enroll you at a gym or in a weight-loss program. You've refused."

Dessie snorted. "Neither would most likely help her, if the high-school summer fat camp didn't do any good. Russian-style fasting is all the rage."

Victoria scraped her plate and pushed back from the table. "I've got to go to work."

She overrode their complaints, excused herself, and fled.

INSIDE THE QUIET VET OFFICE, Victoria gathered herself together before she had to unlock the front door. After spending a few hours with the attack family, she needed to decompress. Dr. Yaz slept away his lunch break in his office.

Without her hat on, the office seemed brighter. She had stashed her cream sun hat in her car since Dr. Yaz didn't allow her to wear a hat bigger than a fedora to work.

A rattle at the lobby door caught her attention. Jeans, sneakers, and a black shirt was all Victoria could see around a massive floral arrangement. Her flower order couldn't have been delivered here by mistake. She crossed the lobby, unlocked the door, and Danny poked his head around the bouquet.

"These are for you. I got a date with my dream girl. Thanks for threatening me." He held the flowers out to her.

"You're welcome." She took the huge arrangement of yellow and blue flowers. The bouquet scent overwhelmed her nose, yet the sweet smell lightened her heart. He'd overcome his fear and done something he thought was impossible and scary.

"See you around." He waved, rushing to his still-running car. She called out after him, "Thanks for the flower-n-dash. Best of luck."

Peering around the massive spray of flowers, she limped over to the counter and put them in a position where she could enjoy the view.

Her mother's small yellow convertible flipped into the lot. Dessie bounced out and walked through the doors, her focus glued to her phone screen. "Tori, you dropped your wallet in your mad dash out of the restaurant."

"And mother couldn't handle me driving without it." Victoria smiled. Her mother stuck to the rules always, so Victoria driving around without her ID would be illegal and unacceptable for her.

"Exactly." Dessie handed Victoria her tiny wallet. Finally seeing the lobby, Dessie's eyes widened and widened, then narrowed.

Victoria knew that look and braced.

"Who are the flowers from?" Dessie's words come out rapid-fire.

Could that be envy? Her sister glowed green with jealousy. Of her! Gloat-fest, party of Victoria. "Oh, these? A friend gave them to me."

Dessie dove for the card nestled in the flowers and ripped the envelope open. "Who's Danny? And why didn't you tell Iggy you're seeing someone?"

"I'm not dating Iggy and since you must know, nosy, Danny is a guy who asked me out and I helped him snag a dream date with someone else." Victoria snatched the card out of Dessie's clutches.

"How nice for you. I have things to do."

With a parting blistering glare, Dessie left.

Bye-bye, ice princess. All the happy, self-satisfied feeling drained out of Victoria. Dessie's bad mood filled the void.

Why couldn't Dessie be happy for her instead of pouty? Victoria received flowers. It shouldn't matter the flowers weren't from a boyfriend. The beautiful arrangement morphed, twisted by Dessie into nothing more than a flower bomb.

She knew she shouldn't care what her sister and mother thought, yet all she'd ever wanted from them was acceptance and love. Exasperated, Victoria hurled herself into her work.

Since the phone call from Dessie announcing her wedding, Victoria had befriended the staff at Jake's, blew past her comfort zone many times, but struck out with dating. For now, dating adventures were closed for renovations. Victoria decided that for Dessie's wedding, she would not bring a date.

She'd brave the wedding alone. Nailing down a plus-one was much too much of a battle. She should focus on something easier, like asking the Pope to pardon Lucifer's fall from heaven.

*C*ats and dogs arrived for their appointments, so Victoria had to brush the craziness of Dessie aside and focus. Finally, after hours of constant tasks, the office started to wind down. Tiny toenails tap-danced across the threshold. Victoria smiled at Ethan and Daisy.

Ethan returned the smile, crossing the lobby to her desk. "Nice flowers. Your date went well?"

"Not too bad. No one escorted off the premises or hit. My date only went home with his high-school crush's number."

His eyebrows rose into his hairline. "It sounds as though your last few dates have been rough."

"If I had to compare them, last night's date was the best date I've ever had." Straightening up her desk, she filed the last red folders away in the bottom filing cabinet drawer. An uncomfortable awareness slithered up her spine. She peeked to the side and caught him checking out her bum.

Victoria fought the urge to tug down her green work polo. Why didn't she pick something nicer to wear today? She took a few more moments to compose herself before she turned back to him. Her face felt hot; regardless, she kept her features professional. "Is Daisy feeling alright?"

"The urine sample was a little off. The doc wants to observe her till Saturday as a precaution."

She reached for the leash. "I'll put her in the kennel then."

"Would you go out with me tomorrow night?"

Unprepared, she answered automatically. "Okay."

His shoulders relaxed. "Good, you can show me around the town. Someone recommended a great BBQ place. I can't remember the name of the restaurant. It has a guy's name in there somewhere."

Gods, are you messing with me? Loki? Shiva? Whichever of the million gods are up there must be yucking it up at my expense. Seriously, you need a better hobby and a funny bone transplant.

While Ethan stood there racking his brain for the name, she volunteered. "Jake's BBQ?"

He released his dimpled grin. "That's the one. You must be psychic. I'll pick you up at seven. If you don't mind me picking you up."

She stretched for her cell phone. "Let me text you my info."

Within a minute, they stood grinning over their phones.

"Take good care of Daisy and I'll see you tomorrow night." He walked out of the clinic.

Victoria took back saying the flowers were duds. They got her a date with Ethan. Ethan asked her out because he wanted to date her. Not because of any outside pressure such as an aunt or mother, or because he thought she looked easy, or he owed someone a favor.

This could be the biggest roller-coaster day ever, given it began with being roasted and lambasted by her family. Just as she was about to give up on dating, he soared in and asked her out. Her luck had flipped a u-ey.

Whistling, she took Daisy in the back for her observation.

The last work hour slid by and Victoria left for the night. A multicolored peacock rode shotgun after she buckled her towering flower arrangement in the passenger seat.

At home, she placed the flowers right on the breakfast bar counter. The smell of roses and baby's breath filled her tiny apartment. Victoria loved it, and the thoughtfulness of the bouquet touched her.

Time to unwind and play some Michael Bublé. Maybe she could glean some important love hints from him. His sultry voice slipped out of the speakers, evicting her worries. Out of her work clothes and into comfy clothes, a spaghetti tank top and shorts. She threw her hair into a simple ponytail and went on a food hunt. The fridge only had beer, condiments, and eggs.

Her pantry didn't stoke her imagination either, so freezer time. Plunging into the chill, she unearthed an ice pack for her foot and a frozen dessert for dinner. After a quick stop to pick up silverware and fill a glass with Irish cream, the golden dinner of the lazy was served.

On her way to the couch, she spotted her sports med tackle box and reminded herself to put it away after eating. She popped the top off her dessert dinner as the doorbell rang. Before she answered the door, a spoonful of orange sorbet went into her mouth.

Wearing a tight scowl and waving her spoon, she went to the door and swung it open. "Dessie, I thought I gave you a key."

Leaning against her door jamb wasn't her sister, but Iggy.

"Um, hey." She stood there with a lame greeting and wishing she hadn't put on her smiling frog shorts.

The corners of his lips tipped up like he was laughing at her. "Nice froggy shorts. How's your ankle?"

She hid her spoon behind her back and croaked. "My foot feels better. I have my ice pack for tonight. I'm sorry. Come in. I have beer in the fridge."

"I'll take one." Iggy followed her in, clearing his throat. "Thanks, by the way, for the flowers. I've never received flowers before. The gesture was both unnecessary and thoughtful."

"Let me just clean this up." She closed the door and whisked the sorbet to the freezer.

He surveyed the mound of flowers on her bar. "Wow. A florist shop exploded in your kitchen. Did you purchase these for yourself when you were ordering mine?"

The beers hissed as she opened them. She handed him one. "No, someone gave them to me."

He noticed the card displayed in a clear holder, edged towards the note, and read the inscription. "Who's Danny? Did you rescue his cat from a tree? Or is he a kid you tutored to pass his math test so he can finally graduate high school?"

Her body stilled. How did he even know she tutored kids in math? Dad. He must have been talking about her.

"Neither. He's a guy I went out with on a date yesterday and ended up helping him reconnect with his high-school crush." She stood opposite him at the kitchen bar, her arms resting on her kitchen sink.

"Awkward." Iggy plopped down on a barstool directly across from her. His eyes drifted lower and widened.

Victoria glanced down and realized her cleavage was about to fall out of her tank top. She contemplated straightening up, but asked herself, what would Dessie do? Experiment time. She leaned over a little further.

She watched the pulse pound in his throat, doing double time.

"Enjoying the view?" Her voice sounded husky and surprisingly not squeaky.

He snapped his very dilated eyes to hers. "Sorry, I couldn't help myself." His cheeks and ears flushed red.

Victoria steered the conversation and herself to safer waters by moving into the living room. She sat down next to the tackle box, slapping the cushion next to her. "I won't bite. Let me get a new dressing on your injury for you."

After a few long seconds, he swiveled in the barstool and walked next to the couch. She patted the cushion again.

He eventually perched on the edge of the couch.

"Relax, let me clean this up." Victoria peeled off the bandage, reapplied the salve to his wound, and when she finished, stuck out her right hand to Iggy. "Friends?"

He glowered at her hand, his expression haggard. Apparently, even being her friend was an imposition. She dropped her hand back down to the couch.

Iggy scooped her hand up. "I would love to be your friend."

Ripples from his touch flowed over her body. Glancing up at him, Victoria could see he wasn't being snide. He seemed honest. "Good."

Iggy leaned closer. "I really like you without a hat on."

"You do?"

"I love seeing your eyes."

Michael Bublé crooned softly in the background. Their eyes locked and his eyes sucked her in with the force of a black hole.

The front door banged open. They both watched Dessie walk in. Victoria knew when Dessie spotted them together because her posture went from dismissive to cobra-coiled. That dangerous body shift meant her sister was about to do something she would not appreciate. Like the time Dessie stole candy, ate it, and stuffed the wrapper in Victoria's bag, so she got the heat for stealing from their parents and the shopkeeper.

Dessie dropped her head to one side, the embodiment of sweet and innocent. "Iggy, I'm surprised to see you here, since Tori got this gorgeous bouquet today from her boytoy, Danny."

Iggy rolled up a glass barrier over his body, and his posture became rigid again. Whatever warm emotion he had moments ago, vanished. "Danny gave her gratitude flowers and she also sent me a bouquet today."

"She sent you flowers?" The stabbing stare Dessie shot Victoria around Iggy was withering.

He sunk into the couch. Victoria pulled the tackle box closer, saying, "We're friends. I can send flowers to my friends."

"Great, then I have a question I want to ask a male friend," Dessie said, her voice as slick as snake's scales.

Dessie strode toward Iggy. She had turned her patented sexy strut up to a ten, with slow and deliberate twists of her hips.

Victoria had no idea where this interaction could go besides south.

"I have something I want to show you and get your opinion on," she purred.

"I don't know how helpful he'll be, Dessie." Victoria squeezed the roll of bandages in the open tackle box instead of around her sister's neck.

"Oh, he'll do fine." She inched down onto the arm of the couch and pulled out a box from her purse. Slowly, she bent at the waist, releasing her purse to the floor. Her chest almost brushed his nose, thus giving Iggy the red-roped tour of her breasts, and like a hypnotized stooge, he couldn't break the power of all that creamy flesh millimeters from his eyelashes.

His Adam's apple bobbed. Red crept into Victoria's vision.

Her sister wrapped his hands around a burgundy box. "What do you think?"

Iggy popped the box top and inside rested a diamond-encrusted watch. "That's...that's...overwhelming."

Dessie scooped up the gift, all excited, and kissed Iggy's cheek. "Perfect, I wanted to dazzle him with my love. Thanks for verifying this will work."

"I've got to go. Vi, I'll see you around." Iggy rubbed his hand on his jeans, jumped up, and scuttled out of the apartment.

Victoria folded her arms, pinning Dessie with a look so nasty it should have come with a Surgeon General warning label. "Where the hell did you get money to buy the gift? And what's wrong with you? You scared Iggy."

Pouting, Dessie slumped into the couch. "Damien gave me pocket change to use how I saw fit. As for Iggy, I'm losing my touch. He's not attracted to me. I can understand him not being attracted to you."

An ice pick formed behind Victoria's right eye, the headache blossoming out. "Why do I put up with you? You're a nasty little stink bug."

Dessie rocketed off the couch. "Bug? Bug? I'm not a bug. You're lashing out at me because you can't get a man."

"And whose fault is that? Twice I've been close to Iggy and you've busted in."

Dessie snorted. "With that hot guy? Find a nice guy for yourself. Don't reach too far or you'll get burned like you did with Garth."

A prime example of why Victoria shouldn't live with her sister. Proximity exposed her to the bitchiness disease. "Garett, not Garth, and until you learn how to talk nicer to me, I'm going to bed."

Ignoring Victoria, Dessie flipped on the TV.

Well, at least nothing else could be crammed into this bizarre day. Unplugging her phone on the way to her room, she noticed a text from Sandra and read.

I have plans 4 ur defeat. They're such beautiful plans. Mua hoo haa haa

She tossed her phone on her bed. Damn, Sandra proved her wrong.

*F*riday afternoon turned into Driving Miss Dessie so they could secure a bridal shower spot. She had been concerned about taking so much time off work, but Dr. Yaz told her not to worry and to take the time she needed, so Victoria focused on driving. Dessie focused on texting. A message came in and her sister's features and muscles scrunched.

Warning. Warning. Danger brewing, Victoria's internal Hyde alarm shrieked.

"Something wrong, Dessie?" Victoria's tone was soft and caring.

"No, everything is fine." She shoved her phone in her purse. Her shoulders tightened, her mouth compressed, and her eyes sharpened into ice daggers.

"What music do you listen to nowadays? Last time you were home, you and Greg were listening to hard rock."

"Damien and I listen to música norteña." She plugged her phone into the car. Latino music with a repetitive beat thudded out of the speakers. Dessie thumped her thumb on the armrest.

Pressing the accelerator down, Victoria prayed for Friday

light traffic. Without the Spanish lyrics, the noise became polka music, which danced on Victoria's urge to maim her passenger.

By the end of the afternoon, they had visited four sites and Victoria had to help Dessie decide and book the posh outdoor restaurant. For someone who dreamed and talked about her wedding for years, Dessie couldn't seem to make any decisions.

To combat normalcy, Dessie decided on a Sunday mimosa brunch in a pecan grove. The weather would be in the low 70s. Perfect. Again, her sister paid for the whole brunch on Damien's black card. Victoria shuddered to think how high his bill would be for all the purchases.

On the way home, Dessie thankfully turned down the music. "By the way, I need your car tonight. I promised Maria, my future mother-in-law, I would meet her at her hotel and have dinner."

"No problem. My date is going to pick me up anyway."

"Date?" Dessie chewed on the word. "How wonderful."

What a bad liar, yet Victoria played along with the fake nice. "He is."

Dessie flounced in place, kicking under the dash. The entertainment value of watching her sister throw a contained tantrum? Priceless. The outburst lay just underneath her porcelain skin, packed with all the anger, all the fury, all the madness of a grenade.

"I bet your date is only going out with you because he thinks you're easy and wants to go to my wedding." Her tone and arms were crossed.

Unfazed by her snide words, Victoria reminded herself that buried under the toxic mouth lurked her little sister who cared about her. Victoria wished she saw more of the nice Dessie. "No one wants to go to a wedding for people they don't know. Plus, I've decided to not bring a date to the wedding."

Bitter laughter met her declaration of freedom. "You're

embracing your spinsterhood. How brave of you to face all of the Alburgas alone."

Being nice failed. Yet Victoria refused to be baited and ground away at least two layers of tooth enamel, keeping her eyes on the road.

Neither of them said anything for the rest of the drive. Victoria, gratefully, slid into a decent parking spot at her apartment complex without any bloodshed.

Dessie's face twisted up, displaying no sisterly concern. "A helpful tip to you, dating newbie. Be more cautious about who you date. If you keep guy-hopping, people will think you're an easy lay." Her rotten words launched off her tongue aimed for Victoria's pride.

With her poison spewed, Dessie popped out of the car, slammed the door shut, and sprinted to the top of the stairs.

"Hey. You can't—" Fuming, Victoria got out, locked her car, and bolted up after her. Adrenaline pounded through her veins. When Victoria stormed inside her apartment with lightning crackling across her vision, Odin would have thought her his kin. Her heartbeat like the drums of war, war, war.

Her place was as still as a church on Monday.

"Dessie, get out here immediately. You can't say that and walk away."

Nothing.

Victoria marched over to the guest room and banged on the locked door. "Open this door, tout de suite."

"No."

"This is my house. You're my guest until I kill you. Open the bloody door or I will find a way in." Death laced her words.

"I don't want to talk to you."

"Esmeralda Isabella Shaw, you're a spoiled brat. Rot in there for all I care. I have a date to get ready for."

The door snapped open. Dessie's tiny frame trembled. "I see.

You act like I don't matter, as though I don't have feelings. Like I'm spoiled. You're just jealous of me."

Victoria stepped closer to her sister. Truth time. "Jealous? Of what? You go through men like a drunk goes through bourbon?"

"Is their attraction a crime?"

"Your crime is leading them on and then decimating them because you leave them for someone who is new and exciting. You're a user."

Outrage burned behind her sister's eyes.

Standing inches from Dessie's face, Victoria donned her frostiest smile and delivered the frozen facts. "You slaughter good men just to get your kicks."

Dessie retaliated instantaneously, slapping Victoria. Hard. Right across the jaw.

Whipping her head back, Victoria cradled her face.

Quickly, the realization of her actions seeped into her sister's pores, as evidenced by Dessie's staring at her hand like she didn't own the appendage or its actions. Her teeth chattered. "I di-didn't mean to hit you." Her words and apology were weak.

Victoria said nothing. She became stone and rage.

Dessie whimpered, "I know. I crossed a line. I'm sorry."

Wrath surpassed Victoria's stony exterior. She deliberately prowled forward, invading her sister's personal space.

Her sister started sobbing. "I'm sorry, Tori. Please don't get mad at me."

For Dessie, acceptable behavior was light-years away at the edge of the ever-expanding Dessie galaxy. No telescope had yet to glimpse her being appropriate or reasonable.

"Out," Victoria growled.

"The stress of the wedding."

The angry vibes radiated off Victoria. She didn't touch her sister. Her energy pressed, pressed, pressed Dessie backward.

Tears of faux remorse rolled down her cheeks. Dessie blubbered, backpedaled, and begged for forgiveness. "I have nowhere to go. No way to get there."

"Don't care. Your problem. Call one of your bosom buddy Barbie doll clones."

"I can't. They're on an overnight retreat at the Red Door." Dessie wept harder.

Victoria leaned over, snatching up her car keys and chucked them at Dessie. "Leave. Take my car. But leave this instant."

Victoria seized Dessie's arm and shoved her whole body through the doorjamb, then slammed the door right in her sister's red and snotty nose. She threw the locks and even secured the privacy bolt. Through her thin walls, Victoria could hear her baby sister sniffling and bawling. She propped herself against the wall and waited. Because she knew her sister.

After a few minutes, a key slipped into the deadbolt. Dessie hiccupped and delayed a full minute before trying the handle. A loud *thunk* emanated from the outside. "Ouch."

A flurry of pounding bounced off the door. "Dammit, Tori. Let me in. This is embarrassing." She pleaded through the door crack. Eventually, heavy footsteps stomped down the metal stairs.

Good, her sister would now take her seriously. Shaking her head, Victoria went to the mirror and checked her slightly reddened cheek. Hopefully, with a little bit of foundation and powder, the handprint wouldn't be too bad. Time to prep for her date.

The pounding on her door ten minutes later had Victoria rushing to see if Ethan was early. She checked the peek hole and discovered Sandra outside. Victoria flipped the privacy lock and let her in.

"Where's your car?" Sandra asked.

"Wherever Dessie is. Why are you here?"

"I'm here to get my charger. By your surly tone and that

sweet handprint, I can tell you fought. What happened this time?" Sandra headed toward the outlet to retrieve her cord and plug.

"I told her she was a man-eating cannibal. She told me I was jealous of her."

"You're both right."

The calm she had desperately held on to while arguing with Dessie died. "I'm not jealous of that egomaniac."

"Liar."

Victoria's temples pounded. Her eyes pinned down her back-stabbing friend. "What did you call me?"

Meeting her stare with all the seriousness of a hearse, Sandra spoke slowly. "A. Liar. Which isn't quite right. The most accurate word for you would be coward."

The person who knew her the best in the world had just called her a coward. Her body temperature spiked to sun surface conditions. "You're judging me?"

Sandra tucked her cord and plug into her purse. "Nope, only telling you what Jesus knows. I've been friends with you since high school. Let me share a simple Victoria factoid with you: When it comes to hiding, you're a ninja."

"I hide what?" She hurled her words at Sandra.

She took the heat, unflinching. "Everything."

"No, I don't."

"Yes, you hide." Sandra mirrored Victoria's crossed arms and defiant stance. "Behind your fake, cheerful attitude, behind your crappy clothes, circa high school, and especially behind your outrageous hats."

Victoria ran her fingers along the feather hat pin she used to secure her hat minutes ago. "I should believe this from the girl who can't keep a girlfriend for longer than two months?" Her voice dripped with sweet disdain.

Sandra's fingers tightened on her arms. "Oh, congratulations on the passive-aggressive conversation deflect."

Mount Victoria erupted and her voice boomed. "I don't need this from you. If I wanted such abuse, I would have let my sister stay."

"Touchy much? If you want to live in the dark, moping and moaning about your sad life, I've got better things to do tonight." Heading for the door, Sandra jingled her keys.

"Get out."

"On it."

Sandra softly shut the apartment door, leaving Victoria alone.

"Stupid. Righteous. Wrong." Victoria couldn't form sentences. She ripped off her hat and threw it at a picture of the two of them in high school. The frame crashed to the floor.

*R*esisting murder charges, Victoria directed all her irritation at her sister and ex-best friend by changing and digging deep for a killer outfit. No-heeled boots, a cute swirly skirt, and hatless.

At a minute to seven, she triple-checked her cell was on vibrate to keep her external headaches from interrupting her night. Her ankle didn't hurt, but she downed ibuprofen as a precaution. The doorbell rang as she opened the door, her anticipation high. Her stomach fluttered.

Ethan wore gray slacks and a sky-blue button-down shirt that accentuated his spellbinding eyes. The two of them had matching appreciative grins.

"You're beautiful. Shall we go for an adventure?" Ethan offered her his arm.

Maybe she became hypersensitive to the word. The dang thing seemed to be haunting her after she read the old letter. Mentally, she pushed the old note aside, crossing to him, her body shaking slightly. She linked arms with him. "An adventure? I love those."

"Alright, my lady, where to?" He spoke the words in a truly horrible British accent.

"Onward to dinner. Jake's awaits, good sir." She mimicked his atrocious dialect.

Keeping up the charade, he marched them down the steps. Thankfully, her ankle felt great in her wide and supported boots.

On his arm, her heart lightened and lifted. She should bottle this feeling and put it in a keepsake box.

Ethan cruised to the restaurant and pulled into Jake's overflowing parking lot with its raised trucks and dirty motorcycles. "I can drop you at the door, so you don't have to walk so far."

Stunned and touched by his sweet gesture, she said, "No worries, I can handle this. Squat, Squat, find me a parking spot. I will sacrifice two beers and a sister."

Instantaneously, a big truck roared out of a parking space.

Ethan swung into the spot. "Who's Squat? And why are you sacrificing something to him?"

Normally alone when she invoked Squat, she now felt sheepish about explaining this silly trick she and Sandra played. Yet he wanted to know. "He's the Parking God. You need to make an offering to him to find a parking spot, and the best part is you never need to give him the things you offered."

"You're going to have to initiate me into your cult. Sounds very practical." He turned off the car.

Relief washed through her that he didn't think she was a freak. "Food first, rituals later."

"Don't move." Ethan got out, walked to the passenger side, and opened her door for her.

"Thank you." A man opening doors and assisting her out of a car was fine by her, woman's lib be cursed. He wanted to be helpful, not degrading. Heck, if someone wanted to carry her in a covered palanquin chair, she wouldn't complain.

Inside, Jake's was hopping. Tugging on the sleeve of his jacket, she navigated through the mess of people to Mary at the hostess desk. Victoria waved to her. "We have a reservation."

"Hi ya, Vi. You're in Susie's section again."

Pressing close to her, Ethan leaned down near her ear. "So, you've been here before?"

Mary wove her way to the rear of the restaurant. The section was quieter than by the stage or jukebox. The same area where she sat with Iggy a few days ago. "Susie will be with you in a few minutes."

Ethan held out the chair for her. Discreetly, Mary shot Victoria a thumbs-up. Once situated, she handed them their menus and retreated to her hostess post.

He scanned the menu. "Since you've been here before, what do you recommend?"

"The burgers are great and the ribs with the spicy sauce are amazing. Are you a fan of spicy things?"

"Only my dates." He wiggled his eyebrows at her.

His compliment banished Victoria's bad date memories and flustered her.

Dodging a running kid, Susie slid to the table, smiling at Ethan, which saved Victoria from responding. "Howdy, my name's Susie. What can I get ya both to drink?"

Ethan ordered a draft beer. Victoria dittoed his order. Susie left with promises of being back soon.

He put down his menu. "What do you think you are going to get?"

She sat at T-minus eight days to the wedding. "I'm thinking the bowl of soup and a chef salad."

"You aren't going to order something slathered in sauce? How about I order for both of us?" His voice was salesman smooth.

Victoria pushed down the memory of Nick using the same

tone, him ordering for her, and his sliminess. Her internal censor said *no, don't let him decide what you want. You make the call. Not him.*

Ethan reached over and touched the back of her hand. "I promise you can change the order if you don't like my choice. Have a little faith. An adventure, remember?"

His touch helped lift the memory of all her nightmare dates. Ethan kept referring to number four from the letter she wrote to herself. *Life is meant to be an adventure.* Fine, she would try this. Victoria tossed her curls behind her shoulder in faux enthusiasm. "Geronimo."

He tugged at her menu, channeling a Cheshire cat smile. "I won't let you down. Boy scout's honor."

The menu slipped through her fingers, and her bravery plummeted. She reminded herself to trust in the journey.

Susie came around with their drinks and to see if they were ready to order.

He handed both menus to Susie. "We'll have the Tin Can for two. Can you please make sure we get half with spicy BBQ sauce for my date, please?"

His meal choice had a little of everything for them to try.

"Anything else, Shug?" Susie's body angled toward Victoria, checking in to make sure she had nothing else to add to the order.

Ethan was no Nick. Having Susie verify that Victoria agreed to the choice was a nice, protective feeling. Victoria said, "I'm good."

Susie nodded, turned, and welcomed the table next to them.

To Victoria, Ethan asked, "You approve of the daring dinner choice?"

"I've always wanted to eat off a trash lid."

"On a trash lid? That'll be an interesting dining experience."

He lifted his chin to the barren dance floor. "May I have this dance?"

Victoria checked in on her ankle and it felt supported and comfy in her boots. "Yes. Though my agreement comes with a verbal warning. Me and the dance floor aren't the best of friends."

"Noted. Don't worry, I'll protect you from the mean wooden monster."

The jukebox played one of Victoria's favorite country songs. Ethan twirled her out and reeled her in. Her skirt spun out like a tulip in bloom. For the whole song, he glided them around in perfect harmony.

A molten stare zipped between the two of them as the final notes played. She ended encased in his arms, with her back to him. She was glad his hard body kept her upright because her bones vanished.

His breath caressed her ear. "You dance well."

Her heart galloped. She shivered, breathing hard at both the exercise and his firm chest pressed against her back. "You're not too bad yourself."

People stared. A few clapped and whistled at them. She wiggled out of his arms aware of the stares they were receiving. She instinctively tried to draw the brim of her hat down but grasped only air. That's right, she wasn't wearing a hat tonight. Sandra accused her of hiding. Maybe she had been.

Ethan looked toward the table. "You ready to rest?"

"Sounds good. Where did you learn to dance?" Victoria led the way to their table.

They sat. "My dad was from Texas; he darn well made sure I knew how to two-step."

"What other dances can you do?"

"Ballroom, tango, and waltz." He put his drink down and reached for her hand. His fingers were still cool with condensation. His touch was chilly and nice on her overheated palms. "I could teach you."

Her stomach dropped out. Giddy panic rose up into her head making her dizzy. Victoria seized her courage. "I would love that."

Ethan ran his thumb over her knuckles. Then his body shifted and he released her hand. "Our food is here." He nodded to the approaching silver garbage lid.

Separation from Ethan helped clear her mind.

Susie set their food down, checked what else they needed, and then bounded off.

On a metal trash lid, food was heaped, as promised. Yellow corn on the cob, half a roasted chicken, ribs, wings, fries, and the best cornbread. Enough food for a family of five.

Victoria loaded up her plate with one of everything, taking a big bite out of the sweet and buttery cornbread, and it was southern-perfect. Which meant there would be no calorie counting tonight. She started at the mound of food on her plate and the tiny dent she made in the trash lid and said, "They must measure people's portions by linebacker's standards if they think this is only for two people. There goes fitting into the dress next week."

Ethan also piled food on his plate. "What's next week?"

"My sister's getting married on the eighth. I'm her maid of honor. Well, I was. I'm not sure she still wants me to be in the wedding."

"You're not sure if you're her maid of honor?"

She set her silverware down, collecting her conflicted thoughts about Dessie. "She's a bridezilla. I love my sister. I want her happy. What's best for her. The problem is she defines herself by her significant other. How can you get married if you aren't being you?"

"Why do you think she defines herself by her significant other?"

"Prime example: new boyfriend, new music stations. Whatever music he listens to will be the only thing she'll listen to. Presently, she's in love with música norteña. Do you know it? The words are typically in Spanish and it feels like every song uses the same polka-march background. Maddening." Her words were the embodiment of disdain.

"She can't be that bad."

Victoria stared at him, befuddled. He defended her crazy sister's antics?

He cleared his throat. "Maybe she's trying to connect to her fiancé."

She unlocked her phone, opened her sister's social media photo album, AKA the selfie page, and handed him the evidence. "Take a look at these." Her tone dared him to deny reality.

Ethan flicked through the pictures, his first reaction shock. Then, when each new picture exposed the thousand faces of Dessie, he looked stunned and handed the phone back. "I have never seen someone change their style so much and so often."

"Welcome to Dessie. Pictures would've diagnosed her with split-personality disorder. But we know the cause is boyfriend rotation."

Dates were not the place or time to waste on Dessie's problems. Victoria picked up her fork again, changing topics. "I'm always interested to know why people move to the desert. Why did you move here?"

He relaxed into his chair. "My job transferred me here. I'm an architect. I specialize in building concert halls."

"What are you working on here in the valley?"

Ethan dove into explaining his work. His gestures became more animated as he explained his project in Tempe.

For the rest of their date, they talked about everything from today's crazy work-driven culture to their favorite constellation. Topics and dialogue flowed easily between them.

The band struck up, squelching the ability to chat. Unlike her disastrous date with Mateo, Victoria would've loved to keep going.

Confidence and a bit of mischief colored his expression. He nodded his head toward the dance floor, asking without words if she would care to dance again. Her ankle felt good, so Victoria rose and offered him her hand.

Ethan taught her new moves and she, in thanks, crushed his poor pinky toe once with her heel. He hobbled a few steps, smiled, and came back to her arms for more. When the floor got truly overcrowded, he inclined his head toward the table. Victoria lifted her chin in a silent agreement, and they walked back together.

Susie popped by. "You two sure were tearing up the dance floor." She blinded Ethan with her spicy and saucy smile. "If you get tired of her, there will be a line to sign up for her dance card."

"I've got my name on every line." His tone was serious.

Victoria sat up a little straighter. Whoa, Ethan wanted to be with her. Odd and nice.

Susie winked at Victoria. "Did the two of you work up an appetite for dessert?"

"What do you recommend?" Ethan asked Susie.

"The chocolate cake is her favorite," Susie mock-whispered to him.

He slapped the table like an auctioneer. "Sold, plus coffee. Do you want a cup?"

"I never say no to coffee. The cake, though; I can't eat all those calories."

He kept his eyes on Susie, capturing Victoria's hand. "Bring two forks, we'll share."

"On it." Susie stashed her notepad in her apron, then melted into the crowd.

"Maybe we should've gotten dessert to go. It's a bit loud in here and I would love to talk to you some more." He laced his fingers with Victoria's.

"That would be nice." Her voice was airy and unsupported. Her lungs had quit functioning.

"I'll arrange it then." Ethan slipped out of his seat.

Her stomach clenched. Was she possessed? Did she really agree to go with Ethan to one of their homes? There was a dizziness and a rush as she contemplated Ethan and her being someplace quiet and alone. What if he tried to kiss her? Or do more than just that?

A cold dread snaked through her intestines. He said he wanted to spend time alone with her and the sin cake. This could be a horrible disaster.

She told herself to relax. Wasn't this what she's always dreamed of? To be kissed by an attractive, interesting guy? Quit freaking out, she berated herself. Her apartment would be best. She felt safe there. The meltdown wasn't necessary. Maybe he wasn't even going to kiss her and maybe she should quit hyperventilating.

*C*heck and to-go box in hand, Ethan returned to the table. To cover her trembling fingers, she clasped them in front of her as they walked through the crowd. Outside the restaurant, the cool spring air shocked her body.

Ethan dropped his jacket around her shoulders and his scent was crisp and sexy male. He waggled his eyebrows at her and whipped out his dreadful Cockney accent again. "All right, Guv'nor, where to?"

His playfulness melted her nerves away. "My place. I can brew up a mean cup or two," Victoria said, her attempted brogue thick and horrendous.

By the time they arrive at her apartment's landing, they were trying to outdo each other with the worst accent.

Ethan stepped in closer to her in the dark doorway. His body heat burned off her laughter and the easy, friendly feeling they'd shared.

"I keep meaning to call facilities to replace the light." Her tone sounded breezy and not a bit shaky like her hands were.

He clicked on his keychain light for her. "Always be prepared."

How prepared was he? Victoria's keys hit the ground. Was he carrying a condom, too?

What was she thinking inviting him to her place?

Ethan scooped up her keys, handing them to her.

"Thanks, I'm a bit clumsy tonight." Key in the lock, she cracked the door.

With more airspace between them, the mood reverted to friendly. He scooched nearer, that tiny shift charging the mood.

Now they shared a classic movie kiss setup. Victoria could imagine the director ordering a camera to zoom in to capture his body, leaning in. Capture his lips, his eyes, her panic.

Screw the sweet butterfly flutters, the frogs were back in her stomach clog dancing.

Ethan's lips brushed against hers.

Everything stopped.

Angst? Bye-bye.

Terror? Gone.

Who knew the way to control hysteria was lip-to-lip resuscitation?

Her first kiss.

He was gentle. Sweet. She sank into the kiss, leaning into his body, lip-drunk. Victoria tentatively mimicked his movements. Her keys dangled from her fingers.

Her cell vibrated. She ignored the interruption, though the call dented Victoria's endorphin daze. Inside, her home phone rang. She pulled away and stumbled into her apartment. Her irritation spiked at the distraction, and yet Victoria felt a bit grateful for the distraction. "Come in."

The machine picked up. "Tori." It was Dessie. "I know you hate me."

"Of course, my sister would call right at this particular moment." Her temper flared, burning off a bit of her post-kiss fog.

Dessie continued babbling. "But you need to call me. Your car. The other car came out of nowhere, I swear—"

The kiss haze vanished. Victoria bolted to the phone and answered. "Dessie, are you alright? Where are you in my car?"

Dessie blubbered.

Cutting in, Victoria's concern tightened her muscles. "Sit tight. I will be there in twenty."

She hung up and the warmth of Ethan radiated from behind her. She ran her hands through her hair, pacing. "I need a ride. My sister has my car. I know it's a real imposition."

He wrapped her in an embrace which calmed her immediately. "I would love to take you to help your sister."

"Thanks, I appreciate your offer." She pushed on his strong chest and faced him.

He tugged on the lapels of his coat around her.

"You'll need this. I can grab mine." She handed his jacket back, went to her room, and donned hers.

On her landing once again, Ethan turned her collar up to protect her neck from the cold. His fingertips brushed the nape of her neck in the process, sending a trickle of warmth down her spine. Linked arm in arm, they made their way to save the crazy bridal damsel.

WHEN VICTORIA and Ethan arrived at the cross streets Dessie gave them, two police cruisers sat on the side of the road with lights flashing. The boys in blue were talking to a kid slumped on the curb who looked barely old enough to drive. Ethan parked, as a minivan stopped centimeters from one cop car's bumper.

Both cops instinctively rested their hands on the butts of their guns and assessed the new threat.

The passenger side of the minivan flung open and a small woman ejected herself from the vehicle. Her eyes landed on the distraught teen. "Child, you are grounded for life." Her voice boomed, filled with parental rage and fear.

The officers relaxed.

The kid's mother jabbed her finger into his chest after every sentence as though it was the finger of judgment. The kid scrunched up small as a mouse, yet there he had no escape. His mother kept at him, her tone gnawing.

Victoria and Ethan walked toward her crumpled car. Anger bubbled up. She never should have lent her sister her car. Her heart sank at the big dent right behind her driver's side door. The car couldn't be driven home. How will she get to work?

Her sister's head popped up, then she ran over and wrapped Victoria in a hug, beginning her sob story. "I left from dinner and since you kicked me out, I called Dad and asked if I could stay with him. I was driving down to his office to pick him up. Then, then, then the kid ran a stop sign. He hit me and spun me around." She wiped her running nose on her sleeve.

Victoria's fury softened. She remembered Dessie doing the same thing when she skinned her shin badly when she was eight. Despite her sister being pushy and obnoxious, she was family, and this wasn't her fault.

Victoria asked Ethan, "Could you grab the box of Kleenex from my back seat?"

He reached into the rear of Victoria's smashed car, handed her a crunched box of tissues, and gave them some space.

"I know you're mad. I'm sorry. It wasn't my fault." Dessie's voice cracked.

Victoria stroked her sister's hair and released a huge huff of tension. "Even though you drive me to contemplate liver abuse, and there are days I would love to maim you, you're irreplaceable and mine. Cars, I can buy another."

Dessie squeezed Victoria tighter. Tears streamed down her cheeks. "I'm a horrible sister."

Victoria didn't respond. She continued to pet her sister's golden locks.

Sucking in a lung full of fresh air and letting it out, Dessie unfolded herself from Victoria. "I don't deserve you."

"Well, bask in your blessing, because I'm here to stay." She dabbed the curve of her sister's cheek, wiping away the salty trail.

Dessie blew her nose and stared in the direction of the cops. "Who's he?"

Victoria spotted Ethan, chumming it up with the officers. "That's my date, Ethan. He drove me out here to make sure you were alright."

"He's cute in a slightly heavy, guy-next-door way. Solid and simple."

"Don't be fooled. He's a lady killer on the dance floor." She shivered at the memory of them on her doorstep and how dangerously good he was at kissing. "Don't even contemplate doing anything more than admiring him from afar, oh bride-to-be."

"I think I could figure that one out for myself." She sent a pipe-bomb glare at Victoria. A glare which seemed innocuous at first glance yet would explode when pressed.

Another car screeched to a halt behind Ethan's car. Their dad spilled out of the passenger side, rushing toward the sisters.

"Esmeralda, are you alright?" Panic and concern were thick in his words, his cheeks colorless.

"Daddy." Dessie dove into his open arms.

He tucked her under his arm. Dessie dissolved into sobs.

"Shh, I'm here." Her dad swayed her from side-to-side in a massive dad hug.

Iggy slid out of the driver's seat of what must be his car.

It was Victoria's turn to give Dessie a little privacy, and she backed away. Iggy started in the direction of Victoria, his stride loose and easy. He stopped by her so they stood shoulder-to-shoulder, watching dad and daughter hug.

Victoria touched Iggy's forearm. "Thanks for bringing him down here."

He hooked his thumbs on his back pockets, angled his body in toward her, and said, "No need to thank me. He was concerned about her. Your sister wasn't just crying, she balled so hard he had to ask her three times where she was."

Victoria could smell him. Every time she stood near Iggy, his sexy smell shorted her synapses.

"Listen, I wanted to talk to you—" His speech and teeth clipped shut. His gaze shifted to the approaching footfalls.

A warm energy zapped her nerves. She could sense Ethan sliding next to her, his fingers skating up the nape of her neck. The effects of his touch snaked down her body, raising her temperature. Even though the night started out cool, she contemplated stripping out of her coat.

Iggy crossed his arms over his chest and did the tiny guy nod of acknowledgment to Ethan.

"Ethan meet Iggy. He works with my dad." To Iggy, she added, "Ethan and I were on a date when I got the call."

Iggy's eyes flattened and his jaw clenched. "Nice to meet you." His words were delivered as though he was a mechanical entity. He didn't even offer his hand to Ethan.

"And you," Ethan said, his tone polite with a hint of smug and he didn't offer his hand to shake either.

Dessie and their dad meandered to where the three stood in an uncomfortable silence. Her dad looked at Victoria and tilted his head toward Ethan.

Victoria answered his unspoken question. "Daddy, this is Ethan, my date tonight. Ethan, this is Robert."

Ethan offered his hand to her dad. "Nice to meet you, sir. Wish it were under better circumstances."

Her dad returned the handshake and registered he should say something. "You're dating my Victoria. Treat her well."

"I will." Ethan tugged Victoria into his side, squeezing her shoulder lightly.

The action was possessive. Victoria glowed.

Iggy snorted, pivoted on his work boot heel, and left. His steps echoed heavily on the empty pavement.

Tugging on her dad's sleeve, Dessie pouted. "Hello, I'm the one who was in an accident."

The tow truck arrived, loaded up the mangled car, and rolled away with Victoria's only transportation.

Dessie and her dad went to complete the paperwork. Victoria swept her eyes over the few people left, to discover Iggy watching her. She waved at him. He busied himself with something inside his trunk.

Okay, he obviously didn't want to be friendly with her.

The paperwork was doled out and Ethan wrapped his arm around her shoulders. "Ready to go? Your sister's in the backseat of my car texting someone."

"I'm glad to see she's calmed down and going home with me."

Still wrapped in the comfort of Ethan's heavy arm, Victoria waved bye to her dad, blowing him a kiss.

With his hand down by his waist, her dad grabbed her windblown kiss, then promptly shoved his hand into his pocket. With his shoulders hunched and his head down, he climbed into Iggy's car.

Silly old man. Victoria loved that fake grumpy dad of hers.

Iggy slammed his driver door shut, cranked the engine, and they rocketed off into the night.

Ethan nudged her to the car and they climbed in. Dessie

snored in the back seat. Victoria smirked. So much about her sister had changed over the years, and yet so much hadn't. Whenever Dessie felt overwrought growing up, she would expend all her energy during the stressful incident and then pass out as fast as a toddler. The nap acted as her reset button.

The soft snores of Dessie were the only sounds on the ride to her apartment.

The streetlights rolled on by. Victoria didn't know what happened with Iggy. Something changed in him the moment he saw Ethan, but she didn't understand. And she didn't care.

Whereas Iggy exploded with energy, Ethan radiated warmth. Lulled by his presence, she relaxed into the seat, letting the day drift away.

Cold air pricked her skin. Ethan leaned into her door. "You're home."

Blinking, she realized they were in her parking lot.

Ethan opened the back door and he gently shook Dessie's shoulder. "Time to get up."

Dessie sat up, slid out, and zombied up the stairs. Her hair stood high on one side.

Victoria unbuckled and got out, too. This was awkward. She felt awkward. Unsure how to proceed, she studied her shoes. "I better get up there since I have the keys."

A warm, slightly calloused hand tilted her head up. Her vision traveled up Ethan's gray slacks and nice blue shirt and locked gazes with him.

His thumb traced her jawline. "I had a great time. We should do this again."

"Minus the car wreck, I'd like that. Though the next week will be crazy with the wedding."

He stepped in closer, shredding her safety zone buffer. Her brain cells scattered. Her body hummed with his nearness.

She wasn't sure what he saw in her facial expression. Most likely a blend of hope and fear.

Instead of her lips, he kissed her cheek. "Let me know if you need any help with the wedding."

From three flights up, Dessie hollered a few tart words. He backed up from Victoria. "Go on. I'll wait until you get in the door."

Not trusting her voice, she nodded. She floated up the stairs. At her landing, Victoria waved down to Ethan. He flashed his headlights and pulled out onto the empty street.

She touched her cheek and then her lips, feeling the imprint of his kisses. Minus having to rescue her sister? Best. Date. Ever.

*W*ith her car MIA, Victoria had to utilize a car-summoning app the next day to get to and from work. Her ankle felt a bit aggravated after the standing around at the accident, but if she babied her foot, she'd be okay again in a day or so. Climbing her stairs after her half day in the office, she planned to spend her afternoon applying to vet schools. Time to get her life in order, then she could unravel this whole dating dilemma. Tonight was dedicated to digging deeper into her future.

Victoria waltzed into her apartment ready to tackle the applications and flinched. All intentions of searching for schools withered. She surveyed the carnage.

The TV blared. Dessie's hair still stuck straight up from last night. The remnants of cereal bobbed in a bowl as Ralph licked up the sweet milk.

The bride drama on the screen had Dessie's rapt attention. They talked about the perfect dress, man, and day, and how nothing and no one would ruin their perfection.

What a perfect time for Victoria to escape. *Let Ms. Bride Hyde stay sucked into her show*, Victoria prayed, as she inched around the couch.

Dessie rotated her neck. "You're home early." Her front wasn't any better than her back. She sported raccoon eyes and yesterday's makeup.

Victoria recoiled from the mess before her. "Saturday is only a half day and it's already one in the afternoon."

Her sister pivoted her torso toward the TV and the bride horror show in an eerily slow speed, her voice bland, saying, "Okay."

Victoria patted her leg, desperate to snag Ralph's attention without rousing the comatose bridezilla. Dessie might look Valium-ed out, but Victoria could taste trouble brewing in the air. The rumble in the distance foretold the impending storm on the horizon.

Her phone played Sandra's song. Victoria's heart dropped to her shoelaces. Not sure that she wanted to talk to her after last night's fight, she braced herself and read the text.

One more day go ahead lose the bet, I dare u XOXO

Serving up threats? Satisfaction zipped from her toes to her fingers as she typed and sent.

U don't scare me + mission accomplished. Floating on cloud 9

Instant response. The phone sang, "Great Balls of Fire." Tone set to triumphant, Victoria answered her cell. "Yeesss."

"You didn't think to call me? Dish. No, wait. I'm on my way." Sandra hung up.

Her fingers itched to flip through the vet school applications. Tomorrow...after the bridal shower brunch. Victoria promised herself she'd deal with the applications then.

Six minutes later, it was like wild animals were slamming into her door wanting in. Sandra spilled into the apartment. "Sorry I took forever. Before you start, where's your emergency champagne bottle? This deserves bubbly."

Dessie twitched. Victoria froze. No sudden movements. She didn't want the bride's attention.

Sandra paused, glancing over at the chaos on the couch, and herded Victoria into the kitchen. She opened the fridge, unearthed the bottle, and popped the cork. Victoria fetched the stemware and poured the bubbly. The beautiful golden bubbles sat in two glasses on the counter.

Victoria raised her champagne flute. "To adventures." She'd nailed number four in the letter to herself.

"To adventures and beyond." Sandra clinked their glasses together.

The effervescent bubbles bounced down her throat, making Victoria giddy, as she relayed the whole date to Sandra.

By the end of the story, Sandra had her hands cupped under her chin. Her exhale was wistful. "He can dance. You are lucky."

Victoria reached for the champagne bottle and discovered it was empty. "Where did all the bubbly go?"

Sandra flopped her head onto one arm, waving her sticky and empty glass around in the air. "You took the words straight from my brain."

Hiccupping, Victoria pushed her glass away from her. "Maybe we should eat something to settle our stomachs and soak up the alcohol."

"Brilliant idea. I'll whip something up." Sandra snatched up the closest phone, which was Victoria's, and unlocked the screen.

With a few pressed buttons, she had the phone to her ear. "Ya, Iguana's Pizza, I want two large pizzas. One with mushrooms, basil, garlic, and olives, and the other, the works. For delivery. 829 E. Miramar, number 313. The account should be under Victoria Shaw."

Slumped in her chair, Victoria drafted up a mental top-three for her to-do list.

1. WRANGLE THE BRIDAL SHOWER WITH NO MAIMING

2. FINISH BACHELORS SO I CAN APPLY TO VET SCHOOLS

3. NO MORE DATING FOR A WHILE, NOT EVEN ETHAN

A solid list for her to start the foundation of the life she wanted.

Sandra punched the off button. "See, I know how to cook."

"Yes, I see you can cook as well as most men."

Victoria's phone sang an old song, and she thought, *whose ringtone is that?*

Sandra answered. "Yo. What do you mean I called the wrong number?" Her tone was dangerously light. With Sandra, if she went quiet, heads tended to roll soon after.

Victoria hoped her phone would survive the call.

Squinting and listening harder, Sandra slumped over the table. "But I hit Iguana's Pizza. Your name is what? Did your mother hate you? Hello? He hung up on me."

"Who?" Dessie surfaced from her TV coma, putting her cereal bowl in the sink.

Sandra waved her hands around, venting her frustration. "Some stupid pizza guy who says he's not a pizza guy. His name is Iggy. Can you believe it? What kind of numb nuts is named Iggy?"

The words Sandra slurred, and the ringtone connection slammed into Victoria's chest. Her blood pressure plummeted. "You called Iggy? He's the guy my mother set me up with."

"Mr. I've-got-issues? I thought his name was Victor."

"Same guy, two names."

Cell in her hands, Victoria texted him back.

I'm sorry. My best friend is drunk and misdialed

"It Ain't You" by the Squirrel Nut Zippers played.

Figured. How's Dessie doing?

A sucker-punch to her throat took Victoria by surprise. She

was grateful he didn't ask about her. And yet disappointed. She typed.

Currently in a wedding coma. Sorry 2 have bothered u

Her phone sang his ringtone again.

K, night

Mind reeling, Victoria decided she better figure out this school stuff, because men were too complicated to decipher.

Sandra piped up. "Sooo, no one's bringing dinner?"

The idea of pizza sounded good. Victoria could handle some calorie therapy. She slid the phone to Sandra. "It's ringing, repeat the order to the real pizza guys."

The pizza arrived. Victoria banished the TV bridal shows. They all hunkered down to watch romantic comedies the rest of the night and create the brunch table gifts.

BRUNCH the next day started at eleven. At eight, Dessie started throwing things in her room. Victoria shuffled toward the mayhem and stood in the doorway. "What's wrong?"

Clothes littered every surface. Pale, slinky dresses slummed with cargo Capri pants on the bed. Flowered tops draped over her pink nighty on the dresser.

"I have nothing to wear." Her makeup and hair were polished and pristine, but Dessie sported a towel around her body. She flitted around, grabbing random pieces of clothing, and tossed them, disgusted.

Victoria grasped her spiraling sister. "What's the real problem?"

"Nothing."

She heard the waver in her sister's voice. Shoving a pile of clothes off the edge of the bed, she plunked her sister down. "If you believe that lie, okay. Know that I'm here for you."

One lone tear broke free, snaking through her makeup. "I know," Dessie snapped. Then she let out a shaky breath. "This is big. In one week, I'll be Mrs. Volpé."

"I thought you were going to keep your name, and if you aren't sure about the wedding, it's not too late to stop." Victoria's voice dipped low and soothing, like how she used to calm down Dessie when their dad missed a recital due to working late.

Dessie slapped on a bright expression. "We talked and decided Esmeralda Volpé sounded fine for me. I'm not stopping. I've got a case of cold feet and I'm not sure what to wear for the brunch."

The untruth was apparent. Yet if her sister didn't want to admit this wedding was too much or too soon, her problem. Instead, Victoria said, "Recommend wool socks for the first, and for outfits, we can help."

Dessie nodded.

Victoria bellowed down the hall to Sandra. "Hey, Sleeping Beauty, time to get vertical. I'll fix coffee."

Sandra grumbled and slammed the bathroom door shut.

By the time Victoria walked down the hallway, the bathroom door opened, and she thrust a mug into Sandra's hands.

Her friend inhaled the vapors. The whites of her eyes became less red and crazy. "Why am I awake?"

"We need to help Dessie decide on her outfit for the brunch."

Forty-five minutes later, they agreed on a peach sundress. It flowed off Dessie's waist flawlessly, hugging all her curves. She twirled happily.

Glad she seemed to be doing better, Victoria tucked her sister's curl behind her ear. "You look great."

"My work's done." Sandra meandered out of the bedroom.

Victoria left, too. In her room, she had a showdown with her closet. The event was outside in a pecan grove, so she'd need a wide-brimmed hat. She rustled through her hat boxes, settling on her big red sun hat. That narrowed down her clothing options, and she decided on an old cream dress. Praying the dress still fit, she slipped the material over her head. It was snug across her shoulders and hips. She rummaged through her scarves, found a long black one, and tied the material around her waist. Extra-pound camouflage, complete.

Sandra slipped out of the bathroom. Victoria bounded in.

At fifteen to eleven, the three of them rushed to the formal brunch with Sandra as the wheelman. When they arrived, waitstaff added the handmade guest gifts to the perfectly decorated table. The bridal gifts Gifts were piled on two long tables next to the bride's seat. A giant row of trees shaded the area, yet it provided ample light.

Victoria dropped into a cool metal chair at the flower-laden table. People trickled in and the crowd would have fit in watching a round of golf or yakking about their latest social ball event.

The first few courses chugged along pleasantly enough, until a shrill, "How dare you?" rang out, shattering the illusion of a peaceful brunch.

At the head of the table, the two mothers-in-law, Maria and Millie, snarled at each other. Both stood leaning over the table, bickering.

Maria hit the table. "How dare you insult my beloved son." At a deafening level, she chewed off every word.

Waving her hand down the table where all talk had ceased, her mother glared at Maria. "Calm yourself. You're making a spectacle of this joyous occasion."

The mother-in-law cage match had everyone glued and judging every moment of this disturbance. The only way to silence fifty of the biggest gossips known to man was to place them in front of a bigger disaster than what they were already talking about: Dessie's nuptials.

Dessie held her head high. Her body quivered with the effort of pretending everything was picture-perfect. Victoria knew that posture—stiff back and irate eyes. She had been on the receiving end of that one often. Victoria wished her sister could enjoy her friends and family at the party.

Seeing no one else stepping in to stop the madness, Victoria started to rise to intervene. The waitstaff rushed out the next course early, so the two hens were able to back down without either losing face. Order restored.

Hushed tones spread. Quick, sharp, viper tongues loosened around Victoria. Phones whipped out, with fingers flying across their screens. People raced to have the inside scoop on the impending doom for Dessie's wedding.

Time to redirect the piranhas onto something else. And with that lovely thought, Victoria winced, stood, and tapped her champagne glass. The crystal cry rolled down the table, and everyone joined in the call. When she had the silence of the gossips, the hypocrites, and all the family, Victoria channeled her best, cheeriest smile.

"A toast to the bride. Dessie, may you have found in Damien your rock, your anchor in the storm, your best friend, and the love of your life. Treat him well and love him. Dessie, you deserve the best in the world." Victoria lifted her glass.

Everyone mirrored her, flutes high.

She added, "We all wish for you a long and happy marriage. May this be love everlasting. We love you and hope this is your fairytale come true. Congratulations, Esmeralda. Cheers."

People cheered, sipping champagne. Dessie raised her glass to her sister and the two sisters shared a silent salute between them. All the women surrounding Dessie swarmed her, talking about the wedding preparations.

*T*he party wound down in the late Sunday afternoon sun. Victoria could feel the countdown to the wedding tick by, T-minus seven days. Victoria and Sandra loaded up both Sandra's and her mother's cars with the massive haul of gifts, including fine china etched with gold, monogrammed silver utensils nestled into a cedar box, and soft, spa-type towels that poked out of a big box. Then there were the more mundane gifts like plungers, cash, gift cards, and sexy lingerie.

Victoria returned to the grove to collect the last gifts and herd her family to the dirt parking lot. Three partyers huddled around a lone champagne bottle: Dessie, her mother-in-law to be, Maria, and their mother. Dessie giggled, clearly in the happy-drunk stage, but Maria and her mother were trashed.

"Time to break up the party. Hey, is that my phone?" Victoria asked.

Dessie gazed down at the phone in her hand. "Oh, yeah. Mine died. I needed to post pictures. Pictures of all the loveliness. I can show you." She punched things on Victoria's screen.

"Stop borrowing my things without asking. You know I hate that." Opening her purse, Victoria held it for Dessie to deposit her phone where it should be.

Dessie stuck her tongue out at Victoria and dropped the phone in. Yes, very mature for the woman who was getting married in a week.

Maria's driver loomed over her, hauled the tiny woman up by her arm, and wrangled her toward the running Lincoln in the parking lot.

Sandra scooped up Dessie. Victoria wrestled with her bone-less mother. Grunting, Victoria lugged her mother along and eventually heave-hoed her into the car's passenger seat.

With Dessie safely tucked into the passenger seat of Sandra's car, Sandra leaned over the roof and looked at Victoria. "How are you going to get home?"

"I'll get my dad to pick me up." She waved Sandra off, closed her mother's passenger door, and popped around the car to slide into the driver's seat. The beige leather hugged her in a welcoming embrace. The heat of the leather soaked into her body. The convertible purred.

At least the Arizona spring afternoon was a treat. Top down, Victoria let the cool breeze whip the ends of her hair and the brim of her sun hat around. All too soon, she pulled into her mother's drive, cut the engine, and immediately regretted the loss of the open road.

Victoria poked her mother's drooping cheek. "Come on, let's go inside."

She grumbled from under her mop of hair, which the wind had tangled. With her mother's normally pristine hair disheveled, Victoria couldn't resist immortalizing the memory with a quick picture, which became her cell wallpaper.

Bear snores rose out of the car.

"Have it your way." Victoria dialed.

The other side picked up.

"Daddy? I'm at Mother's, I need help getting her to her room and a ride home."

"Yeah, okay."

Her dad sounded distracted. Wait, did she hear slamming drawers in the background? "Are you at work on a Sunday?"

He promised to be there soon and hung up. Yep, he was at work. Crazy workaholic.

She patted her mother's messed coiffure. "Don't worry, help is on the way."

Ten minutes later, her dad pulled up as the passenger in Iggy's car. Her heart sank to her toes.

Being around him felt awkward on Friday night at the accident. Victoria had been hoping for some stress relief when her dad showed up, not more stress.

Her dad popped out of the car. "Pumpkin, I can get her out." He strolled up to the car, surveying his ex-wife's frazzled blob.

"She's all yours."

He made a noncommittal grunt and to her mother said, "I see you all had a good time today."

Victoria grinned. "Magical time. Mother and Maria, Dessie's soon-to-be mother-in-law, almost came to blows."

Her dad squatted, then nodded to Victoria, indicating he was ready. She popped the passenger door open. Her mother flopped out.

Catching her like a perfectly timed ballet toss, her dad addressed her disheveled head. "Millie, you've gained a few pounds since the last time I carried you over the threshold. And I'm glad you won't remember me saying that." His entire head went beet red, straining under her mother's dead weight.

Victoria stepped in to assist.

Behind them a car door creaked open. She pivoted to see Iggy striding over. He shot her dad a stern look. "I don't care what you said, you need help."

The two men positioned themselves, one on each side, walking her drunk mother inside. The stairs were a struggle. Almost to the top landing, her mother threw up. The puke landed on her dad's shoes and her mother's deep red stair runner.

Glad to be behind the guys, Victoria patted her dad's shoulder. "You sure you two aren't going to get remarried? That way you could be the one to manage this joy, always and forever."

"Doesn't seem like I got far enough away, because here I am." Her dad hauled his ex upward toward the doorway.

Iggy stifled a chuckle behind a gasp.

Without even glancing at the mess or Victoria, her dad said, "Be helpful and clean up after your mother."

Grumbling off into the kitchen, she rounded up cleaning supplies and attacked the mess while fighting her gag reflex.

A few minutes later, Victoria joined everyone in her mother's room. She lay sprawled out on her bed. Iggy propped himself against the hallway door frame.

Iggy didn't seem to be stiff today. Her parents being present seemed to buffer off his edges.

Her dad came out of the master bathroom holding a bottle of antacids. "Victoria, help me get her into a sitting position."

She prepped her mother, making sure she had her feet flopped over the side of the bed, hair pulled back, and waste bin at her knees.

Her dad stood in front and shook her mother's shoulder. "Wake up, Millie. I know your tummy hurts. I have medicine which will help."

"Go away." Her mother swatted at the voice disturbing her slumber.

Her dad pinched her nose shut. She dropped her jaw open to protest and he popped the tablets into her complain maker. "Chew this."

Dutifully, she chomped and swallowed. He held out a glass of water for her to wash them down.

"You're a good man." And promptly heaved. Done retching, she wiped away the spittle and whined. "My stomach hurts."

Her dad winked at Victoria over her mother's bobbing head. "Here, I have something to help sour stomachs. Do you want it?"

Weakly nodding, her mother held out her hand.

Sucker.

He deposited two more antacids into her waiting hand. Her dad and Victoria shared a naughty daddy-n-daughter secret twinkle.

But her mother saw nothing. Being a good drunk, she lifted her hand up and ate the tablets. Within moments, she repeated the previous cycle, ending with retching.

Stomach on E, her mother squawked for solitude to die, as she flopped onto the bed. Phone, water, and bucket close by for her. Everyone left her to her siesta.

Downstairs, her dad walked with them to the front door. "I'm going to stay and watch over Milly. Iggy, can you drop Victoria at her apartment?"

"I can." Iggy glanced at both Shaws and shook his head at them. "By the way, remind me to never call either one of you to help me out if I'm drunk. You two are the devil."

Her dad and she shared a sly, sneaky glance and cracked up.

"I'm serious. Giving her antacids so she'll throw up? That's mean. You both knew her drunk stomach had a high probability to sour further and she'd end up heaving."

Her dad cocked one eyebrow. "I'm a scientist, I knew the possibilities. We're not mean. I knew she needed the excess alcohol purged."

Victoria and Iggy left her dad on the porch and climbed into Iggy's car. They rode in silence.

She broke the quiet first. "Do you mind stopping somewhere so I can pick up something to eat?"

"I know a great place I think you'll love. If you're not in a hurry."

"That family mayhem was the sum total of my Sunday plans."

They drove to a crumbling part of town off the 101, on the border of Mesa and Tempe. He pulled into a deserted little strip mall. In front of a small, slump-block store, Iggy parked and got out.

Grocery shelves about five feet high were visible on the inside, but no people peered out. Victoria got out, too. "Are you sure they are open?"

Tugging open the front door, he gestured for her to lead the way. "Yep. We missed the lunch rush."

In they went with Victoria first. The store smelled of roasting meat and odd seasonings. Curry, cumin, ginger, and fennel spices were the only scents she could identify.

Past the dried rice and pasta, she turned right and walked toward the tiny restaurant in the back. A little Middle Eastern man with a tan turban greeted her.

"Table for two." Iggy's low voice snaked up her spine.

"It's been a while." The man brightened and hustled them to a table. He chatted with Iggy about the latest computer technology.

With the two of them engrossed in techy jargon, she covertly studied Iggy over her menu. His laugh rumbled and infected everyone around him. She could sit here all afternoon basking in his warm humor.

From the kitchen, a slew of foreign words streamed out. The

man pulled himself out of geek land, excused himself, and disappeared.

"Sorry, he loves to talk computer stuff with me. Have you figured out what you want?" His menu sat on the table untouched.

Victoria pushed her hair behind her ear. "No clue. What do you recommend?"

"The chicken platter is good because there's a bit of everything to try." He reached over the top of her menu and pointed the dish out to her.

She noticed his hands. They were large, calloused, and meaty. Working-man hands. Focusing on anything but the idea of his hands touching her, she swallowed. "What are you going to get?"

"The Mediterranean platter, my favorite."

The man bounced to the table, took their order, and retreated to the kitchen. Alone, she and Iggy talked about growing up in Arizona. They swapped tales about out-of-towners freaking out because the temperature in April can be 90 degrees. Wimps.

They chatted through their late lunch. After food, he ordered them Arabian coffee. They shared favorite science pranks they pulled in school.

The easy flow of conversation felt nice. Something was different about him.

Her phone intruded for the first time since they sat down. "Pardon, the call is from Dessie."

"Go ahead."

She turned slightly away from the table and answered the phone.

Dessie started in immediately. "Where are you? Why aren't you here helping me write my thank you notes? It's bad manners to not send out thank you notes."

"Simmer, I'll be home soon. You want some food to fuel your drunk tantrum?"

Iggy coughed.

"A, I'm not drunk. B, nothing to fattening. And C, hurry up." She huffed, hanging up.

Victoria dropped her phone into her purse. "Her royal pain needs me home."

Iggy gulped down the dregs of his coffee. "No offense, but your sister seems a bit high strung and crazy."

"Sometimes I can almost convince myself we're not related, but she is my sister. She can be as sweet and loyal as she is bossy and bitchy." Victoria waved the server over for her take-out order, excused herself for the lady's room.

While she was away, Iggy had paid.

Victoria dug for her wallet. "Let me pay you back. You've gone out of your way to help me today."

"It's my treat." He put his hand on her arm.

Once their skin touched, they both stilled. The moment stretched. Stretched out and out, until the server brought the to-go order, breaking their contact.

Even though they were no longer touching, the jolt of energy morphed into a dim hum around her, like a lightning storm charging the air, even before the first raindrop. They'd had a wonderful lunch without any awkwardness. Yet one shared touch and every movement after the touch felt stilted and strained.

APARTMENT-BOUND, neither Victoria nor Iggy spoke. To Victoria, Iggy acted like a force of nature that both bombarded her senses and softened her inner defenses.

He pulled up to her apartment complex.

"Thanks for your help today. I'll see you around." Her words gushed out.

She gathered her things, rabbiting out of the car and bounding up the stairs as fast as her heeled shoes would propel her. Victoria didn't catch her breath until she sagged safely against her apartment door. Note to self: avoid the confusing man.

Time to unwind from this convoluted day. She enjoyed Iggy's company and that they had no fallout, which was odd. It seemed like every other time they had seen each other, someone left in a huff.

Her decision to go dateless to the wedding still felt right. Single life was for her.

Kicking off her shoes, she hollered, "Dessie, food." She placed the bag on the counter and grabbed a cool glass of water.

Decked out in USC sweats, Dessie hunkered down at the kitchen bar counter, sniffed a grape leaf wrap, and slung the food into her mouth. Victoria's shoulders dropped. She loved Dessie relaxed and real and not the curled perfection everyone expected to see.

Dessie demolished half of her salad and rolled on her I-want-something smile. "Can I borrow mom's car?"

"Left it in Mother's driveway."

"How'd you get home?"

"Iggy dropped me off."

"You were out with Iggy? What about Ethan? He's nice and kind. You're a shameless floozy, throwing yourself at Iggy." Dessie's voice turned glacial.

Oh, goody, Hyde time had arrived. "Channeling Grandmother Alburga today, I see. What do you care about my budding dating life? Ethan and I don't have monogrammed towels." Too tired to hide her irritated tone, Victoria plunked her water glass down on the counter.

"I don't want you to ruin Ethan."

Ding, a dose of reality coming right up. Victoria leaned over the counter. "Your wedding is in T-minus seven days. Focus on that."

"Too late. Ethan's your plus-one." Dessie sang the words in the tune of a petty childhood taunt.

"No. I told you I'm going alone. I don't need a date. I don't want a plus-one." Her family made her insane. No one listened.

"Your phone says otherwise."

"What?"

Dessie nodded to Victoria's phone on the counter. "Check your texts with Ethan."

Suspicion took root, with its buddies anger and trepidation along for the ride. Victoria unlocked her cell and opened her messenger app. "What the hell did you do?"

There, in a text exchange she didn't send, "Victoria" requested Ethan as escort to her sister's wedding. He'd replied with a maybe and that he needed to check his calendar.

"Why the hell did you do this? Wait, that's why you had my phone at the brunch." Victoria's tone dropped to deadly, as all the diabolical pieces fell together.

Dessie pushed her salad around in her to-go box. "Yes, that's why I had your phone. All the other bridesmaids chatted about their dates and I realized you needed to have one to complete the seating arrangement. No biggie, it's just a date."

Her sister didn't respect her opinion or her boundaries. Victoria erupted. "You, you, you immature, nosy—"

"Don't be righteous. You wore 'the lost cause sister' label. I helped you."

"No, you helped you. I'm going to tell Ethan the truth." Victoria started to text back.

Dessie dropped her fork and pushed the Styrofoam box away. "Ethan will be a great, attentive date. I saw him get territorial with you in front of Iggy. Do you want to say no to a budding relationship? Take my gift."

Her fingers stopped typing. She would never say this aloud, but Dessie was right. Ethan didn't care that she was heavy or degreeless. He liked her sans hats and all. Plus, he would save her from facing her mother's family alone. Her resolve crumbled. "I guess it won't hurt for him to take me if he says yes."

"Good. Then stay away from Iggy." Dessie spat each word out faster than a rabid dog attacking. "You're seeing Ethan. You can't have any other guys on the side."

Her sister's aggressiveness shoved Victoria's temper into overdrive. "You're outrageous. You set me up against my wishes. I acquiesced to your request, and then you proceed to dictate who I can be around. Jawohl, Herr Hyde."

Dessie bolted upright, toppling the barstool over, furious. "Don't. Call. Me. That."

She hated being referred to as Jekyll and Hyde, but Victoria didn't care anymore. She yanked her sister's chain even harder. "Why? You're two-faced."

"I'm not." Hands balled, eyes defiant, Dessie leaned in closer to Victoria, her breath hot. "If you hurt Ethan, I promise I'll let everyone know you're a harlot."

"A harlot? What are you, eighty?"

Dessie kept silent and disappeared.

Her sister acted oddly whenever Ethan's name came up. Defensive and overly protective of him. Did the bride have a crush on Victoria's ill-begotten date? Or maybe it was only wedding jitters.

Ethan chose that moment to reply to her sister's request. Verdict: Victoria officially had a plus-one. A plus-one she hadn't asked for and couldn't refuse.

She felt hollow instead of happy, anxious instead of relieved. No part of this wedding, dating, or her life tracked as she had expected. Yet Victoria found herself thanking Ethan and typing the details of the wedding. After hitting send, she hated herself. So much for showing her sister, mother, and cousins she was fine as is. That she was a woman who didn't need a man to be whole.

And these were the days of Victoria's life.

*B*efore Victoria could lock the front door of the vet the next day for lunch, her mother strolled in. Sunglasses devoured the entire top half of her face. "Victoria, I'm here to take you out for a Monday surprise."

She'd never been more grateful for the backlog of paperwork littering her desk. "Gee, I can't. The wedding has been wreaking havoc with my work. I need to stay."

Dr. Yaz prodded from the back. "Nonsense. Have a great time with her. I can handle the office."

"See? What a lovely man. We'll be taking a long lunch." Her mother waggled her fingers at him.

How the depths of Victoria's eye roll didn't permanently make her lazy-eyed, she would never know. Yet to fight both these titans was useless. "If I go, you'll have to take me to pick up my rental car."

"Let's go then." Her mother whisked her out of the office and into her convertible, flapping her lips nonstop. Officially, nothing had changed in the last fifteen years between them. Victoria let the words wash over her.

A tap on her leg brought her back to the car and her mother. "Dessie tells me you're stringing along that nice Ethan fellow."

In their mother-daughter relationship, dating had always been a huge bruise between them. Her mother insisted Victoria must have a significant other. Victoria insisted she be left alone and yet here she sat being interrogated.

"Dessie's paranoid. Ethan..." Victoria couldn't bring herself to admit that her younger sister set her up with a wedding date and added, "Ethan is my plus-one."

She patted Victoria's leg again. "Good. I would hate for people to think that because your little sister is getting married, you're getting desperate and bringing the nearest man off the street. I do want you to be happy and in love."

Always pushing the find-a-man angle on her left Victoria exhausted.

Her mother shot a glare at her. "Don't forget on Wednesday we have a meet and greet with Damien and all his family. The event will be at a very nice five-star restaurant for dinner and dancing. You'll need something nice to wear."

Terror spilled down Victoria's spine. "How nice?"

Her mother donned the lying mask, resettling into her jacket. "Don't worry, Darling."

Instantly, Victoria started to sweat. She knew her mother planned to badger her into doing something unpleasant.

"Surprise! We're going dress shopping today."

Shopping was how her mother showed love. How she meant the gesture and how it chafed Victoria were two different things.

"No. I did my time. I shopped with Dessie. I'm not shopping with you." Mustering up her best you-must-be-joking glare, she crossed her arms to up the no-go ante.

"I know you dislike shopping. This isn't for you. Do this to support Dessie. To show her fiancé what a great family he's joining. I'll pay for the new dress." Her mother slathered on a dollop of family guilt.

That was the thing Victoria hated. She could see the guilt-trip windup and delivery coming, and yet she still had trouble dodging. Her mother wanted to buy her a new dress? Loved it. Her clothes must come off in the proximity of her mother? Hated it. Yet her mother paying so Victoria could pick any dress she wanted? Intrigued by it.

Victoria slumped down in the convertible. "If, and this is a big if, I go with you, you will not criticize me about my weight."

"Won't think of criticizing you."

She didn't believe her mother and tapped the dash for emphasis. "One word and I'm gone. Gone faster than Daddy caught at a hen party."

Her mother crossed her heart. "Deal. He sure knows how to move, if properly motivated."

"I remember him coming home, seeing all your friends filling his house, practically hanging off the rafters, and he froze. He found his legs after you offered to use him as your makeup model."

They both laughed. Victoria wished she had more moments like this with her mother, moments where they could look at their past and have a reason to smile instead of bicker.

Her mother turned into a massive plaza. "He finally crept home at one in the morning, told me he wanted to make sure they were long gone."

They got out at the Scottsdale Fashion Square Mall valet stand. Head hanging, she followed her mother's stream of words into the rich hipster hell.

Her mother headed straight for the Nordstrom archway. "What do you think of Esmeralda getting married?"

Victoria blinked, buying time. An old trick she picked up from her dad. She decided to go for a neutral response, to test the waters and fish out what her mother wanted. "Dessie is an adult and can make her own choices."

Her mother pivoted, stepping in close to her, the lines on her face deepening. "Don't bullshit the pro here." Her tart tone cut through her standard polite manner. "What do you think about the quick marriage?"

With no other option, she answered truthfully. "Your family will be ecstatic to add her to the wedded rolls. I am concerned, since we didn't have the best model of how to make a marriage last, that now, right after she can legally drink, she's agreeing to a forever decision."

With her long, fake, pink nails, her mother tapped her clutch purse and started toward the store again. "Regardless of what my family thinks, I want Dessie to be happy. I think the gravity of what will happen in six days is seeping in. She's a scared dog biting anything that comes near."

"More like a raging bull." Victoria pouted better than a six-year-old full of huff and injustice. "She keeps going at me like I'm the matador and she's the bull."

Over her shoulder, her mother's face softened into a genuine smile. "Talk to her. She looks up to you."

Was she crazy? Better call the doctors to show her mother the latest fashions in straight, white jackets.

Victoria quickened her pace to catch up. "I can't get within a ten-mile radius before she rips me for being Jezebel. Which is odd, because even though I'm older, she's definitely had more men, dates, and stories than I will ever have with guys."

Her mother whapped Victoria's arm with her purse. "Victoria Abigail Shaw, your sister loves you and worships you."

"I've never seen an altar dedicated to me."

Ignoring the truth and her humor, her mother *tsked*. "If you can't reach her and let her know she can do anything, no one can."

Cue the teenage disbelief. "Because I'm the model of ambition."

"If you wanted to be, you could. Ah, here's the dress area."

Her mother fell into the fluff monologue that required only an occasional nod and muttered response from Victoria about a dress's style. She digested what her mother had said.

Did Dessie look up to her? Could she talk sense into a Sybil carbon copy? Victoria knew nothing about dating, marriage, and the forever ball-and-chain. To initiate that conversation, she'd need to say "Olé" and dodge horns.

Sighing, Victoria focused on her mother. In the dressing room light, her mother still looked gorgeous. Dessie took after her.

Victoria realized her mother must date often. She might be able to offer some insight into her sticky situation with Ethan and Iggy. Even with all the dressing rooms empty, she couldn't broach the awkward conversation for advice. Instead, she asked a question that had plagued her since her teenage years. "Why did you really divorce Dad?"

Her mother stopped hanging dresses for Victoria to try on and then sighed out her tension. "Your father and I love each other. We never worked well together. I knew the moment we got married we'd made a mistake. Then you came along. I couldn't break up our family." She broke off as the attendant came bearing shoe boxes and then left.

"I was a mistake." The statement catapulted off her tongue as soon as they were alone.

"No. The breakup wasn't Robert's fault or either of you girls. I didn't know how to handle being a wife and mother. I was miserable." Her mother sunk onto the cushioned couch, watching her nails as she talked. "Finally, one day, I looked in the mirror and couldn't tell who the person was in the reflection. I was adrift. The next morning, I filed for divorce."

"Did leaving us fix you?" Victoria asked, surprised by how much heat and anger spewed out of her mouth.

Her mother looked up, her eyes clear and sharp. "No. No, it didn't. I still haven't signed up for those interior designing classes I desperately wanted to take all those years ago, and the reason I said I had to leave."

"You wanted to finish school?"

"Yes."

Never had Victoria guessed her mother wanted to be an interior designer. This piece of information made her childhood make sense. Like why the house would be rearranged every year or why her dad would bellyache about stubbing his toes, and yet, even after the divorce was final, he couldn't tolerate changing the house without his ex's help.

She sat down next to her mother. "Why haven't you pursued this dream?"

Her mother stood, brushing off her jacket and the subject. "Life is busy. Let's focus on something important, dress hunting."

After an eon, her mother and the salesclerk both agreed on a beaded, two-piece chiffon gown in a lovely emerald green for her. Twirling in the dress and checking her reflection, she struck a prim and proper pose. "I feel like Cinderella going to a ball. I'm actually kind of pretty."

"As long as I'm Jaq and not Gus, that fat mouse." Her mother tucked a strand of hair behind Victoria's ear and softened her tone. "You look stunning. You're going to wow Damien's family and your date on Wednesday."

"I better see if Ethan can go with me." Victoria hiked the dress up to her knees, dashing into the dressing room to text him.

Her mother followed. She watched Victoria dig for her cell. Her mother paused, her lips pursed to say something, and then gave her daughter a sad smile, shutting the dressing room door. "I'll be at the register, paying."

Victoria didn't know what her mother's hesitation was about. She shrugged and texted Ethan.

R u free Wed night? There's dancing involved

Uneasiness crept into her belly. Ethan seemed to check off what most women say they want in a man. What was her problem? She should've been down on her knees thanking the love gods he fell into her life.

Shoving her mental mess aside, Victoria undressed and shimmied into her jeans and blouse. After a final bobby pin to secure her hat in place, she headed out to her mother with her beautiful dress in hand. "Mind if I swing by the hat area? I don't have one to match this dress."

With one hand on her hip, her mother sent Victoria an exasperated mamma look. "Your hair is beautiful. Why don't you wear your hair down, without any distraction, for this dinner?"

"I love my hats. I saw a few new ones near the escalator downstairs." Victoria jutted her chin out. Her mother always brought out her inner defiant teen.

Conferring with her gold watch, her mother tapped the clock face. "If we don't leave in the next five minutes, you'll have to sit through the country club fundraiser committee, before I drop you to get a car."

Victoria swung the dress onto the counter so fast, she was surprised a bead didn't whip her across the cheek. "I wouldn't want you to be late." Those country club meetings stunk. Victoria would rather have lit her hair on fire than sit around with those pretentious cronies.

"Figured."

Dress paid for and her mother's car retrieved from the valet, her mother dropped Victoria off at the car rental agency. After a deposit and a signature, Victoria had wheels again. She zipped to work, which flew by, and she headed home.

Her phone rang. It was Ethan's ringtone. Pushing the accelerator to the mat, she prayed for no cops. Once she skidded into a parking spot, she dug into her purse and answered.

"Hello?"

"Dancing? I think I can be persuaded. Are both these events formal?"

A mixture of flutters and excitement bubbled up in her. "Dinner, yes, a tux is needed. Wedding, no, business casual is on the invites."

She waited. She would love to have him with her, but meeting her mother was a big deal.

"No problem, I have a tux from a wedding I was in. What time should I pick you up Wednesday?"

Her heart nearly passed out. She wouldn't have to face her family alone. "Pick me up at six."

"Sounds good. See you then."

"Can't wait."

They hung up.

Resting her head on the headrest, Victoria's stomach shifted, making her queasy. She'd only had crushes from afar, so this dating thing left her bewildered. Ethan was attractive, a good kisser, courteous and kind, yet between them, something was missing. Maybe Ethan's glazed eyes when she cracked science jokes made her prefer Iggy.

Life was easier without all these flying emotions and unruly thoughts. Her lips still remembered Ethan's kiss. Her skin still remembered him so deliciously close. The replay of their one kiss looped constantly.

Dragging herself out of the car and up the stairs, she realized that since Dessie's phone call announcing her wedding, Victoria's life had gone from basket-sized crazy to Hindenburg-sized madness.

She'd gone from never going out on a date to having dates every few days. Today, she had a possible boyfriend. A boyfriend. The thought made her dizzy and sounded so juvenile. A sad commentary to get to this point. Victoria, the woman who snagged her first boyfriend at twenty-five.

What if Ethan wanted this relationship to go further? How could she explain to him he was her first kiss? Let alone never having been...intimate before. She didn't want to think about this anymore and let her head bounce off her apartment door. How embarrassing would that be, to have to explain her virginhood?

Her apartment door opened from the inside.

She grabbed the door frame to keep upright and took in the devastation on the other side of the doorjamb.

Dessie's eyes were red and puffy. Her cell dangled from her hand. "The florist called. Their shop burned down. I have no flowers. What am I going to do? I have no flowers."

At this point, Dessie lost her mind. Her tiny sister put paid wailers to shame. Her arms flailed as if an overdramatic anime cartoon possessed her.

Victoria bit her tongue before she blurted out how not having flowers wasn't big a deal. Instead, she shook her crazed sister by the shoulders, shouting over her cries. "Pull yourself together. We can find you flowers."

The crazy storm subsided.

"How?" A delicate bud of hope blossomed.

Victoria wracked her brain for a way to keep Dessie sane, as well as herself sane and both of them out of orange jumpsuits because this situation teetered on the edge of a dramatic explosion. Then, a genius thought worthy of her dad dropped into her brain.

"Let me make some calls. By tomorrow afternoon I think I can produce some flower magic." Victoria steered the leaking bride-to-be to the couch and plopped her down. "I'll make you a cup of tea."

By the time the tea brewed, Dessie sat with her nose in her wedding scrapbook. She caressed the pages, like petting a puppy. "Tomorrow, Damien comes in. He needs his tux fitted. What are we going to do? You don't have a car I can borrow. I don't want to Uber or Lyft everywhere. I don't have flowers. This wedding is falling apart." Her voice was going near dog-sonic again.

Victoria wrapped Dessie's hand around a warm mug. "Borrow Mother's car. Pick up Damien. Show him the venue and get him fitted for his tux. Enjoy the afternoon together. I'll handle getting you your flowers."

Waving around her fistful of snot rags, Dessie sank into the couch. "Look at me, I'm a wreck. But I can always count on you to help. I know I can be difficult, so why are you always here for me?"

Victoria cupped her sister's face. "Because we're sisters and even though we aren't always good to each other, we're here for each other. Plus, if my children ever act like a horde of demons, I'm shipping them off to live with you. Devils deserve to be together."

Dessie gave her a weak and watery smile. "Thanks."

"That's what I'm here for. Besides flowers, are we good to go? When do we pick up the dresses?"

"The final fitting is on Friday, right before the bachelorette party. I booked a party bus." Dessie's energy had rebounded.

Victoria cringed. Bachelorette parties were comfort zone no-nos. Her comfort zone included a couch, movies, girlfriends, and booze. Her un-comfort zone was pounding music, bars, and guys. Disaster served straight up with a garnish of forced-to-go.

She hoped they didn't end up at a strip club. The thought of a stranger shaking his junk in her face made her cringe. If Victoria had to be that close to a man, then they had to be personal friends. As such, she'd feel compelled to invite him to the wedding.

"The bus will pick us up in front of the Hilton. We have it all night. We can party as hard as starlets, except no puking."

"Why is the bus picking us up at the Hilton?" Victoria asked.

"We have rooms at the Hilton for the weekend. The hotel is close to the Wind Song Gardens. I got a block of rooms for the entire family." She brightened as she talked about this weekend and the wedding.

Victoria opened her phone and tapped her note-taking app. "I think I know what I want to get you for a wedding gift."

Dessie perked up, reaching for Victoria's phone. "What'cha going to get me?"

Shielding her phone from Dessie's nosiness, Victoria said, "If you peek at my phone one more time without my permission, I will change my mind and get you a hideous gift."

Dessie's arms hung frozen in the air, like a puppet waiting for its strings to be tugged and pulled. "You wouldn't."

"Go ahead, read my notes. Then find out when you open my gift."

Calculating the threat and its repercussions, Dessie paused.

Victoria tossed the phone at her. "Don't you want to test my malevolent depths?"

She squeaked, ducked, and let the phone fly by. Once it landed, she hightailed her butt into the kitchen. "I'm not going to play your silly game."

Victoria clucked at her retreating sister.

TIP # 26
BEG, IF NEEDED

*L*ight filled Victoria's rental car the next day. She sat curbside at her dad's office after her early release from work, ready to pull off an Iggy heist. The passenger door creaked open and Iggy slid in.

Shivering as a gust of cool March air snaked in the car, she adjusted the heater. "Thanks for showing up."

Iggy buckled and blew on his coffee. "Sure. How can I help you with your sister's wedding?"

She pulled into traffic and wound her way to the freeway. "Your coffee smells great, what shop is it from?"

"A little place your father recommended down the street. Why do I get the feeling you're avoiding telling me what you need me for?"

Once on the freeway, where he couldn't bail without injury, she confessed. "Dessie's wedding is in five days and her florist's building burned down yesterday. I want you to take me to the florist shop you worked at."

Either the coffee was too hot or Iggy had exhaled coffee by the way he sputtered.

"You're hijacking me to go to pick out flowers?" He jiggled

the door handle.

Victoria had already locked him in and was hoarding control of the power locks. She slumped in her seat. "I'm desperate. All the other florists I called last night and this morning laughed at me. You're my last shot at this."

His nose flared. His jaw clamped tight.

"Iggy, please, as a favor to me, help me out." She loaded her voice with so much pity-me, she should have been a spokeswoman for an ASPCA ad.

The rage emissions from the passenger seat lessened. His mouth lost some of its rigid and righteous snarl. "For you, I'll help. Get on the I-10 and get off on Seventh Street," he said, though he was clearly helping under duress.

Victoria suppressed her happy dance.

The traffic was light. Off the freeway and in downtown Phoenix, a massive sign read "My Florist" with an arrow pointing to a blue building. In the windows, huge, beautiful arrangements sat on display. The opulence in the windows appeared odd next to the holey and crumbling sidewalks.

Victoria swung around the back for the parking, got out, and headed around the building to the front of the shop. Iggy begrudgingly exited the car and dragged his feet, grumbling about wishing he had a hat, too.

Bells chimed, announcing their arrival to the shop. Iggy's eyes dilated. His breathing became shallow. The noise rattled deep in his throat, akin to a blender dying.

He looked about ready to pass out or puke. In his ear, she whispered, "You can wait by the car, till I'm done."

Iggy perked up and vanished faster than a cookie in an orphanage.

She wondered what his problem was with this place. The shop sparkled with clean and tidy tables. Victoria had hoped she could have used Iggy as an in with the owners. But that wasn't going to happen.

A man in his late sixties sauntered up to her, wiping his hands on his green apron which read *Flowers are Manly*. "Can I help you, Miss?"

Instantly, Victoria liked him and handed him the crinkled carbon copy form from the previous order. "I hope you can. I have a wedding in five days and the previous florist burned down."

"You must be talking about Peacock Diamonds. I heard about the fire this morning. Come in and sit down. I'm the owner, Ted. I'll see what I can do to help."

A sense of ease loosened the tension in her stomach. He gave off the vibe of a trusted friend. "I can use all the help I can get."

A small worktable that doubled as a desk sat against the back wall. He led her there. He popped on his reading glasses, browsing through Dessie's original order.

He ran his hand over his scruffy cheek. "I can get the flowers in on the Saturday delivery. I wouldn't be able to get them arranged by Sunday."

"But you can get the flowers here by Saturday?" Her words were so hopeful that if she were a dog, she'd have been tap-dancing on the tile.

The owner scribbled on a blank order form. "If I order today, I guarantee a Saturday delivery. Are you going to put the flowers together then?"

Victoria whipped out her phone and texted Iggy. Maybe he would be useful after all.

He can get the flowers in by Sat. Will u help me Sat night put the flowers 2gether 4 the wedding?

Her phone chimed.

Yes if we can leave here all the quicker

She shook her head and wrote.

I'll b done in less than 10

The owner folded his hands over his belly and apron, watching her, and said, "The groom, I take it." His voice was warm with a knowing lift at the end.

Not a question. A statement. Yet she wore no ring.

Before Victoria could clear up the confusion, a woman's voice shouted, "Oh my god."

The owner jumped up. "What's wrong?"

From the rear of the store, a heavy door slammed shut, echoing throughout the whole building.

Victoria followed him into the work area to help with whatever disaster just struck. What greeted her was not what she imagined. A blonde woman stood next to the back door, crushing Iggy in a bear hug. The woman looked about Victoria's age. Thin, attractive, and cutting off Iggy's air supply.

To Victoria, Iggy mouthed, "Help me."

The owner stopped. His eyes locked on Iggy, who was locked in the blonde's arms. "Honey, why don't you leave the boy alone? Victor. I'm surprised to see you." His tone flickered dark and menacing. Gone was the sweet florist from the front of the shop.

Iggy waved awkwardly. "I'm with—"

The blonde dipped Iggy's head down, laying a big kiss on him.

If the owner could have reached the florist shears, Victoria didn't doubt she'd soon be looking at crime tape and news vans over Iggy's death.

The blonde finally released Iggy from the lip lock. "I'm glad you're here. Shall we bury our rocky past? We're older and wiser. I hope you still have my engagement ring. You never know what could happen." She turned and winked at the owner. "Daddy won't mind."

The owner, AKA Daddy, went purple. His blood pressure

must have soared. Victoria swore she could hear the veins exploding in the poor man's head.

The pieces clicked into place. Iggy had dated the owner's daughter, got burned by his boss, and Victoria got the ghost of girlfriends' past.

Victoria stepped into the owner's view. "Say hello to the lucky groom." The fib rolled out smooth and slick as duck feathers in the bath.

Everyone let the words linger in the silence. The blonde wobbled.

Iggy's whole body went slack, and then he puffed up, almost crowing or singing or heel-clicking. From cowering to strutting, he'd recovered at lightning speed.

The owner seemed relieved. His wrath evaporated. His shoulders drooped.

Realizing his moment of grace was upon him, Iggy slithered out of the blonde's hold and slid up next to Victoria. Acting like he belonged beside her, he looped an arm around her.

She ignored his heat seeping into her skin. His hands on her. She blocked all the rightness of these sensations.

Iggy was as happy as a cat with catnip and had the same stoned grin.

To both Iggy and the owner, Victoria said, "I knew there could be bad feelings between the two of you and I didn't want to cause any strife so I asked him to stay outside." Her explanation was logical and reasonable.

The owner awoke from his fog. "No, no bad feelings here. I'm glad you found such a thoughtful bride." He slapped Iggy on the back. "Congratulations, Victor."

The blonde made a croaking noise and scurried into the closest fridge to hide.

The owner regained his professionalism, steering them into

the front of the store. "I'll have the flowers in by four on Saturday. Swing on by then and they're all yours."

Victoria handed over the black card to pay the deposit and forged her sister's signature.

"Best of luck this weekend." The owner handed the final bill and order to Victoria.

Iggy linked hands with Victoria, smiling at her. "I've got all the luck I need right here."

HER HEART BLOOMED AND BLOSSOMED. His words sounded so authentic and so what every girl wanted to hear, that her eyes watered.

They walked outside still holding hands. Victoria waited till they rounded the corner, out of sight of the windows, before slipping her hand from his. She cradled her hand.

Iggy burst out laughing. "Your save was pure genius."

She already missed the feel of his hand in hers. Grumpy at the fact she'd had to lie and the confusion he caused, Victoria hurried toward her car. "I couldn't stand not helping you."

"Why? Because you liiiikke me?"

He would have been more mature if he just pulled on her hair.

"I didn't want to see you suffocate," Victoria said, her voice tight. She unlocked her door and slipped into the driver seat.

"Gee, thanks."

The blonde was the entire reason why she wouldn't risk dating him. There's always another woman who messed things up for her. First her sister and Garett and now this girlfriend relic. Victoria always got the shaft. Her insides were fizzier than a can of dropped soda.

Iggy slid into the seat and turned to Victoria. "You deserve the whole story. As I told you before, I dated the owner's daughter."

"I recall." She backed out and made her way onto the freeway, merging sharply.

"When she and I started dating she was already pregnant with her ex's child and started to pass the baby off as mine."

Victoria slowed down, jolted out of her pissy mood. "What the hell?"

Iggy shifted in his seat. "As soon as she told me about the baby, I did what I thought was right and I proposed. Then she miscarried and the truth came out that the baby wasn't mine and she had used me."

His story stole her words and her righteousness.

Silence answered him.

He squirmed. "I liked you and once I found out who your dad was, I had flashbacks of the stress and the lies and I panicked. Then you moved on, so I respected your choice."

Past tense. Her spirits sank. He no longer liked her. A sludge of confusion swamped her as she exited the freeway. "I appreciate you telling me this story and helping my sister with the flowers. I'll drop you at the office."

Neither one of them said anything else on the short car ride.

She parked her car curbside, right outside the front doors. Iggy hopped out and leaned down to look at her through his open door. "I'll bring the materials to your apartment Friday night."

"Won't be there. I'll be at the Hilton. I'll text you the room number." She stared straight forward, not knowing what she really felt. Not quite anger, not quite sadness. Maybe good old frustration at the unusual space she and Iggy always fell into when dealing with each other.

"Okay, see you then." Iggy closed the door, stepping away.

She slipped into the light afternoon traffic.

SANDRA'S SONG played from her purse. Slinging her purse into the front seat, Victoria snatched the singing phone and answered.

"I'm initiating the Crappy Day Protocol. I need a margarita, stat. Your place or mine?" Sandra asked.

"Yours. Mine could have Dessie and Damien there, doing god-knows-what."

"Drinks will be ready in an hour. Bring normal food. Screw kale or greens or my arteries."

"To-go food fix, can do." Victoria hit end.

After swinging by their favorite burger joint, she sat in Sandra's drive forty-five minutes later. Time to say sayonara to this day. She marched up to the entryway.

Sandra answered the door looking ragged, her hair disheveled. Her age lines had multiplied in the last few days. In the den, behind Sandra, a tornado had left a trail of destruction. The scene snapped Victoria out of her funk. Sandra liked to be neat, not OCD-neat, but the disaster zone inside surprised Victoria.

Victoria nodded at the mess. "What's with the sloppiness?"

Sandra snatched the food bag from her hands. "Work is killing me. My new baby boss told me on Monday that I needed to have a sales pitch presentation done by today at four p.m." She shoved a handful of fries into her mouth, retreating into her townhouse.

Closing the front door, Victoria brushed past Sandra. Her nose led her into the kitchen where already salted and poured margaritas awaited.

Sandra ate and followed. "I worked eighteen out of the last twenty-four hours to get the PowerPoint and handouts done. I handed the presentation to him at noon today as ordered and he scoffed." Fueled by hot righteousness, she tapped into a darker rage. "The boy-child boss chuckled at me."

Victoria's lizard brain flipped to flight mode. Screw fight. Someone laughed at Sandra. Victoria should run as fast as her chubby legs could carry her.

Sandra plowed on, dropping the to-go bag on the island between them and pulling out the containers. "My boss informed me after his laugh that the meeting got canceled yesterday afternoon and he forgot to tell me."

"You put the kid in the hospital, didn't you?" Maybe Victoria should call the hospital and tell them to assign more guards to his room because Sandra had her jaw set to reaper wrath.

"I didn't beat the little tick. I'm not violent."

Victoria guzzled her sweet and salty alcohol and licked her lips. "Remember the time that girl in gym class called you a dyke?"

"She deserved the whipping."

"No argument. Prom pictures that year immortalized your anger."

Sandra grabbed her margarita, sipped it, and did her best impression of cat disdain. "Ancient history. Anyway, I didn't hit the pubescent pimply teenager." She let her fury fall away, smiling. Not a greeter smile. A grin that concealed poison.

Victoria shivered, shying away from the psychopath. "What did you do, Sandra?"

"Nothing, though I was tempted to tell the vice president about my baby boss's two-hour-long lunches with the VP's personal secretary."

Nearly snorting up tequila through her nose, Victoria coughed. "The secretary? The one the VP is having an affair with?"

"Absolutely. And the big boss man would not be happy." Sandra licked the salt clean from the rim.

"Diabolical."

Over the halo of salt and margaritas, Sandra's features hardened into a sadistic glint. "I would say a genius plan. But I'm not going to implement it yet. For now, I will watch and wait, because the little brownnoser will screw up and get taken down by the guys at the top if he continues to be so sloppy."

"Look at you, resisting the urge to wreak havoc. Congrats on growing up." Victoria reached for the pitcher and sloshed out the last of the margaritas into her already empty glass.

In an instant, Sandra went from plotting to concerned, studying Victoria. "You never drink this much, this fast. What's wrong?"

A tangy swallow of the icy drink tore up Victoria's throat. "Nothing."

Sandra checked the clock and leaned closer to Victoria, pinning her glass to the counter. "Liar. It's three and you're drinking hard. What happened? Tell me before you draw an IV for the tequila."

Victoria pushed her drink away, disgusted. "My drinking problem number one is Iggy and number two is Ethan. I don't know what to do or think about either." Her words, emotions, and spirits were low.

"Iggy? I thought he was out of the picture because of your dad?"

"He was. He is, still. I guess." Her head dropped into her hands. "I have these swirling feelings for Iggy, who is hot and cold. Yet after he told me about his dating past, I can understand why he freaked out on me. And then there's Ethan. He's everything I say I want: nice, sweet, kind, comfortable, a good kisser, and I can talk to him."

"I hear a 'but' about to pop up," Sandra said, using her soothing tone.

With no way to suppress the sigh, Victoria exhaled a long

huff. "But I can't imagine Ethan and me together as a couple. It is easy to see us hanging out, drinking beers, and dancing. Especially dancing. Any woman wouldn't miss a chance to be in his arms."

Sandra nodded and poked Victoria's hand with her finger. "How do you feel when Ethan kisses you? Or gazes at you? Or slips his arms around you?"

She tilted her head back, visualizing those moments. "I'm nervous because I'm the center of his attention. I'm afraid what he sees in me is in his imagination. I know, I sound silly." Emotion threatened to turn her into a crying, insecure fountain.

Coming around the counter, Sandra wrapped her friend in a big hug before the tears hit the granite. "No, you're not silly. Everyone has those thoughts. We all feel insecure and vulnerable."

"Really?"

Sandra gave her an extra love squeeze. "Dating's an emotional roller coaster, scary and exhilarating, all at the same crappy time."

Victoria dammed up her tear ducts and corked her anxiety. "Thanks. Now, let's banish this self-pity talk. Do you have your pink dress all picked out?"

She chugged her drink. "I have outdone myself this time. Even bought a pair of stilts to match."

"You're going to be a sight at the wedding. Are you bringing a date?"

"I figured I'd go stag, like you." Sandra headed toward her bedroom.

Victoria's whole body flushed. Her feet took root on the kitchen floor. "There's been a change."

"You're not going by yourself? Who are you going with, Iggy or Ethan?"

"Ethan."

"Why am I finding out about this now?"

Victoria stalled. How Dessie treated her was a massive sour subject with Sandra. She glanced at her best friend and knew in her bones that Sandra wasn't going to understand. "I apparently asked him."

"Apparently?" She whipped around and started across the room to Victoria. "Explain."

"Well, Dessie did the asking for me using my phone. Posing as me."

Sandra's face had question marks popping up everywhere. "Dessie. Helped you. Why?"

Preparing mentally for the backlash, Victoria took a deep breath. "Dessie set me up so her bridal party table would have an even seating arrangement at the reception."

Then Sandra became the quiet-before-the-ape-shit storm. Hands balled, head cocked for maximum attitude, Sandra seethed. "Your sister is a pompous—"

Victoria raised her hands. "It's fine."

"No, my new skinny ass is fine. You aren't going to stop this?" She dropped her ire and searched Victoria's eyes.

"No, I think Ethan taking me is for the best. My family will see I'm not a worthless spinster." The last word nearly made Victoria choke.

"I'm sorry. What did you say, Millie? I thought I was talking to Victoria."

Guilt assailed Victoria, she sounded exactly like her mother. "I know."

"What about your feelings for Iggy? What about telling your family you don't need a man? What about going alone to be yourself?"

Victoria felt every question hit her, darts into her heart. "I don't feel strong enough to be on my own for the wedding and give the bird to my family like you would."

Slumping her shoulders forward, Sandra shook her head in a gentle back and forth motion. "You should wear a chicken suit as your bridesmaid dress then."

"*Cluck, cluck.*" Victoria shoved the doubt and self-loathing down and away. "I'll deal with all that after the wedding. How about you show me your hot pink dress?"

*V*ictoria woke to an anvil ringing in her head at Sandra's, which made surviving work a lesson in willpower. As she was locking up for the night, Ethan texted to verify the details for the in-law dinner, and it doubled down on Victoria's queasiness. She had never brought a guy home to meet the family and now one would be ringside to view her family's crazy circus.

The dinner started in two hours. She had ninety minutes to get herself presentable. Hair, the bane of her existence, was first. She pulled out all her dusty beauty torture devices. Her hair ended up in a simple twist and a few spiral curls, softening her square jawline. She continued her preparation and, with ten minutes till Ethan's arrival, Victoria scrutinized her reflection. She looked slightly better than her normal.

A text from Iggy blinked on her phone. She ignored the message. Whenever her thoughts landed on that gorgeous and prickly guy, a whirlwind of confusion swallowed her. She liked him, yet his statement of how he "liked her" told her to not look back, to close the door on him.

There was a knock on her door. Ethan must be early.

Opening the door, Victoria said, "You're optimistic and lucky that I'm ready."

Blinking at her was Iggy, carrying a vase with purple roses.

Shock rippled through her. The man she didn't want to think about had shown up.

Iggy shook himself and thrust the bouquet to her. "I didn't mean to interrupt. I wanted to bring these over and apologize for not explaining to you better about my past."

He shifted his weight from foot to foot.

She took the flowers. "Come in, I'll put these in some water." She walked away with the flowers yet kept him in her view. "Should I add an aspirin to the water? I read somewhere it helps the flowers last longer."

He stepped inside, closing the door behind him. "Yes, that's right."

Victoria blew dust off a vase and filled it with water.

Ralph let off a tiny yawl of a meow, twitching his tail at Iggy.

He reached down and scratched behind the cat's ears. "What a tiny meow from such a big fellow."

She stepped out of the kitchen to put the vase on the table when Ralph darted in front of her. She squeaked, wobbling.

Iggy caught her and gently helped her onto her heels.

The heat from his touch zapped through the silky fabric. Didn't she know any better than to let him touch her? When he did, the world shrank, leaving her bespelled.

He was close. Too close. The air burned up between them.

His minty exhale brushed her cheek. "Are you OK?"

She licked her suddenly dry lips. "Yes, I'm fine."

The lie blistered her tongue. Victoria presented herself as being fine. Inside though, a whirlwind of emotions and feelings battered her. An overwhelming urge to taste his lips gripped her. Just once, she wanted to see what would happen between them. One simple kiss.

Maybe everything she needed to know could be answered in comparison kissing. Anticipation built in her stomach, hot and heavy.

Her heart pulsed in her throat. There was only one way to find out. Victoria giggled nervously. His hand still burned her skin.

Gliding his fingers down her arms, he broke the spell, releasing her. "I better go before your date gets here."

"Right," Victoria whispered.

He headed for the door and stepped over the threshold.

She watched him leave, a lump, most likely her heart, clogging her windpipe. "Thank you for the flowers. How did you know purple Sterling roses are my favorite?"

Dragging the door closed, Iggy didn't glance backward. "I didn't. But they reminded me of you. They're beautiful, elegant, and sweet. Good night."

Victoria's heart compressed into the size of a flea. The whole encounter left her more confused than ever. She must have been the only one who felt the attraction.

After a few minutes of circular and unhelpful pondering, another knock pulled her out of her stupor. Straightening her dress and taking a moment to calm her heart rate, she opened the door again.

Nothing could have prepared her for Ethan's boyish charm being morphed into GQ good looks with his sharp white tux, red tie, and black slacks.

Ethan assessed her from the top of her hatless head to her sparkly shoes. "You're stunning, Victoria."

The warmth in his words sank into her heart and curled up like a sleeping and content kitten. She ducked to hide her nervousness. "Thank you. You cut a dapper figure yourself. I'm going to have to fight off the other women there tonight."

Then the easiness they always had around each other crept

in, the iron bands around her chest loosening. It's crazy how Ethan soothed her with only his presence.

He held his elbow out for her. "Ready to stop traffic?"

She threaded her arm in his. "Yes."

She locked up and he drove. They arrived at the restaurant fifteen minutes before the reservation. Pacing alone in the lobby, Victoria's dad looked sad. His normal attire of wrinkled polos or free convention shirts had given way to a formal tux.

Victoria waved him over to them. "Daddy, you're as hand-some as ever. You remember Ethan, he helped me pick up Dessie after the car accident. Ethan, my dad, Robert."

They shook hands.

She hadn't realized how much it had bothered her to have never introduced a boyfriend to her family until the two guys mingled, date-to-dad.

The maître d' signaled them over. His nose stuck up in the air, and his posture and expression dripped with judgment at anyone within sneering range. "Please follow me. We are ready to seat the Volpé-Shaw party."

Once at the table, all three men moved to pull back her chair. Ethan beat them all, pushing her seat in for her. Her dad beamed his parental approval smile.

Her dad sat to Victoria's right and Ethan to her left at a table large enough to seat twenty in a cavernous, secluded room.

Her dad straightened his silverware. The metal clinked and clanged.

Squeezing her dad's hand, Victoria smiled at him. "You'll do fine, Daddy."

He squeezed back, nodding.

The room's view of the valley was astonishing. The sun slid down toward the horizon, creating a painted sky. Deep crimson, oranges, and pinks bounced off the scattered clouds, making the kaleidoscope sky breathtaking.

Ethan tugged his jacket sleeve over his watch. "This could be a very small party."

"Both my sister and mother run late." She reached for her purse.

Ethan stopped her. "No fixing others tonight. They can manage being late all on their own."

Before she could respond, the maître d' arrived with a group of people in tow. Ethan and her dad stood immediately. Victoria rose to greet her new extended family.

Maria, Dessie's mother-in-law-to-be, was draped on the arm of a smartly dressed older man. She had squeezed herself into a gold sequined dress, the cut and color of which Victoria would have expected on a twenty-something, not on a woman whose son was saying "I do" in a few days.

The only other person she slightly recognized was Dessie. Normally, Victoria would describe her sister's makeup as slight and tasteful. Not tonight. If a circus clown and a Mexican soap opera star bred, their offspring would've worn that shellac.

Dessie hung on what looked like an Italian mobster's arm, his jaw square. His shoulders were broad. This must be Victoria's new brother-in-law. Damien oozed testosterone.

The Volpés sat as far away from Victoria and her father as possible. The maître d' had to help Dessie into her seat. Victoria noticed Maria seated herself. Bad manners ran in the family. Minus twenty points to the groom.

The bride-to-be didn't acknowledge her guests or introduce any of her in-laws. Uncomfortable moments stretched out, and yet no one reached across the canyon of white linen to say anything.

Victoria decided to play nice. She waved. "Hi, I'm Victoria. I'm Dessie's sister. This is our dad, Robert, and my date, Ethan."

After a moment of stubborn silence, Dessie began the introductions on her side of the round table. "This lovely lady is my soon-to-be mother-in-law, Maria, and here's her husband of thirty-four years, Estevan." She leaned toward the lumbering man at her side. "And the gorgeous man right here is my wonderful Damien."

The bride and groom shared a charged look. Victoria had seen less combustive fireworks in finale displays. Damien whispered in his bride's ear, and she pivoted into his coat, blushing.

Victoria couldn't tell if the movement and expression were from embarrassment or shame.

Damien took over and finished the introductions. "This is my Nana. She's from Italy and doesn't speak much English. Then there is my business partner and his wife. My little sister couldn't join us tonight."

Victoria could see her mother coming, weaving her way through the tables. Then again, even the blind could have sensed her mother in the outfit she'd chosen, a red-and-gold beaded and sequined dress with a slit up past her knee. Between the dress and the Jane Fonda hair, she should've looked perfectly ridiculous, and yet she looked fantastic.

Striking a pose at the apex of the room, her mother waited for a beat and then approached the divided table. "Esmeralda, my darling, you look marvelous."

They kissed each other's cheeks.

"You must be my new son-in-law, you fine specimen of a man." Her mother gestured to Damien to rise.

He moved with sulky teen jerkiness to stand for inspection. Her mother shuffled around him like he was a bachelor about to be auctioned off. "Welcome to the family, Damien." She threw her arms open wide and captured Damien in a hug.

"Nice to meet you," he said, his voice only slightly warmer than the Arctic.

"Be kind enough to introduce me to the rest of your family." Her mother waited with her arm looped through Damien's.

Snared in her web, Damien begrudgingly walked her down the table introducing everyone to her.

Ethan leaned into Victoria's side with his arm draped around the back of her chair. "The introduction reminds me of reality TV, without the commercials."

She laughed, turning toward him.

The room stilled, their mouths a kiss away.

Her mother shoved her face between them. "And you must be Ethan. Be good to my Victoria, she's all I have left now."

Only his eyes shifted to her mother. "Have no fear, Ms. Shaw, I will."

She patted Ethan's cheek, dismissing them, and loomed over her ex.

Her dad jumped up and glided her chair out for her. "You're radiant as usual."

Her mother let loose a throaty giggle. "You old goat, you're such a closet charmer."

By almost seven o'clock, everyone had arrived. Even their war horse uncle, Uncle Aggie, showed up with his back straight in a finely pressed suit. As a retired military officer, he seemed lost without his troops. His body tense, he sat on the edge of his seat, and he constantly surveyed the exits like he expected a terrorist attack or the need to get civilians to safety. Victoria chalked his behavior up to too many years of being a soldier.

Victoria smiled around Ethan at her Uncle Aggie, her favorite Alburga family member. "I'm glad you came."

Her uncle brushed his shoulders to evict nonexistent lint and with a brisk tone, said, "Your mother called me an hour ago and told me I had better show up or else."

Victoria could have sworn the old warrior cringed. She reached across Ethan, patting her uncle's arm. "Good call. No reason to have her vengeance pointed at you in her stressed condition."

Sagely nodding, he continued scanning the crowd of wealthy patrons for trouble.

The first course, soup, came out. Victoria's saliva gland kicked in and her stomach begged. She was very hungry and loved soup.

Sadly, what this place called soup was a cold, pink liquid pureed with no identifiable food in the bowl. Victoria picked up her spoon and took the prescribed thank-you-no-thank-you sip. The flavor was sour. She flagged the waiter over and asked for the wine list.

Ethan sipped the soup, managing to gag it down. "Do you think Damien is Catholic? Because I think this recipe is from the Inquisition."

"Do you think they're trying to scare us away with the horrible food?"

"Maybe."

The next course of tiny proportions replaced the cold pond-scum bowls and was followed by boring and bland entrees and salads.

This dinner party seemed funeralistic with so many people in all black and no one talking over a whisper. The only things necessary to make it a real ceremony for the dead were a body and wailing. The Volpés had closed in on themselves, drawing Dessie away with them.

The only time anyone could speak with Dessie was if they walked over, stood beside her chair, and ignored the hostile glares from the rest of the Volpé clan. With their beady eyes, the family watched, staying silent until the interloper slunk back to their designated space.

Nice, friendly bunch Dessie was marrying into.

Victoria checked on Dessie. Her lips held a bright smile. Her eyes were uneasy and timid. Victoria excused herself to go investigate her suddenly demure sister. Ethan and her dad stood.

Such mannered men made a woman feel respected and important.

Slipping around the table, Victoria tapped her sister on the shoulder. "Can I borrow you for a moment to show me where the restroom is?"

Dessie stole a peek at her fiancé. He waved his hand in her direction, dismissing her. He continued with his discussion, undisturbed. She pushed her chair back un-helped and unnoticed.

Unmannered ape. Victoria forced her anger down into her belly and away from her right hook.

Without a word, Dessie led the way.

Once outside of the ballroom, Victoria let her plastic, happy expression fade. "Earth to sister clone. That's your wonderful he-who-doesn't-fart fiancé?" Her volume ratcheted up.

Her sister whipped her head around, hissing, "Keep it down."

Victoria dragged Dessie into the bathroom and plopped her sister down on the couch. "Do you actually want to marry that uncouth Neanderthal?"

TIP # 28
HOPE SPRINGS ETERNAL

*T*he bathroom was deserted. Dessie's eyes wouldn't raise off her left hand, her engagement ring, her albatross. "I love him."

The couch dipped and squeaked, commenting on Victoria's weight, as she sat next to her sister. Covering her sister's ring with her hand, she said, "I love you. I want the man of your dreams to love you. For Damien, you're a hood ornament."

Dessie's head bolted up and she stared, squawking her protest.

Victoria held her hands up, overriding the bride-to-be's defense. "If you think he is your forever man, I'll support you. If you're marrying him because he asked you, make sure you want to wake up beside him for the rest of your life."

Her sister calmed down, backed down, and squeezed Victoria's hand. "I love him, I will marry him in four days, and thank you for supporting me."

"I'm here for you, husband or no husband." Victoria tugged on her sister's hair like she used to when they were little.

Dessie went to the mirror and touched up her makeup before they headed back. At the table, the waitstaff served desserts and after-dinner drinks. Dessie rejoined Damien. The groom did not even acknowledge Dessie's return and stayed engrossed in conversation with his business partner and father.

Victoria's eyes narrowed. Arrogant man. Ethan held her chair out for her to sit, then continued his chat with her Uncle Aggie.

Fresh vanilla ice cream with touches of cinnamon and pecans waited for her. She snarfed her serving down, decorum be damned. Dinner had been toddler's portions. With her bowl empty and spoon in hand, she longed for Ethan's scoop. He was deep in sports talk with her uncle.

With his right hand, Ethan nudged his ice cream toward her. Beaming, she took him up on his unspoken offer. Thirty-five points to him.

Swapping out dishes, she dug into his portion.

Her mother caught her eye, shaking her head. "Remember, you have to fit into the maid-of-honor dress."

Ethan broke off his discussion abruptly, dipped his own spoon into the dessert, and held it out for her. "You're always welcome to my dessert." Around her, people might have been judging her. She wouldn't know. Her eyes stayed locked onto Ethan's.

She took the offered bite.

He leaned in so only she could hear, his voice practically purring, saying, "There are always ways to work off those rascal calories."

Her body immediately flushed, and she almost choked on the ice cream.

He tapped her nose and smirked knowingly. "Finish it up or no more dancing for you."

Her temperature rocketed as she nodded and ate a spoonful. He'd stood up to her pushy mother. Infinity-plus-one points to him. She finished his dessert and collected her prize.

Ethan escorted her to the dance floor.

They waltzed and Ethan swayed gracefully while keeping perfect time.

The song ended. With his left hand on the small of her back, they walked over to the conductor. His warm touch transmitted tingles through her dress. Ethan tipped the conductor, thanking him for the song.

Tipping the musicians, ten points to Ethan. How could he still be single?

The conductor bowed. "Any favorite songs we could play for you?"

Ethan gave Victoria a smoky appraisal. "How about 'At Last'?"

Heat rose to her cheeks. Another ton of points for him. Maybe she should stop counting.

"Excellent choice, sir." The conductor struck up the song. Ethan's slipped his hands around her, locking her in his embrace.

Under the spell of him, everyone but the orchestra disappeared. The crowd and noise and her worries dissolved into oblivion.

The way he controlled her wasn't possessive. Yet he communicated to her that at this moment, she was everything to him. Led by his focus and skill, she moved like she never knew her heavy body could move—twirling, spinning, and floating across the wooden floor.

The music ended and the room sank into deafening quiet. Plastered against his hard body, both of their breaths were slightly labored.

Then around them, the rest of the dancers clapped, startling Victoria and Ethan. A large open space surrounded them. They must have commandeered the area while dancing. They stepped away from each other, joining the applause for the orchestra.

Victoria fanned herself. "I think I need some water."

"Me too."

With his arm wrapped around her waist, they walked hip-to-hip towards the table. A feeling of contentment flooded her. He felt good. He made her feel good.

Once again with both families, the party vibe appeared more relaxed. People milled around mingling. Except for Dessie and Damien.

Dessie looked chained to her man's arm. Victoria and Ethan passed by the couple as the bride-to-be gave Damien her patient, under-the-eyelashes plea. "Take me out on the dance floor. It looks fun."

Damien shifted his arm under her touch. "Maybe after I finish this discussion." His "maybe" meant a solid no and his patronizing tone sounded more like an overworked parent dealing with a child than a young and loving groom.

Ethan stopped by Dessie and offered his hand, palm up, to the bride-to-be. "It would be my honor to twirl you around the floor until he finishes his discussion." His tone was pleasant, though he sent the groom a man-up sneer.

Dessie grinned.

Damien brooded. By the hard lines around his eyes and mouth, he seemed to understand that there was no tactful way not to allow Dessie to dance with another man except to take his bride out there himself.

Nostrils flaring, he pivoted to his business partner. "Excuse me for a moment, I have a dance card which is suddenly full."

Huffing, he marched down to the pit, snapped his fingers at the conductor, and talked a moment with him. The conductor nodded and flicked his baton on his music stand.

Out came a slow, dry Bavarian Waltz.

Damien lugged Dessie around the polished floor until the last painful note played, then whisked his uncoordinated bride back to his party. The groom deposited Dessie next to Victoria. "I hope you're satisfied. I have some business to finish."

He twirled on his heel, marched across the room, and reinserted himself into where he'd left off speaking with everyone. Everyone but Dessie.

Dessie forced her cheeks upward into a smile. A dam smile, since the fake grin was the only thing keeping the waterworks at bay.

Victoria wrapped her sister in a side hug. "Jerk." The single word rocketed out of her mouth.

"No, I disappointed him. I've never done any fancy dancing." Dessie's misery was evident in her stooped shoulders.

"You could never stand to dance with Dad." She squeezed Dessie's waist.

Ethan's smile ratcheted up to dazzling and he sighted it on Dessie. "How about tomorrow I teach you to dance? I can show you a few basic moves."

Dessie snuck a glance at Damien. Ethan stepped in to block her view of her groom. "Let the lessons be my wedding present to you. I want you to feel confident during your first dance as husband and wife."

Brightening, Dessie perked up like a raccoon hearing a trash can rolling to the curb. "I could surprise him on our wedding day. Thank you, I love the idea." Dessie squealed, hugging Ethan.

Over their fancy, colorful drinks, a few of the in-laws shot them righteous glares.

Slipping her arm through Ethan's, Victoria claimed her date and tugged him to their seats. "The natives are getting ideas. Maybe we should call it a night."

"How about I treat you to the best food money can get at a drive-thru?"

"I thought you'd never ask."

He led her around the room for an obligatory goodbye round. They were about to slip out the door when "Over the Rainbow" filled the air and as expected, her dad and mother twirled on the dance floor.

"Wow, your parents can move." Ethan stopped and watched the pair gliding in sync, laughing.

Her heart lightened watching her parents acting like smitten teenagers or newlyweds or anything but exes. "Who do you think taught me how to dance?"

Outside, waiting for the valet, Ethan let the quiet of the crickets settle around them. "I thought your parents were divorced."

Having heard this a million times, she tilted her head back to study the faint stars. "They are and unexpectedly madly in love with each other. My dad wears his wedding band and my mother calls him first if something important happens."

He took his keys from the valet, tipped him, and opened Victoria's door for her. "But they won't get remarried?"

"No, they say they love their freedom."

They got in his car, hit the drive-thru for food, and headed to Victoria's apartment since she lived closest, and ate there.

Hunger sated, they stepped into the kitchen to clean up when Ethan put his hands on either side of her on the counter, caging her in at the sink.

Victoria's brain reminded her that they were alone. In her apartment. Panic rose, making her heart race. She wasn't ready for intimacy yet.

"It was lovely to have you in my arms tonight." His words purred across her skin.

Not knowing where to look, she gazed over his shoulder at the microwave time. It's ten-fifty. Her mind frantically searched for something to say, and she babbled, "That was very nice of you to offer to help my sister out."

He moved his hands from the counter, resting them on her hips. "I thought my offer could help ease her nervousness about the wedding."

"It will be one less thing for her to worry about." Her voice wasn't squeaky or panicky like she would have imagined.

He slipped his hands to her lower back, shrinking the space between them. "Also, teaching her means I have an excuse to get you in my arms again."

"I'm coming?" The smell coming off him was musky, clean, and inviting.

Ethan tapped her nose lightly. "Don't be silly. An engaged girl dancing with a random man would be improper."

Her synapses malfunctioned. Nothing could tear her riveted gaze from his lips.

A deep laugh finally snapped her out of her hormone daze. His dark chocolate chuckle slid over her skin in a sweet and dangerous caress. "I lost you for a moment."

"Sorry?" Her cheeks burned.

"What's happening in your beautiful brain?" He brushed his chest against her body.

Nothing. She had nothing. No idea what to say, no idea what to do, besides melting.

"Maybe this was what you were preoccupied with." Ethan swooped in and kissed her, tenderly and gently.

Victoria leaned into him and the kiss. Then she had the strangest sense of being glared at, her primitive brain screamed a warning.

Ethan's body tensed, too.

Breaking off the kiss, she twisted around to find Dessie gaping at them. Her body radiated rage.

Victoria slipped out of his arms, taking a step towards her sister. "Is everything alright?"

"Everything's fine." Dessie hit every consonant hard. Her tone clipped.

How she said 'fine' sounded like she had swallowed tacks on purpose. Dessie could have sparked a fire with the pit-of-hell gaze she threw at the two of them before she stormed to her room.

The kissing mood died. Something happened to Dessie after they left the party. Sighing the deep sigh of a Cinderella who needed to tend to her stepsister immediately, Victoria glanced at Ethan. "I guess I should walk you out."

"I can find my way out. Go. Be with your sister." He kissed her cheek and left.

GRABBING a beer and locking up behind Ethan, Victoria swallowed her discomfort and knocked on her sister's door, never knowing which Dessie would answer—Jekyll or Hyde. No noise came from the other side.

"Dessie? You alright?" She bumped the door open further.

A lump hid under the blanket. Throwing the door open all the way, Victoria sat on the edge of the bed and folded the comforter back, exposing her sister. "Want a beer to cheer you up?"

Dessie burrowed her face into her pillow. "Got any ice cream?"

If her sister asked for calories, then Dessie's troubles were serious.

"How about a scoop of cookies and cream topped off with homemade whipped cream?" Victoria knew her sister's calorie weaknesses and wasn't afraid to leverage them.

Tentatively, Dessie peeked up at Victoria. "You're offering me ambrosia."

Good to her word, a few minutes later Victoria had them set up for a sugar download. The sisters sat stretched out on the couches with ice cream, gobs of whipped cream, and a double helping of cherries on top.

They ate in silence for a few moments until Dessie broke the silence. "You don't like Damien, do you?"

Her hair hid her expression and a tang of desperation hung in the air.

Crap. Victoria dodged the question about liking or not liking Damien and instead asked, "Do you love him?"

Dessie pushed the lumps of cookies around with her spoon. "I think I do. But how does anyone know if they're in love for real?"

It was Victoria's turn to drive the cold lumps around her bowl. "Don't ask me. You have more experience being with men than I do."

"Men may want me, but I don't know if they like me for me. Everyone likes you though and you don't even have to try."

Sitting up and taking a sharp, assessing look at her sister, who suddenly complimented her, she frowned. "What are you talking about?"

Dessie stopped shoveling ice cream. "Don't you know why I stopped bringing my boyfriends home to meet the family unless I believed the relationship could get serious?"

"No." It wasn't the fact that Victoria would deliberately call Dessie's newest boytoy by the last one's name if she knew it?

"You're the nice, stable sister. The one everyone depends on. If anyone needs something, you always help," Dessie said.

Her sister had just complimented her twice. Victoria thought she might be feverish from fast-food poisoning. This whole discussion could be a delusion.

Dessie set the bowl down and hung her head in her hands.

"No one calls me unless they want a dumb blonde to be at their party. Everyone disapproves of me and judges me."

Scooting closer on the couch, Victoria placed a hand on her sister's shoulder. "Screw everyone else. Who do you want to be? Because you can be anyone."

She gave a dainty, indignant snort. "No one can change that easily."

"True. But once you have a vision in your head of who that is, it will be easier."

Dessie continued to count the carpet threads.

"If Damien loves you, then he'll love you no matter what minor changes you go through. Because underneath all the outer beauty and inner turmoil, you're wonderful, bright you."

Her sister glanced up, tucking her ice cream bowl into her arm. "Thanks. Even if you sound like a Hallmark movie, that's nice of you to say." Standing, Dessie went and dumped her bowl in the sink and moped off into her room.

Alone, Victoria fidgeted and stewed, thinking about men.

Being with Ethan felt great. He tried to help her sister and had charmed everyone throughout the dull dinner. His kiss felt unexpected, exciting, and wrong, and Victoria had no idea why her gut and brain couldn't quit nitpicking her and Ethan's relationship.

As for her sister's groom, Damien had brute written all over him. Dessie needed to make her own decisions. All Victoria could do was help break Dessie's fall. Families stayed together and helped each other when things fell apart. The Alburgas fixed each other to hide the family flaws. The Shaws fixed each other to bolster the whole family up. As much as Victoria's homicidal tendencies cropped up concerning her family, she'd still superglue her sister's shattered heart back together.

TIP # 29

HEARTS ARE WILD, HENCE RIB CAGES

*V*ictoria arrived home from work on Thursday a scant five minutes before Ethan was to arrive. Dessie lounged on the couch in spandex pants and a tank top. She could have been posing for a magazine ad. Victoria bolted to her room where she donned yoga pants and a tank top. Coming back into the living room, she said, "Help me move the couches so we'll have room to dance."

They pushed, pulled, and kicked the furniture against the wall. The doorbell rang.

Victoria shoved a strand of rogue hair behind her ear and opened the door.

Glancing down at his Dockers and wingtips, Ethan smiled. "I'm overdressed."

"No worries." She tugged him inside.

"We'll just need to plug in my phone for the music."

Victoria pointed to the cherrywood entertainment center. "There is a docking station by the TV."

He hooked the player in, and a waltz rolled out of her speakers.

Ethan gestured for Dessie to join him. "Let's begin with the basics. The waltz is a classic. Now follow my lead."

Victoria's heart tanked. No, she didn't feel jealous. Nope. Not her. Not even a little. She crossed her arms, not sulking.

The first dance should have been hers purely to demonstrate. Yes, purely as a demonstration for her unskilled baby sister to learn from. The younger sister, who never wanted to dance with Dad or learn from him. Today though, she appeared plenty eager to learn from Ethan.

Her petite sister stepped into the circle of Ethan's arms, dropping her head to concentrate on Ethan's shiny shoes.

A tiny smirk popped up on Victoria's lips. Mistake number one.

He gently rocked, transferring his weight from one foot to the other, moving with the tempo. "Close your eyes. Can you feel me swaying to the beat?"

Eyes shut, Dessie swayed with him. "Sure, I'm holding onto you."

Ethan put his wingtip out, stepping toward her in slow motion. Dessie registered his body shifting and moved backward. Ethan grinned, prouder than a parent witnessing a baby's first steps. Again, he stepped forward. Dessie mirrored him, stepping back.

"Good. Now open your eyes and watch mine." Ethan raised his chin, reminding her to stay with him, and slowly, in half-time, they waltzed. Dessie tilted her head up, eyes locked on her dance partner. Her willowy body drifted gracefully across the floor.

Victoria's stomach cramped. The song ended.

Ethan dropped his arms. "I'll dance with Victoria next, that way you can see variations of the waltz. Tell me which one you want to learn. I don't want to overwhelm you with all the different moves three days before your wedding."

Dessie grabbed her water bottle and hydrated.

Victoria sauntered over to him as he cued up the next song. Her heart felt light. He chose her.

"Here we go." He raised his arms, waiting for her to step into his hold.

She placed her hand in his. Victoria wasn't judging her worth on a scale of his attention, but inside the circle of his arms and affection, she felt adored.

Ethan placed his hand on the small of her back, claiming her as his, and took the first step.

Her heart beat faster. Time stopped.

They had only the music and each other. He changed directions, varying his dance style. With ease, Victoria matched him step-for-step.

By the end of the song, they had demonstrated four different styles. Snug next to each other and in the perfect position to share a kiss, a cartoon-style air raid siren wailed. The tender moment shattered.

"My work's calling, I have to take it." Victoria rushed to her phone.

Resetting the music, Ethan waved to Dessie. "You're up again."

Victoria grabbed her cell, slipping outside. "Hello."

"I'm calling from Property Alert. Is this Victoria Shaw?" a woman asked.

"This is she."

"We could not reach the initial contact person for the business Noah's Haven. We're calling you as the designated backup contact. An internal alarm has been tripped. Can you provide the safe code for verification?"

"Fluffy face." Victoria could hear the woman's hard keystrokes.

"Thank you. That matches what's in our records. Are you aware of anyone currently occupying the building?"

Victoria leaned on the cool metal railing. "No, I was the last one to leave."

"There were no external sensors triggered. Would you like to cancel the police that are being dispatched to the address and turn off the alarm?"

"Yes. An animal must have Houdini-ed, triggering the alarm."

The woman kept typing. "Thank you. We have disarmed the alarm and have canceled the dispatch request for the police. Do you have any additional questions?"

"No."

"Alright, if you think of anything, please call us back and we'll be happy to assist you further."

"Thank you."

"Have a safe night."

Victoria hung up and called Dr. Yaz. She gave him a rundown about the alarm. He promised to swing by to check on the clinic tonight.

Crisis adverted. Victoria enjoyed the crisp night air. Her chest expanded, the first time she could breathe deeply in the last three weeks. Must be the Ethan charm. She smiled and headed back into her apartment.

All her champagne feelings burst.

Her sister's head rested on Ethan's shoulder. The two swayed to a romantic song, creating the perfect intimate ambiance.

With Victoria's weight and body shape, there would be no competition. Dessie would always steal the guy's eye and heart.

Victoria dropped her phone. The cell clattered on the wooden table, making them startle and break apart.

Both Ethan and Dessie glanced at each other and promptly found Victoria's wall art ever-so-interesting. The one charged glance between the two of them told Victoria everything. Her baby sister had devoured another man.

Ethan cleared his throat but couldn't clear the awkward tension in the apartment. "I'm done here. Dessie can follow a man's lead and knows the basic steps she'll need for her first dance."

"I bet Dessie can follow any man's lead." Victoria's voice was lethal.

He collected his music player and his jacket off the back of a chair. "Thank you both for the dances."

"No, thank you for teaching me. I don't know how I can ever thank you enough." Dessie sounded as chipper as a rooster about to crow, and she stroked his arm.

Victoria's jealousy and ancient sibling wounds bled. She couldn't stop seeing how perfect those two were together. Dessie's wedding was days away and here she was charming another man.

"For thanks, how about you get married on Sunday and move far away?" Victoria asked.

Dessie slunk away from Ethan.

Ethan shot Victoria a puzzled expression. To Dessie, he said, "I hope your fiancé appreciates what a fine woman he's marrying. I know you did all of this for him."

Victoria grunted.

He crossed to Victoria and kissed her cheek. "Good night. I'll see you on Saturday for the rehearsal dinner."

"You're coming?" Her rage o-meter pegged to Hulk-smash.

"I didn't invite him." Dessie's tone was full of not-me inflections.

He gave Victoria another confused glance. "Your mother invited me yesterday. Is that not OK?"

If her sister wasn't messing with her life, her mother was.

Victoria smiled, wide and fake. "I'll see you Saturday at the Hilton."

He exited.

The image of him tucked up warm and cuddly with Dessie made Victoria want to throw up. All the furniture askew raised her temperature. For her sanity, she decided to hole up in her room.

Sprawled out on her bed, Ralph opened one of his sleepy eyes and emitted a low purr. No longer fighting the anger and despair, Victoria curled around Ralph and sobbed. Confusion and jealousy sloshed around her soul and mind. He meowed at her, curling into a ball at her hip and purring himself to sleep.

After a good sleep, she'd feel better and be that much closer to having this disaster over.

DESSIE SAID they had to meet up at Ms. Z's separately, so Victoria dragged herself to her stupid final dress fitting the next day, still sour about the engraved image of Dessie and Ethan in each other's arms.

Inside the store, Olivia waited in another amazing pencil skirt. "You're the first to arrive. We are extremely tight on time today. Once the others show up, we'll get them dressed immediately."

Dessie busted through the door. Bags cascaded down her arms. "Just finished shopping."

"Mom's not with you?"

"There was a problem with the hotel, so I dropped her off to straighten it out before the Alburgas check in this afternoon."

Olivia swept her arm toward the dressing rooms. "Ready to see your dress?"

"Yes." Dessie gushed sunshine.

Victoria had to dig deep. She had to help her baby sister with her wedding dress. For God's sake, she needed to drop the lemon pucker and slap on a cheerful expression. Do it for Dessie.

Olivia sauntered down the hall to an open room. "I'll guess your shoes are in one of those bags."

Showing off a pair of green and yellow striped high heels, Dessie kicked off her jeweled flip flops and strapped them on. "I wanted something fun for the shoes, and besides, no one but me will see them."

Victoria smiled at Dessie. "Good to see the wedding isn't swallowing your spunky ways."

"Get undressed and let's see how you glow." Olivia unleashed the dress. For such a simple dress, there was a ton of fabric, most of it the train. Surprisingly, Olivia and Victoria could maneuver around the train, and they got Dessie zipped in and fluffed up.

Olivia and Victoria admired their work and the bride.

Tears sprung to Victoria's eyes, crying for how incredible her sister looked and crying at her selfish self. Her little sister would be a missus. In two short days. Dessie deserved Victoria putting aside her petty jealousies and stuffing her wounded ego into a dying star.

Dessie hadn't been brave enough to turn around and see herself. "Well, what do you think?" The bridal jitters were in full force.

Victoria kissed her fingertips. "Perfecto. If Damien doesn't almost faint, he's a robot."

"The mermaid cut is smashing on you." Olivia glanced at the open doorway, as a woman popped her head into the room. Olivia stepped over and they conferred together quietly at the door.

"Check yourself out and see if we're wrong." She twirled her finger at Dessie, urging her to turn.

Her sister closed her eyes, spun around fast, and peeked under her eyelashes. She let out a long breath, visibly relaxing. A massive smile and wet cheeks adorned her face.

Victoria handed her baby sister a tissue, keeping one for herself. "You're gorgeous, just as we promised. You're gorgeous, even when you're a snot factory. I don't know if I should be jealous or appalled. You're an abomination."

Dessie dabbed her eyes and laughed.

Exactly what Victoria was hoping for.

Olivia came over and surveyed the dress. "Fantastic fit, no alterations are needed. Change out of this dress. Your bridesmaids are getting changed and I'll bring them here."

Admiring herself, Dessie twisted and turned, viewing every detail and angle in the mirrors. "Can I change after they get here?"

Olivia checked her watch. "How about you surprise them on your big day?"

"That's a great idea." The bride-to-be beamed.

Olivia left.

Victoria helped extract Dessie from the dress.

A hard knock and the three bridesmaids stomped inside, clad in matching god-awful, light-yellow dresses. The cut of the dress would've been appropriate for a virgin nun, complete with three gigantic flowers, right on the ass.

Hands full of satin, Victoria packed the bride's train into the bag, hiding her face and stifling a righteous giggle.

The triplets steamed. No one dared to say a word.

Olivia broke the stalemate. "Now that you three have tried on the bridal dresses selected by the bride, why don't I take you ladies down the hall to the seamstress? She can take up the hems a bit."

The Barbies looked stabby. For a moment, Victoria predicted bloodshed. Yet without a word, the three stalked out of the room, following Olivia.

The door clicked shut.

Around bubbles of laughter, Victoria said, "I wish I had a camera for that one."

The bride kept her eyes on the door.

"You changed the dresses on them? Mean-spirited." Holding her sides, Victoria took a deep breath, fighting another fit of giggles. "But ever so funny."

Dessie made a noncommittal *hmmm* in the back of her throat.

"You stood up to them like you used to. I'm not sure why or when you ever stopped." Victoria put her hand up to Dessie for a high-five, which Dessie returned with little enthusiasm.

Dessie's phone started talking, making the bride jump. She checked her phone. "It's a text from Damien, I have to run. You OK with bringing the dress to the hotel tonight for me?"

"Sure, sure. I can handle one dress delivery. Call me when you have my room number. Thanks for the memory of them in those dreadful dresses."

Dessie slunk out the door.

Alone, Victoria checked the time and felt a twinge of excitement spread through her body. Olivia had picked for her an exquisite dress. She could sense the good mojo.

Olivia came in and handed her a small black dress bag. "This is yours."

Humming, Victoria unzipped the bag. Humming stopped. Confusion started. "Um, this? This? This?"

"Your maid-of-honor dress." A fake smile was on Olivia's face.

Victoria couldn't stop staring. This had to be a horrible joke. The color was the same light green Dessie wanted, yet the collar had gold beading in the shape of a diamond. She looked at the dress in her hands. Looked at Olivia. Looked at the dress again.

Olivia adjusted her glasses, not glancing at Victoria. "Dessie picked the dress out."

There seemed to be a bad case of not-looking-Victoria-in-the-eye going around. She swallowed the rock in her throat and pulled the dress all the way out of the bag.

God, in full light the thing managed to be worse. The dress would hug her every curve and showcase all of her fat rolls. The style wasn't worse than the flower-ass dress Victoria had laughed about, yet her maid-of-honor dress was awful. From the horribly beaded collar to the cut-away shoulder sections, which exposed only the top part of her arms yet managed to still be strangely long-sleeved.

Victoria sneered at the hideous thing masquerading as a dress. "My sister picked this...this thing out for me?"

"She called the day after you were here. Even though she still had to pay for the other dress, she insisted on reordering. She mentioned something about the dresses being garbage and needing to change them."

Spiteful Dessie. Victoria's retinas burned.

"Would you like help trying it on?"

She extended her arm out to put distance between her and this monstrosity. "It's a fashion train wreck. A train wreck that no reality TV show could fix."

Olivia neither confirmed nor denied the charge.

Her sister wanted this. Victoria could do this. Begrudgingly, she donned the dress. "The color isn't bad on me. But the choker collar is hot and these flower accents clustered on my boob are weird."

If Dessie thought there wouldn't be retaliation when Victoria eventually married, she was sorely mistaken. She would remember this horror show.

Victoria stripped, slung her and Dessie's garment bags over her arms, and left Ms. Z's.

Waddling to her car, her mother's text song started playing. Victoria dumped the bags in the trunk and checked her cell.

Room 414 is ready 4 u. U'r down the hall from the bride

She was down the hall from the devil because only pure evil could have picked the abominable dress. Victoria texted back.

On my way now. U w/ ur family?

Her mother answered.

No, I'm in the lounge, drop by after u check in

She didn't want to deal with her mother, especially after this dress disaster.

If I must

Her mother replied.

C u then

Please let this be a quick chat with her. Victoria could hear the spa calling her name from Ms. Z's parking lot. Thirty minutes later, she stowed the dresses in her closet and headed down to the lobby to see her mother.

By how much peach lipstick was left on her mother's lips, she had to be at least three martinis in.

"You hoo. Vic-toor-iaa. Over here," she drunk-shouted. The type of shouting where her mother thought she was being quiet, but she sounded more like a St. Bernard. Loud and dopey.

Embarrassment propelled Victoria's feet to the table to stop her mother from hollering at her. She doubted she could pay for more than two drinks in such a swanky bar. As she got closer to her mother, Victoria could tell she had aged badly in the last few days.

"You're a dutiful daughter. Just like I was. I knew you'd show."

"I'm not a floor mat." Victoria didn't cross her arms, only her tone.

"When people ask you for help, you say no?"

"Yes."

Her mother clearly disbelieved her as showcased by her raised right eyebrow, squinty left eye, and her lips pressed into a thin line. "You're here."

Victoria dug her nails into her palm and rose. "I need to get things done."

"Stay." Empty martini glass in hand, her mother waved the empty at the passing server, who nodded and headed to the bar for a refill. "I have a few wedding details to pass along to you from your sister."

"She's smart to avoid me." Victoria sank into her chair.

Her mother passed Victoria her phone. On the screen was a picture of a woman, her hair swept back, complete with pearls and cascading curls in a fairy-tale hairstyle.

Victoria handed the phone back. "Pretty. Is this how you're doing your hair for the wedding?"

"No, this is how you'll be wearing your hair for the wedding."

Irritation at a ten, Victoria's eye twitched. "Done by a hairdresser, right? Because if you think I can do this, share the hallucinogens."

"All the bridesmaids will wear their hair like this."

"I'll just wear a hat."

"No. Hats. Allowed. I want to see your beautiful face." Her mother tapped the tabletop. "If you come in a hat, I'll be forced to do your hair for you."

She blanched, touching her tender scalp. "I'd prefer not to be burned."

"You've never let me live down burning you once with the

curling iron." Her mother rolled her eyes.

"I had a bald spot where you fried my hair off. Did Dessie ban hats?"

Her mother stared at Victoria hard, then her face brightened. "I can tell Dessie you're refusing to go along with her prescribed hairstyle. Last time I saw her, she was screaming at the caterer about having to change the plate patterns."

Victoria flinched at the threat. "I'm irritated. Not suicidal. Send me the picture. I'll see what I can do."

"Wedding messages relayed." Her mother leaned back. "How's your office job?"

"It's good. I've figured out where I'm going to apply to finish my undergrad work and then pursue a veterinarian degree. I've already talked to Dr. Yaz about changing my work hours a bit."

"You can't afford to cut your hours." The harsh tone reminded Victoria that her mother never accepted that she grew up and could figure things out on her own.

"There are scholarships," Victoria said.

"You're too old."

"Thanks for the support, Mother. I want to complete my degree. I want to do something with my life."

Her mother waved her hands around in wide, drunk exclamation points. "You want to go to school for another five years. How will you get by? You're barely covering your bills right now. Are you sure you're going to complete this? Or are you going to let this degree waste your time, money, and youth?"

The speech was her internal doubts, vocalized. The questions jabbed at Victoria's ego and stoked her fears. "I can do this." Her words snaked out between her clenched teeth.

Her mother smiled brightly as the waiter handed her a dirty martini. She had a hollow look in her eye and drank. One long sip and the glass was almost drained. "We're similar."

"That's your other daughter. The perfect one."

Her mother stared at the almost empty glass. "School, you won't finish, and I couldn't start." Her voice was a whisper of the saddest caliber, destitute and final.

Her miserable tone struck at Victoria's heart. She had never known her mother to sound so lost. Yet Victoria wouldn't let her mother drag her down. "I'll finish. You're not too old to go."

Dessie texted, informing Victoria that the bachelorette bus would be arriving soon.

"That's Dessie, isn't it?"

"I should skip this tonight." Victoria slumped at the table. A quick whack on her shoulder snapped her upright. "Ouch, don't hit me."

"Don't slouch. Go with Dessie. You keep her grounded and safe. Have a little fun with your sister. Otherwise, you can wait with me for my family to arrive," her mother said with forced sunniness.

A shiver ran up Victoria's spine. The Alburgas cometh. She knew they would eventually show up, yet years of dread balled up in her stomach. "Bridal insanity versus family hell? Dessie plus her friends plus me equals a safer abyss for me."

Her mother shooed her away and finished her drink. "Ciao."

Victoria hesitated. "I can call Dad for you."

"No. Go. Don't forget, you shouldn't flirt too much, Ethan's your date this weekend."

"I know he's my date. Flirting, no. Enduring, yes."

Too loudly, her mother said, "Now run off and do things I would still do. The list is long."

A few heads turned toward them in the bar. Victoria's face must have been a thousand degrees radiating her shame. "Mother." Her one word was packed with a pound of shut-it.

Dessie texted her again reminding her not to be late. Victoria ducked out, ignoring her mother's forced laugh, as she merrily called for the waiter.

a shiny, black bus sat in the valet section of the hotel. Dessie and a dozen of her closest frenemies, plus one unhappy sister, trooped up the stairs. Inside, the bus had maroon couches, a bathroom, a wet bar, and poles in the aisles.

Goody, stripper poles on the bus. That didn't bode well.

The stereo blared out "Girls Just Wanna Have Fun." Being forced to listen to '80s music and stuck with all of Dessie's friends yowling like cats in heat was not Victoria's ideal night out. But away they rode.

The first stop happened to be a new casino and a five-star, high-end restaurant. The place reeked of freshly minted money. Roasted eel paired with radish cream sauce or broiled skinless chicken with cream of peas and mashed potatoes were the night's specials.

What Victoria wouldn't give for Jake's simple food.

The table talk at first leaned toward calorie counts and fat grams. Men, the ultimate squawk subject, popped up. In an instant, the noise level flipped to repelling anyone with a Y chromosome.

Victoria kept her head down. In this conversation, she felt woefully unable to contribute anything of value.

Then she heard a shrill noise and felt the first train wreck barreling at her, whistle blaring.

"Victoria has a boyfriend? Miracles do happen," Avon screeched from the opposite end of the massive table.

Her sister, who sat next to Avon, waggled her fingers at Victoria. Thanks to Dessie, the rat, everyone stared at Victoria.

With a captive audience, Avon preened. "Do you feel proud? You finally joined the ranks of the dating, Victoria."

Play nice, play nice, she chanted in her head. They'd only been out of the hotel for a full fifteen minutes together and already Victoria's tongue bled from keeping quiet.

"We began to believe the rumors from high school, you know, the one about you and Sandra being a hot item." Avon's voice was sweetly vicious.

Victoria couldn't even conjure a false mask behind which to hide her fury. She could feel her lip snarl. "I barely remember seeing you in high school unless you were hanging off some jock's arm."

"At least I had someone's arm to be seen on and wasn't a loner loser like you are," she retorted, her words soft and heated.

Ding, ding, time to speak. Victoria's mind became unfettered. She propped her elbow on the table and rested her chin on her palm, unwilling to take anymore attitude. "Name-calling, how very grown up of you. High school is all you ever talk about. Let's chat about the present instead, shall we? How's life for you today?"

Avon's bitch-itude intensified after the reality slap. "I have a life. I bet you had to ask your date to be your plus-one." The challenge was clear in her snotty tone.

"I did ask him." Victoria slid a layered, pile-of-dung look at her sister. The top layer a hot, eat-shit promise, followed by a dry death threat, and ending in a rancid, ashy assurance of retribution if her sister dared to challenge her.

Avon leaned over to Dessie. "Why don't you show me where the restroom is."

Under the table, Victoria flattened her hands onto her legs, unable to do anything as she watched the two walk away. If her sister squealed on her, letting her secret out about Ethan to Avon, everyone here would know with cheetah speed. They would discover Victoria didn't ask Ethan to be her plus-one, that Dessie did, and label Victoria a failure.

If gossips here found out, her whole family would, too, and eventually someone would tell Ethan. Her spirits dove for the basement. Ethan would know. Victoria's insides quaked. She might not know where their relationship was going, but she wanted to keep spending time with him. He might not want to if he knew she'd deceived him.

Her sister and Avon walked in, linked arm in arm. Dessie looked like a repentant pup. Avon looked like a gloating ape, her chest puffed up and a triumphant roar in her eyes.

"I can't wait to meet Ethan tomorrow. Dessie has told me so much about him." Avon slipped into her seat.

Victoria shot her sister a murderous smile.

Dessie shrunk. "Does everyone know what they want to eat?"

Dinner rolled on. No one spoke to Victoria, though they twittered amongst themselves while directing darting glances and tattling giggles at Victoria.

Bill paid, they piled into the bus. The next stop on the Torture Trolley was Geode, a swank place in Scottsdale.

Inside the gyrating club, fake crystal shards jutted out of the ceiling. A VIP section stood ready for them, fully equipped with a red rope draped around a plush velvet seating area designed to keep the riffraff out.

With room to spread out, the women deserted Victoria. Fine

by her. She sipped her cocktail in peace. Two mind-numbing hours later, she bet on which one of the boozy floozies would fall first. Thoroughly snockered, a few drunk women caved, inviting the lurking guys to pop under the rope.

This would be entertaining. Drunken women plus smokin' hot guys equaled Victoria viewing her own reality TV show. She kept her distance in her lone corner, drink in hand, content.

A tall blond hunk in a striped shirt with one too many buttons unbuttoned dropped next to her, slipping his arm onto the back of the couch. "Hey, beautiful lady, your friend told me you were lonely."

Victoria leaned away, careful not to touch the creeper. "Not lonely. Enjoying a drink. Alone." The strong emphasis on alone.

Clueless, he closed the gap she'd created between them. "I'll show you a good time, but I gotta ask, how'd the bouncer let you in? 'Cause, you're the bomb."

Was this schmuck for real? Dessie hadn't spoken to her since this afternoon at the dress disaster. Maybe Victoria could slip out unnoticed.

As if conjured by her thought, Dessie loomed over her with her martini glass in an iron grip. "Victoria, who is this?"

"He's leaving." Victoria's harsh tone broadcasted that the dummy should take the sledgehammer hint and disappear.

"We're having a good time." The guy slid closer to her.

Victoria scooched away from him and landed hard on the wooden floor.

He offered his meaty, sweaty paw to help her up. "Babe, you OK? Maybe you've had too much to drink."

Dessie threw Victoria an executioner glare, the same look Victoria had put up with for the last two decades. Dessie must've been taking notes from their mother.

She tossed her blonde curls over her shoulder and headed for the exit. "Ladies, let's bounce." The rest of the party fell in line behind the bride-to-be. She bested drill sergeants, her shout having been heard over the pulse of the music.

Victoria begrudgingly grasped the offered hand. Before she could blink, the guy had branded her palm with his number and left, throwing over his shoulder, "Call me."

She had way too many ass problems. Tomorrow, a bruise would be on her ass. Tonight, she must deal with her sister, the original pain in the ass.

By the time she extracted herself from the club, everyone was on the bus, plus a cop. After Victoria slunk on, the driver snapped the door closed and pulled away from the club.

The cop strutted up to the bride, his feet shoulder width apart and thumbs hooked on his belt. "Ma'am, are you Esmeralda Isabella Shaw?"

Dessie let her eyes drink in the broad-shouldered man in blue in front of her. "Yes, Officer."

"You have the right to remain..." He dropped his mirrored, aviator sunglasses down his nose. "...sexy."

"Hot In Here" by Nelly blasted out of the speakers. The cop tossed his sunglasses and hat at the screaming women surrounding him. He launched himself onto the pole, shaking his booty. The women swayed with the beat, shrieking.

Victoria felt trapped in hormonal stew.

Ten minutes later, when the bus stopped, Victoria scurried off first, only to discover outside wasn't any better. They were at a big gray building that had no windows, but enough lights to be mistaken for mini-Vegas. A strip club. Victoria craved a gallon of hand sanitizer.

The cop-slash-stripper led a conga line out of the bus with the rest of the women in tow. Dessie snagged Victoria, adding her to the line. With no other option, she conga-ed inside.

Two men, both dressed like the Village People, twirled their hips on stage at the screaming women. Only the lifetime of crap she would get from Dessie for bailing, and maybe a pinch of curiosity kept Victoria's feet on the sticky carpet inside the dank club.

Most of the women split off, heading for the bar. The three boozy bridesmaids wiggled their way to the front, dragging Dessie who, again, tugged Victoria along. In the end, all five ladies were against the stage's edge.

"Isn't this great?" Dessie shouted in Victoria's ear.

Victoria nodded, drawing a mental path to the bar to order a drink. A new song pumped through the place, "Fire." Three firemen danced out from the wings, holding two chairs.

The DJ's voice boomed out of the speakers. "Fire in the front row." A spotlight shined on Dessie and Victoria.

Victoria became immobile. The crowd around them whooped.

The silky voice continued, saying, "We have a bride plus a stripper virgin in the house. Boys, time to light them up and hose them down."

Dessie leaped onstage, giggling and dancing with the "captain," whereas the other two hulks had to heave Victoria up onto the stage. Victoria caught Avon's eye in the crowd, and Avon blew her a kiss. Victoria bristled. The conniving back stabber had set her up.

She would use this setup in her favor. Victoria smiled defiantly at Avon, strutted to the open chair and sat, beaming. A big black firefighter danced her way. The air was damp and dense, clinging to her, and tasted of musky desperation and longing.

The hunky firefighters shed their coats in sync. Victoria's breathing became shallow, her heart pounding. Not that she didn't appreciate good-looking men. The crowds were the trouble.

The dark stud shimmied closer. He gyrated his crotch in her face and reached behind him, arching his back. She gaped eye-to-cock with him. Perfect, they were officially intimate friends. Ripping his pants off, he whipped them around over his head. This cranked the crowd from howling fans to crazed stalkers.

Like with every great disaster, she couldn't avert her gaze.

With the accuracy of a trick shooter, the scrumptious fire-fighter sling-shotted his pants straight at the loudest, rowdiest, and drunkest knot of shriekers. The mosh pit behind him undulated.

He only wore a banana-hammock on a diet.

Victoria's eyes searched for Dessie to help. No help there. Her baby sister danced, bumping and grinding between the two firefighters. The lights blazed, hot and hellish.

The song wrapped up. The crowd exploded with catcalls.

The two men flanking Dessie dropped a helmet on her head. She had a hand on each guy's butt, grinning like she'd snorted laughing gas. The guys didn't seem to mind and helped her down the steps.

Victoria sent up a silent thanks to whatever deity had blessed her with the fortitude to withstand the torture.

Her hunky firefighter guided her to the edge of the stage. A fan rushed up the steps, nailing Victoria in the chest. She staggered in her heels, hit a slick spot, and crashed into the steel of the firefight-er's torso. She and the fireman went down in a tangle of limbs.

"I'll be off soon, honey." His deep drawl sent a shiver all the way to her pinched toes.

"Thanks for the offer, but no need." Her voice was cool and smooth. She mentally high-fived herself for not freaking out about flattening the stripper.

Noticing their buddy pinned, the other nearly naked men hoisted her up and sent the overzealous fan into the audience.

Upright, Victoria's ankle rolled out from underneath her. Damn, she had injured the same ankle as the night Iggy had saved Ralph from the tree. She didn't think it would bother her, except for the icepick heels she'd strapped on that night.

Two strong arms swept her up. The fireman came to her rescue again. Women screamed, throwing more silk underwear onto the stage. He bowed, nearly tipping her out into the audience, then spun on his heel and marched offstage with her clutching him.

What in Odin's name was happening? Victoria squirmed to break free.

"I'm going to wrap your ankle up. Trust me, I'm a paramedic," he hollered over the ruckus behind them.

"You're in the wrong uniform."

He chuckled and kicked open a door leading backstage. Inside, five strapping men were in various states of undress.

The buck-naked guy didn't seem flustered by a strange woman in the room. He continued digging into the pile of costumes heaped on the couch. "Has anyone seen my chaps? I'm on in five and I can't find them."

Another barely clothed man joined in the lost chap hunt. Two men played cards. The other settled into his nap against the makeup table.

The door slammed shut behind them, muting the thudding music and wails of women.

Setting Victoria on an empty seat, her fireman said, "My name is Charles. I've got some bandages and a cold compress in my bag."

"I'm Victoria. What happened out there?"

"Rookie mistake. You slipped on silk panties." Charles blasted her with a boyish bad-boy smile and unzipped a gym bag.

"Hazardous job you have here."

A bandage in one hand and an instant ice pack in the other,

Charles ratcheted his charm up a notch. "Can't complain. You were at least civilized onstage."

The still-chapless guy piped up. "I hate when they grab my equipment like it's a joystick." Flashing his baby blues at her, he clipped on his chaps. "It is a joystick, darlin', but there's a difference between being manhandled and stroked."

With eyes bugging out and a tongue that had suddenly lost the ability to do anything other than droop uselessly, Victoria nodded her head as though she understood the crazy babble.

Charles knelt and wrapped her ankle up. "Wiggle your toes to make sure there's enough blood flow."

"It's a solid wrap." Victoria stood, heels in one hand. She swayed a little to keep off her injured foot.

"Not a bad sprain. If you elevate it tonight, you should be good in the morning. Should I call you a cab?" His puppy-dog eyes whined that he wanted to help her.

"No, thank you. The bridal party hell rides on." She pumped her fist in the air, limping toward the exit.

He called after her. "Stay off your feet for the rest of the night."

Yes. This ankle thing was her golden ticket to freedom. Dessie couldn't argue with her leaving. "Agreed."

"Don't forget to ice it. If you need anything else, call me." Charles grabbed a card from his gym bag, crossed to her, and slipped the card underneath her bra strap.

"Sure." Victoria headed down the dark hallway, moving closer to the pounding music instead of running away.

DESSIE and the rest stood huddled by the backstage door.

Wobbling her way to them, Victoria winced. Once she was close enough, she touched Dessie's arm to get her attention and shouted, "Sorry, they bandaged me up." She lifted her foot up to show Dessie the proof.

Saying nothing, Dessie nodded, shoving Victoria's purse into her empty hands. Her sister had an eye twitch, warning Victoria that Dessie might be Hyde-ing out.

"Did I miss anything good?" Victoria's voice was cheery, trying to lighten the mood.

Dessie glued her eyes on Victoria. "Nope. I see you and the stripper are close."

Victoria ignored the snide tone directed at her. "He's an EMT and wanted to help me out since I slipped onstage."

"He wants you to call him. To check up on you. Medically, of course." Her sister jabbed at the card under her bra strap.

Oh, she wanted to play the attitude game? Victoria shifted her weight to her good leg and scowled. "What's your deal? You have been clawing at me like I'm a scratching post all night."

"Every time I turn around, another man is sniffing after you. What about Ethan? The man who is coming to the wedding with you?" Dessie's tone was razor-edged.

"You mean the man you invited. Something sparking between you two that I should know about? If so, you have bigger problems than me."

Her sister ground her teeth. Her eyes were diamond hard. Fury oozed behind her sister's cool, composed mask.

"Struck a nerve, I see," Victoria said.

The bride stalked away, heading straight for the booze. At the bar, the bartender poured Dessie a shot. Without hesitation, she slammed the drink down, paid, and whipped back to the cluster of women.

Dessie frowned at Victoria. "Go to the hotel."

Thus dismissing her. She turned to everyone else. "Time to go." Everyone threaded their way to the exit.

Victoria pulled up her car-summoning app and ordered a

car to pick her up, then escaped outside. In the parking lot, the bachelorette group staggered onto the bus, laughing and chatting.

Charles lounged near the car pickup stand. He pushed off the brick wall. "Hey, I wanted to make sure you got out of here in one piece."

A premonition jolted Victoria to survey her surroundings. Dessie shot Victoria a look of pure venom with her hands balled into tight fists. Transported to the battlefield, that look would have been perfectly poised to kill. A lethal combination of hate, contempt, and C4.

Her sister poisoned the crisp night air with one ugly word. "Whore."

"Whore. A term I know you're intimate with. No one has ever needed to call me that," Victoria said, her words aimed square at the bride's pride.

Even in the low, parking lot lights, she saw Dessie's back stiffen. Bull's-eye.

Dessie scurried onto the party bus.

Charles stared at the bus lights moving away. "That's some serious hate. Did you fool around with her fiancé or what?"

At first, a mere bubble of laughter escaped, then Victoria doubled over, unable to stop laughing. "Her thug of a significant other? No. As to what causes the attitude spikes, she gets livid every time I'm near a guy."

He glanced up and down at Victoria. "Jealousy? You deserve the rap?"

"I wish. Until a few weeks ago, I hadn't even been on a proper date." She covered her mouth with her hand, shocked. How could she reveal her secret to a stranger?

Charles' low chuckle resonated in his chest.

Her body heated up and she was glad they were in a dark patch, otherwise he would see her bright red face.

He looped his thumbs into his pockets. "Maybe you should do something to make her jealous."

"Too much trouble. She's the one getting married and is almost done with her degree. Nothing about me stirs envy."

Charles rocked onto his sneakered heels. "Going alone to the wedding? If so, I have a free arm you can look gorgeous on. Plus, I love to dance. Hell, I could rustle up an entourage, if you wanted one."

A stranger offering to be her date? Strange...once she had decided to no longer worry about dating or chasing after external validation, men swarmed around her. Guess confidence was the ultimate pheromone. "I have a date."

"That's good."

"It would be good if my sister hadn't pretended to be me and set me up—I shouldn't have said that."

"But you did."

She waved at the approaching car. "You should have been a counselor instead of an EMT-slash-stripper."

He opened the door for her. "This work tips better. Time for you to ice and elevate."

"Orders I can obey." With her foot throbbing, Victoria slid into the car, grateful the night was over. She couldn't believe her sister called her a whore.

*a*fter confirming the hotel's address with the driver, Victoria opened her phone. No new texts. Just then a text popped up from Sandra.

Hello, R u ever going to call back?

She tapped on her text app to reply. Her texts were grayed out, marking them as read, but Victoria hadn't seen any of them. Fifteen had come in within the last hour while she had been trapped in sweaty strip-club hell.

Exasperation compressed her muscles into steel ropes. Dessie had read them all, but fortunately she hadn't sent any replies in Victoria's name this time. Victoria should have updated her password after the last time Dessie hacked her phone since her listening skills were worse than a toddler's.

The car pulled up to the curb as she finished reading her previously viewed messages. Two were from Iggy, two were from Ethan, and the rest were from Sandra.

Iggy needed her room number for tomorrow in order to make the bouquets, Ethan verified the time for the rehearsal, and Sandra seemed to be in the thrall of some crisis.

Victoria paid, climbed out, and felt too tired to be more than mildly pissed. She'd deal with the nosy Hyde-zilla in the morning.

Up in her room, she rubbed her neck. Sandra texted again. A dozen texts in less than an hour.

"I'll call you, woman," Victoria griped, then dialed.

Sandra picked up and blasted Victoria with trance house music. "Where are you and what's your malfunction, Sandra?"

The music died.

"A drive-thru. So, were you a reverse Hugh Hefner and raked in the men tonight?" Sandra sounded about ten.

"No smoking robe or men hanging off me like the Hef." She flopped on the bed and propped her foot up.

Giggles greeted her grumpy declaration.

Her internal alert system tripped to Level Yellow, with Oh-Hell-No Red on standby. "Why are you laughing?"

Sandra ordered at the drive-thru then spoke to Victoria. "Well, according to your bridal hurricane social site updates, you had men cannonballing into your dating pool tonight and you loved the company."

A low growl started in Victoria's chest and clawed its way up her throat. "That sniveling slug," Victoria hissed.

"I take it the pocket Hyde exaggerated?"

Done, she was so done. "Yes. If she thinks I'm a slut because of tonight, then she's going to Love. The. Wedding. Want to help with my impromptu wedding plan?"

"Is it a good plan?" Sandra perked up faster than a puppy hearing keys rattle.

"A great plan. My sister may disown me afterward. You in?"

Sandra honked her horn, yelling out her window. "Hurry up, I have a master plan to implement."

"I'm famished, order me something." Victoria's tone ready-to-rebel confident. "On your way over pick up matches and lighter fluid."

After a pause, Victoria heard a horn blast and Sandra screaming, "Evil minion needs to add to her order."

"I'll let you go."

"Master." Sandra channeled her best Igor into the phone. "I'll bring all you ask for in half an hour."

WITH HER NEW wedding to-do list stacking up in her head, Victoria could feel the tension that had been building in her body since she received Dessie's phone call start to dissipate. Because no longer would she stay quiet or docile. Nope, it was time to demand respect. Victoria lounged on the hotel bed, boneless, carefree, and no longer worried about what her family thought about her.

Joy fizzed up in her heart.

A pounding on the door brought Victoria out of her planning trance. She hopped over and opened it.

Sandra spilled in. "What you are planning to do with the fire and accelerant?"

Victoria grabbed the food and snapped the door shut with her hip. "Food first, then my brilliance."

"Come on, I have been racking my brain since we hung up." Sandra flopped down on the edge of the bed, eating fries.

Victoria wiped her hands on her yoga pants, opened the wooden armoire, and pulled out the black bag. "Do you want to see my maid-of-honor dress?"

Clapping her hands like an excited toddler, Sandra said, "Show-and-tell time."

Victoria's body blocked Sandra's view. She unzipped the bag, shivered, and extracted the dress. Twisting back to Sandra, Victoria unveiled the awful surprise. "Ta-da."

Jaw on her knees, Sandra blinked rapidly, clearly disbelieving what her visual cortex was feeding her brain. She let out a low whistle. "I think bad chiffon flowers threw up on your dress."

"This dress is a punishment, to teach me a lesson. But Dessie's planned humiliation will backfire. My ungrateful sister is about to learn a hard life lesson."

"Agreed, the dress is hideous. How is that going to teach Dessie, though?"

Victoria swung the dress from side-to-side. The green fabric crinkled and groaned with each movement. "How to treat me well with a side of humility. Dessie has angered the gods with this monstrosity. I believe this dress should be the ultimate offering to Squat. He must be tired of being shafted."

Sandra drummed her feet, hooted, and slapped her hands against the bed. "Yes, Squat should be honored with a bonfire."

They both dissolved into evil laughter. Inhaling food, the two of them strategized where to do the deed.

"Come, my evil sidekick, there's an empty lot close by. A prime ritual site." Victoria snagged the dress, a feeling of power coursing through her.

GIGGLING, they nonchalantly walked out into the dark, empty streets. At almost one in the morning, a full moon shined over-head. After a five-minute stroll, they arrived at the barren lot, littered with shards of glittering glass.

Sandra scoped out the vacant area. "Should we just light the horrible fabric and run?"

Victoria shook her head. "We have to pay respects and properly dedicate the dress to the great and wonderful parking god."

The sound of the bag unzipping was loud and it echoed out

into the darkness. Victoria held the dress up under the dim streetlamp, the color now a pukey green.

"Squat, for bestowing your bounty on us, please accept this token of our appreciation." Her voice filled the space with a reverent and respectful tone.

Sandra presented the lighter fluid to Victoria reverently, head bowed. Victoria hurled the dress to the ground, took up the fluid, and hosed the abomination down. Every inch of the scratchy material dripped accelerant.

"You trying to drown the material?" Sandra asked.

"Can't be too careful. This dress could be of the devil and refuse to burn." Victoria walked backward, leaving a trail of liquid till they were a safe distance away.

Sandra offered her the box of matches with both hands. An offering to the gods themselves.

Slowly, Victoria cracked open the box, selected a match, and struck it to life. She tossed down the flame on the trail. "Thanks be to Squat for the great parking spots."

"Amen," Sandra chanted.

Flames fanned out over the ground, raced toward the dress, and hit the drenched cloth. The material shriveled and wilted. Every angry hiss and crackle filled Victoria with satisfaction. She wasn't allowing her sister, her mother, or her family to dictate her worth or her beauty.

Sandra stood next to her. "Too bad you didn't tell me to get marshmallows."

"That would've been a perfect wake refreshment." Victoria linked arms with Sandra and leaned her head on her friend's shoulder. "Thank you."

"For what?"

"For being here with me. For supporting me. Even for cattle-prodding me."

Sandra laid her head on top of Victoria's head. "It's my pleasure to Taser you, I mean, torture you."

Victoria nudged her friend. "Very humane of you."

"Seriously, I love you and I'm proud of you. In the past few weeks, you've constantly had to hug your monsters and your sister."

"Rough days, for sure." Victoria's words were soft and heartfelt.

"And yet you survived."

"Unlike the dress." Victoria pointed at the charred, smoldering mess.

"Praise be to Squat."

"Praise be."

Sandra turned her head and stared at Victoria. "Now that you've burnt the maid-of-honor dress, I assume you're going skyclad?"

"No, I won't be naked. I have a few ideas."

"There's more to the plan?"

The two of them chatted about dress replacements and basked in the dying glow of the withered material. Victoria felt lighter, better than she had since she dropped out of college.

A few light ashes flew across the open field. Once the last ember extinguished and lay dormant, they stomped on the carcass. Victoria had to baby her wrapped ankle and her athletic shoes gave her great support to crush it. They squashed the dress for two reasons: one, so no little fire devils would flare up and start a weed fire, and two, assaulting the monstrosity felt satisfying.

Ritual complete. The breeze carried the last of the ashes away.

Victoria and Sandra strolled to the hotel and parted in the lobby.

For all the trouble Victoria had gone through in the few

weeks since Dessie's announcement, her ability to play nice had just burned up with the dress. Tomorrow, everyone would meet a new Victoria. Tomorrow everyone would play on her terms.

On to the next step in reinventing herself. Victoria picked up her phone and punched in a new number. The line rang and rang. She almost hung up.

"Hello?" a deep voice asked on the other end.

"Is this Charles?"

"It is."

"This is Victoria. We met tonight and I'm thinking about getting a restraining order against silky panties."

He chuckled. "Good luck with the paperwork. How's your foot?" His words felt warm and inviting like she could have talked with him all night long.

She gathered her courage and her plans for her independence declaration at the wedding. "The foot is elevated and iced. I have a favor to ask."

"How can I help?"

Sweet man. "What are you doing on Sunday afternoon?"

"I'm free."

"Excellent. You offered up a hulky harem. Think I can borrow them for my sister's wedding this weekend?"

Charles' laugh was a low rumble in Victoria's ear. "I'm intrigued, tell me more."

Hope sparked, and Victoria continued with her plan. "Right before the wedding starts, I want all of you gorgeous men dressed up to escort me from the woman's dressing room to the back of the aisle. I figured if my sister called me names, I shouldn't disappoint her by only having a single man as my date."

"I'm in. Sunday afternoons are slow at work so I bet I can find three others, and we all have work tuxes. Hell, I might be able to get a palanquin chair so we can carry you over to your sister."

They laughed and plotted for a few more minutes and by the end of the call, she felt jazzed and couldn't sleep. Instead, she plopped down in front of her tablet and pounded out a few school application drafts. Once she found her GRE results, she'd hit send. Easy task. Why had she hesitated for so long?

She wasn't her mother riddled with doubt and trepidation. She was strong and wanting to live her life on her terms.

When she finally headed off to bed, visions of flower-adorned dresses danced in her head. Thankfully, in her dream, she carried a shotgun loaded with buckshot. Time to let the crinoline fly.

TIP # 32

BE A CATERPILLAR: EAT, SLEEP, WAKE UP BEAUTIFUL

*T*he next morning, in her dark hotel room, Victoria fumbled for her cell and answered.

"Well, hello, Little Miss Sunshine. Partying too hard last night, I take it?" Iggy asked.

Rolling onto her back, Victoria stared at the empty dress hanger, happy. "You could say that."

"What time do you want me to come over with the flowers?"

"Rehearsal starts at five and we'll eat right after. How about seven?" Victoria fumbled out of bed and rolled into the bathroom.

"I was hoping to come up earlier since I'll have a car full of flowers."

"I'll talk to the front desk and have a key ready for you. I'll put it under your name, come up whenever you get here." She flipped on the water for her shower.

"What are you doing?"

Victoria stripped off her pj's. "I'm about to step into the shower."

"Right." Iggy's voice sounded odd, stretched too thin, and the call disconnected.

That was curt. Whatever, she didn't have time to figure out what Iggy's new personality tick was about. He wasn't her problem to solve. Never had been hers to solve. Victoria got into the shower and got ready for the day. Her sister texted. She ignored it.

Time to run errands. Forty-five minutes later, she sat in front of her first stop. Unwrapping her fingers from the steering wheel, Victoria stepped out, rolled her shoulders, and marched inside.

There with glasses perched on top of her head was the woman Victoria was looking for. "Olivia, I have a question for you."

Olivia smoothed down her navy and gold skirt. "How may I help you?"

"Did you receive the original dress you picked out for me?"

"Yes. Is there a problem with," Olivia coughed delicately and added, "the other dress?"

Simple and understated, Victoria loved the description. "The other dress accidentally burst into flames. I'm on the hunt for a replacement. A noncombustible replacement."

Olivia's grin made her eyes twinkle. "An accident? Too bad. Has the bride been informed of this mishap?"

"I'll spare her the news, she's busy enough driving me and the rest of the world crazy."

"If you don't mind me asking, what happened?" She perched on her toes, waiting.

"The dress's aspiration to be a clown's costume had been dashed and took its own life in mourning."

"You don't say." Olivia's voice carried amusement even though her lips were straight and serious.

"If I had but known, I would've never left it alone with lighter fluid and matches. I hope that you have the original dress you ordered."

"Let me check." Olivia led her to an empty room and asked her to wait.

During the wait, Bridezilla texted her five more times. Each time, Dessie asked inane questions, like were the linens delivered or did she order the pale yellow or pale green napkins? Victoria flipped her phone to silent. All these details were completed days ago and Dessie knew this. Her sister was spiraling.

The final text from Dessie thanked Victoria for the early wedding present, a spa treatment at the hotel. Hopefully, her overstressed little sister would find some chill.

Olivia returned with a black garment bag draped over her arm. Déjà vu, except this time the dress she brought out was simply stunning.

Empire waistline. Victoria tried it on and the full-length dress fit her perfectly. Her body trembled. The tears started as she stared at the stranger in the mirror. "I feel beautiful. I've never felt this good in a dress." Her words were thick and watery.

"I'm glad I could help you. You're a knockout."

"You must be confusing me with the bride."

Olivia placed her hands on Victoria's shoulders. "Your beauty is solid. Jackie O-type classic. Your sister's beauty is a more contemporary splash."

She bowed her head, placing her hands over Olivia's. "I'll trust your judgment since you obviously know your job. How much for my upgrade?"

Olivia handed her the receipt. "Your sister already paid in full."

"And at my favorite price, how much better can that be?" Victoria stepped out of the gown.

Five minutes later, she was out on the street, whistling. Dress down, she now only had the rehearsal and dinner to go. Until then, she would devote herself to her own tranquility.

TWO HOURS LATER, bubbles and jets had banished all the stress out of her body.

Victoria rinsed off in a quick shower. Dessie rang while she was toweling off to say that she wanted to come up and "chat."

The only thing Victoria wanted was to keep this night peaceful. She felt great. If Dessie wanted to bicker, she'd shove her sister out of her room. She wouldn't deal with the demented, demanding bride.

She slapped her earplugs in and finished up her hair and makeup. Humming to her music, Victoria opened the bathroom door and stared at Iggy. His eyes widened. Her eyes screamed.

He pinched his eyes shut. "Sorry. I thought you'd be gone already. It's almost five. I'll step outside so you can get something on."

"NO."

Too late, the room door opened and standing, hand raised to knock, was Dessie. Iggy almost slammed into her in his rush to escape. Victoria watched Dessie's facial expression morph from puzzlement to rampage the moment she spotted Victoria, nearly naked.

"Pardon me, I see you're busy." Dessie's voice brimmed with cold hate.

Neither Victoria nor Iggy moved.

"I felt bad about last night, but I was right, you are a two-timing whore. I'm going to tell Ethan. I've kept everything else from him, but not this. This. This is just too much." Dessie's words dripped venom.

She stormed off, propelled by her windy, pious rage. Her stomp thundered off the plush carpet.

Both Iggy and Victoria stood stunned. Victoria recovered first, grabbing her black cocktail dress and throwing it on. But Dessie's back had disappeared through the elevator doors.

Victoria prayed for a drink. She saw the crazy rise up, possessing her sister. Hyde murdered Dr. Jekyll right in her hotel room, killed by the jealousy pistol.

In her room, Iggy stood glued to the same spot where she had left him.

"What happened just now?" he asked.

"Hyde visited us."

His brow pinched down and his mouth slacked.

Victoria slapped on her shoes. "My sister thinks I'm fooling around with everyone who looks at me."

"Are you?"

"No." The two letters were delivered with a sharp bite.

Throwing his hands up, he backed up. "Right, none of my business. I'll go get the rest of the flowers and start putting them together."

They left together. Silently, they boarded the elevator. Victoria noticed Iggy staring at her through the reflection on the elevator doors.

On the next floor, a couple slipped in, giggling. Two floors down, the couple stepped off, glued hip-to-hip. The elevator descended again.

Victoria used their shared privacy to step into Iggy's space. "Why are you staring at me?" Her voice was hostile and ready to leave bruises.

"Because you're beautiful."

His compliment in such a tiny space unsteadied her. "Oh."

The doors dinged open into the lobby. Iggy bolted out.

Victoria smoothed out imaginary wrinkles in her dress and strode out.

The lobby was empty. The clicks of her heels echoed, bouncing off the marble archways. The rehearsal was taking place here at the hotel. Wind Song Gardens had another wedding booked there tonight.

Victoria stopped outside the ballroom and collected herself. She pushed the door open and walked in to find that everyone was clustered in tiny hives.

The three bridesmaids, Avon, Connie, and Joy huddled together, whispering. She still hadn't thanked Avon for the forced stripper dance.

Once Avon's eyes landed on Victoria, the other two swiveled their heads to see how they should react.

"Poor mouse, she's just trying to make a grand entrance." Avon's tone was as slick as a slimy eel.

Kill them with kindness, that's what her dad always said. Victoria threw them a little friendly wave. "Good to see you're no longer wasted and puking."

The three glowered harder.

Victoria breezed past them toward her parents.

The bride was stuck onto Damien's hip. Maybe Dessie would set aside her attitude problem with Victoria for the sake of her wedding. Dessie glanced at the doors and seeing Victoria, lifted her nose and planted her back towards her.

Nope, Bridezilla wasn't in a magnanimous mood.

This rehearsal had better be over with fast. Air rustled behind her. Ethan walked up to her wearing a blue blazer and tan pants. He was dressy and relaxed at the same time.

"We need to talk outside." She snagged his elbow, directing him outside into a secluded nook saying, "My sister has lost her mind."

He laughed. But when she didn't join in, he deflated. "Lost her mind, how?"

"Ever since Dessie met you, she has been on my case if I even talk to another male. I think my sister has a crush on you."

Ethan sputtered. "Are you sure?"

Victoria sagged against the wall. "Iggy dropped by my room to work on the flowers and didn't know I was getting dressed when Dessie showed up. She stormed off before I could explain nothing had happened. She's angry at me, for your sake."

Ethan didn't say anything. He only blinked.

She continued, trying hard to get him to understand. "She also called me some version of slut more times in the last few days than I would care to count, even though you're the only man I have ever kissed."

He didn't move.

She pressed her nails into her palms. "Time to be honest. I didn't ask you to be my escort tomorrow. Dessie did. She took my phone and texted you without my knowledge or my permission."

"You didn't ask me?"

Honesty tasted tart and gave her heartburn.

*T*he dimly lit secluded corner hid Victoria's embarrassment as she told him the truth. "No, I didn't ask you to the wedding. I'm sorry. I should've told you."

Ethan smiled, but the expression was sad. "How could you say no to a date to your little sister's wedding?"

Relief surged through her. He wasn't mad. "Call me a transparent coward. I like being with you, dancing with you, laughing with you. I can't explain it, though. You're every woman's perfect guy."

"Do I hear a 'but' coming? To crush my masculinity?" He propped against the wall, facing her.

Victoria fidgeted, then stilled her hands. She could speak about how she felt. "Maybe I'm the defective one. I think of you as a great friend, not as a great romantic partner."

"Me too."

Relief surged and buoyed her spirits.

Freedom and liberation lay between them. They locked eyes, sharing a timid smile.

Ethan grabbed her hand. "Thank you."

Victoria tilted her head. "I gave you the dreaded friendship line and you're thanking me?"

He gazed into her eyes and said, "Yes, thank you for being strong and beautiful and courageous. Not many women would've told me the truth the day before the wedding. They would've clung onto me, lying to themselves and me because they're afraid of being alone."

She squeezed his hand. "That is the nicest thing anyone has said to me."

He winked and tugged Victoria off the wall. "As your escort for the wedding tomorrow, we better talk more about what you think is going on with your sister."

Reality crashed into her. "That's a harder topic."

"I don't want to confuse your sister. Should I bail tonight and show up tomorrow to be your arm candy?" He was clearly uncomfortable with the situation, based on his hesitation to follow through on his word.

"No, Dessie would cause a scene if you left. Come on, let's not anger the monster, since she needs to rat me out to you."

They strolled to the rehearsal together. The bride watched them walk in with her eyes narrow slits.

The priest, who rivaled a mummy in age, stood hunched over at the front of the room. Damien argued with Dessie. He stabbed his fingers in the direction of his groomsmen and loomed over his petite bride.

Dessie dropped her head to one side and shrank. Damien, with his chest puffed up, strode past her to chat with his groomsmen. His head cocked to the side, a slimy grin lining his lips.

Victoria suppressed the instinct to punch the pompous look of victory off his mobster mug. He couldn't treat her sister like a submissive, blow-up wife. Slowly, Victoria forced each finger to uncurl. She kept her toxic glare on the groom.

Dessie wobbled toward the three bridesmaids.

She should check on her sister. "I've got to see what's wrong now."

Hands in his pockets, Ethan snagged a seat. "I'll be here."

Victoria met up with the knot of women. "What happened, Dessie?"

Her sister bared her teeth at them. "Damien changed his mind and decided his groomsmen aren't going to walk the bridesmaids down the aisle. We had already agreed last week. Now he's changing things."

"We'll be fine without the guys." She gave her sister a little side hug.

The priest coughed. A dry, crackly, deathbed cough. "Places, everyone," he said in a deep Irish brogue. His glasses looked as thick as microscope lenses.

Damien and his groomsmen strolled up to stand next to the priest. Dessie and the rest of the bridal party trucked back to the doors. The three bridesmaids began bickering about who would go first.

Victoria cut in on the squabbling. "Ladies, does the order matter?"

The three stopped. In sync, they thrust their hips out and sneered at her.

Avon spoke first. "Yes, it matters. Whoever goes last must stand next to you, Chubby."

Victoria's eyeballs blazed.

Chubby was she? She'd had enough of these rude, snide, and overweight egos. No one would insult her anymore. *That* Victoria had died last night. She balled her fist and shifted her weight ready to attack.

Dessie snapped, "Joy, you go first. Thanks, Avon, for volunteering to stand next to my sister. Line up."

They all blinked. Victoria relaxed her hand and smiled. The

old Dessie stood in front of her, controlling and bossing around her minions. Proud of Dessie for handling Avon with surprising efficiency, Victoria cued up. Better lie low and stay on the bride's good side.

Joy bounced down the fake aisle, took her place, and the rest of them followed suit, marching in the order Bridezilla had decreed. Dessie walked down on the arm of their dad.

The first monster truck speed bump started with who would hold the wedding rings.

The best man crossed his arms. "My job is to hold the ring for you, Damien. If you're going to do everything, why do you need us?"

"I need you four to stand there beside me and balance out the pictures, that's all," Damien said, his expression and tone bored like he was talking about getting his car detailed, not talking to the man standing up for him at his wedding. "I picked you guys because you all know me and will look great next to me."

The best man looked livid enough to throw a punch. "You're a bastard."

"Nope. I, unlike you, know who my father is. As my room-mate in college, you know how I am. Why is this a problem now? None of you have ever complained about taking my money." He swept his gaze down the line next to him.

Every one of the groomsmen went red and shut up.

"Let's move on." Damien blithely continued like he hadn't insulted the men by his side.

The priest nodded. "We'll do the first few lines of your vows. Did you write your own?"

Dessie ran to her purse and rummaged. "I started mine. I thought it would be sweet to write our own."

Damien rolled his eyes. "We'll do the traditional vows."

"But..." Dessie slunk to her groom without her vows.

Victoria's patience evaporated. "Are you even interested in having a wife? Or do you want the trappings and respect of being married, without the work?" Her words steamrolled out.

Damien leveled a porcupine glare over Dessie's shoulder at her. "I may have to put up with your meddling after the wedding. Tomorrow isn't about you and your jealousy issues. Tomorrow is about me and my bride."

Dessie glanced at Victoria, giving her a little fake smile. The type of smile that begged for her to stop talking. "It's okay. I hadn't finished the vows and you know how terrible I am with words."

For the good of her sister, and to stop Dessie's tears from falling, Victoria swallowed her wrath. Not her battle to fight. Dessie had to decide what she wanted in life. Yet Victoria remembered that pleading expression from childhood and was always powerless against her sweet, innocent, imploring trust-me gaze. "If you're sure. I only want you to have the wedding you've always gabbed on and on and on about since birth."

"I know, Tori."

"Can we move on?" Damien's foot wasn't tapping. His words certainly were.

Dessie turned back to her groom.

The priest cleared his throat and started reciting the vows. "Damien, repeat after me. I, Damien Estevan Volpé, take thee, Esmeralda Isabella Shaw, to be my wedded wife."

He repeated it like he was ordering at a drive-thru, his words clipped and rapid.

"To have and to hold from this day forward, for better or worse, for richer or poorer." The priest continued in his thick accent.

Damien kept repeating the words, sounding worse than a hypnotized parrot.

Not the way Victoria would've wanted her marriage to start.

The priest turned to Dessie. She recited all the same words, yet Victoria could feel her eyes filling with water. Her baby sister's words were overflowing with care and concern.

They wrapped up and walked to dinner at the hotel restaurant. Not even the sight of all her pretentious cousins waiting at the host stand crimped Victoria's good vibe. By this time tomorrow, the wedding would blessedly be over.

Candles sat on the tables radiating a warm glow. Flowers overflowed the centerpieces on the long table. The rehearsal dinner flowed smoothly, despite the stabby glares Dessie zapped at Victoria and Ethan.

Ethan brought his head close to Victoria. "Your sister is giving me the creeps."

"Meet Hyde."

Between courses, Ethan tapped Victoria's hand to get her attention. "How's the speech going?"

She stilled. "Speech?" The word uttered was more of a croak than a scream.

Ethan nodded toward the miserable bride and the cocky groom. "The maid of honor must offer a toast to the couple."

"Doggy scooper."

With his raised brow, Ethan asked her *Now what?*

She studied her sister over the golden rim of her wine glass. "After dessert, I'm helping Iggy with the flowers. When that's done, I'll write the speech."

"Go when you need to." The groomsmen pulled Ethan into a conversation about the current spring training games a few miles away from the hotel.

Victoria tuned the chitter-chatter out.

She knew Dessie was mercurial and an emotional diva, yet she was also loyal, loving, and wanted desperately to be loved. Victoria better think up something better than that cheesiness, because those words described most women in the world.

Switching her gaze to Damien, Victoria grimaced. From what little she had seen, Damien seemed overbearing, arrogant, and a smooth-talking devil. Dessie was marrying a male Cruella De Ville. What advice could she offer him?

Her phone vibrated against her leg, scattering her thoughts. Fishing her cell out of her purse, she saw a text from Iggy.

I need ur opinion on the bride's bouquet

Ethan raised an eyebrow at her, noticing her phone was out.

"It's Iggy. If anyone asks, tell them I had to go deal with a few final details." Victoria slipped out of her chair.

He nodded and returned to his discussion with the groomsmen.

Rich smells greeted Victoria in her hotel room. Vases dotted every surface, transforming her room into a garden paradise. Victoria's shoulders relaxed and she kicked off her pointy heels.

"How'd it go with your sister?" Iggy's tone sounded nervous as he glanced up from his work.

"Received the silent treatment. That's preferable to name-calling." Tossing her purse on the bed, she flopped down in the chair across from him. "How can I help?"

He handed her pictures of bouquets. "I'm trying to figure out what would go best with your sister's dress and style. Pick one." He stood, stretched, and rubbed his lower back with both hands.

She tried to ignore his flat stomach peeking out from underneath his surfer tee. Focus, Victoria, focus. She didn't want to live up to her sister's slanderous accusations.

Studying the three pictures instead of Iggy, Victoria thought of Dessie's order at the flower shop, visualized her sister's dress, at sunset in the red rock amphitheater, and knew the perfect bouquet.

"This one." Victoria handed him the picture of three long-stemmed calla lilies with miniature roses surrounding it.

Iggy leaned over her and his intoxicating smell snared her. "That's what I thought, but I wanted to be sure."

Thankfully, he moved away, releasing her from his nearness trap. He gathered flowers and began to assemble the bouquet. Victoria watched his forehead crinkle. The tip of his tongue poked out. This must be his deep concentration expression because whereas she was acutely aware of Iggy, he didn't register her existence.

Warning, warning, she screamed at herself. Until the wedding ended, she had to keep her mind and hands off Iggy. One crisis at a time.

She still found herself watching him. "You must come to the wedding tomorrow."

Startled, he swung his head from the flowers to blink at her, reminding her of her dad. "I couldn't."

"Please, Iggy. My sister needs to thank you in person for doing this for her." Her voice and eyelashes were low like she'd seen Dessie do to get her way with men.

Grunting and shifting in his seat, he slumped down to finish his work. "There. Done." He tied the last ribbon on the bouquet and put the bunch in a clear glass vase on the desk.

Their eyes met, and the joking light hardened into a flash of smoldering lightning, striking Victoria's heart. She counted her erratic heartbeats.

"I better get going. I added ice to all the vases to keep the flowers cold. You'll need to add more ice in the morning to keep the flowers from opening until closer to the ceremony." Iggy collected his things, never glancing at her. He bent over and dropped his tools into his workbox.

Treated to a nice long look at his butt, she couldn't help staring.

Iggy snapped the box shut and quickly raced to the door. His hand on the handle, he paused, stared at the exit, and then shook himself. Hesitation over, he clicked the door open.

Victoria moved to him and stood close. "Thank you again for all your help. I wouldn't have been able to do this." She leaned into him. She could smell his dark and alluring scent as she kissed his cheek. "See you tomorrow at the wedding."

He didn't say anything for a long moment, just slid into the hall, keeping his unsure eyes on her. "I never said yes."

"I know. I'll see you tomorrow."

He grunted, striding away from her. Moments later, the elevator dinged, and he vanished.

Alone in her room, she slumped against the hotel door and exhaled. "He's more trouble than a chimp with a plan."

Somewhere in her purse her phone vibrated. Digging it out, she found a new text from Sandra.

B there @ 10 tomorrow with coffee n 2 help with last-minute nightmares. Night, Goose

Victoria was lucky. Sandra would make the wedding go off without a hitch. Well, except for Victoria's big surprise guests. That was one hitch she couldn't wait to see happen, unlike her sister's nuptials.

The next day it finally, finally was time for the wedding liftoff. The morning hours zipped by in a blink. At two-thirty, Victoria and Sandra were prepped to deliver the flowers and set up the favors at the site. They stuffed all their clothes, bags, presents, and flowers into Sandra's Mini and still managed to close the trunk.

Five minutes later, they did the whole thing in reverse. Dessie showed up an hour later with their mother in tow.

Their mother flitted around helping Dessie get ready by setting out the veil, unpacking the makeup kit, and generally filling the room with her rambling. "The garden is blooming. This is going to be lovely. The day will be perfect," her mother said, her worry evident by her forced cheeriness.

Victoria silently watched while fighting with her hair and the stupid pearl clips.

The bride sat in her slip. Dessie watched her mother put makeup on her. She sat passively, her eyes locked on her reflection. She dutifully turned up her lips, feigning happiness whenever their mother talked to her through the mirror.

Dessie's makeup looked vibrant and lush and her hair

sleek and beautiful. Chandelier earrings with diamonds and tiny, pale-pink pearls adorned her ears. Yet the bride's twinkle, which was normally there, was dead. No spark or spunk.

Someone rapped lightly on the bridal dressing-room door. Victoria hollered, "If you're anyone but the groom, come in."

Sandra poked her head into the room. "Millie, Robert's here. Thought you would want to make sure his tux is right." Then, her head disappeared.

The mother of the bride sailed past Victoria, muttering about what an old fuddy-duddy her ex was. Her exit left the two sisters alone.

Dessie didn't look well, nor did she have the vibe of a woman about to walk happily to the altar. She stared blankly at the hanging white gown.

Victoria walked over and picked up the empty dress bag off the floor. "Is there anything I can do?"

She didn't move or acknowledge Victoria. "This is forever."

Closing the gap between them, Victoria wrapped her arms around her little sister. "You don't have to walk out there if you aren't sure."

Choking back a sob, Dessie waved her hand and fears away. "It's cold feet, that's all."

She raised her sister's chin, so they stared eye to eye. "Remember, you can walk all the way to your groom-to-be, and if you still have this nagging feeling when the priest asks you if you do, you can say 'I don't'." Her tone was quiet and full of love and support.

"I'll remember your advice. I appreciate you being nice to me even though I've been a bridezilla."

Sandra busted in, but when her panicked gaze landed on the two sisters standing together, she hesitated. The hot pink and black '50s dress hugged her best friend's new curves.

Victoria let go of Dessie's chin and turned to Sandra. "I hate you. You're rocking the new look."

Sandra wore a cheesy grin. "I told you I'm no gutter rat. Sorry, I need to borrow the maid of honor for a moment."

The three bridesmaids rocketed into the room, surrounding Dessie. The bride wrapped herself in a pleasant and relaxed outer armor. Her friends might be fooled, but Victoria detected her sister's depression.

She let Sandra steamroll her outside. Once out of earshot of the bride, Sandra dropped the peachy grin. "We have a problem."

"No surprise. Weddings area series of disasters."

"The groomsmen have vanished."

The news made Victoria stop. She expected late in-laws. Something small and unnoticeable. "They're gone. Not late?"

"None at the hotel. None here."

A few guests cut through close by them. All the men checked Sandra out in her shocking pink getup. From her heels to hair clips, she was sporting pink.

Victoria tugged Sandra close. "Do we know why they're a no-show?"

"I ran into Ethan and apparently, at the end of dinner, the groom and groomsmen had a row. A very loud row and all the groomsmen stormed off, cursing at the groom."

Starting to pace, Victoria pondered the problem. "Not hard to imagine them swearing at the puffed-up orangutan. Did you tell Damien?"

"Yes, and he told me that they'll be here and to leave him alone."

"Buffoon. They aren't coming." Victoria's words were disgust-loaded.

Sandra paced in the opposite direction. "Do we go on without them?"

Victoria tapped her chin. "We should, but Dessie would be disappointed about her seating chart. Remember, Ethan got invited because of the silly thing."

"Got a pocketful of men ready to lend out for the cause?"

Victoria spotted her comeuppance entourage approaching and hoped they could be repurposed. She turned Sandra around. "I do. Meet the wedding's tuxed saviors."

"Who are they?" Sandra whispered to Victoria.

She waved the men over. "Change of plans, Charles. We're moving from man-candy revenge to studs-on-loan. The groomsmen are MIA for the ceremony. Would you boys mind being stand-ins for them?"

The four handsome men huddled.

Charles spoke for the other three, saying, "Escorting pretty women, we're in, but only if you don't strip us before the ceremony. You'll have to wait till after, Sweetness." He winked at Victoria.

Her roots might've been blushing after his comment. "I think I can keep my hands off your Velcro tux for now. This is an even easier gig than you think. You'll start at the altar with the groom and then walk us to the reception."

Charles hooked his thumbs on his vest pocket. "Stand pretty and look dashing. Those are within our skillsets. Oh, and sorry to tell you we couldn't get the palanquin chair for later."

Sandra piped in, intrigued. "I don't know why you'd need one, though I've always wanted to ride in one. I think I'll keep these fellows around." She popped both arms out to them.

Charles took one arm and one of the other hunky guys took the other, and all five of them walked to the amphitheater where the wedding would take place. Sandra knew how to make an entrance. Heads turned and murmurs followed behind.

Her mother frowned at the scene and rushed over. "You've ten minutes to get dressed."

Victoria dove into the dressing room. Dessie and the other bridesmaids squealed out in the gardens, posing for pictures. Blissfully alone, Victoria slipped on her dress. She struggled with the zipper as a soft rap sounded on the door.

"Come in. I need a hand."

Iggy popped his head around the door. "Hi, I..." The rest of his words died.

She waved him in, turned around, and swept her hair up, exposing her back to him. "Can you zip me up? We're about to start."

Silently, he obeyed. His hands trembled slightly when he placed them on her shoulders, done dressing her. Energy from his touch zapped down her spine and pooled in her pelvis.

Some things never changed between them. Victoria picked up her bouquet to break his touch.

Iggy grabbed her free hand, turning her toward him. "Victoria, you're lovely." His words were heavy with truth and thick with desire.

She could feel her body flush and her heart thump, thump, thump, racing up her throat. She pushed all the conflicting, swirling feelings down. "We better get out there before I'm late."

The opening music started. She peeked out of the dressing room. Nearly three hundred people sat in white padded chairs with light yellow and green ribbons streaming down the backs. The weather was beautiful and clear. A stunning March day in Arizona.

The groom stood at the altar arguing with the priest, ignoring everyone else, oblivious to the men standing near him. The fake groomsmen threw her a thumbs-up.

She pushed Iggy out and sprinted for the bride's hiding spot.

The music changed and the first bridesmaid started down the aisle. People whispered, snapped pictures, and there were a few muffled giggles. The next two bridesmaids marched out, heads held high. Victoria slipped into the secluded alcove unseen.

Dessie queued up and gasped at Victoria. "Where'd you get that dress?" Her voice wasn't quite a shout, though her disbelief echoed in the little room.

"Surprise. See you at the other end." She blew a kiss to the bride, stepping out onto the red carpet.

Murmurs followed in Victoria's wake. The good kind. The shocked kind.

"Is she the bride's sister?"

From the Alburgas' section, she swore she heard someone saying, "She's lovelier than I remember."

Not one person gossiped about her weight or her failures or her spinsterhood. Big fat win to Victoria. Sandra clawed the air and *rowr-ed* at her.

She could feel her smile stretch wide. Even her typically tight-lipped military uncle, Uncle Aggie, gave her a relaxed grin. For him, that equated to jumping for joy.

The three other bridesmaids molded their faces into a grim line of disapproval at Victoria and her pretty, pale green dress. Her dress was flower-free with clean lines and classy. Unlike their matching dresses, featuring the ass flowers.

Victoria stepped into place. Charles fanned himself and mouthed, "Smoking."

The music changed to an airy fairy-tale tune. The bride appeared.

In the late afternoon light, her baby sister stood tall, all grown up, and radiant. Her blonde hair was curled under in understated elegance with an orchid holding back one side. Tears formed in Victoria's eyes.

Dessie deserved to be the star in her own wedding wish book and she nailed the vibe. The sun had begun to set, washing the sky in burnt orange and purple streaks.

People held their breath. Couples in the audience drew together watching Dessie march by.

Damien gave up whatever argument he was having with the ancient priest and watched his bride approach. Victoria didn't see an ounce of happiness in the groom. She could see pounds of possession.

Their mother refused to let her emotions ruin her makeup but from where Victoria stood, she could hear her mother sniffling. Their dad stopped stiffly before the steps leading to the altar.

The priest asked, "Who gives this bride away?"

"Her mother and I do." Her dad's voice came out a little wobbly, but his words were clear.

The priest nodded his head, dismissing the father of the bride from his duty. Their dad kissed Dessie's hand and he stumbled to his chair next to his ex.

Dessie gathered her dress, walked up the three steps to join her groom, and took Damien's hand. Hand in hand, the couple stood before the priest.

"Please be seated." The priest's brogue was thick, his words resonant.

Shutters clicked all around them, capturing the precious moment.

A malicious vibe in the groom's section made Victoria turn. Damien's mother, Maria, seethed. Her husband wasn't by her side, sharing the moment of their son's wedding with his wife. No, he stood across the aisle in the bride's section, next to a woman half his age.

The vibrations of death were like standing near a simmering volcano. People politely ignored the rumblings.

The priest continued, "Let us bow our head in prayer. Dear Lord, please grant your love and guidance for this young couple today, that they'll always listen to their hearts, and allow them to remember the joy they feel in this moment. The moment when they are no longer two separate people but are together as one loving person who turn to you for guidance. Amen."

A resounding "Amen" echoed from the guests.

Victoria's stomach unknotted. All was going well.

Then Dessie glanced over at the groomsmen and wobbled. Victoria steadied her from behind and checked the row of groomsmen. All of them, besides the groom, were in some stage of clothing decay. The guy next to Charles had sleeves peeling off.

Oblivious to the startled bride, the priest droned on. "We are gathered here today to witness the sanctity of marriage, which lasts a lifetime and beyond. With pure hearts, the couple vow faithfulness."

Maria erupted, spewing her rage magma. "You dirty swine. You brought your whore to my son's wedding."

Estevan's head snapped up. "Your son? He's my son, too, unless there's something you need to tell me. Did you sleep with my brother all those years ago?"

Great, a soap opera began unfolding at Dessie's wedding. Normally, alcohol was served first, but for today's special treat, everyone got a pre-booze show.

At this point, the priest's jaw flapped in the wind, catching flies. Dessie and Damien froze, their happy countenances melting off their faces. Dessie clutched her dress. Damien's jaw tightened.

Estevan's date nuzzled into him like a cat curling around its tail. She tilted her head up and blew a kiss to Maria. "Calm yourself, you sow."

Maria coiled and sprung, lunging over the aisle toward the tramp, her killing intent clear.

Damien dropped down the three steps and halfway to the other woman. Maria slammed into him, her arms swinging.

"Momma." The single word broke through her hate haze. The groom dragged her toward the altar, stopping at the steps. "You're making a fool of me over some woman. You're ruining my wedding over nothing. Control yourself."

One lone fat tear rolled down Maria's face. Damien walked up to Dessie. Maria stood alone in the aisle, her back to the crowd, facing the bridal party. She struggled to keep from disintegrating in front of everyone.

The bride stepped down and put her arm around Maria. She made cooing noises to soothe the broken woman. "Come on." Dessie guided the crestfallen woman up the aisle toward the exit.

"Esmeralda, where are you going? We haven't finished yet." Damien's tone wielded a brutal and heavy judgment.

Over the weeping woman in her arms, Dessie straightened and stared at her groom like he was a stink bug. "We're finished."

He jumped down the three steps, seizing his soon-to-be wife by her arm. "I didn't say you could leave."

Dessie tried to shake off his grip. "You're heartless. Your father cheated and flaunted his infidelity at your wedding and you treat your mother, who loves you more than life itself, like it's her fault. We're over."

Her baby sister had solid clarity in her tone. Victoria was impressed. No hysterics or ranting from Dessie about her ruined wedding.

Damien's fingers tightened on her arm. Victoria could see his hands turning white. Dessie whimpered.

Enough. Victoria stepped down and tapped on Damien's arm. He turned ready to rip off heads, his features an ugly mask of fury, and met Victoria's solid right hook.

"Don't touch my little sister, scum." Her voice was a savage growl.

"You dare strike me?" Damien glared at Victoria, puffed up like a Pomeranian, loud and useless, but tightened his grip on Dessie's arm.

Ethan, Iggy, and Sandra rushed up the aisle. The groomsmen stepped down behind the groom and tugged him backward, as Ethan peeled Damien's fingers off Dessie.

Once he freed her, Ethan stepped in front of the two huddled women, his hands up in a placating gesture. "I suggest you do as the pretty and pissed lady says and and not touch Dessie."

Iggy stood next to Victoria. He stepped around her, shielding her from Damien, or Damien from her, Victoria wasn't too sure.

Ethan escorted Dessie and Maria up the carpeted walkway, away from the altar.

Iggy said, "You have five seconds to leave before I let Victoria at you again. Then only God will help you."

Sandra, in all her pink fury, was shoulder to shoulder with Victoria, punching her hand into her palm. "Go ahead. Stay. I've got a knuckle kiss for you."

Victoria raised her chin, looking down her nose at this bridal bully. "Leave while your only real blow is to your pocketbook and pride."

TIP # 35
EJECT BULLIES

Damien shrugged off the hands on his shoulders, straightened his tie, and sneered at Victoria. "You're worthless. The best thing to happen today is that I'll never have to see any of Esmeralda's classless friends and family again. I'm leaving."

"I'm glad my sister realized what a slimy and pathetic man you are before being shackled to you in marriage." Victoria smiled broadly, shooing him away like a tattered, dirty rat.

He snapped at his groomsmen. The men didn't move.

"Are you coming or what?" By the stress in his voice and the red in his face, Damien was about to blow. He turned to the men on the dais and actually looked at them.

Charles waved.

"Who the hell are you fools?" Damien's anger dripped from each word.

Sandra said, "Your friends are smarter than you and never showed up."

Victoria added, "Not even your 'buddies' were willing to stand up for you."

"Peons, I can buy the lot of them." Damien stormed off toward the exit. His father and hussy followed the exodus.

Victoria slumped against Iggy. "Good riddance."

The guests started to come out of their shock comas, whispering. Floundering, the priest didn't know what to do or where to go or who to talk to. His mouth kept opening and closing.

Victoria climbed to the altar, addressing the audience. "Ladies and gentlemen, the wedding is canceled. DJ, play that funky music because we're going to party."

The DJ blared "Let's Get It Started" by the Black Eyed Peas.

People started to stir. Victoria kept talking, trying to give them direction. "Please adjourn to the reception. We're going to celebrate fidelity to love."

Sandra, who never needed to be told twice where the dance floor was, led the way with her stripper escorts.

The crowd quietly gravitated toward the cocktail tables, shaking their heads. Only Victoria and Iggy were left on the dais. Soft voices floated back to them.

Iggy stuffed his hands into his pockets. "Remind me to be wary of your fighting skills."

She shook out her right hand, wincing. "His jaw must be filled with concrete."

"I thought I should check the knight-in-heels battering ram." Charles arrived with a med kit in hand.

Iggy stepped to the side, allowing Charles to sit Victoria down on one of the empty chairs.

Charles had her open, close, rotate her hand, and wiggle her fingers. "Nothing is broken. Here's an ice pack. You should be good."

Iggy gave a polite cough, reminding Victoria that the two guys hadn't been introduced.

"Iggy this is Charles. Charles is..." She let the sentence hang.

How did she finish that statement? A medic? A stripper? A friend?

"I came as her extra surprise arm candy." Charles completed her sentence for her.

Victoria could feel her embarrassment from her toes to her hairline. To Iggy, she said, "A story for another time. Charles, this is Iggy. Iggy is—"

"Her boyfriend," he cut in.

A tidal wave crashed over her. A boyfriend. A few weeks ago, she hadn't been on a proper date, then had atrocious dates, then fought with her sister's demons and her own, and now she had a boyfriend?

She settled down, looking directly into Iggy's eyes. "Don't need one."

He had the decency to duck his head at her offended tone. Iggy cleared his throat. "How about you dump your date and let us start again?"

Charles collected his things, bowing out. "Good luck. I hear food calling to me."

His footfalls fading in the distance gave Victoria time to frame her answer while Iggy studied his loafers.

"You want to be my boyfriend? Do you plan on having a ninja assassinate my dad?" Victoria's sarcasm hit a ten.

His head snapped up. "Why would I want to hurt your father?"

"Then you're planning on quitting your job to be with me?"

Realization flooded through his body as his shoulders relaxed and smiled at her. "I'm over my past."

"About time. But I never said that I'm your girlfriend."

"As long as you're talking to me, I can handle that. Shall we head over to the party?" He held out his hand to her.

Victoria accepted. Once they were able to see the cocktail tables and dance floor, her eyes searched for her little sister.

Dessie stood with Maria, but she wasn't weepy as Victoria would have imagined her sister would be minutes after calling off her wedding. She looked happy. Victoria was so proud of her baby sister growing up.

Ethan popped up next to the women, bearing hors d'oeuvres. He offered the ex-bride in white his hand. Dessie accepted. Ethan twirled her out onto the dance floor. Dessie let out a ribbon of laughter. It soothed Victoria to hear her sister's laugh. Dessie sank into Ethan, resting her head on his shoulder.

Victoria watched the two lovebirds dancing. "There goes my dance partner."

Iggy did his impression of Saturday Night Fever, which was a great imitation of geriatrics on crack. He waggled his eyebrows at her. "My dance card is surprisingly wide open."

"I can see why."

He cleared his throat. "You needed extra eye candy. I could've helped."

Victoria studied him from the top of his soft, gel-free head to his slightly scuffed loafers. "You're pretty, just not the best when you're coordinating your limbs to a rhythm."

"Guilty."

The DJ cranked up the music. All the strippers were dancing with the ex-mothers-in-law and and Damien's ancient Italian grandmother. She reached up on one of the groomsmen's sleeves and ripped the fabric clean off him. Everyone stopped.

"Nice one, granny," Sandra yelled.

Damien's grandmother exploded in a big belly laugh, throwing the sleeve at the surrounding tables, and in broken English, shouted, "Now this a party."

With Damien's grandmother leading the way with the strippers, the party continued. On Dessie's and Ethan's fourth consecutive dance, Victoria cut in. "My turn."

Dessie dropped Ethan's hands. "Go right ahead."

Victoria brushed past Ethan and scooped up Dessie's hands. "Good. Let's dance."

They laughed, twirling away from Ethan. He didn't languish alone for long. Sandra snatched him up for a dance.

Victoria set the rhythm and said, "You did well. You stood up for yourself, sheltered his mom, and realized you deserved better."

Dessie stumbled. "I did all that, didn't I? I'm surprised, too."

"Say hello to growing up."

"Speaking of growing up, nice dress. I know I didn't pick that out for you to wear. What happened to the one I ordered?"

"Spontaneous combustion. This was Olivia's pick."

Dessie laughed as they continued to sway across the dance floor. "You're awesome. I can't believe you managed to find a replacement for the horrendous dress I forced on you. And you rolled with the dating, and my insanity, for the last few weeks. I'm sorry for taking over and messing up your life."

She stopped and searched the crowd. "A compliment and an apology. I need the photographer. This is a Hallmark moment we must capture."

Dessie pinched Victoria's arm. "Don't make a big deal out of it. Plus, I'm not done dancing with you."

"Fine, you bossy bride."

They resumed dancing.

"I heard you want to go to school," Dessie said.

"I have my applications prepped for graduate school and I'm registered for a few summer-school courses to replace expired credits and finish up my undergrad." Victoria dipped her sister. "You're going back tomorrow morning to finish *your* last semester, right?"

"On the first flight out and in less than six weeks, I'll be done. You look good with Iggy." Dessie smiled up at her sister.

"You look good with Ethan."

Dessie turned red. "Is it obvious? Are you mad?"

Victoria didn't even flinch at the thought of Ethan with Dessie. Her heart felt light. She spun Dessie out and back. "Blatantly obvious. He and I are square. I already told him you liked him."

"You knew?"

"How could I not know? You were overly protective and interested in him from the moment you met him, which led to me being your punching bag to vent your frustration and confusion, I should add." She spotted Ethan and Sandra and started dancing toward them. "He's a gem. Don't screw this relationship up."

"I won't." Dessie huffed, and yet uncertainty lurked underneath her brave words.

"Good. Swap." Victoria nodded to Sandra.

Victoria spun Dessie out and released. Sandra did the same to Ethan. The two clashed and steadied each other.

"The next dance is for you two. Enjoy." Victoria walked off the floor with Sandra.

"You were right, Vi, Ethan has the moves on the dance floor."

"I know." Victoria noticed Uncle Aggie trying to fend off a small cluster of women pestering him for a dance. "I better go rescue the drowning man."

Sandra glanced over at the knot of women laying siege to him. "If I was straight, I'd chase after the widower, too."

They parted ways, Sandra for the open bar, Victoria for her extraction job.

She tapped his shoulder. "Uncle Aggie, you promised me a dance."

The man was smart enough to know a rescue mission when it stared at him. "Yes, I can't disappoint my favorite niece. Pardon me, ladies."

He marched Victoria to the edge of the dance floor. "Thank you."

"Any time, but this rescue operation will cost you a dance." Victoria held her arms up, waiting for him to step into her space.

"A price I'm willing to pay, Pumpkin." He lined up and took charge of her. "Delighted you gave that bozo a sweet right, just like I taught you."

"You taught me well, against Mother's wishes, if I remember correctly."

Uncle Aggie grimaced slightly, picking the pace up as the songs shifted. "The berating she gave me for teaching you was worth watching you slug that slime."

She went onto her tiptoes and kissed the giant's cheek. "And that's why you've always been my favorite uncle. You could take Mother's heat and come out smiling."

Her uncle blanched. A slender hand tapped on Victoria's shoulder. An elegant woman stood at Victoria's elbow. "I'm claiming the next dance."

His face slipped, and she could see the panic, but she smiled at her uncle. "I see my mother beckoning me. He's all yours."

"Ex favorite niece," Uncle Aggie said to her back.

Victoria walked away, chuckling, and headed for her mother, who was actually calling her over to her table. "Yes, Mother."

Her mother patted the empty chair next to her at the deserted table. Victoria sat down and kicked off her heels. "Where's Dad?"

"He's walking Maria out to her car."

"Typical dad. Well, how do you feel about Dessie not being a missus and ruining the Alburga tradition?"

"Best thing that could've happened to her. You did well protecting your sister at the altar."

Victoria clutched her chest. "You and Dessie complimenting me in one day? Am I dead?"

Her mother hit her arm. Dessie and she were alike in so many ways, physical violence being only one such way. "Don't be cheeky."

Her dad sat down next to her mother and draped his arm around the back of her chair.

Victoria twisted around and didn't see a single member of her mother's side of the family besides her uncle. "How did your sisters take the drama?"

Her mother finished her cocktail. "After the ruckus, your aunts came over to tell Dessie and me how sorry they were for the breakup, boasted about their lavish vacations they have planned for their kids' spring breaks next week, had a few drinks at the open bar, and then left with their gifts tucked under their arms."

"Supportive bunch." Victoria's tone was curt.

"Over the Rainbow" cut into the conversation. The two exes shared a long glance.

Victoria smiled, knowing when she needed to leave them alone. "Go on and dance, you crazy coots."

They did just that. In fact, everyone danced until they were kicked out of the gardens. Victoria had never been to a better non-wedding wedding.

*L*ess than eight months ago, Victoria couldn't have imagined that a single phone call could flip her world upside down. Yet her life was completely different. She was different.

The lobby clock ticked closer to lunchtime. Her work line lit up. She tapped to answer. "Noah's Haven, how may I help you?"

"Tori, are you sitting down?" Dessie squealed into the phone.

A déjà vu wave blasted over Victoria. She kept calm and heard herself smile when she spoke. "Actually, I'm at my new standing desk. You better not be engaged or pregnant, because you've used up your crazy quota. This excitement is hopefully due to your interviews?"

"You know I haven't seen Ethan in weeks, but that's about to change. Starting in fourteen days, I'll be working at Channel 3. I'm moving home to the valley." Dessie's tone was like confetti poppers and streamers flying.

"Congratulations, that's great."

"I won't be on camera for now, but I'm excited to be in town. Ethan's project completes in another six months, so we'll figure out where we are after he's done." A boat horn blared in the background. "I've got to run, my internship rotation with the local TV station is at the wharf today, covering the lucky-fishing-boat contest."

"Hard-hitting journalism in action."

"I know." Dessie's eye roll was clear in her tone. "Love you. Bye."

"Bye."

Dr. Yaz walked from the back into the lobby with a few large envelopes in his hand and flipped the front door lock. "Lunchtime has arrived."

Victoria unhooked the reception headset from her ear and pushed a stack of folders onto the counter between them. "Here's your afternoon appointment stack to review before we open again."

He eyed the paperwork and sighed. "There's always more paperwork. You're going out to lunch?"

She couldn't help bursting into a full-faced grin. "Iggy's on his way to pick me up."

"Is he your boyfriend yet or are you playing hard to get?"

"Not hard to get. I focused on summer school. I only need one more course in the fall to finish up my bachelor's. I should hear any day from my graduate applications."

"You haven't heard back from any of them, including my buddy's fast-track partnership with the University of Arizona?"

"No word yet from any of them, good or bad. The postman must think I'm stalking him. I'm worse than a dog. He turns into our apartment complex and I'm standing at the mailboxes to meet him."

He slid one of his envelopes across the counter to her. "From me. To you."

"Okay." She used her office letter opener and pulled out a

pink paper. Shock cannonballed into her stomach. "You're firing me?"

He propped an elbow up onto the counter. "Finish reading."

Her brain overloaded. "I did. It states right here: you're firing me in four months."

She needed income to live on while in school and had been hoping, if she got accepted to the U of A program, she could still work here on breaks.

A rattle came from the lobby door. Iggy waved through the glass.

"Perfect timing. I'll let him in. This is for you, too." Dr. Yaz dropped the other envelope on the counter and started toward the door.

Her new life plan crumbled and she stood rooted to the tile, staring at the pink slip in her hand. Becoming a vet had always been her dream, but dreams aren't edible. Her mind whirled with a dirt devil of doubts, twirling and hammering all the ways she would continue to struggle as she pursued her degree.

The lobby door opened and a loud door chime *ding-donged*. Victoria had requested the doctor to install the chime so no one could sneak up on her in the office again. She wished she hadn't asked for the annoying sound, because now she heard the phantom noise when she slept.

Iggy slipped inside the lobby.

Dr. Yaz secured the door again, walked to her desk, and nodded at the blank, creamy envelope resting on the desk. "Just open it."

Victoria's heart raced. "After your last letter, I don't know if I want to."

"You okay?" Iggy crossed the lobby and leaned on her desk wall.

"I've been fired." Her voice squeaked.

Iggy raised his eyebrow at the doctor.

Dr. Yaz softened his shoulders, tapping the envelope with his index finger. "I recommend that before you let your mind blast you with extra stress and drama, you open this."

The thick paper felt heavy. Her limbs did what she had done a thousand times in this office, slicing an envelope open. She withdrew the paper and read.

She couldn't talk. Her words jammed up in her windpipe. She sank into her office chair. The tears started. The extremely happy kind.

Dr. Yaz rocked onto his heels, beaming. "Congratulations, you're the first recipient of the Warren Yaz Trust Scholarship. Upon acceptance into a Doctor of Veterinary Medicine program, your tuition will be paid for if you can maintain a 3.0 GPA."

"Really? You'll pay for my degree?" Gratitude made her words thick.

"Serious as a kennel cleaner." Dr. Yaz reached over, plucked a tissue from the box on the desk, and handed one to her. "You're going to be an amazing vet and when you're out of college, I may be wanting a business partner. Who knows?"

Iggy came around the counter and hugged her. "You, lucky lady, can go to school with no more loans."

She felt energized and excited and stunned. "Thank you. Thank you so much."

Dr. Yaz checked the clock. "I have a lunch appointment, and since you've already set me up for the afternoon and tomorrow is light, why don't you take the weekend off and spend it with this fine gentleman? We'll talk again on Monday."

Iggy saluted the doctor and winked at Victoria. "I like those doctor's orders."

"I figured you could be convinced." The doctor laughed, disappearing into the back.

"I can see by your wide pupils that you're still processing. For now, why don't you let me treat you to lunch?" Iggy asked.

"I could use something saucy to celebrate. How about Jake's?" Victoria grabbed her purse, locked her computer, and gently placed the papers from the doctor into her bag.

Iggy unlocked and held the door open for her. "Antler chandeliers, a jukebox, BBQ, and you. Sounds great."

"It does, doesn't it?" Dropping her sunglasses on her nose, she walked through the door into the bright sunny Arizona day.

Victoria sent a text to Sandra.

Tonight it's time to pop the emergency champagne because I've been fired n I have a full paid scholarship for school

Going to the vet office Monday morning would be easier knowing her life had a solid direction. In a few weeks, she would start her last semester to get her bachelor's degree, and then onward to her master's and doctorate. The road would be long, but it would lead to what she had always dreamed of: to be a real veterinarian.

One phone call, two tyrannical family members, a relentless best friend, and a slew of crappy dates had shoved Victoria to get clear on what she wanted and desired in her life. Her high school self wasn't too far off about what was important and how life was an unpredictable adventure, was tumultuous and intimidating, but 100 percent worth pressing forward and expanding her horizons to discover the most important thing—herself.

THE END

DEAR READER, thank you for picking up this book. I'm glad I could share it with you, and I am anticipating writing more soon. Stay tuned. If you enjoyed the story, don't be shy, tell others, leave reviews, and visit my website, MelissaBorg.com. As a bonus, you can sign up for my newsletter and receive a cut scene from chapter 29 where Victoria went to check the reason the office alarm tripped to find Princess loose. https://MelissaBorg.com/bonus/

ACKNOWLEDGMENTS

Though I wrote the first draft in six weeks, it took me years to learn about the writing business, writing, and story structure. I edited. Tweaked. Took classes. Edited. I then sent the manuscript out to agents and my newly-found writer friends and edited more. Thank you to everyone who read the book and didn't say it sucked and instead gave me kind words, pointed feedback, and hand-holding through this crazy journey.

Huge holler to my Rhetorical Mafia and Deep Editing Ninja sisters, my story structure nerds, and all who helped me make this into a better book than I could have crafted alone, such as Lisa Miller, Margie Lawson, Jenn Windrow, Justine Covington, Babette Johnson, Lisa Norman, Mindy Tarquini, Anne Belen, Marilee Beach, and Kimberly Savage—to name a few folks who made sure I upped my writing game.

I would have never even written this book if leukemia, the rat bastard who snuck up on my mother, Andrea Borg, hadn't sentenced her to ninety days to live. Thankfully, she survived to read the manuscript and recover from round one. Yet a few years later, leukemia struck her again, and this time the disease swept her away from us. The creation and nurturing of this book helped me through the uncertain, dark, and harrowing times of her sickness, death, and the continuing aftermath of grief. I owe my love of books and language to her and her unwillingness to dumb down her vocabulary while raising us.

To my family and friends, who always support and believe in me, thank you. Especially to my Sunday girls, Debra Watt, Randi Klein, Noel Neeb, and Rachel McKinney, who have heard the saga of getting this book to publication and have been in my corner cheering me on even when I tell them, time and time again, that I'm reworking the book one more time. To my sisters, Tanya and Erika, who know they may see glimmers of our relationships and conversations on the page and love me anyway, and no you're not getting a percentage of the profits.

To the best husband ever, Lawrence, who doesn't roll his eyes or sigh dramatically at me when I talk about scene or character ideas, story structure, or am tucked into an editing binge for days—I am grateful beyond words. He simply makes sure I'm fed and watered and periodically pried away from my desk. Plus, if I am stuck on something, he'll sit down and brainstorm with me. The couple that plots together stays together.

ABOUT THE AUTHOR

Melissa Borg loves stories that are heartfelt, humorous, and portray vibrant characters. She has always been drawn to stories that explore everyday lives and struggles that are bursting with family, friends, and self-growth. She's an electrical engineer, in degree only. When she couldn't find a job with her degree, she dyed her hair funky colors, found a job managing multi-million-dollar contracts, & was roped into drawing pictures, as part of her job's "other duties as assigned" clause. Nothing is funnier than an engineer muttering dire things at a computer screen, drawing a horse, promise.

Yet her deep love of witty characters and storytelling led her down the road paved in crazy to be a writer. Her background in acting, directing, and zippy conversations, funneled out her fingers and on the page.

Melissa is a fourth-generation Arizona native and she may or may not be suffering from permanent heat stroke. She's surrounded by her family, cats, dog, and the love of her life, Lawrence. Thankfully, he ignores the typing and maniacal laughter from her office and occasionally tempts her way from the keyboard with the lure of food.

You can find information about her and her books at: MelissaBorg.com

facebook.com/InkingDreams
twitter.com/InkingDreams

Made in the USA
Coppell, TX
26 July 2021